Praise for *The Crown o*

"Pick it up. You won't be able to put it down."
– Tom Hastings, Portland State University

"This is an instant classic, a great read for anyone interested in peace and justice." **– Wim Laven, Ph.D., instructor of Peace Studies and Conflict Management**

"I can think of no better source of inspiration for (the topics of peace and social justice) than the Ari Ara series by Rivera Sun, and this latest installation is the best one yet."
– Dr. Seán P. Duffy, Executive Director, Albert Schweitzer Institute, Quinnipiac University

"*The Crown of Light* is a book that contains everything a great novel needs: a heroic female protagonist, colorful supporting characters, adventure, suspense, and most importantly, nonviolence used as a means to solve conflicts. I highly recommend the Ari Ara Series to educators and students!"
– Robin Wildman, Nonviolent Schools Rhode Island

"I have been in youth work forty-five years, and I have never encountered a more important work than the Ari Ara series to share with young people and their advocates."
– Reverend Michael Harrington

"Ari Ara is the bedtime reading adventure for younger generations that completes my circle of peace literature."
– Patrick Hiller, father, bed-time story reader, Peace and Conflict Studies scholar

"The entire Ari Ara Series offers students a warm, exciting, and hopeful adventure, full of problem-solving, love of life, and worthy models of personal growth and peacemaking."
– Scott Springer, The Bay School, Maine

"An amazing family read, and one that we will return to again and again. Thank you for bringing these characters and stories into our lives and imaginations!" – **the Palatucci Family**

"Rivera Sun has done it again. She just keeps getting better and better at weaving powerful stories to remind us that courage, determination, vision, and a taste for high adventure, are all essential elements for waging real peace." – **Rosa Zubizarreta, DiaPraxis founder and Co-intelligence Institute Senior Advisor**

"Ari Ara is one of our favorite heroines and she inspires us daily." – **Savanna Song and Opal Moon, young readers**

"*The Crown of Light* has it all - drama, suspense, heart-pounding action - but most of all this is the story of a group of friends becoming a team that's capable of moving mountains when it counts." – **Rick Brown**

"*The Crown of Light* is masterful. It is an awakening of the mind, spirit and heart that calls us all to action." – **Natasha Léger, Executive Director, Citizens for a Healthy Community**

"We adore this series ... *The Crown of Light* reaches new, much-needed heights in the world of peaceful resolution." – **Romaldo and Carol Ranellone**

"It's a story that touches the heart. I found myself laughing and crying, and felt as though I was part of the story." – **Chiara Kozlovich, 13 year old reader**

"*The Crown of Light* is the latest revelation in what is one of the most urgently important literary series of our time. Rivera Sun has conjured not one but many great leaders for all of us - adults and children alike." – **Ara Savala, Artist in Nipomo, CA**

The Crown of Light

An Ancient Legend, a Lovestruck Heroine, a Journey for Peace

The Crown of Light
An Ancient Legend, a Lovestruck Heroine, a Journey for Peace
Copyright © 2021 by Rivera Sun

Rising Sun Press Works
P.O. Box 1751, El Prado, NM 87529
www.riverasun.com

Library of Congress Control Number:
2021921339

ISBN (paperback) 978-1-948016-16-2
(hardback) 978-1-948016-15-5
(ebook) 978-1-948016-17-9
Sun, Rivera 1982-
The Crown of Light

For Heart & Jeffrey
Thank you for showing me how to build peace.

Other Works
by Rivera Sun

Novels, Books & Poetry

The Ari Ara Series:
The Way Between
The Lost Heir
Desert Song
The Adventures of Alaren

The Dandelion Collection:
The Dandelion Insurrection
The Roots of Resistance
Winds of Change
The Dandelion Insurrection Study Guide
Rise & Resist

Other:
Billionaire Buddha
Steam Drills, Treadmills, and Shooting Stars
Rebel Song
Skylandia: Farm Poetry From Maine
Freedom Stories: volume one
The Imagine-a-nation of Lala Child

A Community Published Book Supported By:

Karen Johnson
Theresa M. Flynn, O.F.S.
Tom Hastings
Jon Olsen
Seán Patrick Duffy
Michael Mirigian
Karen Lane and Chris Walsh
Leslie A. Donovan
Rick Brown
Elizabeth Cooper
Julian and Joann Terranova
Rob and Elizabeth de Lorimier
Rosalma Zubizarreta-Ada
Darien and Glenn Cratty
Barry Buchek
Andrew Moss
Virginia Dixon
Burt Kempner
Harmony Kieding
Scott W Dear
Kiarrow Sereena Rainshine
Raina Doughty and Savi & Opal Holden
Stangl Family
David Spofford
Caroline Corum
David Soumis
Gail and Ken Kailing
Cathy Hoffman
Julia Cohen
Savanna Song and Opal Moon
Kristi Branstetter
Joel Bentarz
Maja Bengtson
Jaimie Ritchie

Henry Gaither
Sally C Kane
Luca Matthies
Kelly Rae Kraemer
Ara Savala & Miarden Jackson
Robin Wildman
"Dr. Mark" Stemen
Romaldo and Carol Ranellone
Leah Cook
JoAnn Fuller
Oliver, Paloma, and Patrick
Amma Guadalupe
Rev Michael Harrington, Director of ALL Children ALL Borders
Laurie Marshall, Unity Through Creativity
Natasha Léger, Citizens for a Healthy Community
The Learning Council
Rebecca Zook
Sunshine Jones
Bob and Sheryl Flocchini
Hilal Sala
Hadley Couraud
Scott Springer, The Bay School, Maine
The Palatucci Family
John Millar
Mia Beale
Anna Lewis Beale, Community Mediator & Grandmother
Jeralita Costa
Natalina
Donna Lynn Price, Author
The Sanborn Sisters
Cindy Reinhardt
Mary Lynn-Masi
Tamara Hitson
Becca Cumley

The Crown of Light

by

Rivera Sun

Table of Contents

Table of Contents, cont.

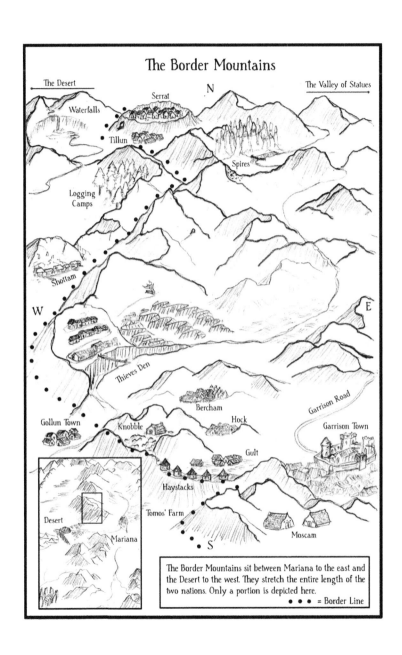

The Border Mountains

The Desert

The Valley of Statues

N

Serrat

Waterfalls

Tillun

Spires

Logging
Camps

Shottam

W

E

Thieves Den

Bercham

Garrison Road

Hock

Gollun Town

Knobble

Garrison Town

Gult

Haystacks

Desert

Tomos' Farm

Mariana

Moscam

S

The Border Mountains sit between Mariana to the east and
the Desert to the west. They stretch the entire length of the
two nations. Only a portion is depicted here.

● ● ● = Border Line

CHAPTER ONE

. . . . .

The Peace Force

Over. Under. Around. Through. Hair flying, arms whirling, legs spinning, Ari Ara danced across the packed earth. The wind tossed blazing white clouds from east to west over the bright blue sky. The glossy boughs of the forest whipped past her line of vision as she turned. The jagged peaks of the Border Mountains flashed by, dark and looming. The steep, slate roofs of the town of Moscam mimicked the crests, sharp and pointed. A handful of village children squatted on their heels, watching the unusual sparring match with fascination. They'd grown up around warriors practicing for battle, but they'd never seen anything like the Way Between.

Neither flight nor fight, the Way Between explored a realm of endless possibilities for navigating the conflicts of the world. It contained ways of cultivating inner quiet and ways to keep war from breaking out. It offered movements for turning aside attacks and skills for building peace. From stopping a fight to ending injustice, the Way Between held countless strategies for solving problems and making change. The ancient practices had

1

lain dormant for a thousand years, ignored and forgotten by cultures swept up in cycles of violence and war. But, like a seed in spring, the Way Between was returning. This summer, Ari Ara and her friends would show everyone the strength, beauty, and power of the Way Between.

Distantly, Ari Ara heard cheers and shouts from the sidelines, but her attention was pinned on Minli of Monk's Hand with the intensity of a hawk. Twice today, he'd caught her off-guard and nearly beaten her at the physical practice of the Way Between. She expected him to run circles around her in the inner skills - Minli was clever as ten monks put together - but this was her strength, not his. She loved the sweaty joy of using sheer physicality to thwart an attack, turn aside violence, and stop harm from happening. She wouldn't let him beat her at this. She had to focus.

Over. Under. Around. Through. Ari Ara tossed the loose strands of her curling red hair out of her blue-grey eyes. She couldn't afford distractions. She may be stronger and quicker, but anyone who underestimated Minli of Monk's Hand because of his one leg was in for a rude awakening. His previous partner had discovered this the hard way, lying on his back on the hard-packed ground, gasping and staring up at Minli in wide-eyed surprise.

Ari Ara leapt like a cat as he tried to hook his crutch around her calf and tug her off balance. He recovered quickly, never losing his poise. Minli was lanky as a heron and could stand on one leg just as silently. Over the past winter, her tousle-haired friend had grown six inches, leapfrogging over her. Now he annoyingly stood two inches taller. At least until she caught up.

Minli swung away from her feint, using his crutch to lengthen his stride beyond the reach of ordinary legs. Pursuing, Ari Ara scuffed her foot in the dust and muffled a curse. Dratted growth spurts! She never knew where her feet were anymore. Just this spring, her limbs had shot out an extra three inches. Her feet blistered in her old shoes then busted out the toes. Just as her new jacket got soft and comfortable, she outgrew it. Her chest, which had ached and chafed for over a year, now jiggled disconcertingly. Her face seemed perpetually pulled and elongated. Her skin had darkened to a deeper shade of bronze from months of riding under the hot desert sun. Her hair, always unruly, had grown even more wild. On a good day, she loved how it leapt like fire. On a bad day, she was tempted to hack it all off.

"Focus!"

Shulen's bellow startled her from her wandering thoughts. She'd have lost the match then and there if Minli hadn't been equally distracted. How Shulen could tell when her mind wandered off on a tangent, she didn't know. Her stern, grey-haired mentor had an uncanny knack for catching her daydreaming in lessons. Ever since they'd met in the distant High Mountains, Shulen's sixth sense never failed to notice when she was staring off into space instead of paying attention. The instant her eyes glazed over during a boring speech, he'd clear his throat disapprovingly. She had tried to argue that mentally reviewing practice moves was a better use of her time than smiling politely at dull words, but Shulen just frowned and scolded her. The iron-hard old warrior never cut her any slack.

"You are the Lost Heir of two nations, the daughter of Queen Alinore of Mariana and Tahkan Shirar, the Honor-Keeper of the Harraken," he chided her sternly, "and the inspiration for this entire summer. You must act accordingly."

It was hard work being an inspiration, Ari Ara grumbled silently. Some days, she wished she'd never come up with this crazy scheme of reviving Alaren's Peace Force.

Thousands of years ago, Alaren, the founder of the Way Between, had put together an "army" of peacebuilders. They carried no weapons. They fought no wars. Instead, they waged peace. They de-escalated violence. They aided people in resolving conflicts before small disputes flared up into battles. They shut down cities and blocked roads to stop kings from marching to war. They restored trust and spoke for peace. They helped enemies heal and people become friends once again. In olden times, it was rumored that the Peace Force, though dispersed across many towns and cities, had been larger than the combined armies of Mariana and the Desert.

This year, Ari Ara and her friends were reviving history as they brought those ancient legends back to life. Thirty people, young and old, noble and common, friends and strangers, had gathered to rebuild Alaren's vision of the Peace Force. They had come from distant lands, diverse cultures, and both sides of the border. They had one thing in common: a yearning to end the cycle of violence between their peoples. They wanted to stop wars before they began, halt skirmishes before they started, and help people resolve their conflicts before they came to blows.

They had trained all spring, here in the town of Moscam, arriving just as the snowmelt flooded the deep clefts of the ravines. They studied relentlessly through the weeks of mud and gnats. They practiced the Way Between under showering petals of apple blossoms and in the pounding rain. Soon, they would travel to Market Day gatherings throughout the region, demonstrating the Way Between, speaking about the Peace Force, and introducing themselves to the inhabitants of these mountains. Most people knew next to nothing about the Way Between. In Old Tongue, it was called *Azar* and stood in contrast to *Attar*, the Warrior's Way, and *Anar*, the Gentle Way. While the other two were well-known, the Way Between had fallen into disuse millennia ago. It had been largely forgotten . . . until now.

This summer, the new Peace Force planned to train hundreds of local folk in the Way Between. Some would join the Peace Force next year. Others would work to end violence in their farming villages and crowded towns. If all went well this summer, the Peace Force hoped to find long-term postings in the Border Mountains for trained pairs of peacebuilders. Next year, the Peace Force could expand, sending groups north and south, east and west, into other areas of the two nations, weaving a web of peace.

"Concentrate!" Shulen barked. He turned to the thirty trainees watching the match, sitting or standing along the grassy edge of the practice grounds. "What does it take to train in the Way Between?"

"Discipline! Determination! Dedication!" they chanted out.

They trained as intensely as warriors, but for peace, not war. They drilled as hard, if not harder. They sweated as much, studied as deeply; ate, slept, and dreamt in the Way Between. In the coolness of dawn, Shulen worked their bodies. The rest of the morning, Mahteni Shirar taught them how to use Azar together in teams. She drew from her experiences freeing the water workers with strikes, and restoring women's rights with sit-ins and singing protests. In the afternoons, Professor Solange Bartou instructed them in the History of Azar, as well as the culture and complicated politics of the Border Mountain region. The three served as leaders for the initiation of the new Peace Force, guiding it with their wisdom and diverse skills. They had won the support of both leaders of the ever-feuding nations. Ari Ara's father, Tahkan Shirar, and her aunt, Brinelle de Marin, had thrown the weight of their authority behind the Peace Force. The two sent funding and supplies, letters of introduction, and permission to cross the border between the two nations. Such an investment in peace was worth more than a century of funding wars.

Minli lunged and nearly caught her. Ari Ara yelped and darted away. He smirked. She snorted. She'd show him. There was no way she was going to let Minli win! With a burst of intensity that startled him, Ari Ara erupted into a dizzying sequence of motions. She picked up her pace, feinting and dancing, up and down, left and right.

Over. Under. Around. Through. There was always a Way Between. Ari Ara used speed and agility to disconcert Minli. That was his weakness: he grew flustered under pressure. Ari Ara dove beneath his lunge. She rolled across the earth. She jumped to her feet and dodged his attempt to catch her in a lock hold. Leaping over his back in a barrel roll, she twisted midair, nudged him off-center, and gently guided him to the ground. She'd never hurt Minli, not with a bruise or a scratch or so much as a skinned elbow.

"Gotcha," she murmured, triumphant.

"About time," he shot back with a grin.

"I was giving you a chance, you old monk," she teased.

She tousled his bird's nest of hair, glad he had grown it out again. With it shorn, he had not only looked like a monk, his head had burned and blistered under the hot desert sun. At least her darker skin kept her from scorching like him. She stuck out her hand to heave him to his feet. Leaning back, she pulled him up. For all his height, Minli felt like he had hollow bird bones. He was hanging halfway to standing when she suddenly froze.

Someone was watching them.

Not the other Peace Force members. Not the villagers. Someone unseen. Nothing else made the back of her neck prickle like that. The sun-gold hairs on her arms rose. She'd felt this tingling on and off all week. Minli had nearly bested her yesterday because of it.

"Um, Ari Ara?"

Minli's voice snapped her back to attention. His hand gripped her forearm as he hung halfway between sprawling and standing. Apologizing, she hauled him upright, reaching for his crutch while he balanced. Shulen's voice droned on about drilling and focus, wrapping up his final remarks. Ari Ara heard only a muffled blur of words as she tried to trace the tingling sensation to its source. She scanned the grassy pastures, the wild shrubs along the forest's edge, the heavy boughs of the fir trees. Nothing.

"I'll catch up," she assured Minli as he and the others headed toward breakfast. "I just want to go over something."

"Yeah, brush up on those moves," he joked. "You're losing your edge."

Usually, she would have shot back a sharp retort to such a tease, but Ari Ara simply flashed a distracted smile and went through the motions of reviewing a sequence until everyone cleared out. The birds warbled tentatively in the branches. The clang and bustle of the town lifted over the rooftops. A hush of wind sighed in the leaves. A lamb bleated from the pastures. A squirrel chittered irritably at some interloper.

Aha, that was it! The hint of an unusual presence in the woods.

Who was it? Ari Ara had a long list of suspicions about who might be spying on the Peace Force. Not everyone was enthusiastic about their efforts. Shulen expected challenges this summer, either from skeptical locals in the border region or from warmongers further afield. In her position as regent of Mariana, the Great Lady Brinelle had backed the Peace Force, but a faction of her nobles detested Ari Ara, abhorred the Way Between, and saw both as a threat to national security. Among her father's people, opinions ranged from tentatively hopeful to downright dismissive. The Harraken had narrowly voted to support the Peace Force at the last Harraken Sing, but many people still thought it a fool's mission.

Anyone could be out there, spying, waiting for a chance to sabotage their work. Ari Ara wanted to know who it was. She let her practice move her toward the edge of the woods. She'd been raised by the Fanten in the distant High Mountains. Their skills at moving unseen were unparalleled. They could slip into shadows and slide through the mists. They could turn invisible, some claimed. Ari Ara's abilities fell far short of the Fanten's, but she could step lightly and move without detection if she tried.

At this end of the training yard, a tiny brook trickled, winding between roots and stones. A clear, still pool had formed where the village children had dammed up the stream to catch frogs. Ears and eyes alert, Ari Ara knelt down and cupped a handful of the sweet, clean water to her lips, savoring the hints of distant ice and minerals brushed from ancient stone. Crouched on a low rock, she splashed the sweat-salt from her face, pretending to have come solely to rinse off. As the eddy's ripples stilled, her breath caught in her throat.

A face stared back at her reflection, cradled in the thick arms of the sprawling oak above her. In the quivering water, a pair of almond-shaped eyes caught her mirrored gaze. A boy's dark brows furrowed together. His skin was the exact shade of an acorn, his face shaped similarly, rounded at his high cheekbones and pointed at the chin.

Ari Ara blinked. A drop of water toppled from her lashes. The pool shivered into ripples. She gasped.

A fox grinned from the trees, right where the boy had been!

She whipped around. A flash of a red and white tail darted behind the oak's dark leaves. She saw the boy's arms reach out as he swung away. The boughs shook. Then he disappeared, leaving her baffled. Had it been a boy? Or a fox? Or both? She leapt the brook and peered up into the tangled canopy. Nothing. Not a rustle. Not a peep. Not a hint of where the boy had gone . . . or if he was even human. People couldn't just vanish like that!

Ari Ara shivered. These mountains ran thick with tales of strange creatures, part human, part beast. Last night, the headwoman's son had regaled them with hair-raising stories of wolf men and bear mothers, witches who turned naughty children into wild pigs, and magic springs that transformed ordinary villagers into shapeshifters. She and Minli had lain awake in their cots in the Sleeping Quarters for hours, whispering back and forth, pretending they weren't nervous about each thump or creak in the night.

Minli didn't believe the tales, not as literal truth. There was always a reasonable explanation for extraordinary happenings, he argued. Ari Ara disagreed. She had seen many strange things in her life. She had worked song magic in the desert, heard prophecies come to pass, brushed up against the spirits of the long dead, dreamed of the ancestors, and ridden a trickster-being disguised as a horse. Anything could happen.

With a shiver of unease - but an even stronger tug of curiosity - Ari Ara rose and entered the woods. Massive oaks dominated this patch, holding their territory with wide boughs that reached down like giant's arms and ran along the ground before reaching leafy fingers back up toward the light. Clusters of unfurling ferns brushed up against a thorny bush with tiny stars of white flowers. She listened for the slightest rustle. A lone bird's tentative warble tested the silence. A whisper of motion hissed at the edge of her sight. The shadows and light shifted behind the thorn bushes. There he was again!

"Wait!" she called out.

The creature bolted. She plunged into the forest after him. The ferns trembled with her passing, leaving a trail of bent fronds in her wake. A rabbit startled out of hiding and dashed desperately for a hole under the roots of a crooked old oak. A grouse erupted from the green grass in a sunny patch. The fox-boy flashed past in a blaze of red as he ran out of the dappled shade into a sunlit break in the canopy.

Ari Ara pursued him. The woods deepened, darkened, and steepened. She scrambled up a slope, slipping on the wet rot of last year's leaves, yelping as she twisted midstride to avoid crushing a black and gold salamander. Her sharp ears tracked the faint crunch and rustle of the fox-boy's footsteps. She grasped for handholds among the twisted tree roots exposed by erosion.

At the crest of the slope, the leafy shrubs gave way to dark pines. Their glossy needles hung low, cloaking their trunks. They grew huddled together, looking like a cluster of ladies in wide skirts. Ari Ara peered through the dense branches, trying to glimpse her quarry among the somber green-black boughs. Just when she was ready to give up, she spotted a patch of crushed mushrooms in the damp moss that carpeted the earth. A trail of footprints led her toward the sound of a running stream. As she burst out among brilliant red reeds, she saw the fox-boy leap the water and head for the meadow on the other side. Giving chase, she jumped the stream and jogged to a halt in the sunlit clearing.

Where did the creature go? she wondered, pulling twigs from her hair and inspecting the patches of wildflowers for crushed stems and bent grass blades.

She scanned the shadows beneath the trees. Emerald moss clung to the roots. If he had passed through here, the crushed stems would have shown his steps.

Nothing.

Ari Ara craned her head back and inspected the boughs

above. In her early trainings in the Way Between, she had learned to look for all the pathways that lay between fight and flight. She had practiced seeing what wasn't obvious and looking for the empty spaces hiding in plain sight. She used this skill now, scanning the forest, the moss, and the edge of the meadow. She studied the area, watching for clusters of shadows where light should shimmer or solid patches of brown where only dappled green leaves should flutter. Suddenly, she stilled, realizing with hair-raising certainty where the fox-boy was hiding. Across the meadow, tall grasses danced in the wind, but one section swayed in a different rhythm, held back by a patch of stalks that had been flattened.

She leapt, quick as a cat, and pounced into the center of the grasses. The boy yelped in alarm as she pinned him. Surprise widened his eyes and dropped his mouth open. His lean muscles tensed for a brief struggle then surrendered.

A peal of sharp, unmistakably human laughter burst loose. His fox cap had been knocked off, lying like an animal amidst a patch of tangled purple flowers. A spray of crushed daisies formed a wreathe around his black curls. Still kneeling on him, Ari Ara let his wrists go and scooped up the cap. It wasn't fur at all! It was stitched with brightly-colored thread, the oranges and reds so carefully crafted it fooled the eye. She offered it back to the boy.

"Who are you?" she blurted out.

His smile flashed, lopsided and toothy.

"Finn Paikason."

"I'm Ari -"

"I know who you are. You're not what I expected."

"Oh?" Ari Ara retorted, wondering just what he'd been told about her.

"I thought the heir to two thrones would have a crown or something."

Ari Ara made a face. It was true, she was a double royal, heir to two nations. But that didn't mean she had a crown or a throne. Her father, called the Desert King by the Marianans, was actually the Honor-Keeper of the nation rather than the monarch. And her mother's people had refused to accept her as the heir to the throne, sending her into exile instead.

"Sorry to disappoint you," she replied.

"You didn't," he answered.

For some reason, his words made her blush. They studied each other with equal measures of wariness and curiosity. Finn looked like he had grown from the craggy stones and furred forests of this land. Everything about him was roughened; hands like wood, tough with callouses; skin dark with sun, cheeks a blaze of wind-chapped red, eyes that looked like bits of sky fallen from a lightning-stabbed storm. His leggings had patches on the patches. His cuffs hung ragged. Grass stains left crisscrosses on his knees. Ari Ara guessed that he was about her age, maybe a year older. He tossed the stray strands of wild black hair off his forehead with an impatient gesture. She had the uncanny suspicion that if she blinked, he'd vanish right out from under her.

Ari Ara scrambled backward, letting him up. He rolled over and rose to his feet, brushing grass and tiny flower petals from his shirt. Finn snatched his cap from her and pulled it low over his eyes. It shadowed his gaze, making him hard to read.

"Well?" she asked Finn Paikason. "Why are you spying on the Peace Force?"

She tossed a grin in his direction. He caught it, but shrugged. Something more grimace than grin crossed his face.

"You could come study with us, you know," she offered.

They wanted to share the Way Between up and down the Border Mountains. They could start with Finn Paikason.

"Why would a *Piker* bother with your nonsense?" Finn scoffed, whacking the grass tips with his hand. He snarled the word out, lips twisting in self-derision.

Whatever a *Piker* was, Ari Ara doubted it was a compliment. He spoke the word as if it had been hurled in his face like cow dung, over and over.

"Peace is for everyone," she started to say.

He leapt the distance between them, eyes narrowed, nose close to hers.

"Don't lecture me, Ari Ara Marin en Shirar," he warned her softly. "You're standing on Paika ground. Your people killed us for deserting your armies, for refusing to fight, and for being conscripted to your enemy's army. You burned our homes, massacred our people, starved us, and occupied us. And now you dare build peace here?"

He stepped back, tilting his chin up defiantly, arms crossed defensively over his chest. Ari Ara's pride stung at his words. She stared steadily back at him, refusing to be intimidated.

"Yes, I dare," she answered. "Peace has to start somewhere."

He let out a bark of laughter.

Ari Ara stiffened her resolve. In the Way Between, one never ran from a conflict. Nor did you attack the attacker, no matter how scared or angry you were.

"Look," she said, offering her hand out, palm up in the greeting of the Harraken, "maybe we got off on the wrong foot."

"I'll say. You knocked me clear off my feet," Finn snapped. He sniffed proudly and brushed his shirt again. She got the impression that he was more affronted by the fact that she'd caught him at all than that her pounce had sent him sprawling. He gave her outstretched hand a disdainful glance.

"Don't bother trying to be friends," he told her curtly. "I'm just a *Piker*."

"I don't even know what that is," she sighed in exasperation.

"Ask your friends," Finn growled. "I'm sure they'll tell you all about the backstabbing Pikers."

Then Finn Paikason spun away and sprinted into the shadowy woods.

This time, she did not follow.

CHAPTER TWO

. . . . .

The Rumor Song

Ari Ara raced back to Moscam. The town nestled like an egg in a bird's nest of mountains. Above the houses, swift-soaring clouds careened over the snow-capped peaks. The slate of the steep roofs served as defensive armor against fire, stretching all the way from high ridgelines down to the stone-carved gutters at the foot of the buildings. Moscam was an old town; the inhabitants claimed to have lived here for centuries. A few houses testified to an even older age with time-darkened foundation stones that bore the names of masons in Old Tongue runes. Others, constructed of wood, had been burned in wars and rebuilt many times.

According to local tradition, the buildings were salvaged from rubble. The stones of the old were laid into the hearth of the new. Moscam's residents mixed the ashes of the past into the mortar of the future, remembering what had happened as life churned ever onward. Local families renamed their dwellings each time they were rebuilt. They spoke to their houses, telling them the stories of their mother, grandmother, and great-grandmother houses. In this way, the histories of buildings and

15

humans entwined like two strands of wool making a strong yarn. To lose the story of the home meant the loss of two lineages not just one. It made Moscam a place of long memories - and even longer grudges.

The War of Retribution had hit the town hard. During the conflict over the death of Ari Ara's mother, Queen Alinore, a sweating sickness had left more of them buried in the forest graveyard than living in the houses. Ari Ara could sometimes feel the restless spirits on dark moon nights, tossing and turning in their graves, crying for water, haunted by the thirst that had killed them.

The town's headwoman had been eager to host the Peace Force. The clamor of the group's voices filled the aching silences in her town. She had rallied her community to clean out their two great halls, one for a dwelling space, the other for trainings and communal meals. She personally swept the cobwebs from the rafters of an empty cottage to offer a quiet meeting space for the three leaders. The funds and supplies contributed by both nations to support the endeavor meant prosperity for her town. And notoriety. The name Moscam no longer evoked images of a sad, empty town fading into the twilight of obscurity. Moscam had become a symbol of hope, revival, and peace.

Ari Ara nearly knocked over the headwoman as she sprinted around a building into the main street. Shouting an apology over her shoulder, she hopped across the stepping-stones over the wide, central drainage gutter. She passed a pair of lads drawing water from the well. She skirted a row of old women spinning in the shade of an overhang. The chatter of their gossipy questions chased her heels. Scouring the narrow streets for signs of Minli's tousled brown hair, she flattened against the wall of a barn while a Moscam lass herded her goats past, headed toward higher pastures.

Beside the Main Hall, at the foot of a stately beech tree, she found Minli reading cross-legged as he waited for lessons to begin. Professor Solange sat next to him on the grass, a caterpillar inching unnoticed through her frizzled and greying hair. The stout scholar looked more likely to be found ensconced in a dusty records room than tromping about the mountains, but Solange had cheerfully abandoned the comforts of her university post to support the peace work. Last year, she'd aided Minli in organizing two peace delegations – one from the desert, the other from the riverlands – to exchange visits. In the desert, she'd burnt redder than Ari Ara's hair and peeled like an onion, but Solange's archival knowledge of history, war, and the Way Between had helped the delegation navigate the trickier moments and challenges. She had smoothed over awkward mishaps, translated for her peers, and provided a steadying force when the trip turned tumultuous. When the Marianan nobles had tried to rescind the Great Lady's invitation to the Harraken delegation, Professor Solange had convinced Brinelle to hold firm. Over the winter, the twelve Harraken visitors had given talks and song concerts, participated in unprecedented dialogues with their enemies, and secured Marianan support for reviving the Peace Force this summer. Ari Ara had heard all of this secondhand from Minli, of course. She was still officially exiled from Mariana, though she knew her Aunt Brinelle was searching for the right political moment to invite her to return.

History lessons with Professor Solange were far more exciting than the dull recitations of war she'd endured at Monk's Hand Monastery. Alaren had stalked these mountains thousands of years ago. After his death, the old Peace Force stayed active for centuries longer. These forests were the backdrop for Ari Ara's favorite folktales and legends. The dowdy scholar took her students on hikes to the places where several of Alaren's adventures transpired. She showed them a cave where Alaren and his family might have taken shelter from snowstorms and soldiers. She tested them by having them fill out maps with markers for as many stories and historical facts as they could remember. She asked them to imagine the realities of Alaren's tales, how it felt to make a lake's worth of soup for hungry villagers, or what it sounded like to hammer up signs for Peace Villages.

"The old legends are full of dashing deeds and daring heroics," she had warned them, "but they skip over the drudgery and hard work. Alaren walked for days to get from one village to the next. He spent hours learning the songs that his Peace Force used. At his Way Station, he sweated buckets pulling up his turnips to feed people working for peace."

This, she insisted, was important to remember. The work of the Way Between wasn't always dramatic and flashy. Most of the time, it was quiet and ordinary.

Ari Ara crouched down on her heels in front of Minli and Professor Solange. She was glad to see the scholar. The middle-aged woman was a walking library on a host of subjects. If Minli didn't know what *Pikers* were, she would.

"What is a Piker?" she asked them.

Minli looked up sharply from his book.

"Not Piker, *Paika*," he corrected. "We learned about them, remember? If you had paid attention in class, you'd know."

The name tickled the edges of her memory. Now that he mentioned it, she had heard it before.

"They are a very ancient people," Solange reminded Ari Ara, "as old as the Fanten - and far older than the Harraken and Marianans, whose cultural identities only began to distinguish from one another when King Marin and King Shirar split the world. The Paika have inhabited the Border Mountains through all of the wars and territorial claims of the two nations. Our tales tend to report only our conflicts with them. Conflicts, mind you, that are narrated from the perspective of our nations, not the Paika clans. Beneath those very skewed tales, what we know is this: the Paika are the world's most skillful trackers. They know the Border Mountains intimately, having spent thousands of years living here. And, they are extraordinary mapmakers. They've had to be."

She sighed again, thinking of how often the maps of this region had been redrawn. The Border Mountains, past and present, were a complicated terrain, the epicenter of thousands of years of conflict. The Paika had weathered the chaos of invasion and occupation, migrating populations, refugees and warlords, and ever-changing laws and rulers. The border lines had been drawn and erased, shifted and ignored so many times that many of the local villagers had simply given up trying to remember which nation they were part of this year. The villagers often fled their homes as war crashed down upon them, moving to fortified cities, then returning to pick up the pieces of their lives in the short-lived lulls between outbreaks of violence.

"Did you see a Paika?" Minli asked, eyeing Ari Ara with keen curiosity.

"I met one," Ari Ara told him.

Solange looked delighted.

"My word! A Paika here in Moscam! I've been longing to speak with them. They're quite standoffish, you know, but so knowledgeable about this region."

Ari Ara hastened to explain that the boy had vanished. The professor looked crestfallen.

"So, why are they called Pikers?" Ari Ara asked, still confused about why Finn had used that word. From his tone of voice, it wasn't a compliment.

"Because in the war, they cut off people's heads and stuck them on poles," Solange answered matter-of-factly.

Ari Ara gagged.

"But the armies also did it to them in punishment," Minli reminded her with a frown. "It's not their name, though. *Pikers* is an insult and we shouldn't use it. They are the Paika."

"Ah, Shulen," Solange called out, spotting the old warrior. "Your dear girl here has spotted a Paika! Isn't that marvelous!?"

Shulen's scarred face folded into a scowl. He crossed his muscled arms over his chest and eyed Ari Ara. The wild, red-haired girl had long held a place in his gruff old heart, but she did have a penchant for trouble. He was not surprised that she – of all people – had run into the Paika. His swift gaze shot suspiciously toward the forest, scanning the trees for threats.

"Oh, come Shulen, none of that," Solange chided, catching his expression. "They're not our enemies."

"The Pikers - "

"Don't call them that," she interrupted sharply.

"The Paika," he corrected grudgingly, "are not necessarily our friends, either."

Solange frowned. She knew Shulen had many reasons to distrust the Paika - scars down his back, friends left dead from their ambushes, and, worst of all, it was possible that the southern Paika clans had been involved in the death of his wife and child. The mercenaries that had chased Queen Alinore and Shulen's family into the High Mountains could have come from anywhere. The bodies Shulen had left strewn under the shadows of the Great Trees had mixed features similar to the Paika, lighter-skinned than the Harraken, darker than the Marianans. They carried no insignias or identifying marks. None had been captured alive. The identity of these attackers was the most closely-guarded secret in the world.

Tahkan Shirar, himself, was traveling in the southern border mountains, following hints and clues that had been uncovered last winter. It was the only reason he'd let his daughter out of his sight and permitted her to join the Peace Force this summer. It was safer here, under the guardianship of his sister Mahteni Shirar and the steely-eyed watchfulness of Shulen.

Stiff as a dog with his hackles up, Shulen grilled Ari Ara about her encounter with the Paika boy. How long had she sensed him spying? Why didn't she mention it? Who was this boy?

"His name is Finn Paikason - "

"A Spires Paika, then," Shulen grumbled, mentioning the needle-like rocks to the north. "What's he doing here? This is far south for a son of *The Paika*."

"Grandson or great-grandson, more like," Solange corrected, calculating the age of the clan leader known by her title, not her name. "*The Paika* would be quite old now."

"He didn't mean any harm," Ari Ara put in. Truthfully, Finn had been a bit hostile, but at least he hadn't tried to hurt her. "He doesn't think much of the Peace Force, though."

She glanced from Solange's bemused face to Shulen's scowl.

"Maybe we should reach out to the Paika and invite them to visit?" she suggested.

Shulen snorted.

"They'd never agree to that, not in a thousand years."

"How do we know if we don't ask?" Ari Ara countered.

The grey-haired man switched subjects, scolding her for her recklessness. She shouldn't be wandering the woods all by herself. She had enemies - an assassin had tried to kill her two years ago. What if the boy had been a mercenary? Or had lured her into a trap? Why was he spying, anyway? Who was he working for? The Paika had always served as spies and trackers for one faction or another. Who was it this time? What if they took her hostage? There wasn't a bandit gang in the Border Mountains that wouldn't leap at the chance to kidnap the Lost Heir for ransom.

"Including the Pikers - Paika," Shulen stated, correcting himself when three sets of eyes narrowed in protest. "They're notorious for taking hostages as protection against retaliatory attacks."

"No one holds a follower of the Way Between against her will," Ari Ara grumblingly reminded him.

Shulen informed Moscam's headwoman, urging her to warn everyone against wandering alone. The town's leader, however, was not unduly alarmed by the sighting. The Moscam townspeople crossed paths with the Paika from time to time.

"We stay out of their business and they stay out of ours," she remarked with a shrug.

The headwoman didn't like the Pikers - no one did - but she wasn't going to go hunting for the boy. He wasn't worth the fuss. Shulen disagreed. Pikers served as spies and mercenaries. What was one of their boys doing, creeping around, following the Lost Heir? He argued that someone should track the lad, but the headwoman warned such efforts would be wasted.

"No one tracks a Piker, not in these mountains," she stated emphatically. "They vanish and reappear like magic."

By the time the bell rang for midmorning trainings, word of the sighting had spread. Gossip flew, fast and furious. As the thirty Peace Force members filed into the hall, their nervous babble bounced off the high ceiling and crashed down around their ears. A small crowd surrounded Ari Ara, bombarding her with questions. New friends and old had gathered this summer. Acquaintances from both sides of the border had leapt at the chance to join the Peace Force. Everill Riverdon, the former

Urchin Queen, jostled at Ari Ara's elbow, prying for details in her choppy, street urchin's accent. Emir Miresh studied her with his warrior-like intensity, eyes furrowed together under his ink-dark hair. Young Sarai Nouran blurted out the tales her desert family told about the Paika. She wasn't the only one with stories. From east to west, north to south, each had a dark tale of backstabbing Pikers.

"I heard they raid villages and take children hostage," said Isa de Barre tentatively, nervously patting her honey-wheat hair into place. As heir to a noble house, she'd grown up around warnings of kidnappings and ransom schemes.

"They do it for protection against reprisals," Marek de Westers declared, straightening his beanpole spine and nodding with an air of authority. As a Marianan noble from the Westlands, he knew all about the raids and dangers his father's merchant caravans faced in the mountain passes. "My father always travels under full guard because of the Pikers. He says they're all bandits and looters."

A wizened old man from Turim City chanted a phrase in the desert tongue, reciting an old saying. Confusion spread over the Marianans faces; few of them spoke Harrak-tala, the Desert Speech. Another Harraken took pity on them and translated. He had come from the Desert Crossroads with his husband, leaving their orchard in the hands of relatives for the summer.

"*Mercenaries, trackers, bandits, betrayers, Pikers can't be trusted,*" he explained.

"Vicious turncoats," muttered a student from the Capital University. "You should see the records on them. They flip loyalty in every war, even mid-battle, selling out the apparent losers to gain favor with the victors."

"I heard it was their betrayal during the War of Retribution that led to our loss," Sarai hissed, mock-spitting in disgust.

"I heard," said Minli severely, the click-thud of his crutch and one-legged stride rapping on wooden floor as he approached the huddled group, "that you shouldn't believe everything you hear."

"Are you saying they didn't betray us?" Sarai shot back hotly, hands on her hips, indignant.

Minli shrugged. He couldn't say for sure, but that was the point: what did any of them really know about the Paika? Rumors and tales, mostly, and a few shallow facts taken out of context.

"Don't you remember the Rumor Song?" a new voice called out, unexpectedly supporting Minli.

A slender youth elbowed into the crowded circle, umber-skinned with a head of copper-tinged black curls. Tala's green eyes flashed with mirth. Neither male, nor female, Tala was the youngest of the thirteen Tala-Rasa, the songholders of the desert, and held in great respect. Accorded pronouns that had no translation in Marianan, Tala went by *ze, zir, zirs*, instead of *he, him, his* or *she, her, hers*. After a few awkward mix-ups and flustered apologies, the Marianans had caught the knack of it and now couldn't imagine trying to cram Tala into the box of one gender. Ze had been sent to the Peace Force by the twelve other songholders, but even without their instructions, Tala wouldn't have missed this for the world. Driven by a sixth sense for history-in-the-making, Tala had forged a fast friendship with Ari Ara Marin en Shirar and then with Minli of Monk's Hand. The scholarly boy and the young songholder shared much in common. The two were thick as thieves.

Tala drew even with Minli, exchanging knowing looks. They shook their heads with matching sighs. Rumors killed peace as fast as soldiers. During the delegations last year, ze and Minli had their hands full quelling lies and gossip. Facing the group, Tala clapped out a rhythm and sang out the Rumor Song in zirs clear voice. It was a chastising little ditty with a catchy melody that taught Harraken children to sort through truth and hearsay. With so many rumors in the air about the Paika, it was the perfect reminder about why they shouldn't believe every rumor that crossed their ears.

I heard . . . I heard . . . I heard . . . A little bird told Alaren.

Absurd . . . Absurd . . . Absurd . . . Alaren warbled back.

The Harraken laughed and jumped in. They'd all sung it as children, though not with Alaren's name. Ari Ara translated for the Marianans. Language lessons were strongly encouraged in their spare time. Since most Harraken had a relative who had gone to Mariana to work in the Water Exchange, many spoke the riverlands tongue. But only a handful of the Marianans spoke Harrak-tala, the Desert Speech. The Peace Force used the common tongue of Marianan in lessons, but everyone strove to learn both languages.

"Before repeating a story," Minli reminded them as the song broke off into laughter, "ask yourself: is this true? Where did I hear this? Was it a reliable source? What's being left out of the tale I just heard?"

Entire wars had been launched on half-truths and lies, the facts only emerging long after a battle of falsehoods had left behind grieving mothers and orphaned children. The Peace Force couldn't repeat malicious gossip that struck fear into people's hearts. They couldn't spread secondhand tales that drove wedges between groups. They had to make sure that every word that came out of their mouths was not only factual, it helped move people closer together. In the tangled web of tensions that stretched across the Border Mountains, someone had to break the cycle of prejudice and misunderstandings. That someone would be the Peace Force.

"But isn't it true that the Pikers - Paika," the university

student corrected hastily as Minli shot him a stern look, "take hostages and betray people in times of war? It's in the records."

"Records can be wrong," Minli admitted, though it pained him to say so. "They can leave out important details."

His glance met Ari Ara's. They'd learned this as young orphans at Monk's Hand Monastery, searching for the true identity of the Lost Heir, neither realizing that she was sitting right there.

"Our Harraken Song Cycles also portray the Paika as traitorous," Tala mentioned, after humming under zirs breath with a far-away look, remembering thousand-year-old lyrics from ballads about backstabbing Paika. "It's unlikely that those are all falsehoods."

"Unlikely, but not impossible," Rill muttered under her breath, skeptical of the veracity of such old songs.

The street urchin's grumble set off a clamor of protest from the Harraken. The Tala-Rasa were revered throughout the desert – to question them was to question *harrak*, the honor, dignity, and integrity of their people. Just because the Harraken recorded their knowledge in song and memory did not mean they were any less accurate than the Marianans' history books. It was an old insult, one the desert dwellers resented deeply.

"We don't have to write things down. Our minds are better than yours," Sarai declared furiously.

"I'm just sayin' the old ballads mighta taken poetic liberties with the facts," Rill replied, hands lifted defensively, her accent thickening in the heat of the argument.

Minli stepped between them. Equally feisty and hot-tempered, the two were always at each other's throats, putting the skills of the Peace Force to test on a daily basis. Twice, they'd come close to sending the two youths home, but each time, the pair promised to try harder, looking shame-faced for their quarrels when they had come to work for peace. No one in the Peace Force was perfect . . . they simply felt that the chance of peace was worth working through their grudges.

"I just meant that the Harraken trust that our Tala-Rasa are telling the truth," Sarai amended in a lower tone.

"At any rate, between the records and the songs, it's the only truth we know," Tala pointed out.

"But there's so much we don't know!" Rill cried out in frustration.

"Ah," Minli chuckled, "now you're getting it. So much of what we think is solid fact isn't as solid as it seems. If the rumors you've been told were a frozen river, would you dare to walk across it? How solid or weak are the 'truths' you've been told? Would you stake your life on them? Would you rush to put your weight upon them without examining them for cracks? If someone shouted a warning to you from the other side, would you stop and look more closely?"

Minli did not need to spell out the example that haunted them all. The Marianans had charged into the desert fourteen years ago, willing to spill blood over the rumors that the Harraken had attacked their queen and stolen their heir. Tahkan Shirar had vehemently denied all those claims. No evidence ever pointed to his people. Nonetheless, the Marianan army rushed onto thin ice and fell through into the deathly waters of war. The black Ancestor River had gulped down the souls of the battlefield dead. Years of tragic, needless violence had ensued.

It was up to the Peace Force to prevent that from happening again.

CHAPTER THREE

. . . . .

Finn's Request

That night, after dinner, the Peace Force gathered in a wide circle around a campfire. A touch of coolness still clung to the air. The cold of distant snowcaps plummeted down into the valley like an invisible waterfall. Stars shone like white sprays of wildflowers in an inky meadow. Ari Ara eyed the black treetops swaying against the even darker sky. She sensed nothing, but still wondered if Finn was out there, watching and listening.

Professor Solange spoke. It had been a long, tense afternoon. Overhearing the Rumor Song, she and Mahteni decided to split the afternoon session, teaching what they knew about the Paika and drilling the Peace Force in how to counter rumors. Minli had taken the lead in some of these exercises. From the beginning, the youths had led certain trainings. Emir and Ari Ara aided Shulen's dawn lessons in the physical Way Between. Tala and Sarai guided some of Mahteni's exercises in how to work together *en masse*. Minli served as Solange's assistant in history and politics lessons. At first, some had murmured in surprise or skepticism, but Mahteni swiftly set them straight.

"Our Peace Force will learn from all of us, with all of us. The

29

youngest have as much wisdom to share as the eldest. Peace is forged not just by those strong in body, but also by those strong in heart, mind, and spirit."

No one had worked harder to revive the Way Between than Minli. Without him, the curriculum would never have been written, the delegations would not have happened, the water rights would not have been secured for the desert, and the water workers would not have been freed. The world already owed this boy a great deal, whether they realized it or not.

The afternoon session, however, had stirred up the hornet's nest of prejudices carried by each culture. Insults of *desert demons* and *river dogs* had been flung. The work uncovered buried hurts and lingering pain from the war years. The youths had lost parents; the older folk had lived through the battles. It was important to confront the past, not ignore it. Only then could they begin to heal.

Looking around the evening circle, Solange could see dark memories lingering in people's eyes, remembering that they had once been enemies in war. Now, they had to remember that they wanted to be friends in peace.

"During this afternoon's session on rumors," she said, "we heard a lot of hard, painful words. Tonight, I thought it would be good to ease that harshness."

The light of the fire gleamed on her face. This was an old practice, she told them, as old as Alaren's time, but it had been lost in recent years. She came across it in a book of ancient poems. Two lovers, meeting for the first time, shared where they were from - not just the geography and place names, but also the scents and sounds of their childhoods, the legends and heroes that inspired them, and the memories that gave them strength. Too often, people assumed they knew the journey someone else had walked, simply because of their accent or skin color or style of dress. But they were all so much more than simple categories of Harraken or Marianan, noble or commoner, warrior or farmer. Around the circle, they held a world of stories and experiences.

As the fire crackled and hissed, Solange asked everyone to close their eyes and remember the sights, smells, and sounds of their childhood years. she encouraged them to think of familiar foods, both daily staples and special treats of feast days. She asked them to remember routine chores and tasks, and the adventures or unusual things that happened in their youths. She let them sit with their memories for a while. A calm quiet stilled the air. Then she asked Ari Ara to share a few words about these recollections, starting with the phrase *I am from . . .* and then weaving her words like poetry.

"I am from . . . " Ari Ara began, "Fanten drums and secrets, black woolly sheep, even blacker high peaks, cold brightness and blue skies, and the rare joy of fresh-baked bread."

A few people blinked in surprise, remembering belatedly that the famous Lost Heir had started out as an orphaned shepherdess raised by the Fanten, running half-wild in the mountains. The next person to share was a grandmother from Tuloon Ravine, the woman who had first heard the Outcry Song breaking the silences of her desert home as the women rose up to demand their rights. The Harraken elder's light green eyes darkened to emerald in the firelight, growing distant with the vast stretches of time between this night and her childhood long ago.

"I am from songs too numerous to name, my family's voices blending together, heat and dust, and the relief of shade, spicy beans and almond sweets, the scent of the *gorchi* bush touched by the rain, and the sip of ritual water shared with all visitors."

The university student from Marianan Capital spoke next.

31

"I am from . . . a house without books, and a hunger to know more, and a life-saving soup when I ran away to attend university."

Ari Ara stared at him. She'd never known this piece of the scholar's past. Gazing around the circle of faces illuminated by firelight, she wondered how many hidden memories each person carried. Like the mountains, a human being was full of concealed ravines, tucked-away springs, and secrets like rare-blooming plants. She could spend a lifetime learning about them and never discover a fraction of their stories.

Next, the grandfather from Turim spoke of old things – he'd been born amidst war and raised in its shadow - apricot orchards lost in attacks, the hiss of arrows over the city, strange days passing in a hush while his parents buried the dead. The dressier from Mariana listened with tears in her eyes and a quiver on her lips. She remembered those wars, too. She spoke of the sound of clacking looms as the grey cloth for soldiers' uniforms stretched out by the mile.

As the sharing spun around the circle, Ari Ara sensed a world growing in the open space between them all. It ached with painful recollections, but it also brimmed with laughter and love. It was alive with memories of horse races in dry lands and swimming in favorite river bends. She lived for brief moments in the experiences of all those in the circle. She heard the buzz of the bees and the sweet-rotten smell of apples at harvest time in the Crossroads Orchard. She felt the delicacy of old parchment under the scholar's fingers as he studied old records in the archives. She heard the chanting of monks in the temples.

When they opened another round on familiar sayings, Rill set everyone laughing with shockingly colorful street urchin curses. Mahteni invoked *harrak-en-harrak, the honor in me recognizes the honor in you.* Everyone grew somber when Minli mentioned the adage of Mariana's war culture: *good soldiers make orphans and orphans make good soldiers.* Then they honored ancestors, known and unknown, by blood and by teachings. Isa and Mahteni could recite their lineages back generations. Rill named the Urchin Kings and Queens before her. Emir acknowledged both his goatherder parents to the north and Shulen as his mentor. The woodworker from the Craftlands spoke of the master carver who had trained him. The Ancestor Wind was mentioned; the Ancestor River was invoked.

By the time Shulen spoke quietly of hearing the stories of Alaren read aloud by his grandmother, Ari Ara felt like she'd been on a thousand-mile journey across nine decades of time. Tears pooled in her eyes, moved by the scenes the stories evoked. The depth of time and breadth of culture filled the air like water poured into a bowl. As the logs burned down to hissing embers, Ari Ara could hardly take a breath without feeling the whole of history moving inside her. They – and their cultures – contained so much more than the horrors of war. Beyond the hiss of arrows and the clang of swords, their lives were constructed of stories told in grandmothers' voices, ridiculous games played with siblings and friends, trades learned at fathers' knees, weaving patterns passed down from mother to daughter, the bridge of a rainbow emblazoned on the sky, and the whispers of ancestors in river and wind.

"This is the work of the Way Between," Solange said in closing. "This is how we see each other as more than former enemies. We may be from different lands, but we have common ground between us."

A slow clap rang out, ironic and mocking. Twisting toward the sound, Ari Ara saw Finn Paikason step out of night's darkness, his young face tight with scorn. The firelight glinted in the glass eyes of his fox cap. Expressions around the circle thudded shut like lids of heavy chests dropped in rebuke. Minli, however, shifted closer to Tala, making space for the newcomer to sit.

"Care to join us, Finn Paikason?" Ari Ara asked daringly.

She patted the log, but the lad shook his head.

"I won't stay long," he declared. "I merely wished to join your . . . game."

A contorted smile flickered on his lips. His stormy eyes turned glassy with unshed emotion. The bands of his wiry muscles twitched along his arms, taut with holding back an outburst. Ari Ara's heart sank and lurched simultaneously.

"I am Finn Paikason, descendent of the first Paika clan. I am from these mountains. The bones of their minerals built my limbs. The blood of their waters flows in my veins. The secret poetry of their winds shushes through my voice."

Ari Ara blinked at the unexpected truth – she could hear the sibilant *ssss* hissing in his accent. He threaded the vowels within each other like a low moan of wind bending around stone and sifting through pine boughs. He was young for the poetry of his words, but he carried his head high and unabashed as he spoke, as if turning a beautiful phrase was as natural as breathing the air in these peaks. Perhaps, for the Paika, it was.

"I am from thickets and deep moss, snow-scraped ridges and shadowed gulches, the bellow of elk and the haunting howl of wolves. I am Paika, and so I am from the longevity of mountains, millennia-old, and ancestors that lived long before yours."

He shot a defiant look at Ari Ara, daring her to challenge his claim. His knew his ancestors' names beyond those who had walked alongside the two kings, Marin and Shirar. He recalled his people's stories of Alaren. They had been here for an eternity by the time the world was split in half. To be Paika was to endure, to survive, to outlive and outlast the passing madness of wars, borders, and nations.

Shulen studied the boy carefully, noting his hot-tempered pride. Ever protective, the older man silently measured the distance between Finn and Ari Ara. He calculated the speed of his own crossing. He plotted his ability to react if the boy's words converted into an attempt on the girl's life. Ari Ara looked entranced; her eyes alight as she listened. A pang of tangled emotions twisted in Shulen, a protective growl, a sting of shock that the wild eleven-year-old he'd met only three years earlier now eyed a boy like *that*, an urge to scold her for it; a yearning to sit her down and explain a thousand things, a sharp regret that he was not her father; a flash of anger that Tahkan was so far away, missing this moment like so many other moments of Ari Ara's life. Shulen shoved the thoughts aside; he didn't have time to sift through them. He had to stay focused on the startling interruption of Finn Paikason.

Finn's next remarks tripped over his tongue, beginning as a condemnation, tumbling into an anguished plea.

"I am Paika," the boy said, "and we are a people shaped by conflict. We are from the clash of sword meeting sword, the twang of bowstrings, the screams of mothers, and the wails of children. We are from fear and hiding. We are cloaked in secrecy and lies of survival. We have learned to have no loyalties but our own. We do what we must because you – Marianan and Harraken, alike – have left us no other options."

Finn swallowed hard, dropping his eyes to mask his shame. Everything the outsiders said about his people was true – and none of it contained the whole truth of the story. The Paika *had* betrayed armies. They *had* switched sides to stand with the victors. They *did* lie as smoothly as they spoke.

What other choice did they have?

Like a fox sneezing pollen-dust, he shook the past from his

thoughts. It was the present that concerned him, the current tangle of truth and lies had brought him here. Vulnerability made him ferocious within his armor of pride. Finn Paikason was nothing if not proud, nothing if not fiercely independent. He'd been able to find his path through these mountains since he could toddle. He had just turned fifteen, but his clan did not hesitate to send him on a lengthy journey south to spy on the Peace Force. He did not like asking for the help of outsiders. Yet, he must. Yesterday, a messenger hawk had swooped down, screeching, bearing instructions from his elders. It rubbed him wrong to be truthful with foreigners, but no one else would even consider aiding the Paika. Finn swallowed hard, uncomfortable. Speaking truth to these people went against centuries of beliefs in his culture. The Paika spoke truth to each other and lies to all others. To be honest with strangers was like stepping naked into the middle of a crowd.

"The Paika are in trouble," he declared, "and only the Peace Force can help us."

CHAPTER FOUR

. . . . .

Stillness & Slowness

To the north, in a terrain of jagged peaks that punctured the clouds, a group of riders swept through the small villages, raiding and harassing the farmers. Normally, the Paika avoided intervening in the constant banditry and roving gangs of thieves. This time, however, they had cause for concern: witnesses claimed the raiders were Paika. The Paika denied it – the raiders were merely masquerading as them, imitating their distinctive embroidered hats and patterned cloaks.

"I've heard your people are the finest trackers in the world," Shulen told Finn sternly after hearing the tale. "Surely you can track down the imposters."

Finn shot the older man an incensed look.

"We would, but the commander at Garrison Town believes we're the culprits. He has banned us from the Fire Peaks Region. We cannot enter to track the raiders, nor question the villagers, nor clear our name. We'll be hanged or worse."

"And what do you want us to do?" Shulen asked the boy.

"*The Paika* requests that the Peace Force go to Commander Mendren and persuade him to lift the ban," he choked on the request, hiding behind the authority of his great-grandmother and clan leader, every muscle in his wiry, sun-browned body tightening, trying not to squirm in the agonizing humiliation of asking for the Peace Force's help. He made the request only because *The Paika* had ordered him to do so. On his cheekbones, a burnt rose blush burned against the acorn of his face. He stared at his boots with resigned despair, fully expecting them to reject his plea for aid. No one helped the Paika. The Paika helped themselves. This was the way it had been for a thousand years. He doubted the Peace Force would be any different.

"We will consider it," Shulen answered cautiously.

"Is that a *yes* or a *no?*" Finn retorted, anxiety driving him to needle the older man.

"Neither, and you'll have to be satisfied with that," Shulen replied sternly.

With the impatience of youth, Finn interpreted those words as nothing more than a delayed denial. He shot them a vindicated glare, spun on his heel, and left.

The arc of the stars swung past midnight before the Peace Force finished the heated discussion over what to do. Were they ready to plunge into this conflict? Raw and untested as a youth stumbling over her own feet, the newly-formed Peace Force had planned to go slow, start small, and achieve modest goals this summer. One couldn't run before they could walk, after all, and they had scarcely finished their training. If they blundered this summer, it could hinder peace work for years to come, giving the Way Between a reputation for failure. Solange and Shulen did not want them to get distracted from their plan to teach, train, and tell stories through the warm season, building understanding and support for the Peace Force.

"Why can't we do both?" Ari Ara cried, speaking out of turn and getting shushed for interrupting another person. Each member had a chance to weigh in on decisions, though Mahteni, Shulen, and Solange made the final call as the official leaders.

"Two feet can't move in opposite directions without tripping," Shulen told her.

Mahteni agreed, arguing that they should stick together, not splinter. She raised another concern, an uneasy worry that nagged her: what if Finn's request was a crafty trap set by the Paika? All rumors aside, the records and songs showed that, throughout history, the Paika had manipulated factions into the tangled web of their schemes. Maybe they *were* the raiders and were simply using the Peace Force to get the ban lifted so they could continue to raid with impunity.

"But Finn said they aren't doing those raids," Ari Ara repeated, obstinate in the face of everyone's willingness to think the worst of the Paika.

"Can he be trusted, though?" Shulen grumbled. He doubted it. The lad seemed clever and sneaky to him.

"We should learn more about the situation before taking action," Mahteni cautioned reasonably. As the newly-founded Peace Force, they shouldn't get embroiled in controversy so early in their efforts.

"Tangling with the Paika is nothing but trouble," Marek muttered. "They've always got a trick up their sleeve and nothing is what it seems."

"But we're the Peace Force!" Ari Ara bellowed in fruitless outrage. "We're supposed to help people. That includes the Paika!"

"And we will," Shulen answered her, "though not necessarily in the manner young Finn Paikason wishes. As the Peace Force, we have to be careful that we don't take sides, working for just one group without listening to the others."

"If we do nothing, we *are* taking a side - the side that's

blaming the raid on the Paika," Ari Ara retorted hotly. "Would you have had us do nothing about the forced labor of the water workers? Or about the silencing of the Harraken women?"

"That was different," Shulen told her. "You did not wear the white tunic, then. If you want to help only the Paika, you'll have to take it off. When you work for peace, you stand for all sides in that choice. And if you don't work for everyone, are you really working for peace? Or just one kind of peace?"

He held up a hand to stem her protests. They had to learn more about these raids, who was really behind them, and what could be done to stop them. Arguing about the ban and the Paika all night wouldn't solve anything. He dismissed the Peace Force with a reminder not to be late for trainings at dawn.

Ari Ara shot him a furious look and stormed off to her cot in the curtained-off Sleeping Quarters. She tossed and turned all night, snarling out arguments to Shulen in her mind. At last, her restless thoughts slipped into grumbling dreams. Just before daybreak, the Fanten Grandmother appeared, cross and red-rimmed around the eyes. The silver-haired old woman could walk through dreams as easily as the forest paths in her home in the High Mountains. Fanten dreams slipped between imagination and visions, prophecy and truth. In the dream realms, they could communicate across vast distances of geography and time. They spent years cultivating their skills in dreamwalking. For their secretive people, dreamtime stood on equal footing with waking life. No one disturbed the sleeping dreamer – which was why the Fanten Grandmother had come across the realms to chastise Ari Ara.

"You dream too loud. Quiet down or none of the Fanten will get any rest."

With her thin knuckles, she wrapped Ari Ara sharply on the crown of her head, startling the girl awake. The old woman's irascible scold echoed in the young girl's ears. Rubbing sleep from her eyes, Ari Ara gasped into full waking and rolled out of bed in the grey dawn. She thrust on her training clothes – a plain undershirt beneath her white tunic and a worn pair of pants with dirt marks on the knees - wolfed down her porridge, and rushed through her chores, hoping to catch Shulen alone before practice.

Everyone rotated through the daily tasks necessary to maintain the Peace Force, including cooking, cleaning, gardening, and laundering. For the Harraken, participating in these activities was as natural as breathing. For others, the thought of doing menial chores was shocking. The Marianan noble youths - Isa and Marek - had never so much as cleaned their own rooms, let alone pulled weeds from a vegetable garden. They swallowed their protests, however. If everyone rotated through washing dishes, they would, too. The first week, Isa had mopped the Main Hall gamely enough, but the morning she was assigned to mucking out the stables, her rosebud lips fell open. Her eyes widened in disbelief. For a moment, an objection hung on her tongue. Then she closed her mouth, steeled her shoulders, and walked to the barn without another word. A Harraken orphan, also assigned stable duty, snorted with suppressed laughter as Isa struggled to lift a sodden heap of straw. His sniggering died as Mahteni's shadow fell on him.

"There is no shame in learning a new skill," the woman reminded him, "but there is little *harrak* in mocking someone instead of helping them."

The boy gulped. A blush scorched his cheeks at the gentle rebuke. Harrak, honor, was dearer than gold to their people. To lose it brought one shame. The boy hung his head and mumbled an apology to the older woman. Mahteni Shirar was next in line to become the *Harrak-Mettahl*, the Honor-Keeper, of their people.

Like her brother, Tahkan, she had a duty to speak gently to people when they lost their way, forgot their values, or acted without honor. She murmured quietly to the boy, explaining how he could restore his harrak. Afterward, the lad crossed the corridor and demonstrated to Isa the proper handhold on the pitchfork. Then he brought the wheelbarrow over and helped. By the end of the hour, Isa was mucking out as fast as her companion, though she'd need hand salve for the new blisters welling up on her tender palms.

"Everything can be done with the Way Between," Shulen had told them, "from the smallest task to moving the largest mountain. Even your chores can be a chance to practice."

The trainees, young and old, experimented with the notion. Neither rushing nor dawdling, Sarai chopped vegetables for dinner. Neither straining nor shrinking, Tala helped the villagers turn their garden beds. Neither pushing nor pulling, Minli guided the sheep toward the lush green pastures. Neither slipping nor shoving, Emir mopped mud off the floor of the main hall. And, the next time the chore rotation sent Isa to muck out the stables, she emerged, sweaty and red-faced, but smiling.

Today, however, Ari Ara didn't spend any time trying to find the Way Between her chores. She rushed through the task of hauling well water for the cooks and raced to the training grounds half-soaked. Finding Shulen meditating with his hands held up in a triangle, palms out to the rising sun, she cleared her throat.

"Shulen, about the Paika . . ."

He sighed and lowered his hands.

"We could at least talk to Commander Mendren," she blurted out hastily, "and see what he has to say. Garrison Town isn't far away. We were already planning to go to the next Market

Day gathering."

"I said we would consider it and we will," Shulen told her firmly, cutting off her breathless outburst. "That answer was good enough for Finn Paikason and it will have to be good enough for you."

She had no more time to argue. The others were arriving and Shulen turned his attention to them.

Today's lesson only aggravated Ari Ara's frustration. Instead of a fierce, fast-paced practice in which she could burn off steam, the training was intentionally designed to reinforce Shulen's opinion that they should wait, be patient, and learn more.

"Only fools rush in," Shulen remarked as the others gathered. "The work of waging peace will be full of crisis and urgency. You must learn to cultivate a measured response. Today, we will practice stillness, slowness, and silence."

Ari Ara wanted to tear her hair out by the fistful. She could feel prickles in the back of her neck. Finn was watching, probably seething as much as she was. His people were in danger and they were doing nothing. It was so wrong, it made her want to throw things.

Shulen ignored her pointed glares, issuing instructions for an exercise in stillness. He sent them to a rocky hillside where sunlight warmed the stones. Each Peace Force member chose a boulder and leaned against it, sensing its weight, gravity, and utter stillness. Every so often - just as the younger members began twitching with boredom - he invited them to shift position. They sprawled over the tops, curled sideways against the bases, or stood on the flat surfaces in their bare feet. Rill fidgeted as much as Ari Ara, but Minli settled in like an old monk. The grandmothers exchanged winks. The grandfather from Turim hid his smile. After weeks of difficult, sweaty trainings, they enjoyed learning an exercise at which they could excel.

"In the Way Between," Shulen told them softly, strolling back and forth in front of the hillside, "it is not always the strongest or the quickest that are the most powerful. Sometimes the gentlest and most vulnerable are the best equipped to handle a dangerous and tricky situation."

They practiced slowness next, lining up at one end of the open field and walking in slow motion across it. Shulen told them the rules: they were to move as slowly as they could without falling into stillness.

"And the last one over the finish line wins," Shulen teased with a smile.

Again, Ari Ara struggled. Only sheer determination not to quit kept her moving like a snail. Rill flopped down on the grass midway through and gave up, groaning with impatience. Shulen hid a smile. When Ari Ara crossed the finish line first, she was told to watch the others.

"Another exercise in boredom," Ari Ara muttered to Rill.

The two giggled, but even they noticed the strange power and grace of the slow pace of two dozen people. Slowness fractured time, sinking pounding hearts out of the headlong rush of haste. Breaths expanded more deeply in chests. Tension lines in faces eased. A sense of calm infused everyone. Strength born of presence, not muscles, built in the slow-motion walkers.

"If I saw people marching in protest like that, it would give me chills," Rill conceded grudgingly.

The pair enjoyed the next training more. The Peace Force split into two groups, one to continue practicing slowness and stillness, the other to challenge them with distractions. Tasked with testing the focus and skill of the others, Ari Ara and Rill shouted and teased, heckled and disrupted. They made faces at Minli, trying to make him crack a smile or laugh. They tossed grass stems at Emir, hoping he'd flinch or duck. At Shulen's urging, they imitated the ways people would try to make the followers of the Way Between lose their temper and lash out in irritation.

"You must maintain your discipline through anything," Shulen instructed. "Your Way Between cannot falter in the face of others' disrespect or anger. Instead, it should deepen. This is how you break the cycle of violence and war, starting with yourself."

Even when the two halves of the group switched roles, Ari Ara found holding to slowness against an onslaught wasn't as dull as she'd expected. She had to heighten her focus as someone yelled in her ear. She calmed her racing heart when a loud shout startled her. She breathed deep and held back her furious retorts when Minli tried to tease her into losing her temper. It was hard work, but by the end of the training, she saw the strength hidden in slowness and stillness.

"When people are upset or on edge," Shulen explained, "moving slowly or standing still can calm things down, lowering the risk of violence."

"Oh yeah," Minli realized, his eyes distant with thought, "Alaren and his Peace Force did that a lot. It's mentioned in the book of stories several times."

"Yes," Shulen affirmed, "it's especially useful when dealing with warriors, soldiers, and guards. They're likely to react to aggressive motions with retaliatory violence. They've been trained that way. It's in their reflexes. That is why it's important to be versatile in how we work for peace. There are a thousand ways to follow the Way Between."

Ari Ara rolled her eyes and held her tongue. While the lesson wasn't all boring, it still wasn't her favorite. There may be a thousand ways to follow the Way Between, but she didn't have to enjoy them all.

After practice, she pelted out of the training area at full tilt, eager to burn off pent-up energy. She sprinted into the cool shade of the pine forest and up a winding trail. The scents of resinous needles and pitch, sweating in the sun's heat, flooded her lungs with each breath. Her legs stretched and her blood pounded delightfully in her veins. She startled a flock of finches from the boughs. She leapt over gnarled roots, swerved around a huge trunk, and skidded to a halt at the fork.

She swept her gaze across Moscam's bustle to see the rising mountains, the wisps of smoke curling up from the villages further away, and the glint of the garrison tower on the eastern horizon, tiny as a speck of dust. One path curled in a loop back to the town. The other climbed the slopes up to an airy ridge of bare stone and hunched shrubs. All at once, the craving for mountain peaks and sharp wind hit her. She longed to go further, but she had neither time nor permission. She made a face. Sometimes, she hated being the Lost Heir - too precious to lose, too young to be trusted . . . or so everyone thought. She could take care of herself! She'd raced across the black ridges of the High Mountains as a small child, never missing a step. She'd ridden from the Middle Pass to the Old Ones in the southern desert. She'd beaten Shulen in the Champion's Challenge. She didn't need to be coddled and protected. Ari Ara sighed. There were days when she wondered how different her life would have been if she *wasn't* the heir to two important lineages.

You'd still be chasing sheep, she reminded herself, *and that's not nearly as interesting as all this!*

Reluctantly, she turned back toward Moscam, but she'd scarcely stepped onto the wide cart road the villagers used to haul firewood when a slim figure broke out of the dappled light of a grove of pale birches.

Finn Paikason.

For a long, awkward moment, they stared at each other. Finn's chin tilted up, twitching as his jaw worked around his hurt pride. Ari Ara bit her lower lip, uncertain.

"I'm sorry," she said, aching over the failure of the Peace Force to offer the aid he had sought.

Finn inhaled sharply. He seemed poised to blurt out a sharp retort. Then his shoulders fell and his head hung.

"Not your fault," he muttered. "At least you tried."

"Don't give up yet. I won't. The others just want to learn more."

Finn gave a miserable little shrug. It would take time and by then it might be too late. He cast a glance at her. On the wings of a separate messenger hawk, he had received instructions from his uncle on what to do if *The Paika's* request was refused. It was a risky plan, though, some might even argue foolhardy, but options were running thin. Finn had risen this morning, ready to carry out this backup plan for protecting the clan, even though he knew his great-grandmother, *The Paika*, wouldn't approve. She had given him a different set of instructions, along with her message to deliver.

Befriend the Lost Heir, The Paika had told him, *we could use her as an ally.*

Finn tilted his head at Ari Ara and swept a glance across her limbs, foot to crown. She reddened at his gaze. For a shocking, agonizing, exhilarating moment, Ari Ara wondered if this was what falling in love felt like. She'd been pondering love with increasing urgency all year, squinting at each of her friends in turn, studying them when they weren't looking, trying to figure out if her heart was racing like the love poems said. She'd spent countless hours obsessively trying to picture her first crush. Would it be a strapping youth like Emir Miresh that made her smile giddily and long to kiss him? Or would it be a cheeky urchin with a lopsided grin like Everill Riverdon that made her swoon? Of course, she didn't want to rule out a mystery like Tala, neither one thing nor the other, but with eyes that sometimes took her breath away. She tried them all on for size - like pulling on one tunic after another, trying to decide what to wear.

Some days, she wondered if it would even happen at all. She was fourteen now. She'd traveled the world. She'd met people from every corner of the earth. But she hadn't felt the heart flutters and swooning delight that the ballads sang about.

Not yet, anyway. Unless Finn counted. Did he? The ballads never mentioned how the sight of him made her feel like she'd stepped on an ant hill, tingling all over. Ant hills weren't a particularly romantic metaphor, though. Maybe there was a reason the poets didn't mention them.

"Come on," Finn said with a grin that definitely made her heart thump loudly in her chest. "You're a runner. Let's run."

And he took off down the trail.

"Wait!" she called, bursting after him.

"Keep up, High Mountain girl!" he challenged her, tossing a grin over his shoulder.

Ari Ara lengthened her stride. She never backed down from a challenge. He notched up the pace. She matched it. Down the length of the open ridge, they ran, not sprinting, but running swift and easy. The wind tossed the grasses eastward. His fox cap was tied to his belt and his black curls lofted and bounced. Her hair slipped loose of its tie and flung wildly with each stride.

They did not speak. At the bend, he gestured and let her lead, falling into a gentle lope behind her. At the next crossroads, he darted ahead and took the left-hand path. Ari Ara jogged in place for a brief, uncertain instant. What if this was a trap? Then she shook her head at the nonsense. That's what rumors did! They sowed doubt and fear where it wasn't necessary. She pushed off the spot and chased after him.

Finn knew the best routes through the woods and meadows. He guided her along a trail she'd never seen on the north side of the river, then picked his way across the boulders near the falls. He fell back and ran in stride with her, following a winding section of trail. Silently, he pointed out tiny bursts of beauty in the woods - a flowering tree in full bloom or a patch of mountain orchids blossoming among the stones. At the next split in the trail, he let her pick their path through the tall, old forest. The trunks swayed in the wind like slow-dancing giants. Their footsteps fell quiet on the thick carpet of needles. A deer startled in the distance, bounding away in graceful leaps.

A grin of delight broke across Ari Ara's features. Unable to hold in the burning blend of joy and thrill churning in her veins, she whooped. The echoes bounced from the slopes, flying through the sunlight and wind like soaring hawks.

At the next turn, Finn tapped her shoulder and pointed the way back to Moscam. He lifted a hand in wordless farewell. Then he ran down the other path, mysterious as he had come.

Ari Ara watched him go, chest heaving, the burning tingle of exertion coursing in her veins, her cheeks bright as the clusters of scarlet wildflowers lining the sunlit edge of the woods.

She decided not to tell anyone about this. They'd make it into something it wasn't, and twist it all out proportion with worry. If she told the others, she'd be banned from leaving the perimeter of Moscam and stuck with either Shulen or Emir hovering over her shoulder at all times.

Better to keep quiet and go slow, she thought with a smile, *and see if it happens again.*

CHAPTER FIVE

. . . . .

Market Day At Garrison Town

"You're watching him."

"Am not."

"Are too."

Rill smirked and nudged her. Ari Ara elbowed her back. A few paces ahead of them, Emir Miresh caught Isa de Barre's delicate hand with a smile and showed her a tricky turn in the Way Between, one they'd learned yesterday. The pair slid through the motion like dancers, graceful and twirling.

Someone whistled. Laughter broke out. The bustle of the Garrison Town Market Day clamored around them. In two long lines, the Peace Force walked down the narrow aisle between booths and stalls. They'd come to spread word of the Peace Force's existence, to tell Alaren tales, and to meet the local community. They turned heads in their gleaming white tunics with the black Mark of Peace, an inked circle with the pattern of rippling river currents on one side and desert sand dunes on the other. With youth and elders, Harraken and Marianans, they made an impressive company. Most traveled on foot. A few of the older members rode to spare their joints, and Minli sat astride the golden stallion Zyrh. Last summer, Ari Ara's blasted trickster horse took one look at Minli and abandoned her for him. Since that moment in the desert, the two had been inseparable. Zyrh treated Minli like royalty.

Ari Ara leapt sideways as a red-faced woman rolled a barrel past them. She tugged a distracted Rill out of the way, noting where the urchin's eyes were glued.

"*You're* the one watching," she shot back at Rill.

"Never said I wasn't," Rill chortled. "*You're* the one denying it while yer ears turn bright red. Nothing wrong with admiring a fine warrior like 'im."

"I'm not - I wasn't - erg!" Ari Ara groaned, whacking Rill's hand aside as the former urchin flicked her burning ear tips. "I was just watching his moves."

"His *moves*," Rill repeated in a teasing leer.

Ari Ara stifled the urge to topple the street urchin into the dirt. Truthfully, she'd been thinking of Finn Paikason's stormy eyes and the length of his stride as he ran off. She told no one about the encounter - except Minli, of course, they didn't keep secrets from each other. All week, she'd been daydreaming about Finn. She kept her eye on the forest and waited for the prickly feeling of someone watching. Once, she'd thought she sensed something . . . only to realize a ladybug was crawling down her back.

She sighed.

Ari Ara thought she just might have a crush on Finn Paikason . . . which was why Rill's accusation that she was staring at Emir Miresh was absurd. She tried to say this to the urchin, but a bellow of voices drowned out her words.

Market Day in Garrison Town was a raucous affair. It was held every seventh day, weather permitting, from the moment the spring floods subsided to the first lasting snows. This close to the East-West Road, both merchants from the riverlands and traders from the desert set up booths for the summer. Herders, farmers, mountain miners, garrison warriors, and more than one pickpocket rolled through.

Due to its sprawling size, the market was held just beyond the walls of the crowded town. Garrison soldiers patrolled the market in uniform. The tangled alleys of the booths spread out across an empty pasture. The pathways were packed to hard earth by footsteps. Grass and swaying wildflowers lined the edges of stalls. The booths were built of wooden timbers. Canvas walls broke the wind in harsher weather and could be rolled back to catch the breeze on hot summer days like this. Each vendor maintained their booth. The stalls that had been in families for generations bore carved beams and mural-painted walls. Newer stalls were held together with wishful thinking and bits of twine. As they entered the market, Ari Ara had seen the Paika spreading blankets on the ground just beyond the rows of stalls. She didn't see Finn, though she hoped she would.

"Paika aren't allowed in the market stalls," Minli had explained, nudging Zyrh forward as he followed Ari Ara's curious gaze. "It was a punishment for betraying the garrison during an ambush in the last war."

"But that was years ago," Ari Ara protested.

Minli shrugged. It was a short time span compared to the standard length of a Border Mountain grudge. He'd read about village feuds that stretched back centuries. And the wars of the Marianans and Harraken had been going on for thousands of years. What were those if not large-scale village feuds?

Ari Ara had craned her neck to study the Paika. Their blankets were actually woven mats of reeds - she saw one woman uncurl hers and anchor the corners with stones. She'd brought baskets of nuts and fresh-gathered greens. The pair next to her bundled wild herbs as a midwife haggled for a bulk price. Leather goods, carved handles for axes and knives, intricately woven baskets - the Paika didn't need booths to keep up a lively trade.

"What the Paika make, they make well," Minli remarked fairly.

Their snaking path took them through stacks of hay bales and barrels of feed, heaping sacks of fleeces and every kind of vegetable imaginable. The summer fields were in high production. Baskets of strawberries leapt off the shelves. People staggered off with boxes stacked in their arms or bags dangling from straining biceps. Rill muttered about the fortunes to be made by enterprising street urchins if only they knew where to look.

Suddenly, the dark-haired girl groaned and smacked her forehead with her palm. Her eyes rolled to the blue sky and back down to the hard-packed earth.

"How's an urchin supposed to compete with that?" she grumbled, cursing colorfully under her breath.

Ari Ara followed the exasperated spit of words to Isa. The noblegirl's bell-like laughter pealed as Emir's hand gently guided her through the sequence again. She wobbled slightly as her ankle turned on an uneven patch. Emir rescued her deftly, his strong arm guiding her back to balance.

"If I pulled such a coy lady-trick as that," Rill muttered, "he'd think I was falling ill."

Ari Ara snorted. True enough. Everill Riverdon didn't need a hand. She'd grown up fending for herself in the bustling streets of the capital. The urchin's muscles were built from scaling the ladder platforms of the Urchin's Nest, racing along the city's rooftops, and clambering through the sewers of the Underway. Rill was sixteen, sleek as a river otter, and rugged as scratchy rope . . . and yet, she had filled out in generous curves that rivaled Isa de Barre's. Not afraid to flaunt them, the former Urchin Queen had simply added sway to her swagger. Ari Ara sighed. She missed the days when Rill thought only silly geese flirted with Emir.

"How can you be in love with Emir Miresh?" Ari Ara grumbled. "You vowed you'd never fall for him."

"Love's a strong word. Let's just say I enjoy giving Isa a run for her noblegirl money."

"Rill!"

"There's a difference between attraction and love, you know," Rill told her sagely. "I'm attracted to everyone - Emir, Marek - but I'd kiss Isa if she winked in me direction. Ancestors, that girl's gorgeous!"

Rill tossed a glance over her shoulder to see if Ari Ara's face held shock. Seeing only a furrow of thought between the younger girl's brows, she continued.

"But love?" Rill snorted. "I don't give me heart out willy-nilly. Whoever gets it is going to have to work hard to keep it. And not just once, mind you, not like in some bedtime story, but as long as they hope to hold me heart, they're going to have to show me respect and trust."

"So, you don't love Emir, even though you flirt with him?" Ari Ara asked.

"Nah. We're having fun is all. He knows it. I know it. That's the key," Rill grabbed Ari Ara's chin and made her meet her sharp brown eyes. "It's all fun so long as both of you knows it's just fun. Don't ever toy with someone's heart, you hear?"

"Fat chance of that with me," Ari Ara muttered.

"Oh, you'll be surprised. Just wait and see."

Ari Ara snorted, unconvinced. People kept telling her to be patient, she'd find out what love felt like soon enough, and she shouldn't be in such a hurry to grow up - but they'd obviously forgotten the unbearable, burning itch of curiosity. Ari Ara didn't like waiting. She wasn't very good at it.

Two years ago, when she was twelve and Rill barely fourteen, a few years' difference in their ages hadn't meant much. But now that Ari Ara was that age, Rill's sixteen years loomed like an impassable gulf between them. Ari Ara could not imagine strutting like a game hen the way Rill did, chest puffed out like that, shirt tight around her breasts, swaggering with her hips, daring every eye to follow her. And they did. Ari Ara spotted the boys stealing glances at Rill when they thought she wasn't looking. They vied to partner with her in practice. Emir, to his credit, had given Everill Riverdon a steady once-over and an occasional flirt, but left it at that. His head was in the clouds of Isa de Barre, anyway . . . a fact not lost on the former Urchin Queen.

"Forget him," Ari Ara urged her friend. "There are other fish in the river."

"Aye," Rill agreed, shifting her gaze slightly toward a saucy young woman sauntering past. "She's none too bad herself."

At Ari Ara's exasperated look, Rill cackled.

"Nothing wrong with admiring beauty in men or women . . . or something in between."

Rill titled her head toward umber-skinned Tala. Before the clever urchin could ask her any pointed questions about who she fancied, Ari Ara changed the subject. She nagged Rill to tell her how the new Urchin King was faring - she'd spotted a messenger hawk delivering a letter to her friend that morning.

Rill had been the first urchin in a long time to step down from leadership instead of losing a challenge from another urchin. The Mother Tree had sent her a dream, telling her to go with Minli and Solange to join the Peace Force, that her talents would be needed. It was an unusual apprenticeship, but Rill wasn't complaining. It included friends, meals, a warm place to sleep, and a bit of adventure. The city-bred girl was a fish out of water in these mountains, though, unused to wilderness and villages.

"Tolly - the new Urchin King - is doing 'bout as well as can be expected," Rill grumbled. "Ancestors help him. The city'll eat him alive if the urchins don't throw him in the stewpot."

Ari Ara hid her grin. Tolly'd do fine. The kid was as tough as a goat and buoyant as a cork. Nothing could keep him down.

"Miss it?" she asked her friend.

"Me? Nah," Rill proclaimed. "Why would an urchin want the stinkin' capital when she could have all *this* adventure? Never seen s'many trees in me life."

Ari Ara wasn't fooled. Rill would miss being the Urchin Queen and all the power that position commanded.

At the center of the market, they paused near an open area set aside for dancing. On a stage, musicians clasped hands in greeting and tuned their instruments, preparing for the dances to come. Benches ringed the space. Ale and wine vendors readied their booths for the noon rush. The Peace Force split into smaller groups to circulate among the crowds. Ari Ara begged Shulen to let her wander with her friends and, after a moment's hesitation, he agreed, ordering Emir to accompany her. Ever dutiful, Emir hid his fleeting scowl, disappointed that he couldn't stay in Isa's group to keep Marek's outrageous flirting in check. Ari Ara read him like a book, though, and as soon as they rounded the bend, she spun on him.

"Look, we're going over there," she waved vaguely in the direction of the training grounds, "go convince *her* to join us."

She didn't need to say who - Emir's gaze already twisted in Isa's direction. He nodded absently and took off. Ari Ara threaded her arm through Rill's and tugged her firmly along, following Minli and Tala toward the roaring crowd watching the Attar Matches. These bouts of fighting were traditional at markets and gatherings. Highly popular, the matches would go on all day, as would the betting on the winners. The sound of cheering surged over the banter of voices haggling and bartering. The groans of defeat drowned out the merchants hawking their wares. The shouts urging on the fighters even overpowered the bellows of the livestock penned nearby.

Ari Ara, Rill, Minli, and Tala reached the edges of the dusty Matching Grounds and found a spot along the tall fence that encircled the area. People leaned their elbows on the top rails or sat perched atop, legs hooked through the second rung. Inside, a pair of fighters pummeled each other. Ari Ara winced as one broke the other's nose. She shut her eyes as the sight of blood made the world whirl. She leaned her back against the fence and looked the other way. Ari Ara hadn't outgrown her nausea at violence; if anything, it was getting worse over the years. She had picked up this disgust for violence from the Fanten. It didn't seem to fade, no matter how far she traveled from the High Mountains. Like her Fanten dreaming, it was growing stronger as she got older.

She studied the faces of the onlookers instead of the two boxers on the Matching Grounds. She would never understand how people could find violence entertaining. Everyone winced as a hard blow landed, but they also cheered when their favorite lobbed a successful punch. People picked sides and chose to feel the pain of the people they liked, not the people they opposed.

That's bad enough during wars, Ari Ara thought, *but it's worse in matches like this, done for pleasure and profit.*

Worse yet, in a mountain region like this, the onlookers likely knew both fighters. The winner and loser might be related by blood or marriage. They were certainly connected through years of living in close-knit communities. Ari Ara shook her head. She couldn't do the mental backflips it took to only feel the blows landing on one side. How could anyone enjoy seeing someone else get hurt?

After one boxer knocked down the other for a ten count, some of the watchers leapt the fence to help carry the defeated man to the healers' tent. Others traded coins as bets were won or lost. In the next match, a pair of swordfighters crossed blades. The clang of steel striking steel rang out. Muffled thuds punctuated the sharp sound as wooden shields slammed together.

As the wagers for the third match started to trade, Rill spoke up in a loud voice.

"They're not so tough, either of 'em."

Cries of objection erupted at the girl's cheeky remark. The two men eyeing each other from the edges of the ring stood over six feet tall with barrel chests and biceps larger than Ari Ara's waist. One was a blacksmith from a neighboring town. The other was a professional wrestler who hired out to the army when he wasn't working the summer Market Day circuit.

"Toughness isn't measured by size alone," Minli put in. "It also depends on determination, resourcefulness, endurance, and cleverness."

"Bah, stop yawping. Let's get on with the match," someone grumbled. "What do you pipsqueaks know, anyway?"

"This pipsqueak could take down the victor, barehanded and without throwing a punch," Rill boasted proudly, clapping a hand on Ari Ara's shoulder.

A murmur of interest rumbled through the crowd. Someone remarked that the looming match between the blacksmith and wrestler would tire out the winner, making it easier for the girl to win her round against him.

"Let 'em fight fresh then. She could take on both of 'em and still come out the victorious," Rill declared with an easy shrug.

A calloused palm slapped a coin down on a nearby fencepost.

"Would you wager on it? That little girl against my man?" the fellow challenged, introducing himself as the wrestler's manager.

He cast a scoffing glance up and down at Ari Ara. No one had figured out who she was yet. Minli tugged at her sleeve, shaking his head. The Way Between was an ancient practice, not a trick to show off like a juggler on Feast Days. The four youths drew into a huddle.

"Why shouldn't I show them what the Way Between can do?" Ari Ara objected huffily. She hadn't liked the arrogance of that man, not one bit. She could topple that wrestler before the count of ten.

"Because, they'll get the wrong impression," Minli argued. "They'll think the Way Between is a bunch of fancy moves, just another form of fighting."

The words came tumbling out of him. The Way Between had to be for everyone, one-legged boys and powerful warriors, elders from the cities and young people from rural villages. People had to see that there were dozens of ways to follow the Way Between, not just one. Inner and outer, individual and collective, all of them mattered. Minli wanted everyone to feel like they could use these practices, too. It wasn't something only famous people like Shulen, Emir Miresh, or the Lost Heir did.

"Physical, outer Azar is just one form of the Way Between," Minli burst out, "and it is the least useful, most dangerous form. It's a tactic of last resort."

"That's why we need to show it boldly here in the Border Mountains," Rill countered hotly, championing Ari Ara's side. "The people here have seen unending violence. Your *last resort* is their daily experience. Unless they know the Way Between can turn aside a punch, knife, sword, or battle axe, it's a long leap of faith to expect them to believe that inner and collective forms of the Way Between can maintain peace."

"I think you give them too little credit," Tala put in quietly. "Those who have seen war and violence firsthand often know it doesn't bring peace. You can't put out a fire with more fire."

"Ari Ara just wants to show off," Minli muttered.

"*I am* the best at it," she stated, crossing her arms over her chest stubbornly. It was true, after all. "People should see how powerful it is."

Minli's face contorted like ten retorts were trying to come out at the same time.

"Never mind," he muttered. "You wouldn't understand."

"Oh, for ancestors' sake!" Ari Ara exploded, throwing her hands up in the air. "Don't pull that attitude: brilliant Minli, thinking too quick for stupid, slow me!"

"Garrgh! You're . . . you're so . . . " he spluttered.

"Yeah?" she shot back. "Well, same to you times two."

She glared at him. He was so clever, fast as a hawk to think of an unexpected solution. She was slow as a mud clod compared to him. She remembered thinking, once, that if Trials were held in the Way Between, Minli would win them without even moving. He would talk his way out of having to use outer Azar. That was the smart way to handle a conflict.

Well, she thought enviously, *we can't all be Minli!*

The wrestler's manager cleared his throat gruffly. The wager awaited. His man hollered from the Matching Grounds, impatient to get to it. Ari Ara craned around to look at him . . . and spotted a familiar acorn-shaped face beaming at her.

Finn Paikason waved from his perch atop the fence rail, one leg folded over the other knee, ignoring the glares the marketgoers shot at him. A gleam of anticipation shone in his eyes. Ari Ara bit back a smirk.

"I'm doing it," she declared to her friends.

Over Minli's protests and Rill's cheers, she stalked over to the wrestler's manager, shook his hand, and vaulted over the fence rail.

"Good luck," Finn wished her as she landed.

"I don't need luck," she informed him, tossing her curls out of her eyes.

And she didn't.

It was all over in under a minute. Leveraging the wrestler's mass and momentum against him, she toppled the big man gently to the earth, twisted his arm back in a bind, and pinned him in a lock. Even if the burly man tried to use his brute strength to break free, he'd snap his bones. It was his choice: concede or cause himself pain. He muttered his surrender. The match was called in Ari Ara's favor. She helped her opponent to his feet, shook hands with the winded wrestler, and brushed the dust off his back.

"Never saw her coming," the big wrestler kept muttering, shaking his head. "Still don't know how the little lass pulled it off."

"With the Way Between," Rill crowed to the crowd, "it is not size, but skill that matters most."

At Minli's insistence, Rill grudgingly refused their share of the wagers, letting the villagers keep their coins. The crowd cheered.

"Shall we wager again?" the manager called out, eager to save face and regain his coins. "This girl against the blacksmith?"

Excitement rippled through the crowd, but someone called out a warning.

"Don't waste your bets, folks. I know her. That's the Lost Heir. She even beat the Great Warrior Shulen. Wager against her if you wish, but she won't lose no matter how big the fellow is."

That took the fun out of the betting.

"Ah, but wouldn't you like to see her at work?" Rill called out. She scaled the fence and walked the rail like an acrobat. "Ari Ara Marin en Shirar is a sight to behold. You'll be telling the tale to yer grandkids."

Rill plied them with all the wiles of a capital-raised street urchin, cajoling, enticing, working their curiosity.

"Tell you what," she announced, tossing them a saucy wink, "let's see her paces, eh? Who wants to test her mettle and see what this double royal heir is made of? Even if she wins, who wouldn't want to go home with a once-in-a-lifetime story to tell? Why, the taverns'll pour you free drinks jus' to hear the tale! The ladies'll beg you to spin this yarn. The elders'll call you in special jus' to hear the words from yer mouth. You're flirting with legend today, folks. Give destiny a kiss, eh?"

Which was how, after three standard matches of Attar versus Azar, Ari Ara found herself dodging a boy who bet he'd smack a kiss on the Lost Heir. Cursing Rill's choice of phrase, and trying to ignore the chortles on the sidelines, Ari Ara scrambled for a way out of this mess.

She hadn't minded the matches against the others - they'd tried their best. One young woman almost landed a swift jab that whipped past her ear with a serpent-like hiss. This, however, was embarrassing. It was a mockery of the Way Between. She would be the laughing stock of the Market Day. The crowd around the Matching Grounds had swelled as word spread that Ari Ara Marin en Shirar was demonstrating the Way Between. She couldn't let that boy succeed in planting a smack on her. She'd never been kissed and she didn't want her first kiss to be here. Not with this impudent Garrison Town boy. Not with Finn

Paikason watching!

She skidded under the boy's arm and flipped him to his back, guiding the fall so he wouldn't even bruise. But he curled around her hand and tried to smack his lips on her arm. She slipped free and danced away.

"Didn't your mother teach you better manners?" she called out to him as he scrambled to his feet.

"I dunno. Did yours?"

The crowd howled at the jibe, some laughing, others hissing at the disrespect for the deceased queen.

"My parents' love story taught me to respect love," she shot back, whirling out of reach as he lunged to grab her. "And everyone knows you shouldn't take what's not freely offered. My kisses aren't yours to have."

"What if I asked really nicely?"

"You didn't."

He sang out the words of a popular folk tune.

"What if I hold you tight, darling?"

"Not happening," she retorted, knocking his arm away. "No one holds a follower of the Way Between against her will."

Cheers rang out from the sidelines. Ari Ara risked a swift glance. A huddle of women had gathered at the fence. A row of girls her age crouched by the lower rail, eyes wide, following her every move. Older women stood behind them, protective, defensive. Ari Ara circled her opponent at a half-jog, keeping beyond his grasp. A spark of anger lit the fire of her tenacity. She'd find the Way Between and deal with this fellow. From the looks on those women's faces, she wasn't the only one dealing with unwanted advances. The match took on a significance greater than her pride.

Ari Ara dove toward the youth, surprising him with her speed. From behind, she snaked one hand along the length of his right arm, holding it taut, as if in a strange waltz. With her other hand, she caught his left fist and curled it up under his chin. She danced backward, sending his feet scrambling as she pulled him off balance.

"I bet you steal a lot of kisses, don't you?" she asked him in a low growl.

He flailed against her grip, but she had the advantage. Without a stable position, he couldn't find purchase to push against. The arena had fallen silent. Something in her face warned the onlookers that the fun-and-games were over.

"Kisses are meant to be exchanged, not stolen. That makes you a thief."

He grunted, a note of panic in his throat. She uncoiled him, sending him stumbling away like a gawky dance partner, her arm extended to his chest, finger pointed at him. His eyes narrowed. He tried to snatch her wrist. She rolled her arm under his hand and slapped him away like a fly. Once. Twice. He paused, pouting, turning in a circle like a tired, angry bull as she paced around him.

"You know what they do to thieves around here?" she asked.

His face paled. Everyone knew the punishment for thievery was getting your fingers cut off, one by one. Four warnings and they'd take the stump of your hand, too.

"You're lucky I follow the Way Between," Ari Ara told him, her voice leaping out, loud and clear, hard and firm.

A shadow of confusion touched his eyes. He stilled. She stilled.

"All I ask is that you release this notion that you can take what should only ever be freely given. I'll stretch out my hand in peace, in friendship, in learning and forgiveness. If you will take it - no kisses, just a shake - you can walk away with your honor restored."

She eyed him.

"Agreed?"

She extended her hand.

He swallowed hard.

The crowd held its breath.

He lifted his hand, shook hers, and walked away, trembling.

Ari Ara nodded and left in the other direction. No one would ever forget the Way Between.

CHAPTER SIX

. . . . .

Commander Mendren

Tales of the match - and the wildfire of gossip it set off -
spread swiftly through the market into the town, all the way to
the fortress. It wasn't long before a garrison rider galloped down
the cobbled streets, out through the gates of the walled city, and
into the crowded market to deliver an imperious order from the
commander. The entire Peace Force was to report to the garrison
immediately.

Ari Ara was thrilled. Here was their chance to speak to
Commander Mendren about the ban forbidding the Paika from
entering the Fire Peaks Region. She cast about, searching for a
glimpse of Finn, eager to tell him. He had slipped away, however,
and she couldn't find him.

Commander Mendren controlled the territory from Garrison
Town north to the Valley of Statues and south to the East-West
Road. He reported, not to the nobles who reigned over these
lands, Lord and Lady of the Westlands, but to the Great Lady
Brinelle. He was a war hero to the riverlands people and a
murderer in the eyes of the Harraken he'd defeated. Mendren
had a reputation for swift and harsh punishment, and fast

retribution toward those who defied his orders. Shulen warned the Peace Force not to bring up the subject of the ban on the Paika when they met Mendren. If they challenged him about it, the commander would think they were insulting his judgment.

"The man is prickly," Shulen cautioned them, "but he follows the law to the letter. No one can fault Mendren on that. He will be furious if we suggest he's not protecting his people. Leave him to me, or we'll get nowhere with him."

But Ari Ara had no intention of leaving the garrison without speaking up on Finn's behalf. She and Minli conferred about it in hushed tones as they passed through the gates of the walled city. The narrow, cobbled streets were packed tight with shops and homes. The horses' hooves rang loud in the quiet streets, iron striking against stone. The sharp scent of chimney smoke settled like a pall just above the rooflines. The town was one huge suit of armor, perpetually ready for battle. When they reached the garrison, it sprang into view on the opposite bank of the river gorge from the town, bristly as a hedgehog. The drawbridge, though lowered, was heavily guarded.

In the tight courtyard of the garrison, every last member of the Peace Force was patted down for weapons. Ari Ara fought the urge to roll her eyes. That was the thing about the Way Between . . . even empty-handed they were still fully 'armed'. The Peace Force members were brought to the Reception Hall - a grisly room with stag antlers and boars' heads hung on the walls. Weapons were displayed in rows beneath them. A ghastly tapestry portrayed a battle scene full of severed heads, curling red embroidery weaving weeping trails of blood into the pattern of the border. In the center, a Marianan warrior lifted his sword in triumph, one foot smashing the face of a defeated Harraken. The desert-dwelling Peace Force members muttered angrily at the sight.

Mahteni cleared her throat.

"Consider this a test," she urged them. "These are meant to provoke hatred and fear. Do not let them succeed. Practice your inner Azar."

The Way Between was an inner practice as much as an outer. It was normal to feel outraged when insulted, or panicked when afraid, or angered over injustice . . . but their work required them to respond skillfully, not hotheadedly or fearfully. In order to find the path between fight and flight, they had to master their gut reactions and deal with the situation wisely. All spring, the Peace Force had trained in keeping their tempers and remaining focused. They studied breathing practices to slow their racing hearts in times of fear. They drilled in scenarios, taking turns hassling each other as they attempted to stay calm and clearheaded. Now, they could put these skills to work.

At Mahteni's reminder, chins lifted. Heads nodded. Spines straightened. The Harraken were nothing if not determined. They had a grit borne of dust and drought. Their spirits were their own, unconquerable by famine or war, and certainly not by this horrible room.

A portly little steward marched in and harrumphed for their attention.

"The commander is otherwise occupied at the moment," he informed them officiously. "You will wait here until supper."

Groans broke out. Shulen held up a hand.

"He demands that we come, then makes us wait?" Shulen asked in a wry tone. "Surely if he was so eager to see us, he can meet with us now."

The steward drew his mouth into a puckered prune.

"He is a very busy man."

"Oh, I think he can find the time," Shulen rebuked him sternly. "We can share song while we wait for him."

He pivoted and gestured to Tala. Ze grinned and launched into an old Alaren ballad about singing down the walls of the heart and opening doors of the mind. The Harraken joined in at once, voices weaving in the eerie and thrilling harmonies of the desert melody. The Marianans waited for the chorus - those quartets of verse had been one of their first lessons in Harrak-tala.

"What are you doing? Stop that racket at once!" the portly official demanded.

No one paid him any heed. Shulen cheerfully informed him that once a Harraken Tala started singing, there was no stopping zir until the end of the song. He pulled out a chair - the little man hovered on the verge of an apoplectic fit - and invited him to relax and enjoy the music. The steward marched out the door, spluttering. Shulen silently wagered that the garrison commander would appear in under ten minutes.

The singing brought people to the hall at a run, perplexed by the sound of Harraken music spilling out the doors and windows. Heads popped in, followed by shoulders. The soldiers' hands hung poised over their sword hilts. Off-duty warriors skidded through the main doors only to halt in astonishment at the sight of the white tunics of the Peace Force. They spread out around the rim of the hall. More people crowded in on their heels.

By the last, soaring refrain of the chorus, the jubilant tune had smiles twitching on the warriors' lips even if they didn't understand the language. The last note held long and proud, perfectly amplified by the cavernous rafters of the vaulted ceiling. A stunned silence followed, broken by a deep, unamused voice.

"Well, Shulen, have you fallen so low that you've turned to wandering minstrelsy?"

Every eye in the hall swiveled to the head of the room. The

garrison commander stood just inside the arched doorway, leaning against the stone blocks. He pushed off and strode down the three steps to the open space where Shulen stood. The warriors wiped the smiles from their faces and snapped to straight-spined attention in a formal wide-footed stance. They crossed one arm over their chests and thumped their hearts with their fists.

The contempt in the man's tone could have shattered clay, but Shulen was made of tougher material. He didn't so much as blink at the jab.

"Mendren."

Shulen made a quick and martial nod as he spoke, an acknowledgment of rank and position by one who respects power while standing beyond its purview. Mendren snorted silently under his mustache, unimpressed. Shulen was a traitor, losing the Champion's Challenge, defying the death law, living in exile, and even pandering to the desert demons when he renounced the Warrior's Way. Mendren viewed the Peace Force scheme as little more than a clever enemy incursion. The Great Lady Brinelle had a blind spot when it came to that girl, Ari Ara. She'd been hoodwinked by the child from the start. All the rumors pointed to it. Lord Thornmar from the Orelands had told him an earful this past winter. The Great Lady had ordered him to allow this motley crew of fools to do their so-called peace work, but Mendren didn't like it, didn't support it, and didn't trust it. He wouldn't sit by idly while they sowed dissension in his territory.

"State your business," he commanded, striding forward.

"You summoned us," Shulen answered dryly. "We came."

The hard heels of Mendren's boots struck the stones in the floor in a decisive clop-thud intended to make them flinch and jump. He circled them, hands clasped behind his back as if inspecting his warriors . . . and finding them lacking. He'd heard they planned to traverse the Border Mountains this summer, teaching peace. As if such a thing could be taught! In Mendren's view, only constant vigilance and the threat of harsh punishment maintained order. Only the presence of his armed soldiers kept the Harraken from invading and prevented the Paika from terrorizing the land. Over his twenty years of defending this region, Mendren had thrown back army attacks, invasions, uprisings, and rebellions. He had battled bandits and routed out warlords. He had marched his soldiers into riots to put down unrest. He would never let down his guard, not after all he'd seen. Peace was won by the mightiest sword, not by unarmed children like this Peace Force.

"What kind of meddling are you planning?" Commander Mendren barked. "What foolish nonsense are you stuffing into peoples' heads? Where do you intend to travel?"

"We are not obliged to answer those questions," Solange murmured to Shulen in a low tone. "The Great Lady and the Desert King gave their permission to work freely, answering directly to them and none other."

Mendren overheard.

"Of course."

An awkward silence fell. Ari Ara took the chance.

"Actually, we did have something to ask you," she said, ignoring Shulen's warning look and crossing the short gap over to the commander. "This ban on the Paika in the Fire Peaks Region - "

"It is necessary for the safety of everyone," Mendren snapped. "They raided several villages and I intend to put a stop to it."

"The Paika say it's not them," Ari Ara replied, "and if you'll lift the ban, they'll prove it."

"Those Pikers have been filling your head with a pack of

lies," Commander Mendren retorted sharply. He turned his hard gaze on her. "They just want free rein to pillage and harass the villagers. No, the ban will stay in place until I deem it safe to lift."

His reply was cold and flat. His jaw twitched, resenting his lack of authority over them. He cleared his throat. A glint came into his eye. Mendren stabbed his thick finger at a map hanging on the wall, pointing at the mountainous terrain to the north.

"In fact, if your Peace Force is planning to enter the Fire Peaks Region, I must insist on sending a garrison squadron with you as an escort. For your protection!"

To spy on us, more likely, Ari Ara thought darkly.

"That won't be necessary," Shulen replied, folding his arms over his chest.

"Of course, it's necessary!" Mendren barked. The row of warriors reflexively snapped to even stiffer attention. "You're not armed, are you? We could run you through right now."

"I'd like to see you try," Ari Ara blurted out hotly.

Shulen sent her a quelling glare.

"What Ari Ara Marin en Shirar means - " he clarified.

"Just Shirar," Mendren corrected sternly. "Mariana has yet to acknowledge her claim of royal blood."

"What she means is that we have ways of keeping ourselves safe," Shulen offered.

"I am not a merchant to be fooled," Mendren growled. "Nor are my warriors mere townspeople you can hoodwink with your tricks."

"The Way Between is not a trick," Minli said as he stepped forward, one arm over his crutch, the other pointing at the map. "It is an ancient practice that ensured peace for centuries in these very mountains. We share your concerns about safety and security, protection and defense. We simply have a different way to achieve those goals."

The commander's critical gaze swept up and down the one-legged boy. His lips curled in scorn and pity. A hint of a grimace flickered in Minli's round face, but he did not look away.

"Because of this," Minli bravely went on, "we must respectfully decline your offer. Your warriors would hinder our work."

"How so?" The commander's voice was sharp and suspicious.

"Soldiers and warriors create an atmosphere of fear and alarm. We seek to build a different sort of . . . sense of trust."

Mendren paused his pacing, brows in a scowl, one boot poised mid-step. The hall had fallen deathly silent.

"Are you jesting?" he barked in disbelief. "My men are the only thing keeping this whole region from joining the desert scum and charging down into Mari Valley to make the rivers run red with blood!"

"That's a bit dramatic - " Shulen cut in.

"Thieves and traitors, the lot of them!" Mendren cursed. "Then there's the hordes of highway brigands and cutthroats that plague this region. And don't underestimate those blasted Pikers! Raiding, stealing, paying allegiance only to themselves. We deal with constant subterfuge and insubordination from those backstabbing - "

"That's not - " Ari Ara tried to interject.

" - louts. They're constantly scheming to slit our throats. You have no idea what you're walking into. The Fire Peaks Region is aflame. The Paika refuse to obey the ban, sneaking back in to raid - "

"It's not the Paika!" Ari Ara exploded.

" - an iron grip is needed to maintain order. You and these . . . " he paused to search for the words to describe the Peace Force members, "naive do-gooders aren't going to change anything. Fools, the lot of you."

"Funny," a new voice chimed in, entering from the main doors amidst a flurry of surprised murmurs, "everyone called Alaren a fool, too. Until he succeeded, that is."

"Korin!"

Ari Ara's shout erupted over the clamor of soldiers whipping out salutes and greetings to the son of the Great Lady. From the look on Commander Mendren's face, and the huffing and puffing of the apologetic steward, Korin de Marin's arrival startled everyone.

Korin had grown a foot, standing taller than Emir and towering over Ari Ara. His cherubic boy's face had lengthened into a striking young man's features. His golden curls, as tightly sprung as Ari Ara's, had deepened in tone. His grin was the same, full of good humor and mischief. As the Great Lady's son, he was next in line for the throne, but Korin had never wanted the burdens of the job. When Ari Ara showed up, Korin had been delighted to toss the crown at her. He'd been bitterly disappointed when the nobles refused to confirm her as the heir and even more upset when she was exiled. The cage of his birth closed again, all the more stifling after his brief taste of freedom.

In his letters to Ari Ara, Korin had been threatening to run off to the Border Mountains in increasingly desperate tones. She hadn't expected him to actually show up! Brinelle had forbidden him from joining the Peace Force. He was the official heir to the Marianan throne. She would not risk his life on the uncertain gamble of the tenuous peace efforts. Certain factions of nobles declared outright that it was all nonsense and would be a complete failure. Brinelle suspected some of them would work hard to ensure it flopped. The presence of both Ari Ara and Korin in one location was too tempting a target for assassins or ambushes or hostage taking. Korin would stay in Mariana where he had duties, responsibilities, and could be kept safe. To occupy him, his mother had sent him on a royal tour, reaffirming support for the House of Marin throughout the nation. His route should have taken him north to the Stonelands - nowhere near Garrison Town.

"Hello, cousin," he said to Ari Ara cheerfully. He lifted an eyebrow as Mendren spluttered in objection. "Oh, come off it, Commander. The nobles' politics change with the weather. They'll confirm her one day. *I* say she's my cousin and that should be good enough for you."

Technically, they were second cousins, sharing a royal great-grandmother, but a lack of other family members let them use the less-formal term of cousin. Ari Ara ran to greet him, and he lifted her off her feet and spun her around. Then he looped an arm over her shoulders, beaming.

"I happened to be in the neighborhood with my royal tour and heard the most delightful tale about Ari Ara Marin en Shirar refusing to let a garrison boy kiss her."

His blue eyes twinkled with mirth. He'd tried to find her at the market, and was told the Peace Force had been summoned to the garrison. Korin's jaw tightened suddenly.

"Commander Mendren, I must have heard wrong, but as I entered, it sounded like you were defying the House of Marin's authority."

Mendren blanched.

"My esteemed mother," Korin went on breezily, "the Great Lady Brinelle, issued firm orders: the Peace Force answers directly to her and the Desert King. Leave them to their work."

"I was only concerned for their safety, Noble One," Mendren remarked smoothly. "The Paika have been causing trouble again."

Korin nodded. He had read those reports - and Ari Ara had, helpfully, sent him a letter carried by her messenger hawk,

Nightfast, relaying Finn Paikason's request.

"The followers of the Way Between can look after themselves. In fact," he dug into the travel bag slung across his shoulders and chest, "the Great Lady thinks they should go to the Fire Peaks Region and get to the bottom of those raids."

He held up a scroll emblazoned with a curling blue river dragon, the symbol of the House of Marin. The Great Lady, while upholding Mendren's decision to ban the Paika from the region, also ordered the Peace Force to look into the matter. If it turned out the Paika were not involved, the Great Lady would tell Mendren to lift the ban at once.

"Yes!" Ari Ara exclaimed. Finn would be thrilled by the news.

Shulen frowned in annoyance. This wasn't their plan for the summer. The work of building trust in these mountains couldn't be rushed. Everything depended on it. This scuffle with the raiders and the Paika was the kind of task a full-grown Peace Force, with allies in every farmhouse, could take on. They didn't have the resources of connections and reputation to draw upon. Not yet. Shulen furrowed his brow at Ari Ara, disappointed in her. He'd seen her sending her messenger hawk, Nightfast, eastward with a letter. She must have gone over his head - and behind his back - to relay Finn's request to Korin. He would have to take her to task for it - later, though, not now in front of Mendren. The man was already grinding his teeth over all this . . . and Korin's high-handedness wasn't helping.

"There, you see?" Korin commented in the tone of someone settling the matter. "The Peace Force wishes to go. The House of Marin commands it. And you, my dear Mendren, have very little to say in the matter."

"If you go without an escort," Mendren warned severely, "it's your heads you risk, you hear? We won't be running to your rescue if you get into trouble."

"We won't," Ari Ara answered hotly.

"If blood spills, it's on your conscience, not mine."

"Are you finished?" Korin said pointedly.

Mendren clenched his jaw. Shulen frowned at Ari Ara and Korin. Their attitudes weren't helping anything. He shot a stern look at the girl, warning her to behave. Ari Ara fought the urge to stick out her tongue. She sighed. Being a Peace Force member was hard work.

"We'll win you over in the end, Mendren," Shulen remarked softly, eyeing the commander's obstinate expression.

"Don't count on that."

"I'm not."

The two held each other's gazes for a long, hard moment. Then Shulen broke away and motioned for the Peace Force to file out the main doors. There was nothing more to say.

CHAPTER SEVEN

. . . . .

Korin de Marin

In the narrow, cobbled streets of Garrison Town, the Peace Force splintered into smaller groups, each dispatched to acquire necessary travel supplies from the market and town shops. Taking thirty people on the road required sacks of oats and other food, tents and sleeping rolls, pack horses, and a variety of supplies and preparations.

Shulen kept Ari Ara pinned to his side – apparently, she couldn't be trusted further than he could throw her. He scowled at the thought of how she'd concealed her actions. Already, that sneaky Paika boy was becoming a bad influence on her. Ancestors knew, she'd always stuck up for the underdogs, but this time, he suspected her trust was misplaced. If she didn't wipe that starry-eyed look off her face, she'd walk smack into trouble, blinded by her youth and naivete.

"And it's not just your life at stake," he told her gently, speaking quietly to her outside a grain merchant's shop, "it's everyone else's, too."

Ari Ara's face grew stony. Her head dropped behind the veil of her curling hair. Shulen couldn't tell if she felt angry over his words or abashed about her behavior. If she were his daughter, he'd - Shulen cut off the thought. She wasn't. Ari Ara was the daughter of Tahkan Shirar and the late Queen Alinore. If he was hard on her, it was only because he had to be. The Marianan nobles might confirm her as royal heir one day. If so, only a few short years stood between her and the throne. She was far from ready.

Shulen drew a deep breath. Sometimes, daunted by the journey that lay ahead of her, he lost sight of how far she'd already come. Standing before him, beneath those startlingly lanky limbs of hers, he still saw the half-wild girl who had once balanced on an ancestor pillar all day, stubbornly refusing to back down from a challenge. Under the hints of the emerging young woman, Shulen still spied the small, exhausted child he had carried up the thousand steps of Monk's Hand Monastery, her head resting on his shoulder, arms coiled about his neck.

But he also caught glimpses of who she might become; a ferocious lioness flexed her muscles inside the uncertain frame of the young cub. Ari Ara was a force of nature, strong as a gale-force wind, fierce as a wildfire, and as unstoppable as a flood. Already, she had changed the fate of nations. Shulen would do *anything* for Ari Ara. If she needed the stars gathered from the night, he would undertake the impossible to help her. If the whole world turned against her, he would stand by her on his own. Shulen was prepared to weather the best and the worst for Ari Ara . . . but that included wading through the unpleasant tasks, such as telling her when her behavior had crossed a line.

"You wrote to Korin behind my back," Shulen said. "Why?"

"Because you would have stopped me," Ari Ara muttered. "But I was right to do it. It worked, didn't it? Now we can help the Paika *and* do all the other peace building work we'd planned."

Shulen chose his next words carefully. Along with the anger burning in her, he saw a hint of a self-satisfied smirk. If she were still just his apprentice, he'd make her run four laps of the town to wipe it off her face. But she wasn't a mere trainee in the Way Between. She was a young leader who had initiated the revival of the Peace Force. The others looked up to her, copied her motions in practices, imitated her attitudes and actions. The lesson Ari Ara needed was deeper than punishment and more difficult to explain. Minli would have grasped it in an instant, but Ari Ara would struggle with it. In her view, the ends justified the means. She would sneak out the window to honor a hastily-made promise. She'd listen at keyholes to find out a secret. She'd set off a stampede of horses to rescue a friend.

"Someday," Shulen cautioned her, "you will discover that you reap what you sow. Means are *always* ends in the making. If you begin by lying and sneaking around, you will wind up in deeper trouble than before."

Ari Ara snorted. Strangely enough, she agreed with him. If she hadn't written that letter, Shulen wouldn't be scolding her now. Although, next time, she would just try harder not to get caught.

Shulen saw the rebellious look in her eyes and his frustration boiled over. She needed to learn these lessons, now, before they came back to haunt her. Better to get in trouble with him than to sink herself into a mess she couldn't get out of. His worry thrust a harder edge into his words than he intended. His concern for her sharpened his tone. Ari Ara weathered his lecture like a rugged boulder on a High Mountain peak. She had to learn to weigh her decisions, he told her; she wasn't a lone shepherdess anymore. Her actions impacted the other Peace Force members. Her words affected entire nations. Her wrong choices didn't just hurt her, they could harm untold numbers of people. With her double-royal blood, she was likely to alter the course of history.

Ari Ara simmered silently. She hated the pressures of her royal blood. She could never live up to the unrealistic - in her opinion - expectations others placed on her because of it. Shulen was twice as hard on her as anyone else. And, as Finn had pointed out, she didn't even have a crown or throne to show for it. All she had was exile and expectations.

"You're not some wild orphan. You're the Lost Heir - " Shulen said.

"I know!" she exploded.

"Don't use that tone on me, Ari Ara," Shulen warned her. He did not tolerate that disrespect from anyone, not from his warriors, not from Emir at her age, and certainly not from her. "I will have to write to your father about this."

Ari Ara threw her head back and groaned up at the rooftops. Why did Shulen have to tell her father? Tahkan had enough to worry about, tracking down the truth about the attack on her mother fourteen years ago. Each time she sent Nightfast winging south with a letter, Shulen added his reports to the bundle, one about the Peace Force, and one about her.

Ari Ara was trying to come up with a good reason why Shulen should hold off on sending a letter when Korin rounded the corner at a jog. Heedless of the tension in the air, the golden-haired youth clasped hands with Shulen and then turned to Ari Ara.

"Look at you!" he exclaimed, holding her back by the shoulders to get a good look at her. "Taller than ever, brown as an ox, and those curls! I see you inherited the family spirals."

He gestured to her wild mop, but a fleeting confusion flickered in his blue eyes. It was his father's side of the family that had gifted him with the crown of curls, not their shared great-grandmother. Fast as the thought came, it vanished, swept out of mind by the sight of Emir Miresh.

Their laughter rang out at the same time, deepened with age, but still brimming with eager friendship. Ari Ara watched the two young men embrace with a pang of guilt. Emir and Korin had been best friends since boyhood. It was her fault they hadn't seen much of each other in the past two years, not since Emir had followed Shulen into exile. Last year, he'd served as Korin's guard during the delegations, but Emir had to leave his friend behind when the Great Lady forbid Korin from joining the Peace Force. The tough decision had torn Emir in half. He'd missed Korin deeply.

"So," Korin asked brightly, looking from one face to the next, "when do we set out?"

Shulen lifted a grey eyebrow.

"We?" he inquired, his mild tone barely veiling the severe note of warning.

"Of course," Korin answered implacably. "I'm not staying behind to schmooze with lords and flirt with ladies. This is far more interesting than the royal tour."

"What will your mother say?"

"Nothing. She's not going to know."

"I'm not lying to the Great Lady for you."

"I'm not asking you to."

"Then you'll return to the royal tour?"

"Not a chance. Think about it, Shulen," Korin said in his most persuasive tone, more determined than Ari Ara had ever seen him. "Next to Tahkan Shirar or Ari Ara, I'm your most significant supporter. If I can make your case to the nobles, that's half the battle of waging peace. It's worth Mum's temporary ire for the long-term gains."

He had a point, Ari Ara thought. She could tell from Shulen's silence that he was weighing Korin's argument. Her cousin

83

pressed onward, explaining how his firsthand experiences with the Peace Force this summer would make him a better advocate for it in years to come. He'd have stories to tell and a certainty born of having lived and breathed Alaren's Way Between.

"I'll be able to tell them I've seen Azar work with my own eyes," Korin said, "and that might come in handy someday. You need an allies in powerful positions and if Ari Ara never gains the royal confirmation, I'll be picking up Mum's role."

His voice dropped in tone, fading into a sigh. Ari Ara hid her grin. Korin had no ambition to become king. He was probably the first of his bloodline since Alaren to dislike the power of the monarchy. The Great Lady Brinelle didn't flinch at holding the regency position. If Ari Ara fell off a cliff, her aunt would simply change her title to queen and carry on with the work of running the nation. Her only son's apathy toward power baffled her.

"What about your entourage?" Shulen asked the youth, thinking of the warriors, servants, and courtiers that accompanied a noble on a royal tour.

"I gave them orders to proceed through the Westlands and Stonelands, lingering at the crystal pools for several weeks. No objections there - they think these orders came straight from Mum as a cover for a special covert mission that doesn't include an entourage."

"And this mission is what, exactly?" Shulen grumbled.

"Joining the Peace Force, of course, but no one needs to know that."

Shulen sighed and lifted an eyebrow.

"You've read too many tales," he suggested wryly.

"Yes," Korin answered darkly, "in the *Book of Secrets*."

Shulen hushed him. They couldn't speak of that in public where anyone – including Ari Ara - might hear. It wasn't called the *Book of Secrets* for nothing.

"I've got it all worked out," Korin stated airily, switching back to his scheme to join the Peace Force. "My royal entourage thinks Mum sent me on a secret mission. They'll pretend I'm still on tour with them to cover for me. Meanwhile, my dear ole Mum thinks I'm dallying with a pretty girl at the crystal pools. With any luck, she'll just send me a scolding message about how to avoid royal bastards."

He sighed and rolled his eyes.

"As if I'd ever be so careless or disrespectful to my lovers."

Shulen cleared his throat at that frank comment. Ari Ara hid her grin. She knew all about her cousin's dalliances - gossip traveled fast and far - and she also knew about Korin's careful approach to his love affairs. Despite his mother's protestations, Korin did take his duties seriously, even if he hid it under a veneer of flippancy and nonchalance. His letters to his younger cousin were crammed full of worldly advice to a double royal. He considered it an investment in the day she'd ascend the throne instead of him. What he *hadn't* told Ari Ara - or anyone - was how often he daydreamed about abdicating the throne and dumping the crown on her head, regardless of what anyone else thought.

Shulen doubted Korin's deception to Brinelle would hold up longer than a week. But the youth had surprised him with his impassioned belief that training with the Peace Force was critically important for the future of Mariana. Korin had given the matter serious consideration. And, since Korin rarely took anything seriously, Shulen found himself strangely moved. Putting aside his reservations, he agreed to let the youth stay. They could certainly benefit from having the patronage of the Great Lady's son.

Besides, even Shulen had to concede that the golden-haired youth had a unique knack for the Way Between. Last year, during the peace delegation to the desert, Korin had shown strong aptitude for the practices of Azar. With the skill of one born into politics, he managed to charm his way into everyone's good graces in the first week. His laughter and humor drew a small crowd to his side wherever he went. And his strength was his unexpected humility. He'd fumble Desert Speech just to get everyone laughing. He'd voice the silly questions everyone wondered but didn't dare ask. He'd tell stories and ham it up with the precision of a theater player, driving the listeners to tears of giggles or genuine sorrow. Shulen had watched the young noble with renewed respect this past year.

"Do you think it's just an act, all this clowning around?" Shulen had asked Emir one day as Korin toppled into the dust during an Azar match with the very smallest Harraken child.

Emir smiled mysteriously. He would neither confirm nor deny Shulen's suspicions, but Korin de Marin was not a fool . . . even when he played the part. Of all the peace delegation members, he was the most likely to be hated as the son of the Great Lady who had launched the War of Retribution. Yet, by the end of the second week, he was the most well-liked. The young man's unexpected humor and humility disarmed everyone. Everyone had bested him at something, received a beaming smile and handshake from the curly-haired youth, and been pressed for a lesson in a new skill.

"I will tell you this," Emir hinted to his mentor, "Korin studied the Alaren stories more closely than anyone. He even took notes and quizzed himself on them. Last winter, he sat down with Professor Solange twice a week to learn the finer points of the Way Between."

Shulen had been taken aback. Alaren tales were full of clowning around. Perhaps Korin's antics were less of an act . . . and more of a coming-into-his-own. Out of the shadow of his mother's expectations, perhaps Korin finally had a chance to find his own Way Between. Through the course of the summer, Shulen realized that Korin de Marin might be exactly the leader the Marianans needed in a world yearning for peace.

"Come along, then," he said briskly to the youths, returning his thoughts to the crowded alleys of Garrison Town and the tasks they had to accomplish before departing. They couldn't dally all day in the street.

Behind his back, the three youths cheered and pumped their fists. Shulen, sensing their hushed thrill, craned around to glance at them.

"What?" Ari Ara asked innocently, spreading her hands and lifting her shoulders.

Shulen just shook his head and strode onward.

"Cousin, we need to work on your lying skills," Korin teased her in mock disgust. "You've a face like an open book."

"Speaking of books," she asked eagerly, "what's the *Book of Secrets?*"

"I can't tell you or it wouldn't be a secret," he answered with a laugh. But she saw his eyes dart away and knew he was hiding something important.

"Come on, tell - "

She broke off as a company of riders clattered past, single-file. Along with Korin and Emir, she flattened against the wall of a shop. Ari Ara nudged them, pointing at the warriors' insignias. They wore the serpent and roses emblem of the House of Thorn. These were battle-hardened men, scarred and muscled, armed to the teeth and road-weathered. An angular man with ropy muscles passed. Ari Ara startled as she caught a glimpse of his face, framed by his dark hood. She craned her neck to watch him ride up the street. The man, likewise, turned over his shoulder to stare at her.

Rannor Thornmar's leather armor creaked as he swiveled. He didn't bother hiding his dislike. Lord Thornmar had done everything in his power to discredit her. He'd hoped to have her executed for treason - though he might have settled for life imprisonment - and had not been pleased by Brinelle's lenient decision to exile her. A sneer twisted Thornmar's lips. His eyes flicked to their white tunics with the black Mark of Peace. For a moment, Ari Ara thought he would confront them, but he made no comment. Thornmar kicked his heels into his horse's ribs and clattered up the cobblestones toward the garrison.

What is he doing here? Ari Ara wondered. His territory was far to the north.

Korin caught her eyes, lips pressed together in a thin, worried line, thinking the same thing.

Whatever Thornmar's purpose here, it didn't bode well for her.

CHAPTER EIGHT

. . . . .

Stolen Cattle

Leaving Garrison Town, they headed north into the Fire
Peaks Region. Sky-piercing mountains dominated the horizons,
cloud-shrouded and snow-capped. Stippled hills crowded
between the broken crowns of ancient volcanoes. Long ago, these
peaks had erupted, blackening the air with ash. Tala sang the
ballad of walking mountains and how the land had rippled like a
river, shapeshifting in shudders and shakes. Ari Ara could easily
imagine such times. Even now, the region seemed unsettled and
sharp around the edges. The bones of the mountains jutted raw
and angular. Scree slopes gashed the steepest faces like scars, bare
of trees and brush. The forces of war had razed nearby villages at
least once per generation. Instead of moss-covered stone
architecture, the buildings were rough-shod, hasty constructions.
No one bothered to carve the lintels or put a touch of curling
trim along the rafters. Not when soldiers might burn the
structures to the ground.

In certain stretches, the border ran along the road. Ari Ara
hopped the rutted centerline, one foot in her mother's lands, the
other in her father's. Then the road would veer east or west while

the invisible boundary between the two nations shot straight over a rocky butte or across an impassable gorge. At these detours, they encountered checkpoints guarded by either Marianan or Harraken warriors. Solange and Mahteni would show letters from their respective leaders granting safe and free passage. Ari Ara would hold her breath, hoping the Marianans wouldn't make a fuss over the nuances of her exile. Occasionally, the guards examined the contents of their travel packs for contraband.

Not everyone passed through the checkpoints. Bandit trails plunged off the road into the forest, circumventing the border crossings. Peddlers avoided import and export taxes by taking hidden paths. Traders took alternate routes through the mountains, their donkeys clopping along behind them.

"What about the Paika?" Minli and Ari Ara asked, hoping to find out more about the elusive people. "Do they travel those roads?"

The solitary peddlers turned and spat to the side. They shook their sun-weathered faces. Paika took their own routes, trails no one knew. They appeared and disappeared like magic. It was uncanny, grumbled the peddlers. Some argued that the Paika weren't even human, not properly.

The further they journeyed into the ravines and ridges of the region, the more rumors they encountered about the recent raids. At the waystations along the road, youths from nearby villages swapped angry gossip over the series of attacks. Woodcutters shouldering axes at the end of a long day muttered about robbed grain or stolen cattle. The farrier who made the local rounds to shoe everyone's horses shared a meal with the Peace Force. She spoke of night patrols and increased vigilance. A traveling healer cautioned them not to approach villages after dusk, or they'd receive an arrow between their eyes instead of a welcome. Goatherds carried stout staffs and belt knives to use if attacked. They told tales of Paika magic and trickery.

"If I see a Piker," one lad vowed, "I'll stick his head where it belongs - on a pole!"

Ari Ara began to think Mendren's ban held some wisdom, after all - it kept the Paika out of harm's way. As it was, many locals demanded that the garrison take further action. They wanted increased patrols, arrests of Paika suspects, and raids on the Paika's homes to search for stolen goods.

"At the very least," spluttered a nervous bridegroom escorting his love from her village to his town, "the garrison ought to put more men along the border. We can't pursue the Paika if they cross it, see. And those good-for-nothing Harraken don't give chase, not on our account."

Mahteni, Sarai, and the other desert dwellers bristled on behalf of their warriors, but at the next checkpoint, they learned there was some truth to the matter.

"We don't work for the Marianans," the Harraken patrol leader stated with a shrug, "and they don't work for us. Plenty of bandits have caused trouble here, crossed over to the Marianan side, and laughed in our faces. We can't do anything. Even a single arrow falling on riverlands territory is cause for war."

Everyone complained about it, but half of them profited from it, too. They bought bandit-snatched goods at discounts. They fled the law by crossing the border. They avoided tolls and taxes by smuggling in the unpatrolled sections. During the War of Retribution, the boundary had shifted west in some places, east in others, dividing families as it moved. The Fire Peaks villagers complained about - and exploited - the new location of the line.

"And the Paika?" the head of one village sighed. "Well, that's another matter altogether. The lines don't apply to them, technically. Paika Crossings happen where and when they please. That's why they're mad at Commander Mendren for banning them on pain of death. It flies against tradition and history. Half the trouble the Paika get into comes from trying to secure their right of free travel from the newest victor of the latest war."

The Paika's ability to freely traverse the mountains was a subject of much bitterness among families separated by the inconvenience of the border. Many rolled their envy into accusations against the Paika, including blaming them for the recent raids. None of these folk had actually seen the Paika attacking the towns. Sifting through the secondhand stories - setting aside the wildest tales - Minli sorted the reports down to one source: a man named Bergen who'd lost his herd of cattle in an attack.

Standoffish and prickly as its owner, Bergen's homestead stood outside the village of Gult. Bergen scarcely glanced up at their arrival, turning his back to them and leaving his dogs to snarl and bark through the wire and board fence. Only when Mahteni silenced them with a bit of Harraken song-magic did Bergen pivot to shade the light from his eyes, scowl, and trudge down from the broken paddock he was mending. He was younger than his stooped frame suggested. He grudgingly called off his dogs and let the Peace Force enter through his gate.

"Not a lot of good you can do about my cattle," he grumbled. "The commander should have sent some trackers, not you folks."

Shulen pried the story out of him. Bergen had been abed when he heard his cattle lowing uneasily in the stormy night. He'd scrambled for a lantern, but by the time he shoved his boots on, it was too late. The cows had been driven into the woods at the end of his fields. He'd seen the Paika in their funny caps and antlered helmets, silhouetted in the flashes of lightning. There were too many to confront, not single-handedly. In the morning, Bergen tried to track the stolen livestock, but the rains had washed away the trail.

"Is it just you, then?" Minli asked, glancing around curiously. "Big place for just one man."

"Grew up here," Bergen muttered. "Family died in the war and I've not married yet. Got a couple lads that come over from my uncle's farm to work, but they go home at dusk."

"The dogs didn't bark?" Minli inquired, eyeing the animals warily. The bristle-coated beasts lay at their master's feet, snarling possessively and making low, suspicious growls in the back of their throats.

"Drugged 'em," Bergen sighed. "The Paika know herb lore. They must have laced a bit of ham with something to knock out my dogs."

Grumbling about wasting his time, Bergen complied with their requests to look around. He showed them the broken gate on the fence and the lone cow that remained. He'd had her in a small shed, treating an udder infection, or else she'd be gone, too. The thieves had driven the cattle up the trail through the forest to the high pastures, before veering off into a tangle of passes.

"They're long gone," Bergen groaned. "And I'm not the only one those blasted Pikers attacked. There've been raids in other places, too. The commander's banned 'em, but that won't stop nothing. Pikers'll do as they please until we put their heads on poles."

Bergen of Gult was a Marianan loyalist; the blue flag flew proudly from the top of his barn. His eyes slipped suspiciously over to that girl, Ari Ara, the false heir who claimed to be the daughter of Queen Alinore. The nobles hadn't confirmed her, and Bergen wouldn't either. Look what she'd done to Mariana already! Freeing those water workers, getting the Great Warrior

Shulen exiled, thrusting the nation into economic turmoil. And she was in league with the desert demons, for certain. Bergen's narrowed gaze fell on the Harraken Peace Force members. Now she was bringing them into the country, touting peace. He snorted under his breath. He wasn't convinced peace was even possible. The best Bergen hoped for was a swift, harsh expulsion of any Harraken invaders. And that took soldiers, not peace workers.

After questioning him further about the cows, the Peace Force took their leave. They spoke to the villagers in Gult, but they learned nothing new. Everyone repeated the same tale of drugged dogs and missing cattle. Before dusk, they made camp by a spring-fed waystation along the road, trying to figure out their next move. Minli kept squinting west, above the tree line, shading the setting sun out of his eyes. Just as the arguments began to spin into endless circles, he spoke.

"Let's go up there," he suggested, pointing to the high ridge that cast its long shadow over the valley. "Isn't there a string of hermitages on the top? If anyone has seen the cattle or the Paika, it's them."

"Ah yes," Solange agreed, pulling out her maps. "The hermits would have a good vantage point."

A plan was hatched to climb the ridge in the morning. Twilight deepened to full darkness and the Peace Force rolled up in blankets and cloaks on the hard ground. The forest hushed and sighed around them. Sleep came swiftly after the long day on the road. Hours later, when the first hint of dawn tingled in the blackness of night, Ari Ara woke to a voice whispering in her ear.

"Shhh," Finn breathed, crouched next to her, eyes darting around the faint glow of the fire's embers.

He tilted his head, indicating that she should rise and follow. She crept after him, nervously passing through the slumbering forms of the others. Shulen would send her straight back to her father if he caught her!

"You shouldn't be here," she hissed as soon as they were beyond earshot. "You're risking your neck with the ban still in place. Mendren won't lift it. The Great Lady sent us to find out what's going on."

Finn didn't bother to hide his skepticism about that. Ari Ara's pride smarted at his disdainful grunt.

"We did find out that Bergen of Gult started those tales of Paika raiders."

"He'll pay for that," Finn snarled.

Ari Ara didn't like the sound of that threat.

"Well," she added hastily, "he says he saw Paika hats in the storm."

"It's easy enough to get ahold of our belongings if you're a pack of raiders," Finn pointed out with a scowl. "What else did the farmer say?"

She told him about the drugged dogs. Finn cursed.

"Liar. Or fool. Or both," he growled uncharitably. "Why would the Paika steal his stupid cattle? What good are cows to us?"

Ari Ara tried to ask Finn what he meant, but he just held a finger to his lips. Alerted to an unseen stirring, he slid into the fold of night, leaving her shivering in the slight chill. Over breakfast, she casually asked Minli the question Finn had raised.

"Why would the Paika take the cattle?" she mumbled, fanning her mouth as she burnt her tongue on the piping hot porridge.

Minli shot her a sour look.

"You should have asked your friend last night," he grumbled in a low tone.

Her mouth fell open. Minli had been awake, sifting through

the details of Bergen's story when he heard Finn's footsteps. He saw Ari Ara rise. For a brief instant, he considered shouting out and waking the others. Instead, he rolled over and pretend to sleep until she returned.

"You promised to bring me next time you saw Finn," he murmured. "What if he was leading you into a trap?"

"You sound like Shulen," she told him.

"Shulen has a point."

"I thought you were on my side."

"Who says I'm not?" he replied.

"So, are you going to answer my question or not? Why would the Paika take the cattle?"

Minli gave her a long-suffering look, but relented.

"It is odd," he agreed, puzzled. "The Paika aren't ranchers. They don't maintain many pastures. They hunt deer and elk, and raise a few goats, but they see cattle as bothersome. Maybe they're planning to sell them across the border or to bandits?"

"Or maybe it wasn't the Paika who stole them," Ari Ara suggested. "Anyone could have drugged the dogs."

"Bergen said it was Paika herbs," Minli reminded her, scooting over to make space for Korin as he sat down.

"Well, they can't be the only people who know about those plants," Ari Ara argued.

"No," Korin agreed, cutting into the conversation, "there's a bunch of formulas in the Book - "

He broke off, changing his words.

"- in this book I once read."

The Book of Secrets, Ari Ara thought. If they didn't get some answers from the hermits on the ridge, she'd just have to get those secrets out of Korin.

CHAPTER NINE

. . . . .

The Haystacks Hermits

The Peace Force followed a well-worn footpath out of the forest and climbed the ridge to the Haystacks. Built of stone, not straw, the round dwellings with peaked roofs had weathered centuries of buffeting storms. Slung low between two mountains, the string of houses looked like knobs on the spine of an old horse's back. The ridge marked the border, the western slope falling down into Harraken territory, the eastern side plummeting toward Marianan villages. The road splintered at this ridge, curving in two directions lower down. Only the hermits bothered to climb up to the wide, open space where the Haystacks hunkered down beneath the fierce wind.

The first hermit who greeted them hollered that the ghost of the old mountain sang fiercely today. As the man ushered them into his hermitage, he bowed to the empty air where the towering crown of a mountain had once stood before an ancient eruption had crumbled the majestic peak. Inside the Haystack dwelling, the howl of wind abated. Only a few of them fit inside at one time. The rest took shelter with Zyrh and the packhorses in a dugout barn on the lee side of the ridge. On a different day, they'd be sheltered on the opposite side, depending on the wind. The currents twisted here, slamming east one day, west the next.

Despite the stunning views in every direction, the Haystacks hermit would tell them nothing of what he may – or may not – have seen. For three hundred years, the hermits had remained neutral in the wars. They stood aside as one army, then the next, climbed to their heights to scour the land below. The hermits did not intervene, not then, not now. The Peace Force was welcome to use their lookout points, but the hermits would tell no tales of those who had passed through.

"Gargh!" Ari Ara complained to Minli later. "That's Anar's Way, passively avoiding the conflict."

She had to holler over the wind. Two abreast, the Peace Force walked in a long, straggling line. The sun silhouetted their wind-battered figures, framing them against the faded blue of the sky as they traversed the ridge to the next Haystack. Hope still remained that one of the other hermits might break silence and share knowledge. They had to try. Ari Ara walked on the leeward side of Zyrh's broad flank. Minli huddled on the horse's back, his cloak pulled tightly around his thin frame.

"Is it Anar or Azar?" Minli shouted. "Neutrality could be a Way Between."

"You can't be neutral on the Mari River," Ari Ara countered, using a line she'd learned from him. "The current'll tug you downstream unless you *do* something."

"But what's downstream, peace or war?" Minli replied. His hood flung back and he scrambled to pull it up again.

Ari Ara shrugged and stopped talking. She didn't know, and it was far too windy for philosophical arguments.

Whipped raw and frazzled, they came to another stone Haystack. Far larger than the previous hermitages, this building had once sheltered the original ten hermits. After years of stepping on each other's toes and yearning for more solitude, they had constructed smaller dwellings further apart on the ridge. The wide, round house was now tended by a single hermitess who used the extra space to dry medicinal herbs and bottle tinctures. A brightly painted wooden trim ran beneath the rafters. A collection of carved statues lined the walkway – all of them making rude faces, Ari Ara noted with a laugh. Mahteni lifted her hand to rap on the blue door. Just before her knuckles hit wood, the door flung open and a cheerful woman hollered out a welcome.

The almond-skinned hermitess had a face like a wizened apple. The wind whipped her grey hair in seven directions as she urged them to come in. She'd clearly been expecting them. The hermitage was swept. Her herb collection had been cleared away and the tinctures shelved along the circular wall. Fresh cushions of straw and burlap had been set out around the low stone bench that hugged the walls of the round building. A huge kettle boiled on a twig-fed hearthfire. A tray of mismatched cups stood beside it, prepared for tea. The woman's Haystack was snug and cozy. Not a single loose shingle clattered on the roof. Every last crack between the stones had been plastered over with clay. When the door shut, the silence startled several people into laughter.

"Settle in as you please," she murmured, pointing firmly to the benches and collecting their cloaks. "You look like the ghost mountain's been haunting you. My name's Nell Banderhook. Some call me the Last Straw Hermit."

Ari Ara and Minli exchanged knowing looks. They'd heard of the Last Straw Hermit. The other Haystack inhabitants had grumbled about this rule-breaking, trouble-making, half-mad woman. Some of them wanted to throw her out of the Haystacks, but Nell had earned her hermitage from the previous occupant in a lineage of succession that stretched back to the founding hermit. Nell Banderhook would not be moved off her mountain by anyone, not hermits, armies, or ghosts. She'd been waiting for the Peace Force with the certainty of a piper with a tune. She knew they'd play together; it was merely a matter of time. After all, everyone said the Way Between was for fools and Nell had been called a fool all her life. It was only fitting that they'd find each other. She poured the tea and launched right in to conversation.

"So, Bergen's been feeding you a line of nonsense about the Paika, has he?"

That got their attention. Shulen straightened up so fast he sloshed his tea across his knuckles and winced from the heat. Nell shook her grey hair and drummed her calloused fingers on her knees. She thought her fellow hermits were daft for refusing to aid the Peace Force. She wouldn't keep silent.

"I saw those cattle being driven across the Lower Heights," she told them. "It wasn't the Paika. What good are cattle to them, anyway?"

"That's exactly what - " Ari Ara snatched back her next words - *Finn said* - and finished with, "I was thinking."

"*If* the Paika are involved - and that's a big *if* - they're more likely to be working for someone," Nell theorized, her brown eyes thoughtful.

"Who?" Ari Ara blurted out, her stomach lurching as she thought of Thornmar.

Nell shrugged. Possibly a feuding clan, she suggested. Ever since Commander Mendren had banned Harraken-style blood debts, the local Border Mountain villagers had replaced duels with malicious pranks. The Paika could turn a pretty profit doing the dirty work for these local rivalries. Nell described the simmering tensions beneath the surface of the seemingly idyllic farms nestled throughout the valley. The feuds had grown so bad that a trio of clansmen – youths, all of them – had even "stolen" their own cattle, herded them into the fields of a rival faction, and raised an uproar over the alleged theft.

"A man hung for that, you know," Nell told them in a mournful voice. "When the truth came out, Mendren was so mad at the trio, he had half a mind to hang them, too."

"I'm surprised he didn't," Shulen said in a gruff tone. He knew the man well.

"He couldn't, not without setting off a wildfire of retaliatory skirmishes," Nell replied. "Bad enough that he took a finger from each of them as penalty for stealing."

Ari Ara blanched at the thought and curled her fingers into fists.

Nell shook her head and rose to refill everyone's tea cups.

"If you want to stop the wars, you'd do well to end these clan feuds. People get away with blaming all sorts of trouble on the Paika, but it's their own nonsense that's set off half the wars in history."

Korin stared at his hands, cupped around the rough clay mug, thoughtful. He agreed with Nell. While the two nations' political tensions drove them to the precipice of war, it was often a small spat of fighting that toppled the whole world over. More often than not, the Paika were involved, or blamed. *The Book of Secrets* detailed numerous examples of how monarchs had purposefully inflamed the tensions in the Fire Peaks Region to justify a broader war, hiring the Paika to harass one group or another. Now that he thought of it, there was even a strategy for paying someone to "steal" cattle, drive them onto enemy land, then invade to "regain" them.

"So, you don't know who took the cattle?" Minli asked Nell, ruefully.

She shot him a sharp look.

"No. But I know where they are now."

"What?!"

More sociable than the rest of the meditative and reclusive hermits, she wandered among the clans in every direction, back and forth across the border. That's why the other hermits called her crazy. While they craved silence and solitude, Nell didn't. She was an herb woman. Wiry and strong, she spent her days climbing the steep paths down into the valleys, tending the sick and healing injuries. She helped mothers bring their babes into the world and guided the dying beyond. In the course of these visits, she teased gossip out of women and girls, heard who was fighting with whom, which lads had come to blows recently, and why one clan was shouting at another. If trouble brewed in her valleys, Nell found out.

"Bergen's cows are in Tomos' pasture on the west side of the Haystacks Ridge," she informed them. "How they got there, I couldn't say, but I'll take you there in the morning to sort it out."

"How can we ever thank you?" Mahteni sighed in relief.

Nell grinned, her broad smile crinkling her face into a hundred lines.

"Tell me about this Peace Force and that old trickster Alaren," she urged. "The night's long and my ears are hungry for new tales."

Nell's isolated community was prone to silence. Who could compete with the wind? But they welcomed new tales from far-off places or times. A fresh story was good as gold on long winter nights.

The Peace Force was delighted to repay Nell in stories. The Haystacks dwellers – even the Last Straw Hermit - were held in high regard by those in the surrounding area. If Nell shared the stories about Alaren and the Peace Force, the valley folk would listen. As part of the Peace Force's training, Professor Solange had ensured that each member could tell a few stories with skill.

"All of you should be able to tell a handful of educational - and entertaining - stories about Alaren and the Way Between," the scholar had informed them. "To practice, you will take turns telling tales and hearing them. That way, we will strengthen our storytelling . . . and our listening."

Listening was an essential skill for the Peace Force. The work of peace required the ability to pay attention in a deep way, to not interrupt, and to hear what was said and left unsaid. The Harraken, with their sharp memories and oral culture, had a distinct advantage over their Marianan counterparts. On the other hand, most of the Harraken could not read written script. So, Solange had the Marianans read aloud from *The Stories of the Third Brother* as the Harraken memorized the tales by ear. Storytelling, however, was more than memorization and regurgitation. Rill had a performative streak that lit up the night. Tala's training gave zir a spellbinding power whenever ze opened zirs mouth. Others struggled, but practice helped.

They shared stories with Nell over a dinner of simple fare, adding their supplies to the hermitess' stewpot. As the evening twilight dwindled and the Haystacks plunged into a sea of darkness, Alaren's tales gave way to talk of a lasting peace. A wistful note crept into Nell's voice. Hard-scrabbled as the slopes of jumbled scree, she had lived through decades of war. The battles stopped and started like thunderstorms, rolling through century after century. The local villagers had rarely lived in the clear sunlight of peace. Brief ceasefires inevitably broke into periods of renewed violence. Their houses were burned so often, people built of stone. Their supplies were raided so frequently, they kept dozens of caches, each more hidden than the last. Nell suspected that even those who were willing to learn about the Way Between wouldn't stop training in Attar, the Warrior's

Way. Prudence required them to hedge their bets. These past few years of tenuous calm had lasted longer than most ceasefires. Still, the villagers hardly dared to release their held breaths, waiting uneasily for the next bout of violence to erupt.

"Alaren believed it was possible to prevent those outbreaks ... or stop them faster," Ari Ara mentioned. Her blue-grey eyes met Nell's. "He thought that if we worked to end our smaller feuds, larger wars would be less likely to break out."

"It's like how a rainstorm in a drought stops a wildfire from spreading," Tala added.

"It's a tinderbox around here, for certain," Solange agreed. "That's why so many wars have started in this region. Conflicts constantly simmer beneath even the most peaceful-seeming surface. It's our job to turn down the heat before it sparks an inferno and burns everyone."

"I watched it ignite over Queen Alinore's death," murmured Nell. "I saw villages burn to the ground. I choked on the black smoke that drifted over the Haystacks for days. There were rumors the assailants came from here, you know. All nonsense."

Nell leaned and spat into the hearth. The spittle popped and hissed. She spoke quietly of the war. The Marianan army had scoured the region, searching for the Lost Heir, trying to terrorize or torture the people into telling a truth they did not own. When the Marianans moved onward, the Harraken rode in. Moragh Shirar and her band of women warriors, the Black Ravens, also sought the Lost Heir. They didn't hesitate to sift through the ashes of the burnt-out villages looking for the child. Back and forth, the two armies clashed. Those who managed to stay in their homes nearly starved when the Marianan troops raided their stores before marching onward to lay siege to Turim City.

Korin shifted uncomfortably, knowing the Marianan army had acted upon the orders of his mother. Mahteni hung her head, acknowledging the harsh tactics of the Black Ravens, her sister's warband. Shulen's craggy face grew taut with harsh memories. No one interrupted Nell as she haltingly recounted her experiences of the war. Hunger and illness had carved dual paths through the local families. Like a scythe in a wheat field, death struck down a whole generation. Sons and daughters had been snatched from homes and conscripted into the military - as soldiers if they could fight, or as able bodies to pack and cook and work for the soldiers. The few who returned came back haunted by the things they'd seen and done. Most never made it home at all.

No one was blameless by war's end. Among the older generation, each person carried pain and each person had caused it. Even actions taken in the name of defense soon blurred with vows of vengeance. Desperate times called for desperate measures, everyone claimed. People did the unspeakable, the unthinkable, and lived haunted by those moments for the rest of their lives. Scars cut deep across the two nations. Wounds still festered beneath the surface.

Around the dim light of the hermitage, jaws worked over trembling lips. Eyes shone bright with unshed tears. Knees jiggled in agitation. Fists clenched. Knuckles turned white. Mahteni breathed out in a long sigh. Her slow exhale reminded her companions that a breath held too long stops the heart from working. A round of sighs and gasps followed hers. A few reddened eyes released their tears. Beyond the stone walls, the wind hissed through the branches of the gnarled apple trees that huddled next to the hermitage.

"I am sorry," Ari Ara spoke into the uneasy silence, "for the war. It was unnecessary and wrong."

"It was not your fault," Nell answered gently. "You were an infant."

"I can still apologize for the war that was fought to find me," Ari Ara replied.

"It was fought to punish others for the pain we felt," Shulen said gruffly. He looked around the circular room. "For that, I am deeply sorry. We were right to grieve. We were wrong to attack in our grief."

The silence stretched long and painful. Buried memories rose to the surface as each person wrestled with their role in the violence and bloodshed. The youth watched the past haunt their elders. Minli gripped Ari Ara's hand. They'd been raised as orphans of war. Minli had no memories of his parents. He felt the ache of this loss more keenly than his missing leg, especially now that Ari Ara had reunited with her father. It drove him to work for peace, so that other children would know their mothers and fathers. Into the silence, he spoke.

"Building peace is what helps me on nights when I miss the parents I cannot remember."

His words unleashed a torrent of emotion in Nell. She, too, longed for a lasting peace. She wished to bring rain to the drought of the region and strengthen it against the re-ignition of violence. The valleys were fraught with sparks and tensions. The clans were always at each other's throats. It was high time for peace.

"This is what brought you here tonight," Nell acknowledged, "and what led me to open my door to you. It's what compelled me to break with the Haystacks' tradition of neutrality. If we do nothing, we will always have war. I want to stand on the side of peace. I want to work for it, like you are. If some cows need to be returned to their rightful owner to keep the peace, I will guide you to where they are."

Nell Banderhook lifted her chin. Some may call her mad, but she knew a good thing when she saw one. All spring, she'd been listening to the tales of the Peace Force, catching bits of rumors and gossip about their curious trainings in Moscam. She'd heard about Ari Ara Marin en Shirar's demonstration of the Way Between at the Market Day matches. Nell mulled and pondered over the odds-and-ends of history she'd heard about the ancestor Alaren. If peace was to come to these mountains at last, she wanted to throw her weight behind it.

"Must you *all* chase these raiders?" Nell asked, her bright eyes sweeping the circle of faces. "Couldn't one or two of you stay here as my guests? If a few of you helped me, we could tackle these blood feuds, once and for all."

Shulen beamed like his birthday had come early. *This* was precisely what he'd hoped for: that the locals would value the Way Between and participate in the effort to build peace. Talk turned to practicalities of who would stay and how they would approach the work. Nell's mind already buzzed with schemes for introducing the Peace Force to people on both sides of the border, at the village schools, the Feast Days and festivals, the local bonfires and weddings. Mahteni asked Nell more questions about the feuds, considering who among them would be best suited to help. The student from the university offered to stay; he'd grown up in a rough town and could speak with the young men. The traditional Harraken circle for resolving conflicts would be helpful, so a former water worker volunteered to train Nell in the process. Nell asked for an older woman to work with her among the mothers and grandmothers, and the dressier from the capital chose to join the small team.

When yawns outnumbered words, they settled down for the night. They slept like sunrays in Nell's ample hermitage, feet toward the central hearth, heads at the outer wall. It was a tight squeeze for thirty people, but they slumbered soundly, comforted by the snug shelter of the old dwelling.

In the morning, Nell led them down the western slope. Tomos' land rested alongside a slender creek, the verdant fields fed by irrigation ditches. The wind tossed the boughs of the higher forests, but calmed in this nook of a farmstead. Tomos was a short, stocky man with a barrel chest and a thatch of red-brown curls. He'd been pounding fence posts when the visitors arrived. He mopped his sweaty brow with his kerchief and offered them all water. He spoke in the style of the mountain folk, his Desert Speech thick and furry, his Marianan dry and raspy.

"What brings you over the ridge, Nell?" he asked her.

"Well, Tomos, it seems Bergen of Gult is missing his cattle. Claims they've been stolen and I think you know where they are."

The man blanched with fright and reddened with fury. He knew where Bergen's cattle were alright – they were in his back pasture, getting fat on his lush grass. Tomos cursed the trader who'd sold them to him for a song. He hadn't known they were stolen when he bought them, but he'd heard the tales of Bergen's herd and hoped they weren't black cattle with distinctive white chests. Unfortunately, they were. Tomos twisted his cap in his hands and swore he hadn't known.

"Could you help return them with no harm done?" he asked anxiously. "Wasn't me that stole them, after all."

Nell and the Peace Force promised to smooth things over with Bergen and make sure he understood that Tomos wasn't to blame.

"Who did you buy them from?" Minli asked. "It wasn't the Paika, was it?"

"No, and I don't know why folks think it was them. They don't tend to deal in cattle."

"So, who was it that sold them to you?" Minli persisted,

refusing to be diverted.

"Can't say," Tomos mumbled.

"Because you don't know or because you're bound to silence?" Minli asked shrewdly.

But the fellow clammed up for good and refused to answer. He was, however, eager to trade back the cattle, especially when the Peace Force offered to compensate him for what he paid. Dealing in stolen cattle was a punishable offense. Tomos was glad to be done with the nasty business.

"Would have turned a pretty profit, though," he sighed mournfully as they drove the cattle off.

Bergen seemed oddly displeased to have his herd returned. His features contorted when he saw the beasts. He muttered an ungracious thanks and barely listened to their explanation of where the cattle had been found. He shooed them off without ceremony, ignoring the local customs of hospitality, not even offering them a sip of water for their troubles.

"Well, that was odd," Minli said to Ari Ara as they left.

She agreed. It was more than odd, it was suspicious. Bergen seemed to know more than he was telling. They couldn't stick around to question him, though. The Peace Force had to travel onward. Nell had heard an interesting rumor as they passed through Gult. The miller's daughter had heard it from a traveling peddler who had stopped to trade a set of shiny buttons for a sack of freshly-ground flour.

Someone had spotted the raiders, not two days' journey away, in the Ruins of Knobble.

CHAPTER TEN

. . . . .

The Ruins of Knobble

Knobble crumbled in a rain-shrouded caldera to the northwest. They climbed up from the high ridge of the Haystacks into constant clouds and weeping, misty rain. The sun rarely penetrated the gloom. Rising fog from moss-lined rivers lifted until it collided with plummeting storm clouds. Water poured from the immense faucet of the sky. The dampness never left their bones. The grey veil never parted. Emir wore a suit of mud from where he'd slipped guiding the horses through a tricky turn. Isa shivered, her hair plastered to her skull. Sarai tried to convince Tala to use song-magic to stop the rain. When Tala refused, she settled for moodily holding her cloak over her head like an umbrella. They slogged through the mud as swiftly as they could, knowing all the while that they were unlikely to catch up with the raiders. But if they were lucky, they might gain a better description that could aid them in their search.

Knobble had been abandoned during the war after an attack left the once-stately monastery and surrounding village in ruins. Before the war, Knobble had bustled with activity, serving as the cultural center of the Fire Peaks Region. All that was gone. The

111

light had gone out of Knobble. Only rain and restless spirits remained.

The place seemed utterly deserted. The rubble of old buildings loomed in jagged heaps, tricking their eyes into seeing hulking shapes of bears and soldiers. Thorny brambles twisted over old chimneys. Moss-gnawed fences rotted, half-hidden in the rain-plastered grass. There were no signs of the raiders. If they had come through, they were long gone.

The Peace Force was not, however, entirely alone.

As Shulen led them toward the half-ruined temple, a man stepped out from the shadows. He was a desperately thin scarecrow of a figure with straggly hair and hollows under his cheekbones.

"Who are you and where did you come from?!" Solange exclaimed, startled.

"I'm Elwys," he answered, "and I should ask you that. I *live* here."

"You ... live ... here?" Solange repeated in an incredulous tone, looking around at the ruins.

He turned toward her, hands outstretched in a piteous shrug.

"Yes," Elwys admitted, his drooping gaze meeting hers. "Always have. I was born here, but I'm alone now. Everyone else is gone - or else their spirit haunts this place."

Ari Ara shivered. The hairs on her neck stood on end. *That's* what she'd been sensing: the spirits, restless and unhappy. As soon as Elwys named it, the sensation heightened. She wouldn't sleep well tonight.

"Then it's you we seek," Shulen called out, striding forward. "We ask your permission to stay the night in the old temple. We offer our stew and fire in exchange for hearing your news. We heard a band of raiders passed through. Have you seen them?"

Elwys' eyes studied the mud.

"Came through, they did. Then they left like all the rest. No one stays in Knobble long. No one but me."

Elwys shrugged dolefully, then gestured for them to follow him into the shelter of the temple. The shattered windows gaped like the vacant eyes of a clean-picked skull, but the walls stood and the roof only leaked in one corner. The Peace Force filed in gratefully, shaking off the rain and wringing out their cloaks. Emir found firewood in a spare room off the main hall and Tala murmured a bit of song to strengthen the sparks into a cheery blaze in the hearth. Cobwebs hung from the rafters in dusty lace. A broken table crumbled in the corner, evidently used by other travelers for firewood. They hung their sodden cloaks across the windows to keep down the drafts. The stones of the floor were slick with damp and mossy at the edges. The temple's old sleeping quarters offered shelter for the horses. Half the roof had caved in, but the remaining section broke the wind and rain. They settled in with good spirits, chattering as they spread out their clothes and gear to dry.

After a round of introductions, Elwys huddled close to the hearthfire. The odor of damp wool cloaks filled the room, but no one complained. The warmth of the soup pushed the chill from their bones. Elwys gulped his down so fast he scorched his mouth, hissing and fanning his tongue frantically.

He had seen the raiders, he reported, a midsized company of about twenty men, no insignias nor colors. Elwys hid, of course. He wasn't stupid enough to stick his head out around a pack of heavily-armed fighters. They didn't seem like Paika, though, not unless they were Paika disguising as northern folk. Something of their features reminded him of people from the Smithlands.

Or Orelands, Ari Ara mouthed to Minli, thinking of Thornmar's territory.

He nodded imperceptibly. Elwys' testimony wasn't enough to

go on, not on its own.

"You might stick around," Elwys suggested in a wistful tone. "They could circle back - happens often enough. Traders and bandits ride out to one village then the next, stopping here in between. Good chance of spotting them if you stay a bit longer."

The prospect of dallying in gloomy Knobble was not enticing, but there was no harm in waiting another day or two. Elwys smiled at their decision, his cheeks quivering over unused muscles. He promptly enlisted their help in repairing his house, the temple roof, and patching together some semblance of a stable.

"Perhaps folks will stop by again if we do," he dared to murmur, visions of Old Knobble's glory floating in his eyes. "If we fixed up the place, troublemakers would stay away."

Empty ruins like this bred problems like mice in a granary. Left untended, old towns collapsed into hangouts for bandits and mercenaries, starting feuds and skirmishes, and fomenting all sorts of trouble. The notorious Thieves Den to the northwest had started out as an abandoned town. Repairing Knobble would go a long way toward keeping the entire region peaceful.

The rainstorm intensified as night darkened, lashing the roof and billowing the cloaks hung across the broken windows. The downpours rolled through in waves, pounding for half an hour, then falling into eerie shushes that whispered over the slate tiles. Ari Ara huddled under her blanket, shuddering, not from the cold, but from the prickling sensation treading along her spine. This was the land of endless war. Dead warriors haunted these hills. Spirits walked through the blackness, muttering under their breaths. As she drifted into exhaustion, she tried to tether her dreambody to her flesh-and-blood limbs. She didn't want to wander tonight. The spirits might not react kindly to the girl who'd caused the war they died in.

She woke with an abrupt start three times, jerking herself out of sleep to avoid dreamwalking. But, in the thick darkness after midnight, she couldn't keep her eyes open. She slid into slumber and her dreambody darted out of the shell of her sleeping limbs.

Even in dreams, the ruins of Knobble crumbled depressingly into the moss. At her feet, a hearthstone had cracked in seven pieces. To her right, the keystone of an arched doorway had split in two. The silence suspended like a held breath. At the edges of her sight, she could sense ancestor spirits writhing. All through the old town, the restless ghosts struggled to rebuild the broken structures of their lives. The unseen spirits strained to lift the stones then moaned in despair. It was an impossible task for the insubstantial beings. Unable to release the tragedy, the spirits tried to carry it with them into the Ancestor River - or Wind. Judging from the way the silver shapes strained to rise skyward, Ari Ara suspected they were trying to join the desert's Ancestor Wind. The weight of the stones held them back, capturing them in the rubble.

Cautiously, Ari Ara tried lifting the nearest stone. As she placed it atop another, a spirit sprang free and shot upward, racing toward the invisible Ancestor Wind, freed.

"I see," Ari Ara murmured, bowing her head.

After that, she didn't get a solid night's sleep in Knobble. Long days of hammering boards onto Elwys' decrepit house blended into dreams of hefting boulders so spirits could slip away. Purple-shadowed bags hung under her eyes. She dozed off at lunch and fell into her stew. She stumbled through the daylight hours, tripping over her feet in exhaustion. At night, the ghosts whispered sad tales of murder and massacre, slaughter and sorrow. Slowly, their thin voices gradually lightened and the constant tingling along her spine eased, so she persevered, staggering with the effort, knowing she was helping the spirits find peace. Finally, the Fanten Grandmother appeared in her dreams, leaping from stone to stone like a cat, silver hair streaming behind her in an invisible, unfelt wind. She poised on an ancestor pillar in a crouch. Her head craned, upward, watching the spirits depart. Then her cool gaze fell upon the girl.

"You need to stop," the old woman informed Ari Ara sharply. "You've neither the skill nor the stamina for this."

"But there are more spirits to free," Ari Ara protested, heaving her weight into a large chunk of fallen stone. "It's working. The sorrow is lifting from Knobble."

"There's more than one way to lift the sorrow, you know," the Fanten Grandmother told her, watching her feet scrabble for purchase in the slick, inky ground-that-was-not-ground.

Ari Ara was about to spit out a rebuttal when her feet skidded. The hard fall knocked the breath out of her. She nearly woke, but the Fanten Grandmother's thin fingers snapped out and tweaked an unseen thread in the fabric of the dreamworld. For an instant, Ari Ara saw the roof beams of the temple in Knobble as her eyes fluttered. Then they fell shut again.

"Stay a moment longer," the spry woman insisted. "We should talk, you and I."

"About what?" Ari Ara answered, wincing as she picked herself up.

"This dreaming of yours . . . it's getting worse, hmm?"

Ari Ara shrugged. She didn't see dreamwalking as a problem. She seemed to be the only lowlander who could do it, but the Fanten dreamwalked regularly. It was powerful. She didn't want to stop.

"You could lose yourself in dreams if you aren't trained properly," the Fanten Grandmother warned her.

"Well, maybe you should have trained me as a child instead of kicking me out of the Fanten rituals," Ari Ara muttered testily.

She hurled her weight against the stone again, rocking it a little. "You could help me, you know."

"You can free spirits in dreams until you become a spirit yourself," the Fanten Grandmother replied with a shrug, "or you could bring the people back to Knobble. They'd lift the sorrow soon enough."

"How do I do that?"

The silver-haired woman tilted her head like a bird and tapped her lips with her finger. Ari Ara rolled her eyes. Of course, the Fanten woman wouldn't tell her. Not without a bargain ... and Ari Ara didn't want to get tangled up in a notoriously tricky Fanten exchange.

"Enough dreamwalking," the thin elder told her, not unkindly. "In due time, everything will become clear as a bonfire in the night sky."

She chortled to herself for reasons Ari Ara couldn't discern. The Fanten Grandmother made a twisting motion with her hands. Ari Ara felt her dreambody lurch and she tumbled out of her sleeping roll onto the cold stone floor of the temple, wide awake. Ari Ara slapped the flat surface with the palm of her hand and muffled her groan. Meddling Fanten Grandmother!

At breakfast, Elwys sat across from her, mumbling on in his usual dreary litany of sighs and moans, recalling the heyday of Old Knobble, the glorious bustle of its streets and the beauty of its people. Ari Ara poked at her porridge glumly, hardly listening to the man's droning voice as he sang the praises of some long-forgotten festival.

" . . . in those days, the Summer Fires sparkled like jewels on the mountaintops and people came from miles around to - "

He faltered as Ari Ara bolted upright, knocking her bowl of gloppy porridge over in the process.

"Fire?" she squawked, hurriedly righting her dish. "Did you

say Summer Fires? Like . . . bonfires?"

"Oh yes, the five fires," he murmured, eyes foggy with memory. "When I was young, we lit the Summer Fires on each of the tallest peaks. Like beacons they were, blazing for all the world to see. Haven't seen them since before the war."

"That's it!" Ari Ara cried out, realization lighting up her eyes. This was what the Fanten Grandmother had been hinting at. They had to build these fires or the spirits would never stop haunting the ruins. "Elwys, we should light them again!"

The spindly-limbed man moaned and shook his head, whispering that it would never happen. Ari Ara stretched across the table and jostled his shoulder to snap him out of his dolor.

"Enough of that," she said stoutly. "Don't fail before you even start."

Elwys shuddered and held his head in his hands, his wispy hair poking out between his bird-bone fingers.

"It takes a village to build and light those bonfires," he explained sadly. "Each stood taller than a man. We spent weeks cutting and gathering the wood."

Ari Ara pointed at the temple full of Peace Force members, young and old.

"Is this not a village of sorts?" she asked him.

The old man, thinned by time and tragedy, gaped at the brimming temple. A trickle of a tear rolled down his cheek as he sensed the truth in her words. For years, Knobble had lacked the people to build and tend the five traditional bonfires. The tipping point between lengthening days and shrinking nights had passed unheralded. During the war, snarling flames clawing at blackness had signaled attacks and burning homes, not ceremonies and sacredness. Since then, it had been a source of shame for Elwys that Knobble had failed to uphold its ancestral rituals. This year, the Peace Force could share the sweaty labor of building the massive bonfires. When darkness fell, torch would touch flame to kindling and a tower of light would gleam bright against the sky. Every village and town for miles would know: Knobble had risen like a phoenix from its ashes. Peace had returned to the town haunted by war. The spirits might finally rest.

CHAPTER ELEVEN

. . . . .

High Summer Fires

The rain began to lessen as soon as they got to work. Messenger hawks flew out to the surrounding villages, calling for aid. Knobble needed the knowledge of their elders. One of the fires would be lit in the courtyard of the old temple, but even Elwys could not remember the precise location of the other four. The old trails had crumbled into the forest. The fire pits were overgrown with brush after years of neglect. But the grandmothers and grandfathers in other villages remembered where they hid. Many a love match had been kindled by the firelight of those summer blazes; many a marriage had begun on one of those fire peaks.

"Let's invite them all," Elwys suggested, a rare smile on his papery lips. "As in the days of old, let's invite all the villagers for a great gathering. Each person can bring a dish, all hands can help serve the feast, all of us can tend the fires together."

The skies cleared to a brilliant blue as the messenger hawks conveyed the invitations. Summer burst into high bloom as the excited replies returned. The meadows blossomed with the wildflowers that would form garlands for the gathering. Heat poured down from the sun, golden and welcome.

Elwys reminisced about the days when Knobble was the hub of the surrounding villages. He asked the Peace Force to stay forever, hinting broadly that Knobble could serve as a base for their work. One of the Peace Force members, a woodworker from Mariana, offered to remain for the summer, building peace and rebuilding the ruins. A Harraken carpenter quickly volunteered as well. With skilled builders on site, perhaps some of the locals would like to return to Knobble. At the very least, more people in the town would discourage bandits and raiders from using the rubble as a hideout. At best, Knobble could foster the skills for peace in the entire region. There were five schools in the nearby area. They could easily teach hundreds of young children within a day's walk in each direction. Elwys wept at the news and kissed the hands of his volunteers. Then he kissed the hands of Mahteni, Solange, Minli, and Ari Ara. He didn't quite dare to kiss Shulen's knuckles, but he pumped the old warrior's hand in gratitude.

The preparations for the feast gave the Peace Force a chance to travel around, collecting supplies, issuing invitations . . . and asking about the raiders. There was little to report. A few people had spotted a midsized company of riders passing through, but they couldn't say for certain who they were. Many bands of mercenaries, armed merchants, bandits, and soldiers traversed the region.

"But those raiders disappeared like Pikers, for sure," the headman of one of the villages pointed out.

Ari Ara refused to accept this hearsay as truth. Why would Finn ask for the Peace Force's help if his people were doing the raiding?

On the morning of the High Summer Gathering, Ari Ara and her friends finished stacking the wood for the bonfires that would blaze on the rocky peaks surrounding Knobble. In the stone rings of the fire pits, they followed the instructions of one of the neighboring village elders, arranging the logs in an interlocking spiral pattern. A layer of dry grass and kindling perched at the top of these woven towers. Lit from the peak, the fire would devour the first layer, fall onto the next, and light it. They also cut and hauled the encroaching brush away from each of the fire pits to prevent sparks from igniting a wild blaze.

By midafternoon, the sun had scorched them scarlet. They were shining with sweat, scratched by thorns, and covered in dust and leaves. As Ari Ara pulled twigs out of her hair, Tala hollered out a challenge to see who could reach the swimming hole near the temple first. Like a herd of deer, they bolted down the trail, laughing and leaping from boulder to boulder. Ari Ara nearly won, but Emir swung her back by the waist and half-leapt, half-fell into the sparkling waters fully clothed. He peeled his tunic off as the others stripped down to under garb and jumped in. Ari Ara caught both Isa and Rill glancing at Emir's muscled chest and rolled her eyes. She dove under the water and yanked the young warrior's feet out from under his smug face.

Minli arrived last, face red and flushed. For a moment, Ari Ara thought he'd been crying. He limped upstream to a quieter pool and lowered himself to the water's edge, cupping the water to rinse his face.

"What are you doing, you old monk?" she called out teasingly. "Get in here!"

He ignored her and she forgot about him as she ducked Korin's splashing. A half hour later, when they emerged cooler and cleaner, he'd already left. Dripping, carrying sopping clothes in one hand and shoes in the other, they walked barefoot back to the temple.

"What are you wearing - ouch - tonight?" Isa asked, wincing

over the stones in the path, leaning on Ari Ara's shoulder.

Ari Ara made a face, not over the rough ground - her feet had been tough as leather since childhood - but over clothes. For the first time all summer, they would put away their white tunics with the Mark of Peace. None of them had anything extravagant in their travel packs, but all of them had a clean shirt, a nice skirt, or a bit of jewelry tucked away. The prospect of dressing-up for the festival sent a rush of nervousness through Ari Ara. Clothes were a sore spot between the two nations. The shared uniform had not only identified the Peace Force, it had also served as an act of diplomacy.

While the Marianans vied for rank and prestige through style, the Harraken found the very notion of showing off with fancy clothes abhorrent. On top of those cultural differences, the Marianans had indentured many Harraken in their fashion houses and mills, demanding unpaid labor in exchange for water in the desert lands. Ari Ara had helped end the Water Exchange, but the sight of Marianan finery still stirred up resentments and unease among the desert dwellers. To diffuse the tensions around these disagreements, everyone had agreed to wear white tunics this summer. Tonight, however, they could wear whatever they chose.

Behind a curtained-off section of the old temple, they emptied their travel bags, shook out the wrinkles from their fancier clothes, and dug out their necklaces or silk sashes. Ari Ara swiftly shrugged on her one nice shirt and tucked it into her last remaining clean pair of pants. Then she took her fingers to her still-damp curls and gritted her teeth as she worked out the worst of the snarls, borrowing Sarai's scented oil to ease the tangles through.

In the back corner of the temple, an age-blackened mirror had been propped up against the wall. They took turns jostling in front of it, braiding their hair and preening. When her turn came, Ari Ara stared at her freckles and made a face at herself. She wasn't . . . ugly, exactly, but definitely odd-looking. She was different. Her name meant *not this, not that,* and she carried the bloodlines of two nations.

Which looks, she grumbled silently, *like they're at war in my face.*

Lots of Marianans had freckles, but they were almond-colored against tan or peach-toned skin. Hers were deep cinnamon atop dark honey. Lots of Harraken had copper hair like hers, but their eyes were green or brown, not river-water blue. One time, she'd complained to her father about the battle being warred across her face. He nearly burst into tears with concern. Then he - unhelpfully - scolded her for such foolish thoughts.

"You carry the beauty of both your families," Tahkan Shirar had insisted in a fierce, defiant growl that dared the whole world to say otherwise. "You are utterly unique."

But Ari Ara didn't want to be unique. That was just a fancy word for *different* - and it was no use talking to her father about that. Tahkan was the epitome of the desert culture's most prized values. He was the spitting image of the ancestor Shirar, and as the *Harrak-Mettahl,* Honor-Keeper, he was a role model for his people. He'd never stood on the margin of things; he'd always lived smack in the center of his society.

People who looked like Ari Ara, on the other hand, had complicated stories of star-crossed love or horrible war stories they didn't want to talk about. She scowled at her expression in the mirror. When she'd brought that up with Tahkan, his response had been even more ferocious than his response to the battle in her face.

"You were born of love!" he had thundered. "Don't let anyone ever tell you otherwise. Your mother's death was a great loss, as was the war that followed, but your mother and I loved you enough to fill a thousand years of time!"

Tahkan was prone to these poetic outbursts. Ari Ara often wished she could just ask her mother these questions and avoid the impassioned tirades. But Queen Alinore had died giving birth to her, so she had to make do with her father's fiery reactions to everything.

"Love shines in every hair on your head, every freckle on your nose, and in every inch of who you are," he had concluded in a strange mixture of sternness and affection.

A royal chamber pot shines, too, she thought, scrunching up her nose in the mirror, *but no one falls in love with it.*

Finn Paikason's cheeky wink flashed through her thoughts. Her heart kerflopped in her chest. What if *he* showed up?! She piled her tangled curls atop her head then let them fall loose, then swept them back into a braid. She teased a few tendrils free, pulled too many out, and yanked the tie loose in frustration. She wanted to get it just right - what if Finn came and she looked like the disheveled wreck she usually did?

He's not coming, she told herself sternly as the memory of his laughter made her eyes grow distant. He was mountains away, hopefully. There was still a death penalty for defying the ban, after all.

She arrived at the feast ravenous. The courtyard in front of the temple was packed to the brim. People from all the outlying villages had joined the festivities. Farmers brought families in hay wagons. Young couples rode double on horseback. Elders perched in the back of donkey carts and told stories of Old Knobble to anyone who would listen. The folk from the villages wore their finery, adorning brightly-colored dresses with strings of beads. Sashes crisscrossed chests and slung over shoulders. Both men and women wore their dark, curling hair long, either braided or falling loose down their backs. Each person, from toddlers to tottering grandfathers, had a broad-brimmed hat cocked at a jaunty angle atop their head.

Everyone brought food to share. Ari Ara's mouth watered looking at the delicious array of sweet breads, verdant salads, fresh fruit pies, berry tarts, roasted vegetables, chilled soups, and wild greens. Bouquets tied with meadow grass adorned the tables. An errant breeze teased through Knobble, swaying the garlands that bedecked the ruins, gentling their tragedy with a hint of hope of better times.

A cheer rose up as the young Peace Force members joined the feast. Ari Ara tried not to blush, feeling strange without her white tunic. After months in uniform, it was almost odd to wear anything else. The chatter fell away to a hush as Isa de Barre came into view. Those closest to her gawked.

"Holy ancestors," Ari Ara heard Emir murmur. A stunned expression hung on his face.

"Close your mouth," she hissed to him. "You look like a fish."

Emir snapped his jaw shut. Ari Ara stifled a sigh. Isa de Barre was hands-down the most gorgeous person Ari Ara had ever met. Not one strand of her honey-wheat hair was out of place. A rosy blush colored her cheeks prettily. Her eyes crinkled in delighted half-moons. Isa had crossed the threshold from girl to woman and it showed. The heir to the Southlands bore the full curves of her mother and looked every inch a noble. Even the dust motes seemed to float around her, reluctant to settle.

Ari Ara tried not to feel jealous. She could sense a smudge on her nose and her belt had ridden up on one side, giving her a piratish look of dishevelment.

Minli was the only one of her friends not dressed up. He wore a clean Peace Force tunic, that was all, and shot her a sour look when she elbowed his ribs and asked him why. He sniffed and refused to tell her. Ari Ara shook her head at him. It was a festival; he needed to lighten up.

"Come on, you old monk - "

"Don't call me that," Minli said sharply. "I'm not a monk and I'm not old."

"I'm just teasing - " she stammered, surprised by the ferocity of his reaction.

"It's not funny," he muttered.

He swung away without another word, leaving her baffled and hurt by his sudden outburst. Minli took his plate over to sit with the elders - *smug little pet*, Ari Ara grumbled silently - and she slid onto a bench next to Korin. Her cousin swiveled and introduced her to Dahn, a lively fellow from a town just outside Knobble. Dahn stood betwixt and between boyhood and manhood, with shoulders too broad for his thin frame and a voice that cracked at odd moments. He could spin a captivating tale, though. Dahn's light amber eyes glowed as he recounted how he'd once ridden a squealing boar through the streets on a dare from his friends. He swept his shaggy, sun-touched brown hair out of his eyes and described how the pig had crashed through the harvest ceremony, dumped him at the feet of the disapproving monks, and escaped into the forest with a squeal.

Korin clapped a hand on Dahn's shoulder and declared that they simply *must* get to know one another; two troublemakers such as they had to forge a friendship. At the other youth's surprised look, Korin spilled out one of his innumerable stories of mischief-making. This one involved soaping the length of a marble hall so he and Emir could slide down it in their stockings.

"Unfortunately," Korin sighed, "Mum's ministers stormed out of the trade talks and went slipping head over heels with their fancy robes askew and their underwear flashing for all the world to see. Emir caught the head minister before she cracked her skull, thankfully. Mum would have disowned me for that. As it was, she blamed me for the economic crash six months later."

Korin winked at Emir across the table. The inky-haired youth made a face, remembering how much trouble they'd gotten in. The Great Lady made them mop up the soap – and clean the rest of the corridors for good measure.

Dahn shot a glance at his boyfriend. Mical, shy and reserved by nature, had sat quietly, listening to the others with his brown eyes bright in his long face. Dahn pulled him close and the two conferred in a low undertone. At last, they came to agreement and Dahn straightened up with a broad smile.

"A bunch of us younger folks have promised to light the highest bonfire," Dahn explained to Korin. "You all should come, the younger Peace Force members, that is. Not that we don't love our elders, but it's quite a hike up there and . . . "

He trailed off. Glancing around to make sure no one was watching, Dahn lifted the edge of his carry sack. A pair of whiskey bottles clinked inside.

"Wouldn't miss it for the world," Korin replied, delighted by the invitation. "After all, we've a duty to the elders to use our young legs to light that fire."

He winked. Word passed swiftly from one person to the next. After the feast, as the older folk dispersed to the other bonfires, the younger crowd gathered to start the climb. Ari Ara remembered with a twinge of annoyance that Minli, sitting over with the elders, wouldn't have heard the plan. She crossed the hall at a jog and tugged his arm, titling her head impatiently.

"Come on, we're all going up to the highest bonfire," she informed him.

He gave her a patronizing, long-suffering look that made her blood boil, but rose and tucked his crutch under his arm. At the edge of the ruins, he gripped her shoulder.

"We should tell Shulen where - "

"No!" she whirled on him, eyes narrowing. "Don't you dare. He'll make me stay here with him for security."

"He'll let us go if we put it to him in the right way," Minli cajoled.

"He'll let *you* go," Ari Ara shot back. They both knew that Shulen would never let her attend without an escort. "You're lucky you're nobody important."

She broke off and clapped a hand over her mouth. Minli's hurt face blinked at her for one horrified moment before a glare pinched his features shut.

"I didn't mean - "

"Shut up. You've said more than enough," Minli grumbled. He pivoted on his crutch and limped away.

"Don't tell Shulen just because you're mad at me!" she called after him.

He froze. Craning his head around, he glowered at her.

"Is that all you care about?" he snarled. "I'm not a snitch."

He hurried off without another word, leaving her biting her lips to keep them from trembling. She hadn't meant it to come out that way. Feeling terrible, she caught up with the others.

"What's up with Minli?" Emir asked, his dark eyes following the boy's angry path. Then, realizing something, he smacked his forehead. "Of course, the trail. He's worried about the climb."

Emir sprinted after Minli, leaving Ari Ara staring gape-mouthed after him. She hadn't even considered that Minli was short-tempered over having to climb the steep trail with his crutch. She was so used to Minli keeping pace with her in practice that she never thought about him having challenges with this terrain. She had seen him rubbing his shoulder, though, and knew Mahteni had given him a salve for it. He never complained, but maybe his missing leg bothered him more than he let on.

Like this afternoon when we all raced to the river and left him behind, she realized with a guilty twinge in her stomach.

She started to follow Emir, intending to apologize. She halted abruptly at the corner of the temple, hearing Minli's voice.

"I don't want Ari Ara to know," he said with bitterness.

"Ari Ara won't judge you for it - " Emir answered in a calm tone.

"The others would, and she'd laugh right along with them."

What?! she thought, eyes widening. *I would not!*

"Fair enough," Emir agreed with a sigh.

Ari Ara's jaw tightened. Is that how little Emir and Minli thought of her?

"Let's just wait a bit and then we'll start up," Emir said. "When you get tired, I'll give you a lift. Before we reach the top, you get down and we'll walk in together. Agreed?"

She could hear the relief in Minli's voice. Ari Ara whirled away and sprinted after the group of youth. A sense of shame chased her heels, but she shook it off, irritated at Minli's comment about her. That wasn't fair! It wasn't even true! When the others asked about Emir and Minli, she answered that they would follow later. Embarrassed and angry, Ari Ara was glad the dusky woods hid her flaming cheeks.

CHAPTER TWELVE

. . . . .

Truth or Toss

The sun plunged below the mountain's shoulder just as they reached the crest. The bonfire stood like a solemn giant, shadowed and hulking. They gathered in a wide ring, the youth of the surrounding villages interspersed with the younger members of the Peace Force. They'd lost all traces of shyness, nerves, and awkwardness on the hike up. A lanky boy with nutmeg skin and braid of ink-black hair taught the newcomers a traditional hiking song, leaving them all breathless and laughing over the tongue-twisting, humorous lyrics. The shortest girl in the group turned out to have the loudest voice, asking the Peace Force members a slew of questions about their lives. Her friend, a tall girl with legs that stretched forever and devoured the trail with each stride, confessed to Sarai in a whisper that the worlds of the burning desert and the cities of the riverlands sounded as exotic as old legends. Outside of being taken to fortified towns as children during the war, few of them had traveled far. They'd spent most of their fourteen to eighteen years of life in these craggy mountains. A dark, snub-nosed boy with a spatter of freckles across his cheeks declared that he would see the whole world one day. Ari Ara didn't doubt it; he had the bold curiosity of a born traveler and a genial nature that would open doors to him, anywhere.

The banter of the group bounced around the clearing near the fire pit. When the last ray of daylight faded from the sky, Dahn lit a torch with his tinderbox and scaled the tower. It lurched under his weight, but held. He lifted the flame high. Then he tipped the torch into the kindling and leapt to the ground. The crowd cheered as he rose from his half-crouch, hands raised skyward. Mical broke out of his shyness and gave him a kiss.

A hiss of smoke snaked from the top of the tall stack of logs. Grass stems flared and flamed out, igniting one after another. Tiny snaps and pops crackled through the tower. Then, in a roar and a whoosh of air, the fire burst loose. Blazing light hurled up against the midnight blue sky. The bonfire stretched the arms of its flames high and tossed sparks to the first glinting stars.

"Look!" Rill cried out.

Ari Ara spun to follow the urchin's gaze. Across the night, the other fires gleamed, one on the peak opposite them, another on the southern caldera rim, a third on the northern ridge, and the fourth illuminating the heart of the temple's courtyard. Beyond the crackle and roar of their bonfire, they could hear horns blowing in the distance. A boy with a lean runner's build put his fingers in his mouth and whistled back. His friends cheered and roared, sending a bellow of sound into the echoing darkness. On the south side of the blaze, a few pinpricks of light glimmered on the distant horizon, lit by far-off villages. Dahn said that the elders remembered a time when hundreds of blazes shone on the mountaintops at High Summer. Only a tiny handful remained.

"How far did they go?" Ari Ara asked him.

"Once, they stretched south to the sea and north to the mystical frozen lands," Dahn answered, shrugging his broad shoulders. "The old legends say: wherever mountains meet and the people stand united, the Crown of Light shines."

Ari Ara's smile blossomed at the poetry of the ritual phrase. It illuminated the reason behind Elwys' sorrow and shame at being unable to light the five traditional fires – without the Fire Peaks, their neighbors, north and south, lost the connection to the entire mountain range.

"Last time the Crown of Light was fully lit was on your parents' wedding night," Dahn told her with a smile. He had been too young to remember, but the older folks still talked about it. "All up and down the Border Mountains, the Crown of Light sparkled like jewels on the crests of the mountains. With Queen Alinore and the Desert King Tahkan Shirar united in marriage, everyone thought that peace would last forever."

He shook his head sadly. The tragedy that killed the queen and the war to avenge her death had destroyed the hope of peace. The fires had not been lit since.

"I've heard the bonfires could be seen as far away as Mari Valley and Turim City," Dahn mentioned. "In that way, the crown encircled not just the north and south, but also the east and west, uniting the two nations."

"We should light it again," Ari Ara declared enthusiastically. "Wouldn't it be something to see it run the whole length of the Border Mountains?"

"I hope we live to see it, someday."

He sounded wistful and skeptical at once.

"Peace isn't as far off as you think," Ari Ara replied stoutly. "We're working to build it, aren't we? Right here and now."

Dahn shot her a doubtful look, but said nothing. It was too fine a night for arguments. Mical pulled out a set of shepherd's pipes made of reeds and twined grass. A girl named Kelli unhooked the small hand drum tied to her belt. Together, the two unleashed merriment into the night air. The tall girl flashed a crooked smile and pulled Rill up to teach her the steps to their heel-tapping, high-kicking dance. Emir, when he arrived alongside Minli, was the only one who could keep up - the dance was a variant of the one his hill tribe practiced in the north.

The bonfire gnawed at the wooden logs, curling tighter into its core until it shrank from the height of a man to the size of a small child. As the late-night star constellations emerged above the horizon, the fire chewed its embers contentedly. The music lulled. The youth gathered close. Amber light illuminated their faces.

In the quiet between a burst of laughter and the next round of banter, a silver flask passed hand to hand, each person swigging and coughing in turn. Sarai refused to sip, as did Tala and a boy from the desert. Many Harraken did not drink, believing that grain should feed children, not be fermented into intoxicants. Minli handed the flask onward, too, stoically enduring the teasing. Ari Ara, annoyed at his sanctimonious attitude, tilted the whiskey back and promptly hacked and coughed on the burning liquid. The others laughed as she waved her hands at her watering eyes.

"What?" she croaked out.

"Just thought the Lost Heir wouldn't choke on a sip of whiskey," Dahn chuckled.

"Huh," she snorted, "you don't know me, then. Did you think I drank whiskey with the Fanten? Or the monks at the monastery? Certainly not with my father, the Desert King. He's probably never touched the stuff in his life!"

The others swapped surprised looks, remembering, belatedly, how Ari Ara went from an orphaned shepherdess in the High

Mountains to the notorious double-royal heir. Dahn wasn't alone in imagining her sleeping on silk beds and dressing in fancy gowns, but, while she'd done that for a few brief months, most of her life she'd been wearing weathered tunics and curling up on hard ground.

Korin looked around with a grin of mischief.

"I know," he murmured, snagging the flask, "let's play *Truth or Toss*. We'll ask a round of questions and you either answer truthfully or toss back another shot of whiskey. We'll start with an easy question: what's your first memory?"

A lullaby. Playing in the grass. A carved wooden horse. A mother. The answers went around the circle, light and easy. Ari Ara's earliest memory was the stillness of the Fanten caves in winter as the Fanten slept through the cold season. Minli confessed that he thought he remembered the pain of losing his leg. He'd told Ari Ara once that he remembered screams and smoke, too, but he didn't mention those.

"Where - and when - was your first kiss?" Korin asked, setting off giggles and blushes around the circle.

Isa elbowed him.

"It was you and you know where - you stole that kiss right under the nose of my ancestor's statue in my front hall!"

"Ah, but does it count if you didn't kiss back?" Emir cut in, narrowing his eyes at Korin.

"Who says I didn't?" Isa retorted coyly. "Where was yours, Emir?"

"A girl named Sheena - you wouldn't know her," Emir told Isa. "She came to work in the Dressiers District one year."

"I remember her," Korin mused with a dreamy look on his face. "She was dubbed the *Most Gorgeous Bosom of All Time* by the Stonelands sculptors. One of them went insane trying to capture her perfection."

He sighed wistfully. Isa glared at him. Rill rolled her eyes.

"How about you, Everill Riverdon?" Emir challenged her, deflecting the attention away from himself.

Rill didn't answer, just tossed back some whiskey with a dark look. Whatever her story was, she wasn't sharing it. Sarai smiled as she mentioned the name of a girl she'd known back home. Minli was next, and Ari Ara expected him to have no answer - he was only fourteen, like her, and spent more time with books than people - but Minli grinned proudly.

"Ellie, the University Library apprentice, on Marin's Feast Day last year."

Ari Ara hid her shock. He hadn't told her about that! Best friends shouldn't keep secrets from each other!

Tala threw a cap of whiskey into the fire, making it flare up, and gave them the traditional line that what the Tala-Rasa know, only the Tala-Rasa know.

"And you, Ari Ara?" Korin asked.

She froze. She didn't have a story. Her ears burned. Everyone else had a first kiss, even Minli. Emir got his at her age. Isa and Korin were even younger. What was wrong with her?

"Oh . . . well, I guess," she reached for the bottle to toss and Rill burst out laughing.

"Never been kissed, is that it?"

Ari Ara stared back like a startled deer.

"Not yet," she muttered.

"Aw, cousin, we're going to have to work on that," Korin teased. "Emir, give her a kiss!"

"No."

Emir's refusal was soft in tone and hard as a kick to the gut.

"You can order me to die for you, Korin," he muttered in a low voice, "but my heart is my own."

Korin made a face at him. Ari Ara squirmed in agony.

"New round," Rill interjected swiftly. "What's the stupidest thing you've ever done?"

The game veered into ridiculous stories with relief. Marek told a tale of accidently tipping a merchant wagon into a pond. Dahn had wound up engaged to the daughter of a nearby town's headman before realizing the love of his life was male. Korin had so many contenders for his "stupidest" prank that their sides ached from laughing before he finished. Ari Ara sat, arms crossed over her chest, staring at the fire, refusing to so much as smile.

When her turn came, she took a swig of whiskey and let them tease her about her madly watering eyes. To her dismay, the water turned to tears. She murmured something about being too hot this close to the fire and rose hastily.

"Ari Ara!"

Emir. Ari Ara groaned as he rose to follow her. She didn't want to talk to him, not after his harsh rebuttal at the fire. She tried to move away, but smacked her toe on a rock. Cursing, she grabbed it and hopped in pain. She sat down, which seemed like the safest thing to do.

"Are you okay?" Emir asked.

"Fine. Just fine," she snapped back. "And why should you care?"

"Ari Ara," he replied in a long-suffering tone. "You're like my *sister*. I'm not going to kiss you just so you aren't the only one who hasn't been kissed yet."

The moon had just risen, spilling silver light across the rustling leaves of the night forest. Backlit by the fire's distant blaze, Emir's expression was unreadable. His voice was shot through with exasperation, though, so she could guess.

"What's wrong with me?" Ari Ara muttered.

"Nothing," he answered, sitting beside her on the ground.

"You're only fourteen and you've been a bit busy stopping wars and freeing water workers and restoring women's rights and building peace. You dance circles around anyone you meet . . . no one's going to steal a kiss from you. Besides," he finished pragmatically, "is there anyone here you *want* to kiss?"

"Er, well," she stammered, skirting the thought of Finn Paikason. "I just . . . didn't want to be the *only* one."

Emir's sigh hushed out through the darkness.

"It'll happen, Ari Ara. Don't rush it. Make it special. Out of all those stories, how many of them were really in love?"

"Maybe Sarai," she guessed. "And Minli?"

"They weren't so in love that they stayed back home," Emir pointed out.

"Were you in love with what's-her-name?"

"Hardly," he scoffed, "and she didn't love me. It was a crush at best, a fling more likely, and over as soon as she realized I wouldn't abandon my job as Korin's guard."

"Have you ever been in love?" she asked, hugging her knees to her chest.

"I don't think so," he answered truthfully. "I don't think it's an in or out thing. The love songs say you just *know*, but sometimes it grows slowly. Anyway, Shulen says real love deepens over time."

"What does he know, anyway?" Ari Ara grumbled.

"Watch your tongue," Emir snapped, defensive of their mentor.

"Sorry."

She'd forgotten that Shulen had loved and lost before she was even born. Emir nodded his forgiveness, masking his dismay. When had Ari Ara developed such a cruel, thoughtless streak? She'd do well to temper that.

"Anyway, don't rush it. It's not the first kiss that matters, after all."

"It's not?" she asked, gaping stupidly at him.

"No, silly. It's the best one that matters."

"How do you know if it's the best one?"

"Practice."

She could sense his silent laughter. They fell quiet for a moment as the moon crested over the treetops. Each leaf in the overstory shimmered with a thin line of silver. Screwing up her courage, she twisted to face Emir, pointing to her wild curls, freckled nose, and the battle in her face.

"Do you think I'm, um, weird-looking?" she asked, chickening out of asking if he thought she was pretty.

"Are you kidding me?" he asked her, surprised. "Ari Ara, whoever falls in love with you is going to fall so hard they'll think they're flying."

She blushed in the dark. Emir stood and stretched, cracking his back and yawning.

"Now, come back to the fire."

Reluctantly, she followed him back to the circle. Ari Ara listened as everyone swapped answers about whether or not they'd ever stolen anything.

"Do you want an itemized list or would a summary suffice?" Rill replied cheekily.

Tala and Minli were bent double with laughter at some private joke. Tala's lips moved near Minli's ear, dark coppery curls tangling with Minli's brown bird's nest. A stab of complicated jealousy shot through her gut, wanting to be the one Tala told jokes to *and* the person whispering in Minli's ear. It was simpler than a crush and more complicated than friendship and she hated the whole muddied mess of it.

"Okay, here's a new *Truth or Toss*," Korin suggested. "What's the most dangerous thing you've ever done?"

When her turn came, Ari Ara answered absently with the first thing that came to mind.

"Tangling with a sand lioness," she said, passing the flask along.

"What?!" her cousin exclaimed, skeptical. "That's not half so dangerous as the death match against Shulen!"

"You didn't meet the sand lioness," Ari Ara grumbled, setting off a flurry of laughter.

"Take a toss, Ari Ara," Minli told her sharply, arms folded over his thin chest, looking at her strangely. "You didn't tell the truth. You've done loads more dangerous things than that."

"Oh, come on."

"Those are the rules," he told her.

Ari Ara called him a stickler, but the others agreed with him. Korin started up a chant: *Toss! Toss! Toss!*

Furious at Minli, she silently reached for the flask and threw back a long chug.

"That's too much," Emir warned quietly.

She knocked his hand away as he reached to take the whiskey away.

"Stop that," he told her in a low tone. "You're too young to be drinking anyway."

She jumped up, mad at him for telling her what to do. He rose to catch her. She evaded him, tossed him a taunting smile, and swigged again. Minli scowled at her and mouthed *show-off*. She ignored him and took another sip of whiskey. Emir tried to grab the bottle. She whipped away, reeling slightly as the world spun. The others laughed and egged them on. Dahn cupped his hands around his mouth and hollered for her to show them the Way Between.

"Even tipsy, she can run circles around you, Emir!" Korin

chortled.

"Don't encourage her, Korin," he growled back.

"I'm not tip - hic!" she hiccupped and dove aside as Emir lunged for the bottle. She got in two more burning mouthfuls before he snagged it. Emir glowered at her.

"You're going to regret this tomorrow."

"Don't be a spoilsport," she shot back.

Secretly, she was relieved to drop down in her place in the circle. Her insides were burning and the ground lurched oddly under her. Her eyes ached from holding back tears and her stomach was clenched painfully. She hoped the alcohol would burn off swiftly.

Sarai was up next in the round of *Truth or Toss*. She knew the most dangerous thing she'd ever done.

"Standing up for my rights," she said somberly.

"Fending off a Piker raid," said Mical with a tight look on his face.

"Hiding the water records," Minli declared.

The youths from the Fire Peaks Region chortled, but it wasn't a laughing matter. Minli had risked imprisonment and exile, even death, to help the Harraken. Next to him, the piper, Kelli, took a toss from the flask and didn't answer. Rill had nearly drowned during flood season in Mariana Capital. Emir had fought in war as a young boy.

"Did you ever kill someone?" Isa asked, eyes wide.

"Yes," Emir said darkly, staring at his hands as if seeing the blood on them.

"How about you all?" Korin asked, turning Isa's surprised question into the next round.

"I haven't!" Isa squeaked.

"Me neither," added Marek.

The orphan from Turim City said he'd seen people fight and

die, but had never killed anyone himself. Rill shrugged and took a toss of whiskey.

"Can't be sure. I knifed a cutthroat before he could knife me and didn't stick around to find out if he lived or died."

Most of them hadn't. No one who had killed someone looked happy about it. When Ari Ara's turn came, she rolled her eyes.

"Of course, I haven't."

"Not true."

Minli's hard voice hit her like a punch. She twisted sideways to frown at him.

"Of course, it is," she retorted.

"You killed your mother when you were born."

An audible gasp of shock ran through everyone. Isa's hands flew to her mouth. A stunned silence fell. Ari Ara couldn't believe he'd said that - even if he was mad at her. She could tell he was, but this was a low blow. She blinked back hot tears.

"That doesn't count," Korin started to say, but Ari Ara leapt to her feet.

"How dare you?!" she shouted at Minli. "You . . . you . . . mean-spirited cripple!"

"Ari Ara!" Emir barked at her, stern as Shulen. "Apologize."

Hot tears of fury burned in her eyes. She wouldn't. She couldn't. Suddenly, everything was too hot, too bright, too loud. A howl of frustration was building in her throat and she didn't want people to hear it when it broke loose. She whipped around and plunged into the forest, hurtling down the trail toward Knobble. Emir called after her - he couldn't guard both her and Korin if she left - but Korin told him to let her go. The temple wasn't that far. She'd be fine.

Ari Ara's head spun. The world reeled. She felt queasy. Distracted by the whirling in her head, she tripped over a stone and fell flat on her belly, skinning both knees on the stony trail and roughing up the palms of her hands.

"Gaaarrgh!" she roared.

The crickets fell silent in the glossy grasses. She smirked, perversely happy that she could get *someone* to shut up. Her face felt flushed. Her back ran with sweat. Ari Ara scrambled back to her feet, certain that if she didn't splash some water on her face right now, she'd burst into flames. She couldn't find the turn-off to the river trail - the landmarks had all split in two - so she plunged into the underbrush, crashing and blundering louder than a fat bear. Briars scratched her bare arms. A twig snagged in her hair and tore loose painfully.

"This is all your fault, you old monk!" she shouted.

No one heard her. They were all back at the bonfire having a good time - like she would have been if not for Minli.

How could he have been so mean? Minli was her best friend, her first friend, the only person in the world who knew that she was really just a strange, half-wild girl who thought *bread* was a delicacy. He'd taught her to read, and risked death to find the secret prophecy about her. He'd promised to keep her humble, to be the one person in the world who ignored her double royal heritage and never treated her like she walked on clouds and farted roses. How could he have said something so cruel?

The night poured down on her flushed skin like a bucket of ice-cold well water. Somewhere close, the river murmured against its bank, lapping and hissing. Her knees turned to jelly and she crawled the last few paces to the river. She soaked her head, dunking her hair under, and drank handful after handful of the cold water, suddenly desperately thirsty.

"Whoa, not so fast. You'll get sick."

She whirled at the voice, leaping to her feet. Her whiskey-drunk head spun and she lost her balance. Ari Ara toppled sideways as her feet slipped out from under her.

Finn's hand shot out and seized her wrist, hauling her back to the grassy bank. His fox-cap gleamed eerily in the rising moonlight, half-askew after his lunge to save her. Ari Ara realized with a sick jolt that she was clinging to him like a lovelorn idiot and let go hastily. Her stomach heaved and she spun toward the bushes, vomiting and retching, coughing on the painful sting of bile.

"Well, you're a mess," Finn commented drolly.

"Go away. Please. Just go."

"Not a chance," he countered. "Someone has to haul you out of the river if you fall in. The Lost Heir isn't dying, drunk and drowned, on my watch."

"Don't call me that," Ari Ara begged. She couldn't bear to think of legends and prophecies and royal duties when she felt this awful. "Ari Ara is fine, Ari Ara of the High Mountains. What are you even doing here? You'll be hanged."

"No, I won't," he countered airily. "They stick our heads on poles, remember?"

The thought was enough to turn her stomach. He leapt back as she retched into the bushes again.

"Best get it all up and out," he encouraged. "That rot gut you were drinking is better used as cleaning fluid."

"How? How did you - "

She couldn't get the question out, coughing and hacking. Finn held out a hand and helped her down to the river to rinse the disgusting acid aftertaste out of her mouth.

"There's little that happens in these parts without the Paika's knowledge," he answered. "Plus, I can smell it."

Ari Ara just about died of embarrassment. Finn made her wade in to her knees and rinse everything off, standing beside her to make sure she didn't slip again. Afterward, soaked and shaky, she sat on the bank as her head slowly cleared and her stomach stopped heaving.

"I'm never - ever - drinking again," she declared in a rasping voice.

"Not for a good, long while, anyway," Finn guessed.

"You must think I'm an idiot," she sighed.

"I already thought that," he answered with a snort. "All that peace nonsense. Now I just think you're as human as the rest of us. I was in your shoes not too long ago. My mother wasn't as nice about it as I'm being."

Ari Ara buried her face in her hands, thinking about Tahkan Shirar's furious reaction.

"You'll feel terrible tomorrow," Finn warned her, "but it'll pass. Here, time to drink more water."

He pulled a little wooden bowl from his belt and ferried cups of water to her from the river, one after another, until she thought she'd burst.

"Wait a little while, then do that twice more," he instructed. "Warm water is best, but I don't think you want to go back to Knobble just yet."

"Ugh. No. I never want to show my face ever again. I feel like a fool," Ari Ara admitted. "Minli said I was showing off."

"Were you?"

"No . . . not much . . . I mean, maybe?" She paused. She had been showing off, now that she thought about it, teasing Emir about the flask. "But Minli was worse! He said something so horrible, I couldn't believe it. He never used to be cruel like that."

"We all change," Finn remarked cautiously.

Ari Ara sighed.

"Yeah. Sometimes, I don't even recognize myself."

He shot her a quizzical look.

"How much have you changed?"

"From when I was just a shepherdess?" she snorted. "You have no idea."

She'd learned to read, become a royal heir, turned Mariana Capital upside down, fought a duel, ridden across the desert, and so much more. Of course, she'd changed. She couldn't live through all that and still be the same person. Sometimes she wished she was, though. Life was simpler in the High Mountains.

"What were you like as a shepherdess?" Finn asked, a note of genuine curiosity in his tone.

Ari Ara appraised him, looking at his calloused fingers, grubby cuffs, and patched knees.

"A lot like you, probably," she said. "A bit wild around the edges."

He grinned at that description. Ari Ara started to talk, quietly, sharing memories of the High Mountains. Stories poured out of her, things she'd never told anyone – except for Minli – about growing up with the Fanten and tending the black sheep. She spoke of dawn light on the jagged peaks, the warm sun after a snow squall, and the depth of the quiet under the cathedrals of trees in the Fanten Forest. She told him about fending off wolves with a stick and a roar. Finn whistled low with respect; she hadn't been more than ten years old.

"Why am I telling you all this?" she groaned after a long-winded story about how much she missed whole days of nothing but wind in her hair and time to run the ridges.

"Because, the moon is up, the night is long, and we have time for telling tales," Finn answered with a shrug. He spoke the words in the cadence of an old saying, echoing something his elders had said to him. He rose to his feet and brought back her next dose of healing water.

"And," he added when he returned, "it's an old Alaren

148

practice, right?"

"Remembering who you are," Ari Ara exclaimed, recognizing the story from the book. "You know about that?"

"Of course, the Paika know about that. Alaren lived here, didn't he?" Finn replied with a disbelieving shake of his head. "He loved these mountains as much as we do."

Finn gave her shoulder a little, companionable shake.

"And we who love the mountains look out for each other, Ari Ara of the High Mountains."

He held out the little wooden bowl with a sense of ceremony. She took it with both hands, strangely moved by his simple, but strong words. He settled back on the grass, leaning on one elbow, a knee bent up, head tilted to look at the stars.

"But there's not a lot of *them,*" he jerked his head toward the festival, indicating the Peace Force members from far-off places, "who truly understand these mountains. Not those city folk or those desert people. Tell 'em you're from the mountains and they think you're half beast."

Ari Ara nodded. She understood. The Marianans in the capital had shrieked with delighted horror when they heard how she'd grown up. They patted themselves on the back for *rescuing* her from the Fanten. They didn't understand that she sometimes missed the High Mountains with an ache sharper than ice-cold river on the teeth. They didn't know how to sit in silence like she and Finn were, just listening to the mountains breathing in the night.

After a long, quiet spell, Finn made her get up and fetch her third gulp of water herself. Then he walked with her to the trail she'd blundered past, accompanying her all the way to the edge of Knobble. He halted at the outskirts.

"You'll be fine from here," he stated. "No one wants to see a Piker."

"That's not true," she countered. "Many of my friends would love to meet you. Everyone's curious."

"The Paika's secrets are our own," Finn muttered.

"Fair enough," she sighed.

She smiled shyly. He grinned back. Ari Ara stuck out her hand, palm up in the gesture of warriors. Finn shook his head and tsk-tsked with his tongue and teeth. He turned her hand sideways and shook it.

"That's how we do it in these mountains," he told her. "At least between friends."

"Alright . . . friend," she answered, "and thank you."

He squeezed her hand briefly then whirled away. Within a few strides, Finn Paikason vanished into the gulp of darkness.

CHAPTER THIRTEEN

. . . . .

The Village of Hock

The next day was hard. Harder than she expected. Everyone was short-tempered and irritable, nursing splitting headaches. Shulen was annoyed when half the youth failed to show up at morning practice. He sent Ari Ara back to rouse Korin, Isa, Marek, and Rill. They all groaned and shoved her away - none of them had used Finn's trick of drinking several gallons of water. Ari Ara ached all over and had a dull headache, but apparently, she'd gotten off easy. Korin moaned about hatchets in the skull and Isa groaned that she felt like she'd been trampled by mountain goats.

When she returned to practice with their excuses, Minli muttered that she deserved to have a hangover after she'd swigged so much whiskey. Shulen overheard. After he'd finished reaming her out, Mahteni took her aside and told her she'd lost *harrak*, squandering her honor, integrity, and dignity through her foolish choices.

"I just wanted to try it," Ari Ara mumbled.

Mahteni's green eyes searched her face for the truth. Ari Ara blushed.

"I just . . . everyone else was drinking," she stammered.

Mahteni cleared her throat and lifted a coppery eyebrow. Ari Ara squirmed. Her aunt knew full well that Sarai and Tala wouldn't have been swilling whiskey. Ari Ara amended her comment, trying hard to stop her downward slide into trouble.

"I just didn't want to be the odd one . . . I didn't want to be different."

"You are different," her aunt told her bluntly. "You will always be different. The question is what you do about it. Do you try to blend in, knowing you're doomed to failure? Or do you accept the beauty in how you stand out?"

After letting her ponder those words in uneasy silence for a spell, Mahteni made her write to her father, telling Tahkan Shirar, in her own words, what had happened at the bonfire. It was not a punishment, her aunt told her, it was a way of helping her rebuild her *harrak*. Ari Ara couldn't tell the difference. She thought she'd die of mortification. She stared at the blank scroll for hours. Mahteni sat quietly beside her the whole time, humming under her breath. A Harraken never strayed far from song; it ran like a river through the fabric of their lives.

One tune tumbled into the next. The sun shifted overhead. Nightfast flew over, abandoning his perch on the temple roof where he'd fussily avoided the noise of the festival. He bobbed his dark, feathered head at Mahteni and screeched softly in an avian croon. Ari Ara glanced up from her blank, teary-eyed stare at the scroll. The words of Mahteni's hushed song finally sank in.

Her aunt sang the Woman's Song, the verses they'd written together when her monthly blood first came. Mahteni breathed a little song-magic into the lines, invoking the women in Ari Ara's life - her mother, Alinore; her aunts Brinelle and Moragh; the Fanten Grandmother – calling upon their strengths to help the girl in this difficult moment. Ari Ara cringed at first, thinking of the disappointment or judgment those women might hold for her. What would they think of her foolishness? Then Mahteni's voice sang out the chorus and Ari Ara remembered that the Woman's Song offered support, not judgment.

She drew upon the Great Lady's determination, and dipped the brush into the inkpot. When she faltered after the first words, Ari Ara borrowed a bit of her Aunt Moragh's fierceness and started writing again. She told her father how she'd let the others egg her on, how her pride led her to take swig after swig of the burning whiskey, how sick she'd felt, how stupid it had all been. She told him what Minli had said and scrawled out the last line, the part she truly feared: *Is it my fault? Did I kill my mother?*

She handed the letter to Mahteni, but her aunt shook her head and pointed to Nightfast.

"This is between you and your father now," she said.

As Nightfast flew south, shrinking to a black speck before vanishing, Ari Ara felt like he carried her heart in his talons, too. All of her shame, fear, and worry was tied up in that letter. At lunch, her stomach was in such a knot, she could scarcely eat. Minli passed by, avoiding her eyes.

"You *meant* for me to get in trouble," she muttered furiously, rising and standing in his path.

He gave her the silent treatment at first, not answering.

"Fine, be that way," she spat, exasperated. "You were mean to me at the bonfire and you're being mean to me now."

"Oh right, this is all my fault," he retorted, sarcasm dripping.

"You're the one who said that horrible thing about my mother!"

"It was true!"

"It was mean!"

"You were, too!"

"You first!"

They glared at each other for a long moment.

"Well, you needed to be taken down a notch or two," he insisted. "You're such a show-off."

"You're just jealous," Ari Ara shot back, stung and squirming inside.

"Jealous of you?" he laughed. "A barely literate girl trying so desperately to fit in with everyone that she's lost all sense of who she is?"

Tears sprung to her eyes. Why did Minli always know exactly how to hurt her feelings? It wasn't fair to make fun of her reading - she'd barely had a minute to study since her exile.

"How can you say things like that?" she yelled at him. "You're supposed to be my best friend."

"Yeah, well, you're supposed to be my best friend, too, but you don't act like it."

"Neither do you."

"Fine."

"Fine!"

They stomped off. It was a horrible day from start to finish. She spent most of it cleaning up from the festival, picking up plates and scrubbing pots and lending a hand when the villagers took down the wilted garlands. Her shoulders ached from hauling tables back to the temple and she fell asleep the instant her head touched the pillow. To top it all off, she dreamed that the Fanten Grandmother was scolding her for drinking.

"Your body can't handle it, you little fool!"

Two days later, she and Minli were still at odds with each other. Ari Ara didn't want to admit it, but she missed him, even though he was right there, frowning at her in practice, glaring over lunch. She gave as good as she got, of course. He still hadn't apologized for what he said.

"Why won't you patch things up with Minli?" Emir

demanded, catching her alone. All day, he'd been wrestling with the decision to intervene with the pair of them. It wasn't his business, but this squabble couldn't continue. It reflected poorly on the whole Peace Force. If two of its fiercest advocates couldn't stop snarling at each other, the Peace Force didn't stand a chance of helping whole nations avoid war.

"He was mean to me at the bonfire," Ari Ara grumbled. "How could he say I killed my mother?"

"That was horrible," Emir agreed, "but he's not the only one to blame. Minli's been mad at you for weeks for the way you've been thoughtlessly, leaving him behind and ignoring him. You know how much it hurts to be on the outskirts. Think about how Minli must have been feeling."

She said nothing, staring at the ground. The silence stretched for a long time. The wind rustled in the treetops. Ari Ara toyed with the dirt between her toes, stubbornly refusing to reply.

"Want my advice?" he asked.

"You'll give it, anyway," she muttered.

"Make good with Minli. He's still your best friend. You're both still kids."

"I am not!"

"You are, too. There are years between you and Korin. Isa's nearly grown."

"Rill - "

" - was grown up before she could talk," Emir stated with a snort. "Sort things out with Minli, Ari Ara. You can't pretend to follow the Way Between if you don't."

Before she could erupt in protest, he left. They didn't have time for this quarrel. The Peace Force had work to do. Word had come that the mysterious raiders had attacked another village. The story traveled to them thirdhand from the son of a farmer whose cousin lived on the outskirts of the village of Hock. The cousin had seen the thatched roof of a barn go up in flames and heard the clamor of the villagers racing to the stone-and-slate temple for protection. Locals armed with pitchforks and axes had joined the warrior monks, ready to defend their families. But something odd had happened: the raiders never attacked.

"It was like those raiders didn't care about the goods," the son of the farmer told the Peace Force. "They didn't take much more than travel supplies from a few larders. Didn't make sense – the temple's worth looting and some of these villagers carried a fair bit of coin on them as they ran. At the very least, they could have grabbed the cows."

It was strange. No one could make heads or tails of it. The villagers reported seeing the embroidered caps and knee-high boots favored by the Paika. Again, fingers pointed, but it could just as easily have been bandits dressed as Paika. Were they working for hire? Or, was someone impersonating them?

"It's a perilous ploy, though," the farmer's son pointed out. "The Paika'll have their heads for pretending to be them."

"The Paika are banned from the Fire Peaks Region," Professor Solange reminded him.

The man laughed at the notion.

"Paika go where they please. Laws and borders don't mean nothing to them."

Ari Ara could see Minli puzzling over the reports as they packed their travel sacks and prepared to investigate what had happened in the raided village of Hock. She longed to ask him what he thought of all this, but she wouldn't. Not until he apologized for that horrible remark about her mother. Once or twice, she caught him looking at her with a wistful expression. Then their eyes met like crossed swords and they both turned away.

When the Peace Force arrived in Hock, the monks at the

temple grudgingly fulfilled their duty of hospitality, grumbling all the while. Ari Ara half-suspected that, if not for Korin's presence, they would have disregarded the Great Lady's command to welcome and assist the Peace Force. Some of the Hock residents had come to the High Summer bonfires at Knobble. These folk greeted the newcomers warmly, offering hospitality. The rest of the villagers eyed them suspiciously. The strong-muscled blacksmith grunted out his greeting and turned back to his forge. A cluster of spindly old grannies silenced their stream of chatter and refused to speak. The rotund, red-cheeked miller told them point blank that the Way Between was less than useless – it hadn't prevented the barn from burning, after all. A pair of sallow-faced cattle herders openly mocked Emir Miresh for following the traitor Shulen. A trio of golden-haired sisters snickered nastily as they shoved Sarai into the mud for being Harraken. A passel of grimy children flung clods of cow dung at the two orphans in the Peace Force.

When Minli went to the schoolyard to question the students about what they'd seen, a tough, stocky bully named Nat sneered in his face. Ari Ara heard the commotion and drew closer, hovering on the edge of the rapidly-tightening circle. Nat carried a grudge on his thick shoulders; he'd been punished for rude behavior by being left behind when the rest of his family went to Knobble. He was more than willing to take out his resentment on Minli. Ari Ara folded her arms over her chest, listening as Nat snarled out his grievances.

She spotted the boy's lunge a split second before he kicked at Minli's crutch. Minli hopped back a pace, startled. Ari Ara didn't wait for the bully to strike again. She leapt forward, standing between the two boys. Even if she was mad at Minli, she wasn't going to let Nat harass him.

"That's enough," she told the stocky boy firmly.

"You can't tell me what to do," Nat scoffed. He jutted his wide chin out, belligerent. "You're not even the real Lost Heir. You've got no crown, no throne. You're nothing."

Ari Ara gritted her teeth. She couldn't care less what was on her head, but she resented the implication that she was an unworthy imposter. She'd never lied about who she was.

"I don't need to be royal to stop you from being a bully," she declared hotly, ignoring Minli's muttered plea to let it go. "Any *decent* person would do the same."

Nat balled his hands into fists, narrowing his eyes. As if a silent signal had swept the schoolyard, the children and youths swarmed around. Sarai and Rill came running over, sensing trouble. No one chanted *fight, fight, fight,* but it hung on their lips as their heads craned nervously, keeping watch for the teacher. Shulen was at the other end of Hock, talking with the monks. The other Peace Force members had spread out across the village.

"Walk away. Now," Minli hissed at her.

She shot him a disgusted look. She wasn't going to back down from this fight. Not when she could win it without throwing a punch.

"You don't scare me," she told Nat haughtily, tossing her red curls out of her eyes. "I'm a follower of the Way Between."

Ari Ara lifted her chin and cast a challenge of a look around the circle of students. She'd stand against every last one of them if she had to. She'd take on the whole town, from the warrior monks to the farmers, right down to the blacksmith's apprentice. She'd show them what the Way Between could do, alright.

"The Way Between isn't for weaklings or fools," she said loudly.

"Or for hot-tempered, pig-headed girls," Minli grumbled under his breath. No one heard him.

"And I'll match you to prove it. On the training grounds by the temple. You first?"

She pointed her finger at Nat. His brown eyes glanced nervously around. Like all bullies, he was a coward at heart. His friends egged him on, though. Sarai and Rill wore smug expressions, half-hoping he'd take up the challenge. No one messed with Ari Ara Marin en Shirar.

The horde of children ran for the training grounds. Nat followed, shoved forward by his cronies. Minli grabbed Ari Ara's arm and hissed arguments in her ear against this folly. This was the wrong way to handle things, he said. You don't make friends by beating them with physical Azar.

"Who says I want to be friends with that lout?" she countered, indignant.

"We're the Peace Force," Minli implored her. "For ancestors' sake, you're the Lost Heir. Crown or no crown, you've got to be bigger than this."

"Well," she snapped, "maybe I'm not. And maybe I'm going to show these villagers that we can't be pushed around."

She shoved his hand off her arm and sprinted ahead, leaving him behind. She was tired of everyone telling her how to behave. In the face of the villagers' blatant disdain, something had to be done. If Minli wouldn't do it, she would.

Word of her challenge spread like wildfire through Hock. Within minutes, everyone from grannies to monks to mothers with babies had gathered at the temple. Shulen marched over, frowning, and held a fierce, whispered debate with Mahteni and Solange over whether or not to let Ari Ara's hot-tempered challenge proceed. He could tell that most of the Peace Force members were for it. The Market Day demonstrations at Garrison Town had been a success, after all. And, from veiled insults to outright derision, all of them had endured the scorn of the people of Hock. Tempers ran short. Pride flared. The Peace Force members wanted to prove the insults wrong. Besides, if Ari Ara backed down, she'd be mocked as a coward and the villagers would think the Way Between was worthless. In the end, Minli was the only member arguing against it. The rest longed to see Ari Ara take the arrogance in Hock down a notch or two. No one doubted that she could do it. She was a legend at the Way Between.

Minli was furious. He snapped his mouth shut and refused to stand with the other Peace Force members. Their pride and folly were leading them into a mess. Even if Ari Ara won the matches, what would that achieve? Restoring their pride by crushing another's wasn't the Way Between. Minli's eyes stung with frustration. His mind raced, searching for a different solution, a way out of all this. He sat on one of the large boulders that marked the edge of the training grounds, crutch leaned up against it, arms folded over his chest.

Ari Ara stretched out her muscles and limbered up, studiously ignoring Minli. She knew exactly what he was thinking; they'd had this argument before. In his view, the Way Between had to be for everyone, outer Azar was the least of its skills . . . and she was nothing but a show-off.

Then, to her complete surprise, Minli rose abruptly and limped to the center of the training grounds. A hush fell.

"Who will stand against *me?*" he asked in a loud voice.

No one moved. A murmur of sound rippled through the inhabitants of Hock. Minli's jaw tightened as he heard the words *cripple* and *not fair to pick on a weakling.*

"No one? Then I've won the first round without moving a muscle. In the Way Between, our vulnerabilities give us strength. The less people want to fight with us, the more battles we've won before they begin."

"You couldn't have stopped those raiders, though," someone called out.

Minli turned to face the speaker.

"Neither did your warrior monks and farmers with pitchforks," he replied. "Those raiders, whoever they were, retreated of their own accord. Aren't you curious why? Help us find out."

Intrigued murmurs rose up. Minli's sharp ears, the ones that heard the painful jabs about his crutch and missing leg, picked up on them.

"The bandits in the hills might know, you say?" he echoed back, cupping his hand to his ear. "What might they know?"

"Why they didn't take our coins!" a woman cried.

"So, you think the bandits did this?" Minli asked.

"Aye, or else they'll know who did," a gruff carpenter answered with a curt nod.

"Shall we ask them?" the boy suggested with a slight smile and a shrug.

"I dare you to try!" a young man, one of the pack who had mocked Emir, challenged. "Those bandits will slit your throat."

"The followers of the Way Between are not so easily killed," Minli answered easily.

"You're not afraid of them, then?" a mother exclaimed, her eyes round with alarm, clutching her small child close. "Going to face them without so much as a belt knife?"

"Of course, I have some fear," Minli answered, "but it's what you do with your fear that makes you courageous or not."

"Then you'll go?" called out one of the girls who had shoved Sarai in the mud. A glimmer of grudging respect shone in her eyes. "You'll face them?"

"It would be more productive than standing here, facing down your fists and knives and pitchforks and warrior monks.

Why are we fighting each other when we could be working together?"

Ari Ara burst into a grin before remembering that she was still mad at him. This was Minli at his finest, redirecting the conflict, turning aside the impulse to attack, stopping these demonstration matches before they began. Minli kept talking, working out a plan of action until the villagers forgot they had come to beat the Lost Heir, and realized the Peace Force could help them solve their problem.

Late that night, long after the gathering had shifted into a shared meal, the former animosity of the villagers gave way to curiosity. From the weaver's apprentice to the blacksmith's son, each person asked their questions about the Way Between. Over stew and salad, the Peace Force explained how they worked to resolve conflicts and stop violence. They told old tales – some of which had occurred in these very hills – and by the time the pies came bubbling out of the oven, plans were in the works to hold a series of trainings in Hock while a small team went to speak with the bandits. When the villagers departed for their homes, yawning and blinking, but with buzzing thoughts, the Peace Force crowded around Minli, praising him on his quick thinking and skillful use of Azar.

"You found the Way Between even through our own pride and folly," Solange told him, glancing at Ari Ara, but shaking her head ruefully at them all. Everyone had gotten caught up in their tempers and bruised feelings. Only Minli had refused to go along with it.

"Ari Ara flipped that huge wrestler onto his back," Emir declared, "but even she hasn't single-handedly flipped an entire village out of conflict into cooperation."

"Yes," Shulen agreed. "Some of us can win a match without throwing a punch. You won the day without moving a muscle."

Listening, Ari Ara swallowed hard. She hadn't known it was possible to feel so many conflicting emotions at once: pride in Minli, lingering anger at him, jealousy at the praise heaped on his head, irritation that he'd stopped *her* from the matches, embarrassment that she'd egged Nat on instead of doing what Minli had done. But mostly, she missed her best friend. Ari Ara wanted to feel pride in his achievements and stand there next to Minli, telling him to wipe that bashful look off his face – he deserved all this praise and more.

Feeling like the whirlwind of emotions would tear her apart at any moment, she mustered up her courage and walked up to Minli. A quiet fell as she approached. She felt the others' eyes on her, watching, wary, suspecting an explosion, hoping for a miracle. Her Aunt Mahteni smiled faintly and nodded, encouraging her to do what was right, to act with *harrak*, honor. Shulen wore an inscrutable look, as if he expected the best and feared the worst from her. Minli's happy blush turned guarded and uncertain.

"That . . . that was amazing, Minli. Well done." She almost choked on the words, all the nastier parts of her feelings seething beneath her longing for her friend. But she wrestled them down and made it through the moment.

As the chatter started up again, she leaned in close to Minli.

"Can we talk?" she whispered. "Not here."

He regarded her steadily. Then he nodded. Later, after the others had gone to bed, they left the temple, walking out into the summer night. Minli's distinctive footstep crunched over a patch of gravel. She sat down on a bench overlooking a darkness-cloaked slope and tried to find the words to apologize.

"So, what do you want?" Minli's cold tone was brusque and shocking.

Ari Ara flinched. When someone who was usually so kind

withdrew that basic warmth, it stung all the more sharply. Despite her irritation with him, Ari Ara shivered. She struggled to speak.

"If you have nothing to say for yourself, I'm going," he stated.

He turned.

"Wait!"

Minli paused. Ari Ara gulped. He wasn't making this easy! He was supposed to be the one who was good at inner Azar, not her.

"Look, Minli, I'm sorry," she blurted out. Echoes of the Atta Song, the Harraken ritual of apology and forgiveness, rang in her ears. She squirmed. She had heard the song a thousand times, even sung it, but she'd never been this uncomfortable. It was easier to apologize for the War of Retribution than this!

"I . . . I wasn't very nice to you on the night of the bonfire."

He lifted one brown eyebrow.

"Or before that," she added with a sigh. "I shouldn't have called you a cripple. I was mad and I wasn't being very thoughtful and I hurt you and I'm sorry."

She groaned inwardly as all her apologies blurted out at once. She felt like she was being squeezed through a cider press. She reached for her inner Azar, taking a deep breath and trying not to panic. Her heart thudded in her chest as she waited for his reply.

"Okay," he said in a quiet voice.

"Okay what?" she squeaked back.

"Okay, you're forgiven, but don't do it again," he gasped out. A shine of tears clung to his brown eyes. His chin quivered as he spoke. "Don't make me feel like a weakling - "

She hung her head.

" - don't ignore me, don't call me an old monk - "

"I won't. I promise," she interrupted swiftly.

" - don't tease me just to make others laugh. Don't say mean things about me."

"Don't you say them either!" she burst out, a flicker of fury in her tone. "What you said about my mother - that hurt, Minli! It hurt a lot and you *knew* it would."

Suddenly, she was angry and sniffling and wiping her eyes with the back of her hand. Minli looked ashamed.

"I'm really sorry about that," he said in a small voice. "That was wrong."

"It was horrible!" she cried. "It was beneath you."

"I know. I shouldn't have said it and it's not even true. It's not your fault she died."

Now they were both crying. Minli's eyes turned red and his mouth quivered. Ari Ara buried her face in her hands. She felt him sit down next to her on the bench. When their sobs had reduced to mere sniffles, Minli spoke tentatively.

"Can we be friends again?"

She reached over and threw her arms around him.

"Ancestors, yes!"

She pushed back and regarded him in the moonlight.

"And, for the record, what you did today was amazing. Hands-down the best use of the Way Between I've ever seen."

"Thank you," Minli replied evenly. "And don't you forget it!"

Ari Ara threw her arm over his shoulders. How could she? She'd remember that match for the rest of her life. In the end, it had restored their friendship. When they returned to the temple, their eyes were dry and their heads held high. They'd found their Way Between.

CHAPTER FOURTEEN

· · · · ·

The Bandits

In ancient times, Alaren dealt with a plague of bandits. Harsh tax burdens turned farmers into outlaws. Poverty drove workers to become thieves. But then, the thefts were used to justify more armed patrols. Military incursions chasing bandits across border lines triggered wars. The kings demanded more taxes to pay for armies. The people grew more impoverished. The bandits rose in numbers. The cycle spiraled through the ages, one century after another, leading to war after war.

Ari Ara felt dizzy just thinking about it.

She couldn't shake the nagging sense that this had all happened before. The bandits. The wars. The raids. Even the Way Between. How many centuries had passed since Alaren's skills were last taught in this region? She thought back through the long history of conflict. Each time the Way Between showed up, the chances of peace rose and the odds of war diminished.

Ari Ara craned around, looking down the road, hoping to spot the small team of Peace Force members returning. Three days ago, Minli, Shulen, and two others had departed to find the bandits' hideout. Ari Ara had begged to go, but she'd been overruled.

"We can't risk them taking the Lost Heir hostage," Shulen said, refusing to budge on the matter. "Emir will stay here to protect you and Korin."

Mahteni cut off her spluttered objection that she could look after herself.

"Better safe than sorry. Your father would never forgive me if anything happened to you," Mahteni told her.

Ari Ara sighed and surrendered. She'd received a long letter from her father. She had dreaded opening it, fearing a tirade. Ari Ara had even avoided taking it from Nightfast until the hawk perched on her head, screeching and fanning his wings, talons yanking painfully at her hair. But, when she finally read Tahkan's words, the tight coil of anxiety that had lived in her belly for weeks released. Tahkan, perhaps suspecting that she'd already endured numerous scolds on the subject of drinking, simply told her the story of how he and Moragh had stolen a barrel of beer. They had been years older than Ari Ara, but curious about the forbidden drink. Moragh had dared him to see who could chug down the most and they'd both been violently sick.

Your grandfather told us that the ancestors had cursed us, Tahkan wrote, *and in our ignorance, we thought he meant our agony would last forever. Even when we recovered, we thought the ancestors would strike us down if we so much as looked at beer.*

He told her how he had rebuilt his harrak after the shame of that episode, spending a year tending a field of grain and delivering it to children and elders. All that grain, the entire field, would have made only a few barrels of beer. Instead, it fed whole families for a year.

Her father also answered her most burning question: she had not killed her mother by being born. The attackers who chased Queen Alinore had weakened her, left her exhausted as labor pains started, and kept her from the aid of midwives. The blame lay on them, not Ari Ara.

And I am closer than ever to finding them, Tahkan assured her.

Until then, he urged her to stay safe and listen to Mahteni and Shulen.

Which meant, she reluctantly conceded, *staying in Hock while the others went to speak with the bandits.*

"Face it," Korin teased her, "your valuable head is stuck with me and the others in Hock. We'll just have to make the best of it."

And they did.

Minli's skill had shifted the blowing winds of gossip from derision to curiosity. The residents of Hock wanted to know more about the Way Between. They hovered on the sidelines of dawn practice, watching the famed Lost Heir turn aside attacks. When the grandmother from Tuloon Ravine did the same, they mustered the courage to join in. Professor Solange gave a lesson in how the Peace Force had worked in this area long ago. The villagers asked many questions, realizing their ancestors were part of these stories. In the evenings, they learned how Alaren had been caught by bandits, stuck on a lonely road with a broken leg. The stork-like man had saved his skin by telling the robbers that he'd come to chronicle their lives. Later, those chronicles had documented the unjustness of the harsh laws and tax burdens that drove people into banditry. Alaren established a self-reliant village where the bandits could leave the life of robbery behind. Then he appealed to his brother, King Marin, to lift the unjust laws.

"Minli isn't hoping to do all that this week, is he?" one of the villagers exclaimed.

"Er, no," Professor Solange answered. "I think they've got enough to accomplish on this trip. But, perhaps someday, you and the villagers could work on ending banditry in this region."

Minli and the team had been gone three days now, and everyone in Hock was on edge. They stumbled through the seconds, minutes, and hours of the day in a state of distraction. The kitchen monks put salt in the pies instead of sugar. A granny knit her granddaughter's hair instead of braiding it. The dairy maid tried to milk a pig. When the schoolteacher absentmindedly told the class that horses were born from eggs, Mahteni suggested that they all come to Azar practice to take their minds off things.

They gathered in a grassy meadow outside the schoolhouse. A light breeze swept puffy clouds across the sky. The mountains loomed on the horizon, rising and falling in husky blue swells. The schoolchildren perched on their heels, giggling and chattering, excited at the unexpected break in lessons. A smattering of older villagers gathered as well. The warrior monks stood in a row behind them, cajoled into joining the practice by the monk who had lived at Monk's Hand Monastery before he joined the Peace Force.

Mahteni held up her hands for silence.

"The Way Between works best when we work together," she told them. "Alaren didn't achieve peace all alone. He trained thousands of people to work in small and large groups, using their collective strength to prevent war."

His Peace Force had marched back and forth over these very mountains, bringing people from one area to support the efforts of another. They established peace villages, stopped one faction from launching an attack against the other, and even stood between two armies on the battlefield. They had pressured kings to make peace and organized entire cities to go on strike against war. These stories had inspired Mahteni's own organizing efforts across two nations, leading to the end of the Water Exchange and the restoration of Harraken women's rights.

Much knowledge had been lost since Alaren's time, it was true, but they could still learn from the remnants. The Marianans had the book of folktales. The Tala-Rasa recalled the old songs. Shulen remembered the physical trainings. And people like Mahteni were learning as they went, discovering new ways to use the ancient practices in their own time.

What we can't rebuild, we can invent anew, Mahteni told them, straightening her shoulders.

"Today, we are going to recreate some of the events in Alaren's stories," she said to the group. "By acting out the scenes, we'll learn how to use the Way Between in dangerous situations."

"Like warriors drilling?" asked a monk from the temple.

"Yes. And, like whole armies practicing large-scale maneuvers," Mahteni answered, "we are going to work together as a group."

"Like the time Minli and Rill got the students and street urchins to stand between the Harraken water workers and the angry Marianans?" Ari Ara asked, remembering the dramatic showdown.

"Yes!" Mahteni replied, eyes shining.

"We shoulda practiced beforehand," Rill confessed with a wry grin, winking at the children of Hock. "Woulda helped us. As it was, me heart was pounding so hard, I thought it would burst. Me 'n me urchins were as likely to throw something as the rest of the crowd!"

"Let's use that experience then, and practice," Mahteni suggested.

She asked Rill to explain what had happened. Two years ago, Ari Ara had won the freedom of the Harraken water workers in a one-on-one duel with Shulen, but when it was time for the water workers to leave, the shocked and angry Marianans had threatened to attack. Minli and Rill had courageously led the students and street urchins to stand between the two groups, forming a protective corridor through which the Harraken could exit the city.

Isa raised her hand uncertainly.

"But, didn't the Great Lady Brinelle intervene? She ordered the warriors to stand down and told her people to neither help nor harm the water workers. Should someone pretend to be her?"

Mahteni smiled.

"Let's imagine, for the moment, that she wasn't there or hadn't acted. This is for training purposes and it's unlikely that we'll always have the Great Lady to rely on."

"Yeah," Rill pointed out, rolling her eyes, "we certainly didn't *plan* on Ole Brinny taking our side."

As the Hock residents chortled at the street urchin's cheek, Mahteni told them to form groups. They would replay the scene over and over to explore what happened, what might have happened, and how each group could have acted differently. Each time, they would change roles, rotating through one of the four parts: water workers, students, street urchins, and angry Marianans. She made sure that anyone who had been there on that day took a different role. Isa was assigned to be a water worker. Ari Ara wound up as a street urchin. Sarai took the part of a student. Rill played an angry townsperson. Instead of throwing shoes or hard objects - like the actual Marianans had threatened to do - Mahteni made them throw blades of grass.

"Maybe we'll work up to a mud fight," she said with a wink as Ari Ara and Rill eyed a nearby puddle with mischievous grins.

They began. Those playing the Harraken water workers tried to walk across the meadow. The angry Marianans started throwing grass and shouting at them. The students and street urchins ran forward and linked arms in a long chain, getting showered with grass. After a period of mayhem, Mahteni whistled through her fingers to call a halt.

Nervous laughter broke out. They formed a circle again, sharing their experiences. A Hock lass twisted her apron in her hands as she sheepishly confessed to enjoying hurling grass a bit too much. Isa said it was a lot scarier being in the water workers' shoes - she hadn't realized how being a Marianan by blood had made her feel safer in that situation. One of the monks asked if they should keep their hands free to block the grass.

"It would look like you were cringing," someone pointed out.

"Not if you did it like a statement, like a firm hand saying stop," a granny replied, making the gesture.

"Let's try it in the next practice," Mahteni suggested.

So, they did, testing it out and discussing it afterward.

"What did it feel like to lift your hands like that?" Mahteni asked.

"Powerful."

"Firm."

"Clear."

"Well," Ari Ara added with a shrug, "it was hard not to duck or flinch as the grass stems flew at us."

"When you flinched," Rill admitted, "it just made me want to throw more things at you."

"What about when they didn't flinch?" Mahteni asked.

"Oooh, that was powerful," a muscular young woman, the blacksmith's apprentice, exclaimed. "I stopped throwing grass for a bit . . . it was hard to keep going against such a clear message."

Around and around the conversation went, interspersed with new variations and practice sessions. In one trial, the townspeople charged through the students and urchins. In another, those in the protective lines unexpectedly sang an old Marianan lullaby as the townspeople stared at them, dumbfounded. In a third round, the students walked up to the townspeople and tried to talk to them. Korin set everyone giggling by pretending to be a stuffy old noble lady and fainting in a dead heap, distracting the Marianans from their assault. One time, the water workers bolted across the space, startling everyone. Next, they walked slowly and calmly. The roles rotated. They spoke about what kept their minds clear and hearts calm - deep breathing, sensing their feet on the earth, a prayer or silent chant. They discussed what worked and didn't work. They tried out wild ideas.

A few times, the practice runs broke down into chaos. Ari Ara dropped out of character to stop a pair of children from colliding as they bolted into motion. One time, the village boys took their roles as angry Marianans so seriously, they shoved the others to the ground. Emir used physical Azar to pull them aside to cool off.

After several hours, the sun slanted west and Mahteni called a final halt. She ended the session with an assignment: to come up with a list of five - one for each finger on a hand - ways to stay calm amidst the fray, to center their hearts when scared, and ground their focus in chaotic situations. They could use their hand as a memory device - like a rhyme or a string tied to a finger- to remember those five practices. They could test one another's memories over the next few days, learning each other's tricks in the process.

"Or," Mahteni said wryly, shading the sun out of her eyes and squinting toward the road. "You can try them out right now."

A rush of excitement struck as they saw what the desert woman had noticed. The small team had returned from the bandits. Backlit by the blaze of the western sun, Minli's tousled hair caught the gold. Zyrh's hide glowed. Shulen lifted a hand in greeting and a flashflood of children came running. Amidst a clamor of questions and shouts, Minli delivered the long-awaited news.

The bandits had not attacked Hock, nor were they inclined to do so in the future.

"Why would we risk our necks for so little?" the bandit leader had scoffed.

Merchant caravans winding along the trade routes were far more tempting. In fact, the leader declared, if anyone needed proof of his gang's whereabouts on the night of the Hock raid, they could go to Shottam, the mining town across the border, and ask the unhappy merchants who'd lost their cargo to the bandits. Like as not, they'd find the Hock raiders, too.

"We'll look for them over the border," Shulen promised the villagers of Hock. "As the Peace Force, we can freely cross and search."

"And, we have an additional task in that direction," Minli murmured in an undertone to Ari Ara.

His words lit the itch of curiosity in her, but she had to wait for hours to satisfy it. First, the tales of their journey had to be shared. The monks at the temple cooked cauldrons of stew and sliced up fresh bread for the whole village. Minli, Shulen, and the others told how they'd found the bandits' lair, stumbling onto it as they tromped around a bend. The leader, a lean fellow named Joss Robberman, had inked markings across his skin, as did many of his band. Their hideout was rough, but serviceable, tucked away in one of the hundred caves chiseled by time into the hills.

Minli surprised the bandits with his bold wit and charmed them with his stories. Joss took a keen interest in how Alaren had convinced the bandits of old to leave the life of banditry behind. He asked questions about the town Alaren helped them found, Second Chance Village, examining how it was organized, what it produced, how it made money, and how it stayed self-sufficient. The tales stretched long into the evening and still the bandits asked for more. The next morning, Joss invited Minli to return someday. His rough and hardened men seconded the notion with surprising enthusiasm.

"When you return, you can tell us the rest of those tales, lad," the bandits said.

"When I return," Minli promised quietly, "it will be because you're ready to make new legends of your own. What was done before can be done again."

The men laughed and called him a dreamer; they'd never give up their robbery, they claimed. But Joss Robberman looked thoughtful and Minli suspected the stories had lodged like seeds in his mind, waiting for the right moment to grow.

As for the additional task in the direction of Shottam, that story waited until the Hock villagers had dispersed. Then in the great hall of the temple, the entire Peace Force assembled. The team that had negotiated with the bandits relayed the unexpected request they'd received. A messenger from another village had caught up to them just as they returned from the foothills near the bandits' hideout. Her horse was drenched with sweat. Shaking with exhaustion, the rider told them that she'd galloped through the night to reach them.

"We heard you have no fear of bandits," she panted, her skin grey with fatigue, "and we wish to ask for your aid."

The woman and her kin lived in Bercham, a crumbling collection of houses up a winding road through a nearby mountain pass. After a series of failed crops and hard years, they had decided to pack up and leave. They would join a larger town across the border, merging with clan relatives on the Harraken side. The families were ready to depart for Gollun Town, but they couldn't.

"We are afraid to leave," the messenger told Minli and the others. "The road is plagued by bandits. We can't risk losing our last possessions."

"But," Minli wondered, "what is there to steal? It sounds like you have little left."

"The bandits don't know that," the woman sighed. She was weathered and worn, dressed in patched clothing and thin-soled boots. "They'll see our wagons and attack. We're afraid they'll kill us first and search our pockets later."

Bercham's headman had requested a squadron of garrison soldiers to protect them, but Commander Mendren refused. Since they were defecting from Mariana, the gruff military man had argued, and joining the Harraken across the border, they were no longer his concern.

"But we heard the Peace Force was in the area," the messenger had explained, "and fearless when it comes to bandits. Would you travel with us? Better you than nothing."

Shulen had grimaced at the skepticism in the messenger's voice, but agreed. Long ago, Alaren had walked alongside refugees providing unarmed protection. The newfound Peace Force could do the same. The bandits knew who they were, and, thanks to Minli's tales, thought well of them.

They set out for Bercham at dawn, waving farewell to the villagers of Hock, promising to send word of their search for the raiders. Two of their members had been asked to stay longer. The husband and husband couple from the Desert Crossroads agreed. They could teach the Way Between to the monks and children, and anyone else who wished.

As they departed, Ari Ara looked back over her shoulder with a smile. She thought of how every small team of Peace Force members shone like a tiny light in troubled places, restoring trust, sharing skills and stories, and helping communities solve their problems without violence. From Hock to Knobble to the Haystacks to Moscam, they gleamed like candles on a dark night, offering hope.

The morning birdsong swelled around them, an auspicious chorus for the start of the journey. When they reached Bercham, they found residents waiting by the village gates, ready to go. Dressed in worn clothes and weathered boots, the parents lifted small children up on top of the heaped-high belongings piled into wagons. Elders clambered up onto the seat next to the drivers. A few rode ponies, draft horses, and donkeys. Most walked, carrying sacks slung across their backs or balancing woven baskets on their heads. This cross-border community blended the look of the desert and the riverlands. The women had the prominent cheekbones of the Harraken and the almond eyes of the Marianans. The children ranged from umber-skinned like Tala to pale peach like Isa, sweeping through all shades of tan, cinnamon, maple, and bronze. Ari Ara realized with a tingle of surprise that several of the women had hair as red as hers and Mahteni's. One of the men had a nose just like her father's.

The Peace Force members spread out among the villagers, positioning themselves at the outermost edges of the group where their white tunics would be conspicuous. As they set out, wary resignation lifted into a mixture of relief and hope. A warm welcome awaited them. The gentle day encouraged them. Late summer painted a touch of gold onto the verdant greens. The road unfolded before them, and, though it hurt to leave their old homes, they spoke eagerly of building anew among their relatives. They chatted with the Peace Force as they traversed the snaking road through the forest, rearing up over a ridge, then plummeting down into the next valley. With their laden pushcarts and heavy wagons, they traveled slowly, at the pace of grandmothers and children.

After lunch, they entered a craggy land of giant boulders and deep-chiseled ravines. Alpine meadows lay pocketed between steep cliffs and narrow river passes. The woods grew dark and dense, dominated by thick fir trees. The hairs on Ari Ara's neck would not lay flat. She felt unseen eyes watching them. They saw signs of the Paika, but no Paika. Peculiar twists of bone and grasses lined the roadside. Crossed branches tied with white sinew had been stuck upright among the stones. Rocks hung from trees, knocking together with a hollow *thock*. The villagers confirmed; here, Paika territories overlapped with bandit hideouts. These were dangerous places where you were as likely to get your throat slit as make it through unscathed.

But they saw no one in these winding ravines. The Paika had no quarrel with the Peace Force, after all. As they traversed the trails of tangled briars and sharp rocks, the villagers regaled the Peace Force members with heart-thumping tales of bandit raids. It was no wonder Bercham was relocating. The garrison did nothing to stop attacks; it was too far from the Garrison Road. The Harraken patrols could not cross the border, so the region was lawless and tumultuous.

They passed the turnoff leading north to Thieves Den, the notorious stronghold of robbers and smugglers. There was no road sign, but the villagers pointed it out. Ari Ara itched with curiosity as they described the town clinging to a cliff across a four-hundred-foot gorge. It could only be accessed by a rope bridge. She tried to wheedle a detour out of Shulen, arguing that maybe they could discover who the raiders were, but her mentor curtly dismissed the notion.

"Thieves Den is dangerous. We're not going."

An hour later, the forest abruptly ended, giving way to a coiled canyon peppered with giant boulders and eroded rock formations. The hairs on Ari Ara's arms began to prickle. Soon, she was certain they were being watched. As the caravan descended a steep switchback along a waterfall, her nerves twanged with unease. Boxed in like this, they made a perfect target for an ambush. As the carts and wagons rolled into the next part of the tight canyon, Ari Ara heard a shout.

The rocks crawled with bandits. Clad in oiled leather, they seemed to step out of thin air, bows drawn, yelling. But the Peace Force had prepared for this. As one, they lifted their hands wide open, chanting: *we have nothing, we have nothing.*

The Bercham folk joined in, until hundreds of hands were raised, palms out toward the startled bandits. Taken aback, their yells and hollers petered out. A new voice spoke, deep and laughing.

"Well, well, we meet again," Joss Robberman called out.

The bandit leader leapt from a boulder and landed in a crouch before Minli. The bandit glanced up with a bemused look. He swept off his hat and touched a knee to the dirt as if greeting a lord. Minli blushed and waved off the foolishness of such a gesture.

"What are you doing with these folk?" Joss asked the boy, his grey eyes sweeping across the group.

The Bercham villagers kept their hands raised, watching the exchange warily. Minli explained the situation, leaving nothing out, not even the villagers' fear of the bandits, nor the reality of their poverty.

"You could waste your afternoon tearing apart their bundles," Minli said to the bandits, "or you could trust my word and let us pass."

Joss studied the white tunics of the Peace Force, the scared and weary faces of the villagers, and the brilliant blue of the sky. Ari Ara spotted a look of thoughtful calculation in the wily bandit leader's face.

"I will do you one better, lad," Joss promised Minli. "If these villagers are as poor as you say, you've saved us all a lot of bother. I will let you pass and make a deal with you, as our forebearers did in Alaren's time."

To the astonishment of everyone, Joss made a vow: wherever the unarmed Peace Force traveled in their white tunics, his bandits would let them pass. Joss' band could guarantee his own territory from here to Thieves Den. The offer did not extend to mixed companies, however. If armed warriors rode or marched with them, the deal was off. No wealthy traveler or rich merchant would dare cross the mountains unarmed. Not yet. But Joss could afford to carve out a narrow space for the poor, the villagers, and the vulnerable to move through the pass unharmed.

Ari Ara hid a smile. This Joss was a clever fellow - and a calculating one, at that. Like the bandits in Alaren's time, he had little to lose and much to gain in forging a friendship with the Peace Force. She studied the scarred and inked man with renewed respect. Joss whistled through his fingers and his bandits melted back into the hills. The caravan of wagons lurched forward and the encounter faded into the stuff of legends and dreams.

From there, the road unfolded gently. The birds sang out in the bushes. A herd of deer lifted their heads on the ridgetop, the stag's antlers outlined against the blue sky. Korin walked amidst the village children, amusing them with absurd questions about farming that soon had them shrieking with laughter at his city-bred silliness. He asked if potatoes grew on trees and if he could wear a sheep on his head instead of a wool cap. If he shook a chicken, would it lay scrambled eggs?

They spent the night at a well-tended way station, then crossed the border with little incident, though the Marianan guards muttered disapprovingly about abandoning one's country and the Harraken patrols eyed them suspiciously for coming from their enemy's side of the border. The Bercham villagers bore the remarks stoically. A decade ago, the border wouldn't have separated them from Gollun Town. The oldest grandfather had lived through so many changes that he'd been born Harraken, married under Marianan law, and switched nationalities twice more, even though he'd lived in the same house all his life. Borders came and went. The people endured.

At the last curve of the journey, just as sunset washed them all in golden light, a small boy gave a shout from his lookout perch atop the tallest pile of belongings. Their kinsfolk in Gollun Town had gathered for their arrival, welcoming them with cool water to wash the dust of the road from their faces, resting spots for weary elders, and the happy tears of reuniting relatives.

The Peace Force received many handshakes and thanks for their assistance. Two of their group agreed to stopover in Gollun Town to accompany people back and forth along the roads through bandit territory. In time, they'd work to set up local Peace Force members who could do this task – these Border Mountain communities frequently traveled back and forth to visit family, trade goods, and join rituals and festivities. It wasn't their fault the shifting border had split their clans in half. The Peace Force was invited to join the welcome feast, but they declined. Shottam was calling. They had raiders to find.

They put the last hours of daylight to good use, traveling up the road. They made camp in a forested grove half a day's journey from their destination. They curled up in their sleeping rolls, watching the stars wink in and out behind the leaves of the swaying trees, thinking proudly of their work with the villagers of Bercham and Hock.

They woke in darkness to the roar of an attack.

CHAPTER FIFTEEN

. . . . .

Riders In The Night

The scream of a horse ripped the night. Ari Ara bolted upright, heart in throat, only to duck down instinctively, flat on her belly, as hoof beats pounded past her head. She heard battle roars and bellowing voices. Flaring torches whipped in dizzying circles. She scrambled to her feet, blood coursing through her veins, closing ranks with a groggy Minli and a panicked-looking Sarai. She heard Isa's scream leap out then throttle back as she caught it halfway. Their training kicked in: don't panic, breathe deep, observe what's going on.

Horsemen circled their encampment, galloping around the grove's edge in a blur of fire and motion. The startled Peace Force members stood shoulder-to-shoulder in a tight ring, backs to the embers of their campfire, faces tracking the riders. Mahteni and Shulen positioned themselves half a step forward, arms flung wide in front of the youngest members. In a strange clarity born of alarm, Ari Ara saw the tic twitching in Shulen's cheek above his tightly clenched jaw. The veins in his hands popped out over his gripped fists. He opened his palms with effort. The ghosts of battle memories haunted him. His old

183

reflexes had kicked in and he was trying not to react with Attar, the Warrior's Way. Ari Ara acted swiftly before he lost control and lashed out. It took discipline to respond with the Way Between, even more so when the nightmares of war still hissed in one's blood.

"Who are you?" Ari Ara called out to the raiders, mostly to distract Shulen from his instinctive reactions. She kept her tone light and even, at odds with the situation, as if she were merely greeting a passel of laughing village children.

Her words quavered a bit at the end, but no matter. The others caught on and followed her cue, greeting the marauders with a gentle welcome at odds with the moment. They could not see the riders' faces. Each wore a mask and hood, some plain cloth, others elaborate wooden carvings, half-beast, half-human. A couple bore crowns of antlers. One wore a wolf-skin cloak.

The riders did not answer, weaving their horses into two rings, one spiraling leftward along the tree line, the other curling rightward close enough to force Mahteni to fall back a pace. They blew into mountain goat horns, eerie and frightening. They began to chant two words in Old Tongue with a Paika accent: *morren bourg* - stay away.

All of Ari Ara's hairs stood on end. She could feel Minli shaking next to her. She dipped under his arm and let her solidarity steady him and his weight anchor her. He swallowed his nerves and squeezed her hand in thanks.

The riders drew their swords and pounded their shields, loud and slow at first, then quicker and quicker. Emir bellowed for them all to get down, out of easy reach of the blades. They crouched low. Emir and Shulen exchanged looks, ready to fight despite the odds.

"No!" Ari Ara called to them. She started to move toward them, to hold them to their vow of Azar, to stop their Attar. The tempo of the pounding shields reached a fevered pitch. Any moment, blood might spill.

Then, at a sharp whistle, the riders peeled off, galloping into the darkness.

The rattled Peace Force stood in stunned silence in the grove. For a long moment, no one moved. Then Shulen broke the spell by bolting into motion, grabbing Emir and a few others, and setting off to patrol the perimeter. Mahteni quieted the nervous babble of voices that erupted, asking someone to build up the fire and put on a pot of water for tea. She gathered the rest in a circle and swiftly, before the details faded from their shock-heightened memories, she asked them to describe the raiders.

They had been tall and stocky, heavily muscled, probably all men. Their skin had been covered from head to toe with gloves and masks. The scent of the torches' smoke had indicated that the pitch came from the eastern side of the Border Mountains, not the west. The horses weren't from the desert, Sarai mentioned with a sniff of pride, or they'd have been far more beautiful. A few faint smiles cracked on the Harraken faces.

"By the ancestors!" Marek swore angrily. "What were those filthy Pikers playing at?"

"Paika!" Ari Ara shouted, defensive.

"Refrain from slurs," Solange reminded Marek, but gently.

She understood his frightened outrage, but name-calling wouldn't help. If anything, it would deepen the eerie monstrousness of the harassment, dehumanizing the people under the masks further, heightening their own fear. Marek scowled, arms crossed over his chest, glowering as Ari Ara insisted that they didn't know the riders were actually Paika.

"If it walks like a duck and talks like a duck, it is a duck," Marek argued in a belligerent, resentful tone. "You saw those carved masks, horns, antlers. All Paika."

"I don't think those were Paika," Minli said slowly, uncertainly, lifting his hand to forestall the outbursts of the others. "There was something . . . off about them."

"I agree," Professor Solange put in. "Paika clans are quite specific in their dress. They would never pair a bird mask with a wolfskin cloak, for example. Nor would they wear ceremonial clothes, like antlered crowns, on a raid."

"That Old Tongue was definitely their accent," Tala mentioned.

"Accents can be faked," Ari Ara grumbled.

"What was it they were chanting?" Minli asked.

"*Morren bourg*," Solange answered. "Means *go home* or *get out* or *leave our territory, you're not welcome here.* It's a bit complicated."

"Clear enough to me," Rill muttered.

"Why is it complicated?" Minli asked, curious.

"Because of why they might have said it," the professor answered.

The Paika avoided fights over land ownership, so long as they could freely travel through their ancestral lands. They had lived through centuries of occupation, regions that changed political hands each decade. To survive, they'd adopted a policy of negotiating their autonomy with the rulers of the day, usually trading services for freedom. Such bargains usually paid off. They were expert guides and trackers, after all.

"And hired swords," Sarai muttered darkly.

"Is that why they want the Peace Force gone? To profit from war?" Isa asked, thinking of the Marianan nobles who sabotaged Ari Ara's bid for the throne in order to protect their ability to make money on weapons sales and war plunder.

Solange shook her head, bewildered.

"Historically, the Paika have been supportive of peace, any

peace, no matter who's calling for it. They trace their culture back to Alaren's day, you know, and see more gain in peace than in war."

No one had answers to the riddle of why the Paika had threatened and harassed them.

"Because those riders weren't Paika," Ari Ara repeated wearily, tired of the Peace Force failing to live up to their ideals of fairness and openness. She tried to insist that the Peace Force send a pair of emissaries to the Paika to ask their opinion, but the others shot the notion down like an arrow-pierced bird.

"They'll just lie."

"Or kill us."

"No point to it."

When he returned, Shulen agreed with Ari Ara, Minli, and Solange. He didn't think the assailants were Paika. Something wasn't quite right about them. He had followed the raiders' trail as far as he could in the darkness, then circled back, looking thoughtful. The trail of horse hooves in the woods had led down to the main road, but heavy traffic had churned the mud into a mess of markings, and it was futile to search further. Emir and two others had been posted as sentries. If the riders returned, they'd have warning. They wouldn't be caught unaware again.

"In the morning, we'll see if we can find out more in Shottam," Shulen told everyone. "One thing is clear: we should not let this deter us."

If the goal of the harassment was to get the Peace Force to cower like dogs, they had to stand courageously. If the attackers wanted them to run away and go home, the Peace Force had all the more reason to remain.

"If you give into bullying, it multiplies. You've taught your opponents that it works," Shulen explained. "We will shift our approach - post sentries, prepare plans, practice how to respond -

but we will not let them deter us from our work."

At first light, they mustered the energy to head toward Shottam. The stale jitters of fear ached in their bones. Circles hung under everyone's eyes. No one had been able to go back to sleep.

Shottam served the miners of six surrounding mines, providing food and housing, but mostly separating them from their paltry wages. The taverns lured their aching bodies down the mountains with enticements of drink and gambling. The shops overcharged them on everything from flour to medicines to small luxuries like soap. Though situated on the Harraken side of the border, the town was controlled by a mining company run by the House of Thorn. After the war, the powerful nobles had twisted the treaty to include their right to operate the Shottam mines. The Orelands ran many such mining towns located beyond the boundaries of their lands. They owned the mining rights, the rough camps for workers, and the general stores that gouged prices sky-high.

Korin told Ari Ara that Thornmar and the House of Thorn had been maneuvering to annex these lands into Mariana for years. Tala retorted that the Harraken would never let them go; there was a sacred shrine on the western slope of the mountains. Korin lifted his eyebrows. From the looks of it, the Orelands planned to take the mountain away piece by piece, one cartload of ore at a time.

Even though it had plied its wares to miners for half a century, Shottam still felt slapped together. After heavy rains, the streets turned into a quagmire of mud. People traversed the town on plank walkways that ran the length of the roughshod buildings. Narrow boards stretched like bridges over the muck between the streets.

Shulen sent teams of Peace Force members to each of the

three taverns, and others to speak with shopkeepers and boarding house matrons. He assigned Ari Ara and Minli to watch the passersby while he and the monk from the High Mountains made inquiries at the wooden shed that served as a tiny temple. The Shottam monks provided funeral services, posted letters by messenger hawk, and tried to keep the miners' spirits up. It was a hard task. The workers came from the region, picking up mining work when coin was scarce and crops failed. The young men hefted rock picks thinking they'd labor for a season and return home rich. Many never made it home at all, dying from cave-ins, sicknesses that spread through the camps, brawls and fights, and the coughing disease that came from certain dusts in the dark tunnels.

They were a glum and downtrodden lot, trudging with weary, clumping footsteps along the boards. They splashed water from rain barrels onto their faces and turned the kerchiefs around their necks inside out to wash off the worst of the grime. Smeared with streaks of sweat, they spoke little until they stumbled out of the taverns, roaring with whiskey's jollity. Their joy and lives flickered like moths against the flame of mortality, brief, fragile, and desperate.

"It's a sad place, this," Minli remarked in a quiet voice as he and Ari Ara sat side by side on a rough-hewn log that served as a bench.

Ari Ara started to agree then broke off. Across the muddy quagmire of the street, a flash of motion grabbed her eye. There was Finn Paikason, in broad daylight, running lithe as a fox along the boards.

"Come on," Ari Ara told Minli with a nudge.

"What? Why?" he squawked as she tugged him to his feet.

"To find some answers about last night," she replied, pointing. "*That's* Finn Paikason."

Minli traced the direction of her arm, shading the grey glare of the overcast sky out of his eyes. Finn leapt in a zigzag, crossing a broken pathway from one side of the main street to the other. His arms flailed for a second as the board slipped sideways in the mud. He found his balance and jogged onward, intent on his task.

"Let's talk to - " Minli's voice faltered, trailing off.

"What? What is it?"

He pulled her down the walkway, ducking behind a stack of logs piled as high as the buildings. Minli turned her and pointed over her shoulder to what he'd seen. Ari Ara gasped.

"Well," Minli sighed, a note of disappointment in his voice, "I liked Finn a lot better before I saw him talking to Rannor Thornmar."

Ari Ara couldn't believe it. She couldn't deny it, either. In the shadows of a narrow alley, Finn Paikason stood in front of the frowning Thornmar, head thrown back, bartering or disagreeing about something. The taller man flashed a coin. Finn shook his head. A grimace rippled through the scars on Thornmar's face. He dug into his pouch and added another coin to the deal. Again, Finn shook his head. Only at the third coin did Finn shrug and accept. He left Thornmar without a bow or by-your-leave.

Ari Ara and Minli scrambled out from behind the logs, hurrying down the series of wooden porches along the store fronts. Neither needed to ask the other what to do: they would confront Finn. Here. Now. And get answers, once and for all.

They caught up with the Paika youth as a jam of cross-traffic struggled through an intersection of two walkways. When his turn came, Finn clasped hands with a skinny man with a wracking cough. The pair swiveled, gripping arms for balance and leaning out around one another. After reversing positions,

Finn darted down the boards, reaching the porches not far from Ari Ara and Minli. A huddle of miners congregated between them, though, backed up as they tried to cross the street.

"Finn!" Ari Ara shouted over the clamor, lifting a hand and waving wildly to get his attention.

He whirled at her voice. A look of shocked consternation whipped through his face. He glanced around swiftly, craning over his shoulder to scan the street.

Looking for Thornmar, Ari Ara suspected sourly.

Finn dove into the crowd like a diver plunging into a pond, resurfacing inches from Ari Ara and Minli with a broad grin.

"Ari Ara of the High Mountains," he chuckled. "You're the last person I thought I'd run into in Shottam. What are you doing here?"

"Someone attacked us last night," she answered in a short tone, cutting straight to the chase. "A group of riders in Paika gear. Minli and I told everyone they couldn't possibly be real - "

"They weren't," Finn cut in. "I'd bet my hat on it."

" - but then we saw you talking to Rannor Thornmar."

She finished with a scowl, folding her arms over her chest. Finn's dark eyebrows furrowed. Minli drummed his fingers on his crutch.

"What were you discussing with Thornmar?" Minli demanded.

"Paika business," Finn answered warily. "Why? What's it to you?"

"Thornmar hates her," Minli spat out. "He'll do anything to hurt her. He tried to have her assassinated once."

Finn looked taken aback. He glanced anxiously at Ari Ara.

"It wasn't anything like that," he assured them. "And if he's no friend of yours, then he's no friend of mine."

"What did he hire you for?" Ari Ara asked.

Finn's face darkened.

"Not for what he thinks, that's for certain. Not now that I know how it is between you two."

"Be careful with him," Minli warned, sensing that Finn was going to trick Thornmar. "He's dangerous."

"Don't you worry about me," Finn laughed. "I was born into danger, learned to walk by dodging war arrows. I've made it this far, haven't I?"

Minli shook his head at the youth's bravado. Ari Ara grinned.

"This is Minli," she said, belatedly making the introduction.

"I know," Finn answered. "He's well known to the Paika. He gave us the benefit of the doubt when few others did. The Paika are grateful for that."

Finn tugged them out of the path of two irritable miners complaining about pipsqueaks blocking the walkway.

"Look," he added, seeing their guarded expressions, "we didn't have anything to do with what happened last night, but if you tell me where you camped, I'll go see if I can track them for you."

"We tried," Ari Ara groaned. "The trail vanished."

"You aren't Paika," Finn pointed out. He flipped his black curls out of his eyes with a proud grin.

Ari Ara's breath stuck in her chest. She shot a glance at Minli, suddenly nervous. Her tousle-haired friend was weighing up the Paika youth, measuring him with his quietly intense gaze. She wanted each boy to like the other so badly that she lost her ability to say anything. Feeling ridiculous, she shifted from foot to foot. Finally, Minli put her out of her misery by meeting Finn's eyes with genuine curiosity.

"So," Minli remarked, "are all the Paika as skillful as you? You seem to slip in and out of places better than the Fanten."

Finn beamed at the praise. His wariness broke like sunlight through storm clouds at Minli's pronunciation of *Paika*, rather than *Pikers*.

"I've a special knack for it, but yes, my people pass on this knowledge from one generation to the next."

"I'd like to meet them, someday," Minli replied. "The Paika are remarkable."

"I'd like that, too."

Ari Ara exhaled in a relieved whoosh that made both boys laugh. She couldn't bear it if one held a grudge against the other. For a spell, they chatted like any young people on a porch, bored and waiting for their elders to finish running errands. Finn asked about where they'd seen the raiders, planning to go check it out. He huffed indignantly over the description of the fake Paika garb. It was more than false, it was an affront to his culture's fashion sense.

"If I dressed that badly, I'd get thrown out of the clan," Finn groaned, rolling his eyes.

Minli launched into questions about Paika dress codes and customs, hoping it would help prove that the raiders were imposters. Ari Ara listened, but fashion had always gone in and out her ears. She liked Finn's look, though, with his travel cloak bundled up over one shoulder and tucked up in his belt.

All too soon, Finn sighed and cast a glance at the overcast sky. The pale orb of the sun was sinking lower. Much as he wanted to stay, he had to get going.

"When will I see you again?" Ari Ara blurted out, feeling stupid for sounding like a lovesick ninny.

Finn shot her a wink that made her heart thump in her chest like a fish on dry land.

"When you least expect it," he answered.

Minli did not stop teasing her until Shulen returned. Then

they reported meeting Finn and repeated his denial of Paika involvement in the raiders' harassment. To Ari Ara's relief, Minli didn't mention Finn's dealings with Thornmar.

"He'll think it's suspicious," Ari Ara whispered to Minli as they followed Shulen to his next stop.

"Yeah, and he might not like that Finn's tracking the raiders," Minli agreed, holding her back a pace so the stern warrior wouldn't overhear them.

"We can just wait until we hear from Finn about what he finds," Ari Ara replied in a hush. "If he figures it out, then Shulen won't be so wary of him. Finn will send word when he knows more."

"Or deliver the news in person," Minli suggested, chortling as her cheeks flamed at the thought. "You're hoping he'll just pop up!"

"Am I that obvious?" she groaned.

Minli snorted. She was head over heels for Finn Paikason, that much was clear.

"Your eyes get round as walnuts," he told her, "and you stand there like a dazed fawn, blinking at him like you think he's going to disappear."

"Which he does," she pointed out. "Do you think I should, you know, flirt or something?"

Her voice rose in pitch, half terrified, half thrilled at the thought. Minli gave her a doubtful look, but asked her to show him what she meant. Her attempts at mimicking Isa or Rill made him laugh until his ribs hurt, until he was gasping for breath, until she couldn't help but smile a little and laugh with him.

"I think . . . " he gasped out, "it's better just to be yourself. Otherwise, he'll wonder if you got hit on the head and knocked silly."

CHAPTER SIXTEEN

. . . . .

Chasing Rumors

Shottam yielded a few leads. A shopkeeper mentioned a large company of riders had stocked up a few days ago. A night watchman saw them ride out at dusk last night. A miner nursing a hangover reported hearing them pounding through again in the wee hours of the morning, headed north. Chasing these rumors, they traveled onward. One tale led them to a clan feud, another to a cover-up for a prank gone wrong. The identity of the real raiders remained elusive. It grated on them all like an itch they couldn't quite reach.

They left two Peace Force members posted in Shottam: the grandfather from Turim and the monk from the High Mountains. They would assist the monks in the tiny temple and keep their ears out for tidbits about the mysterious raiders. Mahteni urged them to listen deeply to the miners; they were being mistreated and, like the water workers in Mariana, the Way Between could be used to help them change things. They would need to be careful, however. Thornmar would not be pleased if he heard they were meddling in his mining town.

Ari Ara could feel their company shrinking, growing leaner,

lighter, and swifter. Two by two, the Peace Force dwindled, leaving a web of peace workers behind them. Ari Ara hoped the strands they wove would be strong enough to stop these raiders from propelling the region toward more violence.

They climbed the mountains into a terrain of no man's land. Here the border vanished entirely. No one could say for sure where it lay. Nor did the locals hold strong national loyalties either way. They stood up for each other and left patriotism to those whose nationality didn't change with each war. The Peace Force traveled along lonely stretches of roads broken only by an occasional shepherd's hut or remote farmstead half-crumbled into ruins. When they turned onto the Dust Road, the border reasserted its presence. Built by one of Shirar's descendants during an era of Harraken occupation of these lands, the wide road still bore cobbled stretches between the lengths that had fallen into disrepair. The Peace Force helped a merchant caravan fix a broken axle and heave their carts out of the ruts. They stopped in the most prosperous of the scattered villages and visited the stone-walled, one room schoolhouses to tell Alaren tales to the children.

Following an herbwoman's suggestion, they searched the forests, passing through a string of logging camps. At a tavern near a clear-cut slope that broke Ari Ara's heart, they kept two factions of loggers from bashing each other's skulls in over disputes about lumbering territory. In the scree of a landslide on the far side of the mountain, they talked a gang of youth out of an ill-planned raid on another crew's stores, instead helping them barter for work-trade.

Their acts won them respect. Their stories started to run ahead of them, greeting them like echoes from the mountainsides.

Tell the one about . . . the children now urged.

Is it true that the Way Between can . . . the mothers queried as they rocked the babies' cradles.

How did Alaren stop that fight . . . the young lads asked as they walked alongside the Peace Force members.

Several times more, the masked riders encircled the Peace Force camp, chanting *morren bourg, morren bourg,* stay away, stay away! They never attacked, only harassed. Shulen suspected they were under orders not to harm the Peace Force. The raiders' goal seemed to be intimidation, trying to frighten the followers of the Way Between into disbanding or leaving the region. Only once did a raider break rank and lift a spear butt to strike out. Emir erupted into action with stunning speed, catching the blow mid-swing and blocking it. The raider nearly fell from his horse, but righted his torso with a painful wrench. The band's leader shouted out a command and the riders wheeled off.

The Peace Force drilled and prepared to weather these frightening encounters. They learned to disperse into the woods, denying the raiders an easy target. They turned the tables on the band and began to track them after they left. One time, Emir and Shulen gave close chase until they lost the riders in a forked ravine. During another encounter, the Peace Force drove harassers away by chanting *calleen alum, calleen alum.* In Old Tongue, it meant *come closer and share your stories.*

When the harassment failed to deter or intimidate the Peace Force, the raiders gave up. Instead, they targeted tiny villages. Sweeping through hamlets and shepherds' camps, they left a trail of terrorized people in their wake. On the Harraken side of the border, fingers quickly pointed at their ancient enemies, the Marianans, accusing them of hiring these marauders. Whether the raiders were truly Paika or mere imposters made little difference, said the shepherd whose hut had been burned to ash. Mahteni Shirar and Tala sat with him, singing songs of consolation while the rest of the Peace Force rounded up his scattered flock. He thanked Ari Ara Shirar, daughter of his *Harrak-Mettahl*, for carrying back the youngest lamb in her arms. They managed to calm his outrage, and urged him not to spread unproven rumors about Marianan schemes, but fear still spread like an infectious disease.

Soon, they came across farming villages drilling in Attar, the Warrior's Way, convinced that a Marianan invasion loomed on the horizon. Korin de Marin spoke for his nation, promising that the army had nothing to do with this, and that war was the last thing the Great Lady wanted.

When the raiders slipped back over the border and harried the eastern villages, the fearful suspicions flipflopped. Here, the Marianans thought the Harraken had hired the Paika to assault them. Maddeningly, they willfully disregarded the reports of the attacks on desert dwellers. Crisscrossing the border, the Peace Force raced to quell the rumors before the entire area exploded. On the Harraken side, a fierce band of warrior women patrolled the region, ready to spill blood over the attacks. Their leader was Mahteni's sister, Moragh Shirar. She vowed to put heads on pikes and threatened to cross the border to do so. Mahteni sought her out and talked her down from the assault, arguing that entering Mariana with her warband would trigger a reprisal from the garrison. She begged Moragh to let the Peace Force continue their work. The ferocious warrior woman reluctantly agreed to stay on the Harraken side . . . for now.

"I swear, sister," Moragh Shirar warned, standing amidst the smoldering ruins of a village, "if we find out the Marianans hired the Paika to do this, they'll pay dearly."

This was how wars started.

As the Peace Force scurried up and down the mountains, chasing whispers and rumors of raiders, Ari Ara searched the skies for a messenger hawk from Finn. No word came. She dispatched Nightfast to her father, keeping him appraised of what was happening, and hoping he'd come north to keep the Harraken from doing anything rash.

The summer withered into browns and golds. Traces of melancholy touched the slanting sunlight. Apples blushed on the branches. The highest slopes woke with white frost then flamed with sunlight and brilliant oranges. Leaves turned scarlet and tangerine, fluttering earthward like flocks of butterflies. In a month, the cold would sweep down from its upper aeries and fan its frosty wings across the valleys.

Ari Ara overheard Shulen, Mahteni, and Solange mulling winter placements for the youth. Who would go where, and with whom? They'd received a number of invitations to place small teams in villages and towns. With the tensions escalating, all of their trained members would be needed to keep the region from reprisals and skirmishes.

Peace Force members came to the three leaders with requests and suggestions. Sarai wished to stay in a small village. Rill boisterously requested a bustling market town. Tala withdrew zirs name from consideration - the other Tala-Rasa wanted zir to return to the desert for the Harraken Sing at Winter Solstice. Korin reluctantly agreed that he had to go home and attend to his neglected duties. Minli would stay with Solange in Moscam, writing letters and sending advice to those with winter postings. Shulen was hoping to hunker down in the quiet of his stone cottage near Alaren's Way Station. Ari Ara didn't ask about her winter fate. She knew it was too much to hope for a posting. She'd return to her father in the desert, accompanied by Mahteni.

A shiver of loneliness slipped its icy finger down the back of her neck. She shook it off and blinked away her thoughts. It was not yet time to fly away like the crying geese in the greying skies. The autumn was still young - though frost iced the upper heights, it was harvest time in the villages. Each time they stopped to inquire about the raiders, the Peace Force also lent a hand. They dug potatoes and pulled turnips. They chopped firewood and herded sheep in from distant pastures. It was a time of hard work and merriment in equal measures. They pushed the dwindling daylight hours to the last shred of light. They gathered chestnuts in the twilight and pulled up armloads of carrots in the early dawn. Ari Ara chopped and dried and stored the harvest with the other villagers, thinking of Monk's Hand Monastery and the Fanten's autumn dances. She dreamed of them, their rhythms pounding through her restless nights. She worked harder the next day to drown out the tingle that lingered in her bones upon waking.

One blazing afternoon, summer roared a last farewell in a dazzle of warmth and light. They sweated as they crossed a winding mountain pass on the Harraken side of the border, heading eastward over rugged terrain, following reports of the raiders. They were forced to scale the steep slopes of one mountain, descend the next, and repeat the process. The Border Mountains were riddled with pathways like this - shorter for those who climbed like mountain goats than for those riding in wagons on the roads. Huffing and puffing, they were relieved when Solange insisted on an afternoon break.

"We have to stop," she stated firmly. "We're close to one of the marvels of the Border Mountains. Some may never pass this way again."

"I sure won't," Rill muttered, wiping her sweaty forehead with her sleeve.

A short detour up a side trail led them to the base of a plunging waterfall. Fine mist lifted in clouds. A series of plunging cataracts toppled from the main torrent, carving out deep pools in the white, calcium-rich stone. Moss-lined boulders surrounded the aquamarine waters, lapping up the plumes of spray. It was utterly enchanting and a much-needed respite from the grit of the dusty roads.

Solange and Mahteni stood in the shallows with cuffs hoisted to their knees. Isa and Rill plunged in, yelped at the cold, then lounged on their cloaks in the sun. In a match of the Way Between, Minli perched on Emir's shoulders and tried to outmaneuver Korin as he clung to Marek. Ari Ara reveled in the refreshingly cool water, then decided to climb the embankment above the frothy base of the waterfall, intrigued by the carvings in the rock face. Spirals and dotted snakes, sunbursts and triangles all marked the surface of the stone cliffs. She ran her fingers around one spiral as large as she was tall. Lichens clung to the edges, hinting at the antiquity of the carvings. There were newer markings, the shapes still sharp white, not blackened by sun over centuries. She studied them, dripping, goose pimples raising slightly in the mist. The sun warmed her back, but this late in the season, a touch of chill clung to the shade.

A pebble stung her shoulder. She winced and whirled to spot its source. There was nothing above her, no collapsing slope or tumbling gravel kicked loose by deer. A second stone hit her between the shoulder blades, right on her Mark of Peace.

"Ow!" she yelped, slapping a hand to her back even though she couldn't reach the spot.

"Hssst! Over here!"

The voice came from the waterfall - or, more accurately, from just behind its curtain. Finn's eyes curled into half-moons over his grin. He glanced below, then stretched out a hand.

"This way," he urged, "watch your step on the slippery parts."

He hushed her with a finger to his lips, gesturing for her to come closer. She picked her footing carefully, sliding over the slick stone until she passed behind the narrow break in the pounding water. Her eyes blinked and adjusted to the gloom. The sound of the falls roared deafeningly, amplifying off the cavern walls. Finn led her back and to the left, where a bend of the cave blocked the tumult. A fern-lined crack in the roof let in a sliver of sunlight.

"I never expected to see you here," she exclaimed, trying to keep from grinning like a fool. She failed, but since Finn beamed back with equal exuberance, she didn't feel too silly.

"This is an old Paika haunt. That was one of our clan elder's life spirals you were touching."

"Oh, I'm sorry!" Ari Ara stammered, wondering if she'd been disrespectful. A blush began to spread from her heels to her hairline.

"No, no, it's fine," he assured her. "Tracing the spiral is supposed to give you good luck and longevity."

"Have you been hiding in here since we arrived?" she asked. They hadn't noticed anyone darting behind the falls as they gawked in awe at them.

Finn shrugged.

"There are other ways in and out."

He didn't elaborate, but Ari Ara saw his eyes flick to the blackness at the back of the cavern. There must be tunnels. She envied him his intimate knowledge of this land. Every hillock and river, tree and peak must be as familiar to him as the High Mountains had been to her.

"I came to deliver a message . . . and a warning."

His voice bounced loudly around the stone, echoing strongly: *warn, warn, warn.* Ari Ara winced at the menace of the sound.

"About what?" she asked in a hushed tone. She shivered in the damp.

Finn pulled his cloak out of his travel belt and handed it to her.

"Thanks," she replied, slinging it around her shoulders. The wool was surprisingly soft, woven into a complex pattern of greens and browns with a strand of red snaking through it all. Wearing it in the woods, he'd be nearly invisible.

"After I left you in Shottam, I tracked the raiders' trail. It led to Thornmar."

She gasped, thrilled that he'd found the connection, but Finn held up a cautionary hand.

"I never saw him with the raiders, but they both popped up in the same places far too often for chance," Finn said, his face worried. A flash of anger shot lightning-like through his gaze. "He's up to something. He's had a number of clandestine meetings under the cloak of night. And wherever he goes the rumors explode that the Paika are behind the attacks."

And that wasn't all.

The rumors rippling out in Thornmar's wake blamed the Peace Force for the unrest. He was hissing his poisonous opinions in the ears of commanders and merchants, telling them the scheme was a trap. He called the Peace Force ineffective weaklings, fools, no good meddlers. Finn ticked the disparaging remarks he'd heard off on his fingers as he recited them. Some people listened to Thornmar, believing the Lord of the Orelands when he claimed that Ari Ara and her friends were worse than useless, they were a plot to distract the soldiers. A growing number of people grumbled that all this peace nonsense was making the two nations soft and vulnerable to attack.

"*That* is a line straight out of Thornmar's book," Ari Ara muttered. She'd heard him say those exact words to her face, once. "He's trying to undermine our efforts!"

"There's some good news, though," Finn reported. "A lot of

people aren't buying it. From here to the Haystacks, many of the villagers are singing your praises. The Peace Force has done a lot of good this summer and folks are quick to point it out. Not everyone thinks you're a bunch of naïve fools."

"But that's what you think of us," Ari Ara pointed out, rolling her eyes.

Finn made a face.

"Maybe, but at least I'm willing to be proved wrong. I'm not sabotaging your pointless efforts."

She grinned. He was coming around.

"Besides, the Paika got dragged into this, so now it's Paika business," he sighed, tugging his dark hair in frustration.

"If only we could find out who those raiders really are. We've tried and tried, but gotten nowhere," Ari Ara groaned.

"Don't blame yourself," Finn reassured her. "The Paika clans haven't found out either, and we usually know every twig that breaks, every horse that tosses a shoe, and every archer posted on the heights from north to south and east to west. They're skillful at concealing their identities, this lot."

"Do you think Thornmar hired them?" Ari Ara asked, voicing the concern she and Minli had been mulling on for weeks. "Or is he just turning the situation to his ends?"

Finn chewed his lower lip thoughtfully.

"Could be either. This sort of thing happens all the time. Marianans and Harraken use the Paika to foment war, either by hire or by proxy like this. It's convenient to them to make us the villains of their tales." His voice turned bitter and mocking. "They say: *we've got to invade and deal with those troublesome Pikers.* Then one army occupies the territory until the other army objects and comes to kick them out. And on and on it goes."

"You think it's happening again?" she wondered, eyes wide.

To her surprise, he shook his head and kicked a pebble

across the rough cave floor. He didn't think this was the same, not exactly. The Peace Force was the real target. The fear of war was a side effect. Thornmar wanted them discredited, ridiculed, and gone from the Border Mountains. After all, the Orelands made their fortunes on war, forging armor and weapons. Peace was bad for business.

"Can you keep watch on him?" Ari Ara requested.

Finn shook his head.

"I've got Paika business to attend to," he replied, "which brings me to this."

He pulled a sealed scroll from his travel sack and handed it to her. It was from the headwoman of Serrat, a fair-sized town nestled in the bowl of an extinct volcano to the east. The festivals of Serrat were notorious for wild celebrations . . . and even crazier fights. At this year's Autumn Festival, Headwoman Kharis hoped the Peace Force could break that reputation and prevent some of the brawls.

"If even one life is spared," Ari Ara read aloud from the headwoman's message, "it would be something to celebrate. The residents of Serrat wish to show our guests that we will not let this continue any longer."

Two years ago, the village had asked the warriors of Garrison Town for aid. The soldiers simply busted skulls and left several dead. Last year, the commander refused to get involved. Mendren had told Kharis that breaking up drunken brawls was hardly a matter of national security. They would, of course, investigate and punish any murderers. The culprits, however, just slipped off into the mountains or hid out in Thieves Den. Headwoman Kharis was at her wit's end.

Ari Ara beamed at the invitation. This was precisely what the Peace Force needed to counter the rumors Thornmar was trying to unleash.

"But I don't get it," Ari Ara said, looking at Finn in confusion. "Why are you delivering this?"

"Headwoman Kharis hired the Paika when her messenger hawks kept getting intercepted and lost. We've worked with her for years. And, I volunteered," Finn replied, a slow blush of a smile spreading over his face, "because it gave me an excuse to see you."

Ari Ara gaped at him, momentarily robbed of words, unable to think of a response.

"I've got to get back. The others will be wondering where I am," she stammered at last. "Come talk to Shulen and tell him - "

Finn shook his head. He didn't trust Shulen the Butcher and Shulen didn't trust the Paika.

"Just keep your eyes open and come to Serrat to counter those rumors that the Peace Force is pathetic. No one'll dare say it to your face, so you've got to be one step ahead of them."

She nodded and pulled off his cloak, handing it back as they circled around to the falls. Just as she was about to slip behind the curtain, his hand shot out.

"Thank you for being a friend of the Paika," he said, mouth close to her ear so she could hear him over the roar.

Her heart fluttered at his closeness. Not quite daring to kiss him, she pulled back and clasped his hand.

"Always and forever," she promised.

With a wink and a grin, he slipped off into the caves.

Ari Ara climbed down the embankment, scroll clenched gingerly in her teeth, already dreading Shulen's inevitable outburst when she told him Finn was the messenger. To her surprise, the stoic old warrior did not erupt at her over the encounter. He merely gave her a long, disappointed look - which was infinitely worse - like he expected her to know better by now. And he didn't need to say anything because Mahteni scolded enough for the both of them.

"What were you thinking, going into that cave?" Mahteni gasped, angry in her alarm.

"I was thinking that *someone* in the Peace Force needs to make friends with the Paika!" Ari Ara said through gritted teeth.

"He could have kidnapped you, or shoved you off the cliff, or ancestors know what! You need to be more careful, Ari Ara," she scolded. "I promised your father we'd keep you safe this summer. It could have been a trap."

"It wasn't," Ari Ara reminded her. "It was a message. He was trying to help."

It was a frustrating conversation all around. At least they agreed to bring the Peace Force to Serrat for the Autumn Festival. Even if they distrusted the messenger, the message was genuine; Solange recognized the headwoman's seal. As for Finn's warning about Thornmar, Shulen and Mahteni considered it thoughtfully, but not everyone in the Peace Force did.

"It sounds like a ploy to shift the blame off the Paika and onto a Marianan noble," Marek argued, loyal to his fellow noblemen. "Pikers - Paika - always have some trick up their sleeve."

"Yeah, with them, the truth is always three lies deep," Sarai added, shaking her head soberly. "Our old songs are full of examples. The Trickster loves the Paika."

"You'll see," Marek muttered darkly. "Time will tell what games the Paika are playing."

And they didn't have to wait long.

CHAPTER SEVENTEEN

. . . . .

The Autumn Festival

Serrat nestled like an egg in the cavernous bowl of an old volcano. Two roads led in and out. One headed south toward the Garrison Road following a pass blown open by an ancient spill of molten lava. The other road entered from the west through a tunnel. A craggy rim cut the wind's bluster and funneled rainwater into terraced gardens and underground cisterns. A hidden balustrade ran its length, carved between boulders, serving as a defensive perimeter in times of war.

Tonight, celebration fires would encircle those ramparts. At sunset, horns would blare and bonfires would be lit, one after another, in a dazzling ritual that stretched back to the town's founding. A thousand people made their homes in the multistory buildings crammed into the town center. In addition, people trekked across the Fire Peaks Region to attend the festival, coming from as far south as the East-West Road. In these last hours before dusk, the town bustled with final preparations. Ale brewers and bakers hawked their wares. Musicians tuned their instruments. Women fussed over head wreathes of colorful autumn leaves. Children chased each other through the alleys.

The entire town burst with boisterous excitement, tingling with anticipation for the celebration's start.

In the days before the Autumn Festival, the scattered members of the Peace Force had reunited. Leaving their postings, they traveled the distances from Hock, Knobble, the Haystacks, Gollun Town, Shottam, and beyond. They bore tales of their efforts over the past weeks and months. Those who had stayed with Nell had settled several clan feuds. The Knobble pair reported about the weekly gatherings that brought people to the temple to study the Way Between. The husband and husband couple in Hock had turned children into messengers of peace, learning Alaren's tales in school and then telling them at home in the evenings. The Shottam team and a few miners had begun crafting plans to use the Way Between to reduce price gouging in the mining town's stores by boycotting the worst offenders. Those who had stayed in the logging camps on the Harraken side of the border had intervened in the violent fights common to the woodcutter crews. Like rain stopping sparks from catching fire, each team broke the cycle of escalating violence. With the two nations growling about the raiders, they had played a small, but critical role in preventing the smoldering conflicts from igniting into war.

In preparation for the festival, Shulen drilled them all hard. Mahteni put them through endless role-plays of the situations they might encounter. They worked through ways to pull back brewing fights from the brink of violence. They reviewed how to spot trouble on the horizon and diffuse it. They practiced remaining inwardly alert and outwardly calm. Shulen instructed them in basic healing skills in case anyone did get injured, showing them how to halt a bleeding knife wound, how to put a temporary splint on a broken bone, and how to help someone breathe again if necessary. The goal was to de-escalate tensions before fights started, but if injuries occurred, it was better to be prepared than unable to respond in crisis.

"No drinking, no dancing, no flirting," Shulen intoned. "You are on duty."

His stern glare swept the faces of the youth. They squirmed, remembering the High Summer bonfires. Privately, he was glad their duties would help avoid a repeat of that fiasco. He assigned Emir to be Korin's partner, knowing the black-haired youth would also assume guard duty over the Great Lady's son.

"You're with me," he informed Ari Ara. "Stop grimacing. You know all the reasons why, so don't argue or I'll make you stay behind."

She grumbled but acquiesced. Better to go with Shulen than not at all.

"Be humble, act with honor," Mahteni urged them. "Remember, you are not the Guard, the Watch, or the army. You're not here to stop lads from stealing sips of ale or to arrest people for trading without a permit. Nor are you here to serve as judges. You're just here to stop violence. Back people away from blows and let them sort it out. The headwoman already has her elders prepared to handle the disagreements according to local customs."

These traditions had ancient roots in Alaren's practices, fortunately. Unlike the laws in Garrison Town, the punishments weren't hanging or life imprisonment, but justice circles and making amends. This was another reason the town was keen to work with the Peace Force. If the garrison patrolled the festival, they'd knock heads to "keep peace", causing as many problems as they claimed to solve.

Just before the feast began, the Peace Force assembled for one last inspection. Shulen had been pestering them all day, ensuring tunics were scrubbed to gleaming white, boots were polished, scuff-kneed trousers were at least patched if not swapped out, and hair was trimmed, washed, and combed. He was driving everyone crazy, but in his eyes, the Peace Force needed to put its best foot forward tonight. People from up and down the Border Mountains planned to attend the Autumn Festival. They would carry the stories of the Peace Force back with them to family and neighbors. Not only would the Peace Force members be working to prevent violence and de-escalate brewing conflicts, they'd also be acting as ambassadors for the Way Between.

"Conduct yourselves accordingly," Shulen instructed them sternly. "Be merry, yes, don't hold yourself too aloof, but keep a clear head and a watchful eye. Your actions tonight could set in motion a decade of peace or a decade of war . . . which do you want?"

"Peace!" was the resounding reply.

At dusk, the setting sun poured through a gap in the western peaks, carving a corridor of gold in the gathering shadows. A low, mournful horn sounded. The reverberating tone echoed against the slopes. A second horn moaned out, the bellowing sound overlaying the fading notes of the first. The eerie and haunting music seemed to have emerged from the mountains themselves. The cheerful chatter fell silent. A nervous twitch tingled in the evening air. Heads turned toward the arched tunnel gate to the west. A murmur of surprise rose up.

Ari Ara stood next to Headwoman Kharis, both shading the sunset's gleam from their eyes, squinting into the tunnel gate. Kharis' children had grown by the time she stepped into her leadership duties. Streaks of grey laced through her dark brown hair. Wrinkles fanned out from her eyes and mouth, hinting at more hours spent laughing than scowling. Thoughtful and decisive, she was held in high regard by the bustling town. A soft gasp of surprise loosed from Kharis' throat as she recognized the new arrivals.

"Who is it?" Ari Ara murmured to the headwoman.

"Paika," Kharis answered. "They're announcing themselves with the Curling Goat Horn."

She pointed into the light. A figure backlit by sun pivoted, blowing another low, bone-aching blast through a spiral instrument made from the curved horn of a mountain goat. Ari Ara squinted at the herald's mount . . . that wasn't a horse! The creature's barrel chest boasted a shaggy mane. A hairy beard clung to its chin. Ari Ara gaped at the massive mountain goat, shocked by its size. As the herald blew the horn again, the beast lifted its head and bellowed back.

A thunder of voices -humans, beasts, horns - roared. The company of new arrivals stepped into the golden light like legends come to life. Ari Ara shaded her eyes, blinking and squinting, mouth hanging open in astonishment. The man in the center rode a tall, antlered creature – a bull elk. The rider wore a crown of antlers, too, the points silhouetted in the light. A figure on a shaggy mountain pony flanked the elk on one side. On the other, a woman sat regally on another curly horned goat. As they strode forward, the rest of their company came into sight, each more astounding than the last.

Embroidered hats and helmets, extraordinary as Finn's fox cap, transformed them into the mythic creatures of the Border Mountain legends: the Wolfwoman, the Bear Brothers, the Serpent Sage. Ari Ara had learned the tales from village grannies all over the region. Now, the stories rose to life, riding proudly into the wide-eyed crowds at the festival. The Paika's heads were crowned in eagle-winged caps. They bore shields styled in tortoise-shell carvings. They wore robes sewn in the patterns of feathers, scales, and rippling fur. Cloaks bore designs of shoals of fish, flocks of birds, and herds of deer. Tunics shimmered with images of falling leaves, spiraling waterways, and swaying grass. The patterns danced in the light, tricking the eye. Ari Ara suddenly realized what a pale imitation the raiders had made. Their lone hats or wolf cloaks were nothing at all like real Paika garb. If the Peace Force had known more about the aloof mountain folk, they would have seen the difference immediately.

The lead rider drew even with the headwoman. He was a large man, muscled and weighty. A bristly beard covered his chin. A cloak of patterned silver and ochre rippled like the elk's hide. Bands of copper curled around his wrists, embossed with blackened spirals. Atop the elk, his antlered helmet towered as tall as the beast's. He loomed over everyone. Ari Ara scarcely dared to blink, half-convinced she was dreaming.

"Greetings," he said in a voice that rumbled like the horns. "Have no fear. We come peacefully. In my father's time, it was tradition to invite the Paika to the Autumn Festival."

"In that tradition, I welcome you," the headwoman replied formally, carefully.

She gestured for the Paika to make themselves at ease. The riders dismounted, stroking furry flanks and bristly noses as they tethered their beasts to fence posts. One man stood watch over them, scowling so fiercely that even the most precocious children huddled in a cluster, whispering, not quite daring to approach. The leader waited as his band settled, then swung his leg over the antlered elk's back. Ducking under the white bristles of the creature's muzzle, he paused to scrutinize Ari Ara.

As he did, the great head of the elk swung slowly around, nostrils quivering. He stretched his neck out and delicately sniffed at the girl. Ari Ara held very still. A small smile bloomed on her face. The elk's warm breath blew across her skin. Ari Ara could see her reflection in the black mirror of the beast's eye. The rider studied the animal's expression then pivoted back to the girl.

His eyes flicked, dark as the elk's, from her red curls to her not-quite-desert-dark skin. She could not read his thoughts, only his quiet scrutiny. He'd heard of her, no doubt, but had Finn told him anything more than the common tales about the Lost Heir?

"I am Ari Ara Shirar," she told the man, courteously.

She extended her hand, palm sideways like Finn had shown her.

"I am Grindle Spireson."

He reached out and clasped her hand. His bare fingers curled around hers, roughened with hard work.

"What are you after in these mountains, Ari Ara Shirar?" he asked with a warning rumble of disapproval. "Building an army to take back your mother's throne?"

"Ancestors, no!" Ari Ara exclaimed fervently, appalled at the notion.

He quirked a bushy eyebrow at her and she belatedly remembered how many aspiring kings and queens of the Marin lineage had mustered armies in this region over the centuries.

"We are reviving Alaren's Peace Force," she stated firmly. "That is all."

She paused for a beat, then added another point.

"And, we're trying to clear the Paika's name. It's not you doing those raids, is it?"

He shook his head and levelled a look at her, his expression speaking volumes. Gratitude mixed with wariness. A wisp of hope crossed paths with the worn ruts of cynicism in his lined face. His gaze fell on the insignia of the Mark of Peace on her white tunic.

"That emblem has not been seen in these mountains for a

very long time," he murmured.

"Alaren came to me in a dream and told me to bring Azar back into the world," Ari Ara said truthfully, openly.

"Alaren himself, eh?" the leader replied. "How much do you know of the old scoundrel?"

"Not nearly as much as I'd like," Ari Ara confessed with rueful honesty.

To her surprise, the big man roared with laughter. The booming outburst startled the ale master into dropping a mug with a clatter. As if loosened from a spell, chatter rose around the town center. A few called out tentative greetings. Others whispered and murmured. Ari Ara saw Shulen nudge the others out of their gape-mouthed stares and into their duties.

"We'd all like to know more about Alaren, wouldn't we?" Grindle Spireson chortled.

Ari Ara couldn't figure out what was so funny about that. She asked him. He clapped her shoulder with a firm grip and steered her toward a table, hollering over his shoulder.

"Finn Paikason! See to the elk."

Ari Ara's head spun round. Finn waved. Shulen eyed him stonily. The wiry lad dug into the pocket of his vest and held out a ball of herbs. The elk's velvety lips trembled toward it and followed Finn. Ari Ara cast a glance after him, dying to talk to him. Shulen gave her a pointed look, and reluctantly, she resumed her discussion with Grindle. The burly bear of a man settled at one of the rugged outdoor tables. The headwoman gestured to the townspeople working the feast and ale barrels. They leapt forward. Soon the table was laden with bread and drink, roasted vegetables and fresh greens, spice cakes and puddings.

"We've been taking bets on when you'd come begging to hear our Alaren tales," Grindle told Ari Ara, thumping the wooden table with his fist for emphasis.

"You have stories about Alaren?" Ari Ara blurted out, eagerly. "We'd love to hear them."

That was an understatement. Minli wouldn't sleep until he memorized the new stories. Professor Solange would be beside herself with excitement.

"You think it's like that, eh?" Grindle said archly, shaggy eyebrows rising to his hairline. "Now that you want them, you expect us to spill our hearts out to you?"

He snorted into his ale mug.

"If it helps bring peace, isn't it worth it?" Ari Ara countered.

"Peace is a dream, girl," he growled. "For two thousand years, your people - east and west - have been coming to the Paika promising peace. You ask us to be your guides, trackers, mercenaries, and spies, but we never seem to get much peace out of this. We get occupation, double taxes, famine, persecution, and execution. Lies and malicious rumors about our people spread far and wide."

He shook his head, his crown of antlers swaying.

"No, Ari Ara Shirar, you don't get to ask us questions. You get to make peace the hard way. You *prove* yourself. Then you can ask something of the Paika."

He rose to standing and - as if showing her how little she mattered - hollered out a greeting and strode across the town center. She sat alone, ears burning with embarrassment and sparks of anger.

Shulen, who hadn't said a single word during the exchange, watched Grindle Spireson carefully.

"Come on," he murmured to Ari Ara, "let's tell the others to stick close to the Paika. With so many people angry about the raids, I'd wager there'll be trouble before the night's out."

The sun plunged below the horizon. Darkness cloaked the

town. The autumn horns blew, low and sonorous, around and around the rim of the caldera, one sound chasing the next, the echoes catching up in a dizzying and dazzling whirl of bellows. The beasts lifted their throats and answered. The town dogs howled. The people roared. The first light blazed upon the caldera's edge. The next flared up on its heels. The fires illuminated the rim until it sparked on every horizon, beautiful against the night.

As the horns subsided, the festivities commenced in earnest. Great barrels of ale and wine poured out. Mugs and glasses were raised in toasts to the harvest, health, and happiness of all. Each person made their way to a strange little carving of a furry beast standing on its hind legs and splashed a drop of spirits on it for protection. Ari Ara learned that the creature kept out the winter demons who could swoop down on frigid nights and steal souls from bodies.

The Peace Force had their hands full with the boisterous crowd. Over two thousand people had gathered, all tangled up in old grudges and ancient feuds. Minli and Emir leapt between two youths throwing punches over insults to each other's mothers, turning aside their blows with the Way Between and convincing the pair to leave each other alone. Mahteni and the dressier stopped a rising squabble among a cluster of women with swift questions about the pattern of the weave in their lovely dresses. Isa stopped an argument by asking one of the quarrelers to dance and promising the next waltz to the other. Korin cut off a fistfight by balancing an apple on his head and trying to do a jig, baffling and distracting the brawlers until they forgot their dispute. Each of the Peace Force members played a role in thwarting the numerous conflicts that could have escalated into violence.

Having the Peace Force in Serrat served the Paika's interest, too. They had come to clear their names, set rumors straight, and remind the townspeople that there was more to the Paika than cruel tales. It was a bold move at repairing the frayed bonds between them and the Border Mountains villagers ... and without the Peace Force's aid, it would have led to more problems.

Ari Ara had never been so proud of her friends. She knew many of them carried personal grudges against the Paika, but they set those aside for the night. Over and over, they diffused rising tempers and prevented quarrels from coming to blows. Sarai reminded a belligerent set of men that no one knew who the raiders really were. Solange redirected a squabble between a Paika woman and the Serrat healer by asking about herbal cough remedies. Shulen called upon a handful of Peace Force members to move two groups apart as grievances boiled toward blood feuds.

Ari Ara only used physical Azar once, when a cartwright with a grudge pulled a knife behind Grindle's back. Ari Ara caught his arm and pulled the stabbing motion askew, pivoting on her feet to turn the man to the side. As he stumbled with the unexpected intervention, other Peace Force members pulled Grindle away, preventing his reflexive counterattack. Headwoman Kharis took the cartwright and Grindle to a justice circle to find out what had prompted the attack, and the festival continued, unmarred by a stabbing. If the Paika stood a chance at regaining local respect, it was because the Peace Force was hard at work, preventing fistfights, brawls, and duels.

Amidst it all, Ari Ara enjoyed the evening. She praised the cooks for their sweet rolls and harvest soup. She sat with a circle of grandmothers who had once met her mother, Queen Alinore. She sang along when Tala and the Harraken answered the request for desert songs.

Toward midnight, the band in the town center struck up a thrilling tune with leaping chords. The music ran across the open space and threw its arms around Ari Ara's heart like an old friend. A pair of fiddles swooped and dove like birds in the wind. A set of hand drummers pattered out interweaving rhythms. A horn player burst forth in a cascading tumble of notes. Couples clasped hands and formed pairs in whirling rows.

"Dare to dance, Ari Ara of the High Mountains?" a mischievous voice challenged her.

Finn extended a hand, chin tilted up proudly and a half-smile teasing his lips. Ari Ara grinned at his words. Not *care* to dance, but *dare* to. She cast a glance behind him. The Paika riders guffawed over their ale and struggled to hide their chortles at Finn's bold request of the Lost Heir. She swept a measuring glance up and down him. Finn dressed as finely as the rest of his kin. A scarlet tunic shone with gold threads in a pattern that matched his fox-cap. His trousers lengthened the stretch of his already-long legs. Copper bands adorned his wrists. Ari Ara could have admired him all night, but his toe tapped impatiently in a polished boot, waiting for her answer.

"Hope you can keep up," she told him.

Finn offered his hand with a flourish.

"It's not me who should be worried," he warned her with a twinkle in his storm-tossed eyes.

Then the music struck up and she had to save her breath for dancing. Finn was a fine partner, bold and unabashed, moving through the steps and swings with the confidence of one who'd learned to dance at his mother's knee. He hit the turns with assurance and tapped out the kick-stomp on the chorus with an easy nonchalance. Each time his arm threaded around her waist, Ari Ara felt like a flock of butterflies swirled inside her. When her hand met his above their heads, she never wanted to let go.

In the tightness of the spins, his face neared hers and everything beyond his lips, eyes, and his woodsmoke scent blurred in a whirl of light and motion. Old legends echoed in her thoughts, reminding her that before the Way Between was a tool for peace, it was a dance between something and nothing, this and that, the known and unknown. Ari Ara finally understood how Alaren and his beloved Fanten wife had danced the Way Between for hours beneath the stars.

As the last strains of the song faded, Ari Ara and Finn stood grinning at each other like fools. He looked on the verge of speaking, but the music picked up again. His eyes clouded and he spun to face the stage. The fiddlers had been joined by another instrument, lower, deeper. A Paika musician had taken the stage, strumming chords countered by twanging rhythms beat upon the strings and wooden body of her instrument. The fiddlers pivoted on their heels and nodded to the Paika player, recognizing the tune and joining in. Off they soared, the music a wild chase, a pounding haunt, replete with eerie bellows of horn and the bays of hounds loosed from the sidelines by Paika whooping at each chorus.

Ari Ara had never heard anything so terrifyingly wondrous. Her heart hammered in her chest. Strange longings flooded through her, memories of running the black peaks, wind tangled in her hair, no one and nothing stopping her from dangerous leaps across ravine and gap, only her inner certainty in the length of her limbs and the strength of her body. She wanted to howl with the thrill of it, the sense of unfettered freedom, of fleeting light and the cold catch of autumn air burning in her lungs. The feeling of urgency quickened her blood, as if the days of fast-falling darkness urged her to live - live now! - before snow flew and coldness gripped the land.

Suddenly, the steps of the dance could not contain all the

longing and living that burned in her. She leapt and whirled, arms flung wide, back arched over air, hair flying in her face and blazing like a torch. A space opened around her as she let the music carry her motions faster, wilder, beyond the patterns of the Paika dance into the wide-open terrain of the Fanten Dances that followed no rules except the demands of the heart.

Howls roared in approval of her unexpected improvisation. Horns sounded, reverberating in her bones. The music kicked up its heels and quickened its pace. The musicians shifted into the next tune, a crazed melody, whipping and driving. They played in a mad frenzy, gripped by the spell of the song. Ari Ara rode the sound, reeling, laughing, leaping -

- then Shulen caught her midair and hauled her out of the dance. She fought him, furious at his interruption, spitting protests in his face, but he pulled her back to the benches, to the edge of the light, and held her shoulders steady as she railed.

"Listen to me. Listen."

His voice sounded a hundred miles away. She blinked, slowly focusing on his serious expression. His tone worried her. Her chest heaved, breathless. The heat of the dance chilled in the cold touch of wind.

"Listen to me. Come back."

He snapped his fingers in front of her lost gaze. He patted her cheek, firmly, with the flat of his hand.

"Why did you stop me? Let me go!" she tried to wrench free, to return to the music that tugged at her beating heart, to grasp the swiftly-fading euphoria that had filled her.

"It's not for you, this dance," Shulen was saying, his voice scared and commanding at once. "The musicians shifted to a new tune and the end of that dance . . . it's not for you. It's not your ritual, not your culture."

"Wha - what?" she stammered, a fog of music and motion

suddenly clearing, leaving her shivering.

"There is an end to this dance," Shulen told her, pivoting her to watch, but keeping his grip on her arm, "a Paika tradition, a Wild Hunt."

The townspeople had backed away, leaving the floor to stand soberly on the sidelines. The Paika danced in a frenzy, eyes wild and far away. Even Finn looked possessed, his limbs blurring with the speed of motion. Suddenly, the music halted. A tense, held breath of silence hung in the air. Eerily, the Paika stilled, panting, and their heads turned as one, fixating upon a single man, a Border Mountain villager: Bergen of Gult.

Ari Ara gasped in startled recognition at the man who'd lost his cattle near the Haystacks. What was he doing here?

Bergen bared his teeth and lowered into a half-crouch. The strange instrument whined in a single, wailing note. A horn unleashed a lone moan. Bergen spun and sprinted out of the light, hurtling into the howling darkness. The Paika were after him in a flash, charging into the night.

A scatter of relieved laughter lifted from those who remained behind. The Paika musician bowed to the two fiddlers, then slipped away. The headwoman murmured a ritual prayer in a low tone.

"What . . . what just happened?" Ari Ara asked, shaken.

"The Wild Hunt is an old Paika tradition, a way of putting justice into the hands of the spirits," Shulen told her. "The music starts, builds, and when it ends, the Hunt begins. Bergen wronged the Paika by spreading those rumors and they will chase him long and hard. When the Paika drop off, one by one, exhausted, the ancestor spirits will decide the man's fate. Perhaps they will throw him into a ravine. Perhaps they will tell him how to atone. Perhaps they will condemn him to years in hiding, scared of Paika justice."

"Oh," Ari Ara said in a very small voice.

Shulen glanced down at her.

"You didn't know and they didn't mind. Many dance with them in the beginning. But I could see a Fanten trance coming over you. I did not care to chase you over the mountains when so many ancestor spirits also roam this night."

Ari Ara cast an uneasy glance toward the blazes on the night-cloaked rim. In her experience, strange things happened on autumn nights when the veil between the worlds thinned.

Be careful out there, she thought in a silent message to Finn.

CHAPTER EIGHTEEN

. . . . .

The Book of Secrets

Dawn broke in a haze of smoke. The Peace Force had done as they promised - not one person had died at the Autumn Festival - but in the dark hours before dawn, a messenger galloped into the caldera of Serrat, horse whinnying in alarm.

Tillun was aflame.

All who could came at once. The village of Tillun stood just west of the tunnel gate. Most of its residents had been in Serrat celebrating. Shocked, they scrambled to reach their homes, but the fire had devoured one building then the next. There was little anyone could do but watch.

Stunned villagers risked burns and injuries trying to save the remaining homes. Everyone pitched in to salvage what they could. The ruins smoldered acridly. The sky overhead hung hazy and dull. Coughing fits punctuated low, worried discussions. The Peace Force worked alongside everyone else, unloading supplies sent from Serrat, helping healers tend the injured, and aiding Tillun residents in relocating. The people of Serrat found lodgings for the displaced families. With the season grinding relentlessly toward winter, only a few structures could be rebuilt before the snow fell deep and thick.

Ari Ara and Minli had just started to round up straying chickens, when Shulen gripped them both by the shoulder and told them to come with him to speak to the headman. The rumors about the fire's cause had spread faster than the flames. People blamed the Paika – who had all vanished suspiciously after the Wild Hunt. The man they chased, Bergen of Gult, had kinfolk that lived in Tillun. People suspected the arson was part of the Paika's retaliation.

"Mind your temper," Shulen cautioned Ari Ara. The last thing anyone needed was one of her heated outbursts in defense of the Paika.

"There may be some truth to the rumors," the headman sighed wearily after accepting their condolences. "The few neighbors who did not go to Serrat say they saw men clad in animal skins riding strange beasts."

"But why would they do this?" Ari Ara cried.

"They're a tricky, backstabbing lot," the headman complained. "They promise on one breath and break their word on the next."

"I just can't believe it," Ari Ara sighed, looking around at the devastation.

"It is odd," the headman conceded, a perplexed look crossing on his face. "What grudge would they hold against us? None that I know of."

"They did chase that fellow," Shulen reminded him. "Bergen. He has family from the area. The Paika know he spread false tales about them stealing his cattle."

"Everyone spreads false tales," the headman snorted. "That doesn't warrant burning down an entire town."

"And the witnesses you mentioned," Minli asked thoughtfully, "are they certain they saw Paika riders?"

"Elder Mullie and Granny Ena reported seeing horns and antlers. Now, maybe their eyes aren't as good as they used to be, but they were never ones for telling tales. And, we've evidence."

The headman led them around the smoking ruins to where a trunk had been dragged out of the fire. On top of the closed lid, an antler with bloodied tips lay next to a bedraggled cap Ari Ara recognized at once.

Finn's fox cap.

Or one just like it, she amended, reluctant to leap to conclusions even though her heart sank. She picked it up and turned it in her hands. The headman wore a grim look. He shook his head and sighed.

"I must go. There's so much to be done," he excused himself, clasping hands with Shulen. "Any help you can offer is welcome."

He strode through the ashes. Shulen trudged over to the two elders to question them. Minli said nothing as he picked up the antler and studied the base. He set it back down and stalked carefully through the ruined buildings, looking at the edges of the churned-up paths. Ari Ara tucked the cap in her belt. Finn would want it back. She had no doubt that he'd find her, eventually. She followed Minli as he slowly retraced their steps up the road. Instead of returning to the chickens, however, he circled the entire perimeter of Tillun, studying the ground.

"What are you looking for?" Ari Ara asked him.

"What's not here," Minli answered cryptically. He gestured for her to join him, pointing at the northbound road. "Here's where they rode out after the attack. Use the Way Between. See what's missing?"

Ari Ara studied the imprints on the trail, a cacophony of hoof prints and splattered mud. She slipped into the Way Between, looking for the answers between what was obvious and known, seeking the negative spaces in the story they'd been told.

Suddenly, she gasped. She ran up the road, examining it carefully. She trotted back, eyes alight. Minli had seen it, too!

Witnesses had reported seeing strange creatures and an antler had been found, but in the mud, there were only horse hooves. No narrow goat or elk prints. The antler, Minli pointed out, had not broken off, but had been shed. It could have been picked up anywhere. The blood was fresher than the bone; someone had dipped those tips. As for the fox cap, perhaps Finn had dropped it or it had been stolen. They raced to tell Shulen about the tracks. The older man's lips drew into a thin line as he considered the implications.

"It's not evidence enough," he cautioned them, lifting a hand to stop Ari Ara's outburst, "not on its own. But it is intriguing."

"But what if Thornmar is behind these imposters," Ari Ara blurted out. "Shouldn't we find out if he's involved?"

"Silence your tongue unless it has truth to tell," Shulen chided her. "The last thing we need is more unfounded rumors."

"But we've got to do something," Ari Ara cried.

"I agree."

"You do?" she gaped at him in surprise.

"Yes. I'm going to send Korin back on his royal tour through the Stonelands, into the Smithlands and Orelands. If the nobles are muttering, he'll hear it."

"I doubt it," Ari Ara said. "The nobles won't talk of it. They hire lackeys to do their dirty work, like Varina did with that assassin."

"I remember. That's why I'm sending Everill Riverdon with him."

Ari Ara gasped. Now *that* was a good idea! The former Urchin Queen could walk in all circles. She was stealthy and clever. If there was a rumor to be found, Rill would smoke it out. If truth existed, she'd track it down.

Korin came to find her that evening. Even in the haze of dusk and ash, Ari Ara could see by the look on her cousin's face that Shulen had explained his task. They were both filthy, covered in soot. Ari Ara wiped the ashes off her nose and smeared it even worse. They'd have a hard time scrubbing the charcoal smudges out of the white cloth of their tunics.

Korin pulled her aside, passing her a waterskin as they climbed a slight rise. The forest, thankfully, had escaped the flames and flying embers. They sat on a rock overlooking Tillun, out of earshot of the temporary shelter where the Peace Force had set up camp to free lodging rooms in Serrat for displaced residents. They were used to camping on the road and the villagers would appreciate roofs over their heads tonight.

"Ari Ara, there's something you should know," Korin said quietly, his eyes haunted by the charred village in front of them. "This is straight out of the *Book of Secrets*."

"What is that? And why wouldn't you tell me earlier?" she asked with a touch of exasperation.

"It's forbidden," he replied. "As to *what* it is, it's something that should have burned to crisp instead of this town."

A half-choked sob caught in his throat.

"It's something I will burn, if I ever become king. I hope you destroy it if you gain the throne."

The House of Marin had a book - the only copy in the world - full of tactics and ploys for starting wars in ways that could be blamed on the Harraken or the Paika. It contained historic examples of how Marianan leaders had used the Paika to agitate fear and confusion. It gave tips on how to stir up the populace's hatred toward the enemy when war fervor waned.

"It's the opposite of Alaren's book of stories," Korin explained, his features shadowed as the forest. "There's a whole section on how our ancestors did precisely what's happening now. The fire, the raids, the rumors, all of it. It's been bothering me all summer. It was all familiar and I couldn't think why. Then I remembered."

He hurled a pebble at a boulder. It clattered against the hard stone and fell. The noise sounded loud. Driven off by the smoke, the birds had left the woods in eerie silence. Korin blamed himself for the fires. He should have seen this months ago. He could have stopped everything.

"The raiders, the attacks," he told Ari Ara, "they're part of a ploy in the *Book of Secrets*. It's even got a name: the Corroding Challenge."

The Corroding Challenge described how to use a mysterious, unsolvable problem to undermine the authority of a group or ruler by starting a blaze of skirmishes that couldn't be stopped . . . or a series of raids by fighters that couldn't be caught. Unable to deal with the threat, the ruler was seen as incompetent. Thus, a temperate general was replaced by a hothead. A peace-loving king was deposed by a warmonger. A voice of reason was tossed to the wayside by an agitator calling for violence. In this case, the Peace Force's reputation was being slowly crumbled each time the raiders attacked a village. It was all spelled out in the *Book of Secrets*.

"You think Thornmar's read it?" Ari Ara asked bitterly.

Korin buried his face in his hands and groaned.

"The House of Thorn wrote it for the House of Marin," he told her in a muffled voice. "The book doesn't name names, but the Thorns have always been high-ranking military commanders. If the kings or queens needed a war, they'd be the ones to start it. Openly or secretly."

"What about my mother?" Ari Ara asked suddenly. "Was the plan for her death in the *Book of Secrets*? Is there a plan for sending attackers after a pregnant queen, hoping she'll miscarry or die in childbirth?"

He lifted his head and shook it.

"No, there's nothing in there about Aunt Alinore," he told her hastily. "I checked, but it wouldn't be in our records, would it? Mum wasn't behind that attack. They were like sisters, very close. Mum's done her share of questionable things, but sending those mercenaries after Alinore wasn't one of them."

As twilight deepened and the villagers splashed into the cold stream to rinse off the ashes of their homes, Korin told her as much as he could remember from the *Book of Secrets*. She had to know what they were up against. Subterfuge, lies, misinformation, fear mongering, cloaked attacks, skirmishes, killing peacemakers: the book distilled the worst plots of a thousand years of history into an instruction manual for launching, fighting, and winning wars.

"It's a nasty business. I wouldn't tell you if you didn't need to know this stuff." He shuddered. "And if anything happens to me -"

" - don't even think it - "

" - I've arranged for a letter to be sent to Mum after my death, telling her I adopt you as my heir. If I have any unexpected falls off cliffs or strange illnesses, they weren't accidents. If they say I committed suicide, don't you believe it. I'm staying alive to marry Isa de Barre one day, trust me on it."

Ari Ara heard the anxiety behind his bravado. She squeezed his hand, suddenly wishing he didn't have to go to the Stonelands and Orelands to try to dig up the truth. She hadn't realized how dangerous his task truly was, how much courage it required, or how vulnerable he'd be as he searched for answers.

"Take Emir with you," she said impulsively.

"You need him here."

"No, I don't," Ari Ara replied firmly. "I've got Shulen and the

Peace Force. You need him. Not just for protection, but as a friend."

Korin said nothing for a long moment. Then he nodded. She was right. The tight knot in his chest eased slightly at the thought of having Emir Miresh at his side. Their mission was still perilous, but a good friend would make the situation less terrifying.

There was one more thing he had to ask of his cousin, a message she should deliver, one that would be believed coming from her.

"If anything happens - no, don't interrupt, this is important - tell Mum I love her. Truly. Despite all our scuffles."

He was serious enough that she didn't wisecrack.

"I promise," she vowed.

Ari Ara and Korin sat in the dark for a long time. Sometimes, they talked. Other times, they just leaned against each other's shoulders in silence. Her thoughts churned round and round, circling crowns and the weight of them, the burden of royal blood and the restless yearning to bolt like a skittish horse. With the specter of danger hanging over Korin's head and his declaration that he'd make her his heir, the future of the Marianan throne haunted them both. In their hearts, neither was even certain they wanted to rule. In their secret fears, neither felt worthy or ready.

Sometime later, as the stars crawled slowly overhead, Ari Ara fell asleep. She woke at dawn. Korin looked like he'd kept vigil all night. He was changed from the carefree boy he'd been. There was a glimmer of steel in his eyes. For one strange moment, he reminded Ari Ara of the Great Lady. Then he smiled a tired, lopsided smile and the impression vanished. Below, the Peace Force stirred.

CHAPTER NINETEEN

. . . . .

The Valley of Statues

Shulen decided to have the Peace Force escort Korin to the Stonelands. They could use this opportunity to introduce themselves to the House of Mara and counter the siege of loose rumors that surrounded them. Korin finagled a temporary pardon from the Great Lady to allow Shulen brief entry into Mariana. After all, Shulen's official exile was only supposed to last one year and he'd already served that time. Ari Ara was still banned. In her reply letter, Brinelle curtly informed her son that he could sooner convince pigs to dance than get the nobles to allow Ari Ara to set foot in the Stonelands. She could come as far as the Sentinel Gates and no closer. Korin decided not to push his luck. So far as his mother knew, he was writing *from* the Stonelands surrounded by his royal entourage, awaiting the arrival of the Peace Force.

Despite her exile, Ari Ara was looking forward to the journey. The stone carvers of the region were legendary. Even without entering the main city of the Stonelands, she would see many sculptures on the way. Minli had read all about them and told her they would pass over two thousand by the time they reached the Sentinel Gates. The Valley of Statues, he assured her, would amaze her.

It began on the woodland trail that led to the valley. A small stone dog sat loyally at the crossroads, marking the turn, a grey tongue lolling in his mouth, a perpetual grin curling on his face. Twisting and turning, Ari Ara spotted more sculptures winking out from the bases of trees or carved into the massive boulders that dotted the forest, covered with moss. A stone bear standing on its hind legs reared up among the shadowed trunks. A row of leaping salmon decorated the rocks of a tiny creek. Ari Ara tripped over a carved tortoise as she craned around to gawk at a pair of lovers arching for a kiss, tormented for an eternity frozen a mere hairsbreadth apart. A warrior statue taller than Shulen guarded the next turn of the path. Its head had been lopped off and now rolled on the pine needles of the forest floor, gathering lichens. Korin struck poses with the statues, sticking his head between the gaping jaws of a giant serpent, riding the back of a leaping sturgeon, smacking a kiss on the stone cheek of his great-great-great grandmother.

When they entered the valley proper, everyone gaped in wonder. Every inch of it was stone. Every inch of it was carved. Immense, they could see neither the length nor the breadth. Shulen did not rush them as they looked around. He did not let them wander, however, nor stray from the main path.

"The Valley of Statues could take you a lifetime to explore . . . even without entering the caverns that open into the mines," he told them.

A din of noise clattered up from the valley, the picks and chisels, hammers and mallets of hundreds of stone carvers. Generations of masons and sculptors trained in the Stonelands. Each student added their mark to the valley, first as an apprentice, then as a journeyman or woman, and lastly as a master. The path the Peace Force followed curled through the Masters Plinths - giant monuments carved by undisputed masters of the trade. Chiseling downwards from the first sculptures the stone workers acted as a human erosion, reshaping the entire landscape. They carted away hills of rubble. They moved boulders the size of houses. They funneled rainwater into pools, canals, and tunnels that drained into farmlands below.

Ari Ara and the Peace Force threaded through silent herds of galloping horses, frozen beasts, and giant curling dragons. They walked between statues of famous kings and queens. They passed by monuments commemorating famous battles. They paused to watch a sculptor chiseling away flakes of stone as a roaring lion slowly emerged. A pair of apprentices shyly showed their rough handiwork on a practice boulder full of countless years of uneven marks made by beginners.

They detoured up a spiraling staircase that curled around the outside of the most ancient Masters Plinth. At the top, in awe, they placed their hands in reverence on the first carving in the Valley of Statues. It had been made long ago by the original sculptress, Marinmara. From here, they stood level with the top edges of the valley, peering down at the labyrinthine paths between the thousands of statues. Ari Ara understood why Shulen would not let them wander. It was a forest of carved stone, larger than a city. Solange pointed out the Sentinel Gates to the east. Tall as mountains, they stood in eternal vigilance. Sentry posts were chiseled behind the eyes of the giant guardians, protecting the entryway into the Stonelands.

"Several battles have raged through these statues," Shulen told them somberly. "Armies retreated into the valley where the stones offered cover and the caverns could shelter thousands. But, on more than one occasion, the stone became their tombstones as the armies were trapped under siege. Some wandered deeper and deeper underground, never to be seen again. There is a legend that one army marches still, rumbling beneath the earth from time to time."

At the feet of the Sentinel Gates, Ari Ara said her farewells to Korin, Rill, and Emir. She wished them luck and safety in their efforts. Korin promised he'd be back before she could miss him.

"Stay in sight," Shulen commanded her, "and out of trouble."

Ari Ara stifled her sigh. Mahteni was staying with her. How much trouble could she get in?

The Peace Force passed between the bases of the Sentinels. At first, their footsteps crunched loudly in the sand and gravel. Then, as they vanished around the bend, the stone's immensity swallowed the sound. The mist descended. A sprinkling rain loosened in the sky. Groups of stone carvers passed by as they abandoned their work for the warmth awaiting them in the artists' halls and homes beyond the Sentinel Gates. The Valley of Statues quieted. Soon, Ari Ara and Mahteni seemed to be the only living creatures left in a realm of frozen statues. Ari Ara shivered and pulled her hood up over her hair. Mahteni cast about for a sheltering overhang and settled on a narrow ledge where a block of stone had been chiseled out. It broke the wind and slowed the damp.

After twenty minutes of waiting in the chilly rain, Ari Ara's boredom got the better of her patience. She wanted to look around, at least. She stood up and strode over to a statue of a sea serpent.

"Where are you going?" Mahteni asked.

"Just looking."

"You heard Shulen, stay in sight and out of trouble."

"Well then, you'd best come with me," she shot over her shoulder in a teasing tone. Her mischievous streak flared into action, along with her Fanten skills.

"Ari - "

Too late, her aunt cursed. The girl had slipped out of sight, letting loose a giggle to make her aunt give chase.

"Not funny, Ari Ara," Mahteni called.

No one answered in the gloom.

Mahteni heard the crunch of footsteps and rounded the corner of a large plinth.

No one.

Where had the blasted girl gone?

Ari Ara smothered her laughter behind her hand. She watched her aunt pivot one way, then the other, searching for her. She'd never find her. Ari Ara tossed a stone over Mahteni's head and silently guffawed as the woman stalked off in the opposite direction. Using Fanten skills, Ari Ara crept away. She'd be back before Mahteni knew it! Her aunt needed to learn how to have fun.

After three split forks in the paths, Ari Ara realized she'd better leave markers or she'd get lost. She scanned the ground. Among the flakes and chips of paler stone, were scattered black shards, carved from a seam of obsidian that ran through the broader strata of grey. Ari Ara filled her pockets with it and left a trail of three pieces whenever the path split. She wandered gleefully and peered at each statue with curiosity. The rain brought out their colors, turning the greys into surprising hues of sage or slate. The forks in the path led her deeper and deeper into side alleys. Here, the carvings were half-formed, buried in moss and fallen leaves. She brushed aside a cluster of ferns clinging to a stone ledge and found a merry band of revelers cavorting in the cliff face. She ducked under sweeps of hanging ivy and discovered statues of famous queens of Mariana. Grinning, she went to the end of the row and posed next to her grandmother, Elsinore. There was no carving of Alinore, though, and she dodged sadness by diving into a narrow passage to examine a statue of intricately entwined snakes.

The first flash of autumn lightning startled her. The gloom had deepened. Thunder rumbled overhead. The rain sharpened, occasionally spitting out sleet. She had just reached a branching path that ran along a cavern's edge when she heard her name.

"Ari Ara!"

She whirled.

"In here."

She spotted Finn gesturing from the mouth of the caves, looking nervously around. She darted over, ducking beneath the ivy-covered opening.

"What are you doing - "

She never finished the question. A hand clamped over her mouth. The scent of sharp herbs flooded her nostrils. The world spun topsy-turvy. Then everything went black.

CHAPTER TWENTY

. . . . .

Hostage

Stupid. Stupid. Stupid.

Ari Ara's head spun as she silently cursed. She squeezed her eyes against the whirling. The scent of bitter herbs burned in her nostrils. Her stomach heaved. She swallowed back bile.

How could she have been so stupid! She'd walked straight into a trap. Everyone had warned her that the Paika couldn't be trusted. She hadn't believed them. Now she'd been tricked – and by Finn, no less! Fury flooded through her veins. She cracked an eyelid open. She was laying bound and trussed in a candlelit cavern below ground. Her throat stung. Her eyes ached. Her ribs screamed as if someone had slung her over their shoulder like a sack of grain and jogged for hours.

Which might be true, she thought with a wince.

Her fingers and toes prickled with cut-off circulation. She forced herself to roll over - her body hollered in protest - and search for a way to break free. A nail, a sharp stone, anything?

She heard footsteps.

"She's waking."

She struggled to place the gravelly voice. She recognized its timbre and accent.

"Can't set her loose, she's slippery as a hare."

"Her hands are swollen. Those bonds'll drop her fingers off if we leave them."

Ari Ara licked her cracked lips.

"I want," her voice rasped, "water."

One nudged the other. They crouched down to hear her weak voice.

"Eh? Come again?"

"Water," she pleaded.

Her tongue felt thick as a sheep in winter wool. That rag scented with bitter herbs held a vile potency. She thought of Bergen's dogs and his claim that the Paika had drugged them. Could he have been right? If so, Finn had lied . . . and lied . . . and lied. She groaned and stopped thinking about it as the cavern spun and her guts heaved.

"You think she's alright? She looks green at the edges."

Finn. She'd know his light voice anywhere. How could he betray her like this! After she'd trusted him, trusted all the Paika! She'd stood up for them when no one else would! How dare Finn lure her into the cave so they could knock her out with those nasty smelling herbs! All the harsh warnings she'd heard echoed in her ringing ears: backstabbing Paika, betrayers, tricky, can't be trusted.

She heard heavier boots approach. A figure lowered to a crouch. This time, she identified his rough voice: Grindle Spireson. A vial flashed into sight. She winced and pulled away.

"It's the antidote," Grindle told her. "Hold still."

His calloused hand cupped her chin and forced her to inhale the vial's scents. The room stopped spinning. Her stomach ceased heaving. She could open her eyes without squinting painfully.

"Kidnapping me is a terrible idea," she told them bluntly. "Taking me hostage won't help anything. Untie me."

"I want your promise not to run."

She glared at him. He looked pointedly at her whitened, bloodless fingertips.

"Or, I could leave you bound until those fall off."

"Fine. I promise not to run."

"Or use the Way Between on me and my company."

She made a face. Then she nodded. She didn't have many options.

"Swear in Harraken," Grindle insisted.

Ari Ara sighed. A vow was binding in the desert language. If you went back on your word, the ancestor spirits would haunt you, plague your home, and curse you with bad luck.

"Fine," she agreed, choosing her words carefully. "I promise not to run away or use the Way Between on you or your men when you untie me."

Grindle nodded and drew his knife. With two sharp tugs, he sliced the ropes. Ari Ara gritted her teeth over the painful burning sensation of the blood rushing back into her extremities. She looked around - she hadn't promised *never* to run, just not right after they untied her. Growing up with the Fanten had taught her a thing or two about secret meanings and word play.

She swiftly realized, however, that she was in no shape to run anywhere. She had no idea where they were, no supplies, and she doubted she could stand up. Better to use this opportunity to find out why the crafty Paika had done such an idiotic thing. Kidnapping the Lost Heir was madness! They'd bring the wrath of two nations down on their heads.

"Who had the stupid idea to steal me? Was that you, Finn?"

She glared up at him. He stared back with a desperate look.

"We have no choice, Ari Ara. After the attack on Tillun,

people are threatening to attack our people and raid our homes. We're taking you hostage to prevent that."

"You're more likely to *cause* that!" she exploded. Between Shulen's fury, her father's protective outrage, and the Great Lady's swift military reprisal, the Paika had just dug themselves into deeper trouble than before.

"Ari Ara, come on," Finn begged.

"You *lured* me," she spat back. "I trusted you and you trapped me!"

"You can still trust me," he cried hastily. "We're not going to hurt you. We just need you to stay with us until things cool off."

"You . . . could . . . have . . . just . . . asked . . . me," she gritted out between clenched teeth. "I would have come to help you."

Finn shot Grindle a triumphant look.

"The lad said as much," Grindle admitted grudgingly, "but Shulen would never allow it."

"Don't underestimate him," Ari Ara replied. Shulen might go along with it just to advance peace.

Something hardened in the Paika's faces.

"We never do."

When she could feel her hands again, she clasped the proffered waterskin and chugged it down. The cool liquid calmed her racing heart and cleared her head. She shot a sour look at Finn. He squirmed uncomfortably. She felt slightly mollified. Drugging her hadn't been his idea, even if he had gone along with it. Maybe she could turn this disaster into an unexpected opportunity to work for peace. At the very least, she had questions she wanted answered.

"Did you set that fire?"

"No," Grindle answered shortly, "though there are plenty who think we did."

"I found this at Tillun," she said, pulling Finn's cap from her belt. She'd kept it close, never knowing when he might pop out from behind a tree.

Finn's face lit up beneath his tangled black hair. Then the light faded as he realized what she was implying.

"We had nothing to do with that fire," he stated, defensive. "I lost my cap during the Wild Hunt."

At her stony look, he spluttered.

"It's Paika justice, Ari Ara," he protested. "Bergen of Gult started those rumors about us when his cows were stolen. He knows more than he's saying about who took them. He didn't want to talk to us, so we gave chase."

"Did you catch him?"

Every Paika in the cave scowled.

"He disappeared."

Grindle's tone discouraged further questions.

Where is he now? Ari Ara wondered. She tried not to imagine him at the bottom of a ravine.

"Look," she insisted, "I don't mind staying with you, but you've got to tell Shulen and Mahteni."

She shuddered at the thought of how worried they'd be.

"They think you're lost in the Valley of Statues. Let them think that for now," Grindle declared with a shrug.

They did not stay long. As soon as she rubbed the color back into her feet, they filed out of the cave through a long tunnel. Ari Ara did not recognize any of the peaks. She rubbed her throbbing skull and wondered how far they'd traveled while she was unconscious. And where? They were headed toward the Paika's homes in the Spires, she presumed, but they could be anywhere. Paika routes were legendary in their secretiveness, following elk trails over backsides of mountains, cutting across roadless ravines, and skirting through hidden tunnels. She only knew that they headed south and west . . . and up, always up.

The party numbered eight, including Finn. The first night, they camped under the sheltering boughs of a pine forest then met up with their pack of beasts and the woman who tended them. Ari Ara eyed the huge, curly horned goats and massive elk nervously, but she was told to ride Finn's shaggy, sturdy pony with him. They climbed trails so steep her neck stiffened and her thighs ached from clinging to the pony's back. The Paika's mounts were bold, balking at little and finding footholds in bare rock. They were a breed apart from the desert's long-legged racers; they bore more resemblance to the wild goats perched on the sheer cliffs overhead.

The air thinned and snow began to fall. At these higher altitudes, autumn storms bit cold and hard. Rain in the valley became snow on these towering ridges. First, a few gentle flakes spiraled down as if bewildered. Then, the storm thickened into white swirls that lifted and plummeted, revealing invisible currents of air that poured like cataracts through the sky. Ari Ara watched the snowfall thicken uneasily. Soon, their tracks filled as swiftly as they passed. If not for the beasts, they could have floundered in the drifts and frozen in the night. The long-legged elk broke the trail. The shaggy goats tramped it down. The short-legged horses brought up the rear. The Paika's odd steeds weren't a mismatch after all, but carefully balanced to form a company of varied strengths and abilities.

Twice, they paused to let the goats pick a path across a sheer cliff. On the far side, the animals lowered light, wooden drawbridges when their riders whistled, stepping onto the bases and pushing with their weight. The bridges sprang back as they slipped off onto the opposite embankment, leaving the ravines impassable to all who followed. When they reached a network of well-packed trails, the elk fell to the rear, resting while the horses led the way.

At dusk, they halted. The company built a windbreak shelter out of snow and led the beasts behind it. Then the Paika set to work, piling the snow into another mound and packing it down. Ari Ara watched, mystified, then joined in, doing whatever Finn did. She hadn't a clue what they were up to, but the motion warmed her blood, beating back the chill that pinched her fingers and toes. When the mound stood as tall as a small shed, the Paika dug out the interior, forming a cave of snow.

The storm started to clear. The clouds parted and the sky opened above them, black and harsh. The temperature plummeted. Grindle Spireson eyed the glinting stars. Snowstorms held back the worst of the deadly cold, but a clear sky threw down the gauntlet of its icy eternity and challenged their mortality to a test of wills. Everyone except for a single lookout would sleep in the snow cave tonight, sharing warmth in the battle against freezing.

Several of the Paika worked together to build a fire and boil up a stew. From the scent, Ari Ara suspected they traded with the Harraken for the powdered beans and vegetables; Tala carried a pouch of this mix. Each Paika carried a small wooden bowl that also doubled as a drinking cup. Most of the men simply passed a flask of burning whiskey around, but Ari Ara had learned her lesson at High Summer. Finn boiled an herbal tea and offered her some in his bowl. It would keep her body temperature up while she slept, he said.

The tea made her drowsy and she curled up gratefully on the heap of sleeping rolls that covered the floor of the cold cave. She didn't even see Finn pulling more blankets over her, nor notice when the rest of the Paika crawled in like a family of bears, lending their heat to one another as the night shone hard and frigid beyond.

In her dreams, she soared, her dreambody flying through a light snowfall like a messenger hawk. Somewhere, Shulen was worried about her. This knowledge groaned in her bones like a toothache. In the dreamworld, she followed her sense of his worry like a signal tower gleaming in the night. She spun through the storm in a curious dance, moving back to move forward, her motions delicate as wind, light as tiny flakes. There was no earth or sky, just blackness and white snow. She dodged the snowflakes with the Way Between, slipping over, under, around, and through. It slowed her journey, but she sensed that if she touched one cold, crystalline flake, she'd wake. And she had to reach Shulen before she did.

Then she saw him. He spun slowly through the snow, searching for something . . . her.

"Shulen!" she cried.

His head whipped up. A snowflake hit her nose.

She woke.

"No!" she groaned.

A drop of snowmelt from the roof had hit her face. The Paika slumbered on in a chorus of snores and wheezes. Finn curled in a ball like a little fox, one mitten cupped over his nose to keep out the cold.

Ari Ara shut her eyes. She had been so close! Pulling the hood of her cloak over her face to prevent further drips from startling her, she slowed her breathing. If she could just drop back into the dream . . . .

She drifted. All was quiet. Silent. Motionless. Black. She'd slipped into a dreamworld that unfolded smooth as the surface of a still lake before dawn. When Ari Ara pivoted to look for Shulen, silver rippled from her feet. She stood on water-that-was-not-water. Directionless, she hesitated. A shimmer caught her eye, gliding and sliding like an ice skater. It was the Fanten

Grandmother. Ari Ara called out to her and suddenly - instantly - the old woman was inches from her nose, frowning as usual.

"How did you get here?" she grumbled.

"I used the Way Between."

"Huh. Of course, you did," the Fanten Grandmother said, snorting with sudden understanding. "Why?"

"I'm looking for Shulen," Ari Ara answered. "I have to tell him something."

"Can't it wait until morning?" the Fanten Grandmother questioned her sharply.

"He's not here. I mean, I'm not there. We're not in the same place."

The Fanten Grandmother studied her for a moment as if weighing all the options, none of which she liked. At last, she sighed.

"Tell me your message. I will deliver it."

Ari Ara scowled, skeptical. She didn't exactly trust the Fanten Grandmother. There was always a price for a favor . . . and often a trick in the bargain.

"What do you want in return?" she asked warily.

"You will keep our meeting a secret," Fanten Grandmother said. "No one can know that you dreamwalk, especially Shulen."

Ari Ara blinked. That was a small thing. Shrugging, she agreed. She had no idea why the Fanten Grandmother wanted her silence about dreaming. The old woman didn't elaborate.

"Tell Shulen that I am fine," Ari Ara said, "that I went to visit the Paika, and that I will return. He shouldn't worry or send anyone in search of me. I am safe and unharmed."

"Anything else?" the Fanten Grandmother replied with a yawn, stretching catlike.

"Just make sure he believes the message is true, not just a dream."

"Oh, he'll believe," the old woman answered with a glinting smile that made Ari Ara uneasy. "Now, run along."

The Fanten Grandmother gave her a nudge. Ari Ara toppled backward and fell through the black water-that-was-not-water. It parted like a pile of featherdown. Silver shimmered in the wake of her passage.

She woke to a beam of dawn light sparkling through the entrance of the snow cave.

CHAPTER TWENTY-ONE

. . . . .

The Spires

Up and up and up. Ari Ara's thighs screamed in protest. She pressed her lips together and made no sound. After three days' journey over hidden paths, far from the eyes of anyone, they had reached the Spires. The Paika's homes were heavily guarded, defensible perches chiseled into huge needles of stone. At the base, each Spire stood round as several buildings before narrowing to a single person's width at the top. The clan dwellings were carved into the stone two thirds of the way up. Rope bridges linked the eighteen Spires together.

They'd left the beasts in cozy, straw-covered stalls at the base of a perilous set of stairs built into the rock. Some of the near-vertical steps switch-backed up the cliff; others spiraled around the outside, hidden behind outcroppings and chimney ledges, tucked in dark fissures and concealed by walls that looked like eroding stone. If you didn't know where to find the next twisting step, you'd never make it up. Some stairs were little more than toeholds and ladder rungs hacked into the damp, slick rock. Ari Ara refused to look down. She kept her eyes pinned to Finn's feet in front of her. She placed her hands where he placed his hands. She put her boots where he put his boots.

When they reached the top, he tossed her a glance of unabashed admiration and offered her a hand up the last step. With his help, she clambered onto a narrow porch that encircled the Spire around the dwelling space. There were easier paths, Finn confessed in a whisper, even a lift lowered with ropes and pulleys. The Paika did not reveal those to newcomers, however. Taking them up the hard way deterred them from returning.

"I've seen grown men turn green with fright and refuse to climb," he told her. "You've a stomach like a goat."

She decided to take that as a compliment.

The door of his home bore a spiral carving like the one she'd traced at the waterfall. Ari Ara followed Finn inside. A crowded entryway, dark and windowless, opened between two doors. Here, they kicked off their damp boots and removed their outer clothes. Finn gestured for her to drop her cloak on the hook beside his, then opened the inner door.

A screech of delight startled her. A small body flung through the air. Finn caught a slight imp of a girl - his sister from the look of her - and whirled her around. Ari Ara ducked the girl's feet and snatched a felted slipper from the air as it flew off.

"Who's she?" the girl asked when Finn set her down.

She eyed Ari Ara with a suddenly wary stare. The girl's attitude was mirrored by the entire room. A tautness crept up Ari Ara's spine. They'd entered a common area - the Hearthroom, Finn told her - half-kitchen, half-gathering space, centered on a large fireplace carved into the stone. Drying herbs, pots and pans, and storage flasks hung from the rafters of the low ceiling. A pile of carpets formed a sitting area. A woman stood facing her, arms crossed over her ample chest, her acorn-shaped face hinting at kin relationship to Finn. A passel of children stood frozen like deer, wary at the sight of a stranger. Behind them, a pair of older grandaunts, twins straight down to their wrinkles, set their knitting down.

Finn pulled his kerchief from his neck and wrung it in his hands, looking uneasily from one woman to the next. Even Grindle looked nervous.

"Things being as they are," Grindle mumbled gruffly, "we thought she ought to stay with us awhile."

He avoided saying the word *hostage,* but everyone knew Ari Ara was security against attack.

A stony silence met his words. No one moved. Ari Ara was measuring the distance to the door when Finn's sister gripped her brother's arm and shrieked.

"You have a *girlfriend!*"

The room burst into sound. One of older children clapped a hand over the girl's mouth. Another hissed at her in an unintelligible mountain dialect. The grandaunts cackled merrily. Finn protested.

The tall, broad woman held up her hand and silenced them all. She towered over the rest of the clan. Her head ducked slightly at the rafters. Her mouth drew into a thin line below her narrowed eyes. Ari Ara caught the sharp look she shot at Finn and *knew* this was his mother.

"Truth?" she asked her son, jerking her chin at Ari Ara.

"Just a friend."

The woman put her hands on her wide hips, cleared her throat, and eyed him expectantly.

He sighed.

"Ari Ara Marin en Shirar, meet my mother, Tessa Paikalyn, granddaughter of *The Paika,* first mother of the Spires clans, head among women, healer and midwife."

He recited his mother's credentials over the exclamations of the others. Suddenly, Ari Ara found herself surrounded, poked

251

in the ribs, red hair fingered, her clothes lifted at the edges in observation. Only Tessa remained still and unmoved, glaring at her sister's husband, Grindle.

"And you brought her here? Why?"

The room fell silent at her chilly tone. The hand patting Ari Ara's head froze.

"These are uncertain times," Grindle began.

"And you thought stealing the Lost Heir would help? Did you miss the War of Retribution?" she retorted sternly. "We'll be attacked by all sides."

"I just thought - "

"No, you didn't think, fool," she hissed at him. "That's the problem."

"I wanted to come," Ari Ara blurted out. Every head in the room swiveled back to stare at her. She swallowed. "I've wanted to meet the Paika since spring. How can we build peace without you?"

The women around the room exchanged looks. They'd said the very same thing all summer. The Paika had to be part of the peace effort or it would fail. Round and around in circles, the clans had argued, some for making contact with the Peace Force, some against it. *The Paika* sent her great-grandson to spy on the trainings in Moscam, and, if possible, befriend the Lost Heir. Some, including Grindle Spireson, thought it a fool's errand. Better to kidnap the girl and hold her hostage for protection, he'd grumbled.

And now, Tessa thought sourly, *the idiot had done just that.*

She gestured for Ari Ara to continue.

"Yes, Grindle Spireson knocked me out with some nasty herbs," Ari Ara admitted with a groan of distaste. A few chuckles broke out. Tessa silenced them with a sharp glare. "But I agreed to come and will tell my friends that I am here willingly, for your protection and safety."

"Why?" Tessa asked, eyebrows furrowing.

"Why not?" Ari Ara answered with a shrug. "I've heard that if you come in friendship to the Paika, you are met with friendship."

She'd also heard that the Paika were backstabbing liars, but she didn't mention that.

"Please allow me the honor of being your guest," she requested formally. "At least until the Peace Force uncovers who is burning villages and pretending to be you."

Tessa shot Grindle a scowl of a glare. He matched it with a shaggy glower. No one else breathed or moved.

"Take her to *The Paika*," Tessa commanded her son. "If she decides to welcome the Lost Heir, I will too."

On the far end of the Hearthroom, Finn pulled back a richly woven curtain and ushered her in under his arm.

Ari Ara blinked as her vision adjusted to the darker room. The quarters were modest and well worn. A window at the back let in pale light. A fire crackled merrily in a corner hearth, fed by the finely-chopped wood stacked neatly beside it. On a ledge just beneath the ceiling, hundreds of stone and wooden figurines, small as chess pieces, formed a row of ancestor statues watching over them. Under the window was a sleeping platform with ornately-carved wooden drawers set into the frame. Finn tugged her forward.

"This is *The Paika*," he informed her. Finn spoke her title with the deference due to the head of all the Paika clans.

A wizened face with bright eyes turned toward them. The old woman's wrinkles rippled as she beamed at her great-grandson, reaching out a hand as gnarled as a weathered cliff-clinging pine. She patted his cheek and asked him about his recent journeys. The usually flippant Finn was strangely gentle, respectful of the elder. He stoked the fire in the hearth without being asked and tucked the loose ends of the blanket back in around his great-grandmother.

"This is Ari Ara Marin en Shirar," he murmured. "She's come from the Peace Force to meet you, and us."

He nudged Ari Ara forward. The old woman's gaze locked on the young girl. The color of an ancient, age-darkened pine forest, the elder's eyes studied her with the weight of history behind them. Ari Ara felt like she was drowning in time, the past rendered present through the wisdom crackling in the old woman. *The Paika* sat with the stillness of stone. If she carried the past, the girl contained the future. It coiled in Ari Ara's wiry frame, waiting to unravel. The blue-grey eyes in that smooth, young face would see the unfolding of profound changes in their world. With her bold, wide-legged stance and that defiant lift of her chin, Ari Ara would wrest a remarkable lifetime out of the unknown. She had the strength to reshape cultures and that rare, raw and wild spark that could catalyze immense upheaval, for better or for worse. *The Paika* saw all this as she took the measure of the girl. She weighed her spirit on the scales of time and wisdom. The balance tipped in Ari Ara's favor. *The Paika* gestured for her to speak.

"Greetings," Ari Ara said cautiously, sensing the power of the old woman. This was the leader, not just of Finn's family or the Spires clans, but of *all* the Paika from here to the frozen north and southward to the sea. She had to choose her words wisely, not just for her own good, but for everyone who sought peace. "I am grateful to meet you. I request the honor of welcome in your home."

She didn't mention the abduction attempt; nothing good would come of that.

"And what do you intend to do here, I wonder?" *The Paika*

murmured. She spoke more to herself than any other, but Ari Ara answered.

"Listen and learn. I understand that the Paika have many tales about Alaren. Perhaps I will be worthy of hearing them someday."

"It has been a long time since the Paika followed Alaren's Way Between," the old woman mused. "Too long."

Ari Ara's hope surged in her chest. She didn't dare speak.

"It will be good for us - and you - if you stay. And listen. And learn."

She paused and glancing at Finn, noticing his hopeful smile.

"I will let her stay on one condition," *The Paika* told him, lifting up a gnarled finger. "You, Finn Paikason, will join her Peace Force."

Finn groaned.

"I'm a warrior - "

"Not yet."

"I will be. Like my father."

"Your father was a tracker who happened to fight in a war," she informed him sharply. Her great-grandson spluttered in protest. She grinned toothlessly. "But he was also my favorite grandson-in-law, as you are my favorite great-grandson."

"You say that to all of us," he muttered.

"And it's always true," *The Paika* cackled, delighted with her own logic. She quieted. "Go to the Peace Force, Finn. You will become braver and better than any of your ancestors could ever dream of being. Not since Alaren's time have the Paika had an opportunity like this."

"Why can't someone else go?"

"Are you Finn Paikason or not?" she barked.

The fire popped at the same time. The two youths jumped, startled.

"I am *The Paika*," she reminded him. "I see things you do not. Perhaps, one day, your wrinkles will give you the right to sit here and argue with my ancestor spirit. Until then, you listen to me: work with this girl. She will make you into the legend you long to become - not the warrior you fantasize about, but a legend like few others."

Finn reluctantly nodded his assent. He'd do as the elder requested. A sharp glint appeared in his great-grandmother's eye. She'd hold him to the task with all the patience of someone old as stone.

The two youths returned to the Hearthroom. Relief broke like dawn light across the dark faces of the family when they heard their elder's decision. The air still buzzed with the remnants of their whispered arguments. The color returned to Grindle Spireson's worried face. Tessa Paikalyn shook her head, still convinced that holding the Lost Heir hostage was sheer folly, but she laid an extra plate at the table for their guest.

Ari Ara sent a messenger hawk - one of the Paika's, since Nightfast had not found her yet - to Shulen and Mahteni straightaway, reassuring them. She explained where she was and emphasized that she chose to stay at the Spires of her own accord. That night, as she drifted slowly into sleep, curled on a mat next to Finn's little sister, the Fanten Grandmother came to find her.

Thin-legged as a heron, eyes sharp as a hawk, the old woman stalked through the shallows of the dreamworld's black lake carrying a blue-green frog in one hand. Ari Ara didn't quite dare ask why. She was as irascible and inscrutable as always. Shulen, the Fanten Grandmother reported with a scoff, had been out of his mind with worry. The Peace Force had scoured the Valley of Statues looking for her. They searched under the guise of admiring the carvings; no one dared admit the Lost Heir was missing once again. When the Fanten Grandmother came dreamwalking, Shulen had been desperate for news.

The wily old woman had traded the knowledge of Ari Ara's whereabouts for a promise that Shulen would not do anything rash. Ari Ara was in no danger, she insisted to Shulen. He could go see for himself, if he cared. The Spires were a five-day journey from the Stonelands by the main road. He could try the Paika route, the Fanten Grandmother had informed him snidely, but she didn't recommend it. He'd get lost fast as a toad could hop.

"He wanted me to relay his lengthy instructions to you," she grumbled to Ari Ara, "but I told him I'm not a messenger hawk. Just stay out of trouble."

She had, however, promised Shulen that she'd keep an eye on Ari Ara.

"As if I didn't have more important things to dream about," she grumbled. "You're fine, girl. The Paika won't hurt you. They need you on their side."

The Fanten Grandmother was right. The Paika treated her with every courtesy, borrowing homespun clothes from a cousin close to her height and trying to feed her second helpings of every meal. But it was the way they included her in their daily tasks that made Ari Ara feel most welcome. Finn's mother tossed an apron at her and taught her how to knead bread. She rode the rope-and-pulley lift to tend the beasts with Finn. His great aunt showed her how to knit, patiently untangling her mistakes and correcting her grip on the wooden needles.

From time to time, Ari Ara caught glimpses of the Fanten Grandmother checking in on her. She could sense the silver-haired old woman watching her silently from the shadowy corners of her dreams. Occasionally, she'd question Ari Ara about what she'd learned that day. Once, the old woman even pulled Ari Ara's lips back to check her teeth like a horse - but upon waking, Ari Ara suspected that was a plain old dream, not Fanten dreaming. Maybe. That silvery, mocking laughter certainly rang true.

As the days stretched on, Shulen did not come to fetch her, but he did send Nightfast with a message. The black-winged hawk had returned from the southern desert, screeching with annoyance that Ari Ara wasn't where he expected to find her. Shulen dispatched him with instructions to head to the Spires.

Stay where you are, he wrote. *Mahteni will come to you when she can.*

He did not say when. Ari Ara gulped at the thought. Her aunt was undoubtedly mad at her for playing that trick on her in the rain at the Valley of Statues. She noticed that Shulen had not addressed the letter to her name, and further on, he urged her not to sign the return letter. Some of the hawks were being intercepted; messages were going astray. He did not want news of her whereabouts falling into the wrong hands.

He wrote that the Peace Force was splitting into smaller teams, scouring the countryside for information about the raiders, regrouping to compare notes, then dispersing for a few days. Tension twanged like a bowstring over the attack at Tillun. This close to winter, raids like that were devastating. The Paika patrols came to the Spires with more reports of attacked villages. Tempers boiled over. Each nation blamed the other, and everyone blamed the Paika. The Marianans demanded that the garrison take action. Commander Mendren sourly remarked that the Peace Force should be able to handle this. The Peace Force appealed to him to lift the ban so the Paika trackers could lend their skills to solving this mystery. Mendren refused.

Learn what you can from your hosts, Shulen wrote to Ari Ara, *for their knowledge is sorely needed.*

She kept her eyes and ears open as Finn took her across the

swaying bridges between the Spires, into the dwellings of his aunts and cousins. She paid close attention to the murmurs and mutters of the patrols rotating in from the road. She eavesdropped on the trackers as she fed an apple to a gangly, young elk in the stables.

Mostly, she learned the ways of the Paika. She rode one of the massive, shaggy goats, and learned how to blow a Curling Goat Horn so loudly it echoed off the mountainsides. Finn made sure she was never bored. He sat next to her at meals, took her to the lookout tower, and showed her the carvings of his ancestors. He also told her the names of the peaks in the Paika traditions. The tallest ones were Grandfather and Grandmother Mountains, the next lowest shoulders were Son and Daughter Mountains. The eroded ridges further down were the Grandchildren. She asked him why one mountain was a grandmother and another a grandfather. He explained that it depended on which face of the mountain you were looking at. If there was a stream or river from the snowcap, it was a Grandmother Mountain. If not, it was a Grandfather. In the spring, when the snowmelt flooded every ravine, all the mountains were grandmothers for a week or so. In the dry season, the grandfathers presided over the region.

"If you learn to greet the mountains correctly," he told her, "the mountains will always look out for you."

Finn's stormy eyes sparkled with delight as she boldly learned - and lost - his little sister's favorite dice game. He taught her the steps to their mad jigs and ignored his aunties' teasing when he asked her to dance. *The Paika* watched them with a tendril of hope and a tangle of plotting. She needed the Lost Heir's favor and allegiance. This brief stay would not last forever, and, when Ari Ara left, she wanted the girl to know the good qualities of the Paika. They were loyal to their own, protective, fierce, and clever. They were kind and generous, and caught in between the rocks and hard places of warring armies. The Paika required allies beyond their clans. The friendship of Ari Ara Marin en Shirar would go far in protecting her people.

Finn was charged with keeping her safe - and ensuring that Ari Ara remained at the Spires as security against attacks. It was a tall order for a young lad, especially since he and she both knew she could use the Way Between to slip away at any time. But *The Paika* had seen the way her great-grandson looked at the red-haired girl. She'd noticed how Ari Ara's eyes stole glimpses of the curly-haired Finn. She chortled to herself and let the feelings they didn't yet dare to confess bind them together and keep Ari Ara here by her choice.

At the request of *The Paika*, Ari Ara told the Alaren tales that she knew. She spoke of the Peace Force often. Some thought it utter nonsense. *The Paika* argued staunchly in its favor. A moment of peace, the old woman said, was worth more than all the centuries of war put together.

Each day, under *The Paika's* watchful eye, Finn learned a new skill in the Way Between. He protested at first, but a deal was a deal, and he had given his great-grandmother his word. Finn had picked up a few things through all his spying on the Peace Force. He knew the examples Mahteni Shirar used in her exercises. He could move through several of Shulen's physical sequences. He recited Solange's history lessons with the keen memory of someone often tasked with reporting back what he'd heard.

"So, you *were* spying on us," Ari Ara exclaimed as they practiced outer Azar in the tight space of *The Paika's* quarters.

"Yeah, she made me," Finn admitted, tilting his head at the old woman and dodging Ari Ara's attempt to tap his shoulder in the training. She didn't tell him she was moving slow as mud compared to her usual speed. She wanted to boost his confidence. Shulen had done it for her when she first began to study the Way Between. Slowly, she'd increase her speed as he increased his.

"It is wise to keep an eye on any newcomers to the Border Mountains," *The Paika* remarked in her papery voice. "And, our people have a long history with Alaren's Way Between."

"I've heard," Ari Ara exclaimed, halting. She conceded the practice to Finn and stood before the elder respectfully. "Will I ever get to hear those stories?"

"Tell her the first Alaren tale, great-grandmother," Finn cajoled, tossing a grin in Ari Ara's direction. "The one about the Paika Huntress."

"I have told you many times," *The Paika* chided Finn, "they are not Alaren tales. They are the stories of how the Paika used the Way Between to survive."

Ari Ara's heart thumped loudly in her chest, excited. The old woman's voice was scarcely louder than the shushing wind beyond the window. She had to listen carefully not to miss a word.

"Please," Ari Ara pleaded softly. "I would love to hear the tale. Alaren's book of stories makes no mention of the Paika."

"We Paika," the old woman responded curtly, "are all through that book. You will not find our name, but we are the villagers, the bandits, the children, the refugees, and more."

She turned her gaze to the fire. The Paika had their own versions of these stories, no two quite the same. She cast her memory back across the decades, back to a time when she sat on a different carpet by the same hearth, back to when her ears were younger than the red-haired girl's, back to when she was wiry as her dark-eyed great-grandson. Back then, she was just Olena, and her great-grandmother was *The Paika*, old beyond belief. She cackled quietly to herself. She believed now, oh yes. She believed how time could erode one's face like a mountain, and how each furrow held a decade's worth of living. She believed how one's bones could ache from carrying the weight of history and how the vast library of story cracked one's voice through the telling and retelling of tales to children too young to understand how this story might save their lives.

"Once, long ago," *The Paika* began in a tone that bridged the past and present, and stretched into the future yet to come. Her words were her great-grandmother's. One day, the rhythm of her storytelling would drum in the cadence of Finn's great-granddaughter's tales. "In distant times, Alaren was young in these lands, a newcomer, always racing against time, often stumbling around, lost in these mountains."

She spun out the story, suspended between times, her memory sitting where Ari Ara sat, wide-eyed, leaning forward, eager for the next word. The snow had danced outside the window then, mesmerizing.

"Getting from here to there sounds simple until there's a mountain in the way. Then, you'll want a companion who knows these ridges and ravines like their own hand."

Her great-grandmother had held out her wizened and trembling hand, palm down, and now *The Paika* did the same. Ari Ara's eyes traced its contours then fell to her own smooth hand. Her gaze grew distant, thinking of the maps of the area. The rise and fall of the closest five peaks formed a sort of hand, she realized.

"Alaren tried to take a shortcut from here to there, and nearly broke his neck," the old woman continued. "He got so tangled in thickets and briars that he made his life twice as hard. He floundered and bumbled until a Paika huntress heard him. Well, to be fair, every creature with ears could hear him between this mountain and the next."

She tapped the knuckles of her fourth and fifth fingers.

Ari Ara thought of the map. If that gesture had been handed down accurately over the centuries, this story would have taken place near where the Spires stood.

"The Huntress stepped out of the forest and couldn't help but laugh. Those briars had Alaren caught in their little snares, sweating and scratching, bleeding and cursing. Where was that man's Way Between now, eh?"

She chortled. The Huntress had asked Alaren this and the jibe stung him worse than the thorns. But, hung on tiny tenterhooks, tangled to the roots of his hair, snarled by his shirt, Alaren couldn't deny the truth of her words. He started to laugh, too. It was ridiculous to be in such a predicament, a fellow like him, trained in the Way Between by the Fanten Daughter herself.

"The Huntress," the old woman went on, "studied him. She looked him up. She looked him down. And, by and large, she liked the look of him. There was a beetle crawling up his cheek and a bird had landed in his hair. When a mouse sat, trembling, on his left foot, she decided: if the animals liked Alaren, he was worthy of helping."

The Huntress set him a challenge. If Alaren could use his Way Between to get out of that thicket, she'd show him the paths through the mountains. The young man agreed. Slowly, he quieted his heart. He felt the sun gently stroking his face. He noticed the thorns sending him their pinprick warnings: no further, come no closer. Carefully, he eased back, lifting cloth and skin away from their barbs.

Sometimes, he thought, *one had to go backward to go forward.*

Cautiously, carefully, Alaren slid between the thorns, over, under, around, and through the brambles. He lifted them up between the spines, holding the smooth part of the stalks. He ducked beneath one vine and curled between the next two. It was

Rivera Sun

a tender, peaceful dance, finding the Way Between those thorns.

"Come now," *The Paika* told Ari Ara and Finn, "do it with me."

She lifted her arms and imagined those brambles, mimicking Alaren's forward and backward motions, lifting and ducking, stepping and bending. Ari Ara joined in. Finn watched, smiling even if he did keep his arms crossed stubbornly over his chest.

"At last," *The Paika* finished, growing still again and nodding approvingly at the girl, "Alaren was free. The Huntress gave him balm for his scratches and spring water to slake his thirst. Then she kept her promise. She showed him the ways through the mountains, traveling with him on many adventures, helping his Peace Force vanish and appear, slip away unseen, and follow invisible roads over ridges and ravines."

The Paika Huntress became a friend for life, the old woman told the two youths, for anyone who could find his way out of a thicket of thorns could find a way to work for peace. Indeed, many times, they felt caught in the sharp briars of violence with the barbs of swords and the pricks of arrows all around. But, backward and forward, forward and backward, over, under, around, and through, Alaren, the Huntress, and the Peace Force found the way out of their troubles.

CHAPTER TWENTY-TWO

. . . . .

The Map Room

The season grew colder and darker. Though the days burned bright and crisp, cold gnawed at the edges of the night. Frost adorned the meadows in the mornings. The leaves turned maroon and golden. Wind hissed through the crack in the doorframe until Tessa made Finn block it with some cloth. The Hearthroom brimmed with warm bodies and murky light. Heaped-up furs and rugs kept off the chill of the stone floors, but the elders still hunched by the hearth, rocking infants and tending toddlers, furthest from the drafts.

Shulen's letters conveyed worrying news: Mendren had deployed soldiers to guard the villages and pursue any attackers. Clashes had occurred, not with the raiders, but with Harraken warriors when a group of Mendren's men chased a pack of bandits across the border.

This is precisely why we didn't want the military involved, Shulen reminded Ari Ara.

Now, the Harraken were threatening to invade Marianan lands in retaliation. In response, Mendren closed the border, denying entry and exit to everyone. This heavy-handed choice set off a wave of outrage and outcry throughout the Fire Peaks Region. The Peace Force was headed to the garrison to try to convince Mendren to reopen the border before the locals erupted. Mahteni, using a bandit trail, snuck across to the Harraken side to speak with her sister and other leaders. One more disregard of the border by either nation would be grounds for war. Shulen asked Ari Ara to remain at the Spires.

The Paika may need you as security against reprisals, yet, he wrote, disheartened. He was now convinced that the Paika had nothing to do with the raids. He, too, had read the *Book of Secrets.* He recognized the telltale signs of the Corroding Challenge. Korin and Rill thought they had found something interesting in the Orelands, but they needed more time.

Hurry, thought Ari Ara. *Time isn't on our side.*

The Paika watched tensions fester with mounting alarm. They shifted their travel routes deeper into the mountains, following hidden paths and wild goat trails. They brought out old maps and taught the less-traversed ways to their clans. On a chilly afternoon of brilliant blue skies and whipping hills of clouds, Grindle told Finn to go nine Spires over to fetch a map that showed a disused route they wished to review. Finn tilted his head at Ari Ara. Grindle frowned for a moment, then nodded.

"Might as well take her along. Show her some of our maps. It'd be good for her. And drop a copy of the one I asked for at your cousin's on the way back. They'll want to see it, too."

Finn tossed her the Fanten cloak and shoved his arms through an oiled leather jacket with a deep hood. They crossed the rope bridges, buffeted by the blustery wind. Scarlet leaves flew past, hurled skyward on updrafts before tumbling earthward again. They split at the next Spire's balcony, racing around the two sides in a game of speed. Ari Ara beat Finn by a fraction and led the way over the second bridge. He eked out the lead around the third Spire and by the time they reached the ninth balcony, they were breathless with laughter, sprinting, and the wind.

Inside the Spire, a spiral staircase led down the cool, solid stone. The stillness hung heavy. Midway, Finn stopped and unlocked a wooden door set into a landing. A narrow, curving room encircled the core of the Spire. The outer wall held windows that let in light. The inner wall contained shelves of rolled scrolls.

"Are these *all* maps?" Ari Ara asked in a hushed voice. Something about the room reminded her of libraries and archives. Minli would love to see this!

"Yes," Finn replied. "We are the world's finest mapmakers."

He made this declaration quietly, humbly, as if this truth should be so apparent it transcended boasts and pride. To Finn, it was a self-evident fact. He might as well state that the sun was bright or the river was wet. He spun to the shelves and pulled a leather-bound scroll collection from the high shelf above a small mantle. Setting the roll on a battered desk, Finn untied the thongs and uncurled the protective covering. Afternoon light tumbled in the windows, illuminating the parchment as Finn's sturdy hands gently opened the scrolls.

It was a map of the East-West Road, laid out in detail across seven sections. Finn released one end and curled the roadmap to the side. Ari Ara gasped. Beneath the first scroll lay a map of the Hand, the set of five Grandmother and Grandfather Mountains shaped like knuckles and fingers. Every cliff and slope, canyon and rock fall was accounted for. It was a work of art, not just a map. Finn grinned at her stunned expression.

He rolled back one layer after another of the bundle of scrolls, pulling them apart and spreading them out on the table. Finn weighted them down with river-polished stones from a basket gathered expressly for this purpose. Each map he showed was stranger and more wondrous than the last. There was a map of animal migrations north and south along the Border Mountains as the seasons shifted. There were maps of fish spawning routes and meadows favored by elk. One map documented medicinal herbs across the slopes of an entire mountain. Another, crafted by generations of mapmakers, portrayed the serpentine dance of the Fool's Gap River over a thousand years of constant meandering. There were maps that sliced the mountains open like apples and revealed their insides. Other maps showed the altitude of the peaks, the height of the cloud layers, and the strata of minerals deep under the earth. There were maps that were so odd and strange, Ari Ara paused to puzzle over their meanings.

"Time!" she exclaimed when she finally worked out the significance of an unusual, spiraling design. "That's a map of time that chronicles - " she counted the spiral rings, " - seven decades of major events. Instead of north, south, east, and west on the top, bottom, right and left, this shows winter, summer, spring and autumn on the four sides."

"Exactly," Finn answered, nodding at her.

Marriages and clan alliances, stories and legends, the dreamworld, earthly haunts of spirits, the locations of armies during a war, star constellations through the year, loyalties and broken trusts ... the Paika were artists who documented relationships between places and people in such detail that Ari Ara began to see the world in new ways.

"These," Finn told her, gesturing to the room of maps, "are just a fraction of our collection. The rest are hidden in a place where neither mice nor humans can meddle with them."

Her eyes shone. Her breath caught in her chest at the thought of the hidden knowledge such a trove contained. The things their world could learn from that collection! The Paika would never reveal the location to an outsider, though. She remembered a comment Professor Solange had made once, mourning the lack of records about Alaren.

"Without peace and the trust it requires," Solange had said ruefully, "so much knowledge is lost."

"Finn," Ari Ara exclaimed, grasping his hand. "Thank you for showing me this. I've never seen anything like it, not at Monk's Hand Monastery nor at the Capital Library - and their archives are famous."

His face turned scarlet, a shy smile blossoming. His eyes darted away, ducking under his long lashes to study the sunlit window with more intensity than it deserved. He cleared his throat and tried to speak.

"Uh, it's, uh, nothing," he stammered. His voice squeaked. "We should get back."

He pulled his hand out from under hers and brusquely rolled up the maps. Without meeting her baffled eyes, he slid them back into their compartment and bolted around the curve of the Map Room to track down the one Grindle had requested. They ran back in silence, stopping only to deliver one of the maps. They burst through the door of his cousin's Hearthroom in a cloud of icy wind. A trio of Paika trackers sat at a table in a cluster, talking in low tones as Finn slid the map scroll onto the far end. With her hood pulled up over her red hair and, dressed as she was in borrowed clothes, they mistook her for one of Finn's cousins and barely glanced up. On the table between them, a heap of gold coins was piled high. A tough woman with braided, dark hair held up a sample to test its authenticity.

"That'll stretch far," remarked the man beside her, pointing to the stacks.

"Aye, no need to raid for a while," the third tracker spat in a sarcastic tone, rolling his eyes over the rumors that the Paika were raiding villages.

Finn tossed them an askance look. Unused to the cutting humor of the Paika, Ari Ara missed the sarcasm in the man's tone. From where she stood, she couldn't see his exasperated eye-roll. Before she could speak, Finn hustled Ari Ara out the east door. The sharp wind sliced her throat and stole her breath away. She said nothing until they reached Tessa's Spire. Then, in the lee of the entryway, shucking off their boots and jackets, she caught Finn's eyes.

"Raiding?"

"He was joking. He's as annoyed about the rumors as the next Paika."

"Wasn't that stolen gold?"

He tossed her a disdainful look.

"Paika don't steal, not if we can help it."

"That was a lot of gold coin," she pointed out.

"So?" he shrugged frostily.

"It came from somewhere . . . "

"That's Paika business, not yours."

He slammed through the inner door. Ari Ara shivered in the frigid air, thinking of something she'd overheard in a village, once: *the Paika get coin somewhere and there's only one way to put your hands on that much gold.*

Banditry. Raiding. Theft.

Finn's stormy temper slammed up and he wouldn't talk to her all evening. At dinner, he wedged his little sister between them and hardly spoke a word. He tripped over his feet in his haste to leave the table and rushed off to help his uncle haul wood - a chore he detested and had wriggled out of more times than anyone could count.

Ari Ara frowned as the door banged shut after him. She cleared the dishes in silence, a furrow lodged between her brows.

Finn returned with an armload of firewood, dumped it noisily by the hearth and scooted out the door again. His effort to avoid her was noticeable. His great-grandmother tracked it all with watchful eyes.

Later, he refused to dance a jig with Ari Ara even when the whole family hooted and whistled and tried to insist. He left her standing awkwardly, cheeks flaming, and barged out the door muttering about needing air. An uneasy silence fell as the door banged shut. Ari Ara felt mortified. The family suddenly bustled about with unnecessary clatter.

What was the matter with him? Ari Ara wondered, confused by his sudden abruptness. Had she said something wrong?

She reviewed the short list of Paika customs she might have unwittingly botched. She shook her head, unable to think of any. Besides, Finn hadn't taken offense at the small blunders she'd made before. She'd served the wrong old auntie first the other morning and he just laughed and smoothed it over with his customary charm. Two days ago, when she had asked one question too many for the Paika sense of propriety, he just tweaked her nose and told her to keep it on her business, not theirs. So, what was bothering him now?

There was only one way to find out. Ari Ara clenched her jaw, screwed up her courage, and followed Finn out into the aching cold.

He stood with his elbows leaning on the balcony rail and his head tilted up at the stars as if searching for answers.

"What's your problem?" she demanded, pressing her back against the rail, arms crossed over her chest, hands tucked under her armpits for warmth.

"This'll never work, Ari Ara."

"What? Holding me hostage?" she snorted.

He shot her an anguished look.

Ari Ara froze, wary as a deer scenting danger in the air. The heat of her body blazed against the night. She struggled for words. He interpreted her silence as anger. Reckless, heedless, thoughtless babble poured out of him to fill the uncertainty of the gap.

"It's been great having you here, don't get me wrong. You're . . . different. You've got lonely heights and ice-cold snowmelt running in your veins. There's a certain wildness that no amount of Marianan manners or Harraken honor can erase."

Ari Ara couldn't stop the smile from growing on her face. She'd spent months hoping to hear him say this. She'd dreamt of it, tripped over her own feet fantasizing about it, tied her tongue in knots trying to creep closer to this moment.

"But . . . "

Her heart plummeted like a stone in a lake as he went on.

"You're the *Lost Heir*, and I'm just a Paika."

"Do you see a crown on my head?" she protested. "Half the world doesn't even believe I'm the heir. At the rate Mariana's going, I'll never be confirmed. So, don't hold it against me!"

She wanted to hurl something at him . . . maybe herself. Ari Ara gulped and wrestled down the overwhelming urge to fling her arms around him and tell him she didn't give a flying pig about her royal blood.

Finn shook his head and sighed, toying with a loose bit of wood on the railing, avoiding her eyes.

"We have . . . there are too many secrets between us and not enough trust. I can't be honest with you."

"Yes, you can," she blurted out. The aching cold seized her throat from the inside.

"No, not about Paika business," he made a strange, awkward gesture of frustration, unable to say more. "There's so much I can't tell you. It's like trying to walk over a floor of knives."

"Like the gold?" she guessed.

He nodded soundlessly. She shifted and sighed. Her warm breath hung white on the black cold. It felt like a Fanten dream, surreal and stark. But, in dreams, the cold never stabbed her nostril hairs like needles.

"I'm good with secrets, Finn."

It hurt to say his name, yet she wanted to say it a hundred times over and thread her freezing fingers in his dark curls and tuck her shivering limbs against his.

Get a grip, she hissed silently to herself. Out loud she said, "I grew up with the Fanten, remember. They have more secrets than the Paika."

He groaned, pounded the rail with his fist, and shoved off. He stalked around the porch rim.

"Hey! Don't run away!" she shouted at his back, jogging after him.

He whirled, eyes angry.

"Yeah, because that would be just like a Piker, eh? Running away, sneaking around, stabbing you in the back?"

"No, I didn't say that."

"Stay away from me, Ari Ara Marin en Shirar," he snarled. "Go find some noble boy to break your royal heart, alright?"

He spun, sprinted around the Spire, and bolted down a rope bridge without looking back.

"Garrgh!" she exploded, stamping her foot.

The night silence hung thick around her. Ari Ara's stomach lurched with the realization that the entire family had probably heard them shouting. She felt like pounding her head against the stone. She shivered, pivoting left and right, trying to figure where to go - she couldn't face Finn's mother and aunties after *that* exchange, not in a million years. Ari Ara had just turned to descend the spiral stairs to the beasts' stables - where at least she wouldn't freeze to death or die of embarrassment - when *The Paika's* window swung open.

"Get in here, girl!" the old woman insisted in a quaking voice, "before we both freeze."

CHAPTER TWENTY-THREE

. . . . .

The Changes & The Crossings

Ari Ara hesitated then sighed. She shoved her shoulder through the opening and squeezed in. Toppling onto *The Paika's* bed, she obeyed the elder's command to shut the window. The old woman was stirring honey into tea. A cascade of wrinkles folded in her brow as she lifted a knowing eyebrow at Ari Ara.

"You heard?" Ari Ara groaned.

"The louder bits, yes," *The Paika* confirmed with a wry grin. "Why is my great-grandson being such a dolt?"

"He blathered on about not being able to tell me his secrets," she repeated furiously, stoking the embers of the fire - as all Paika youth were expected to do when in the presence of an elder - with more vigor than necessary. Throwing a log into the hearth, she sent a shower of sparks up the chimney. Then she flopped down on the carpet, stretching her frigid fingers out toward the warmth.

"He's right about that," *The Paika* remarked unexpectedly. "You're not Paika. We don't keep secrets from our clan, but we also don't share them with outsiders."

"I wouldn't tell anyone!" Ari Ara exclaimed in exasperation.

The Paika said nothing for a long moment, thinking. Finally, she spoke.

"My people have many secrets that are never spoken of beyond our clans. Never."

She emphasized the word. Ari Ara saw something flicker in her eyes, a memory of punishments and wild hunts and betrayals.

"There is one secret, in particular, that Finn is loath to share."

"I know all about the gold," Ari Ara interrupted. "It doesn't bother me - too much - I mean, of course, I don't think it's right to steal, but - "

"Paika do not steal."

The old woman's voice cut sharp as an axe into hardwood. Ari Ara fell silent.

"You think you know what you're talking about," *The Paika* scolded, "but you do not."

"I'm sorry," Ari Ara apologized. "I just meant I won't say anything or think worse of you."

"The gold is not what's bothering Finn," the elder sighed, swinging her head around to stare at the fire.

Ari Ara hoped the old woman would tell her what *was* bothering Finn, but the silence lingered. The air turned thick with Paika secrets. Once or twice, the elder's head swung toward her, papery lips parting as if to speak. Then her jaw tightened. Her lips sealed. Her head gave a tiny, regretful shake. She could not tell this girl *that* secret. Not the one about her mother. Not in a thousand years.

The Paika teased out her braid to comb her white hair. Ari Ara's eyes flicked toward the door to the Hearthroom, but voices rose up so she made no motion to leave. She'd wait until the others had gone to bed before returning. Restless, Ari Ara scrambled to her feet and prowled the room. *The Paika* watched her steadily, running her silver-backed, boar's bristle brush through the ends of her hair. The old woman said nothing as the girl feigned curiosity in the ancestor statues she'd already examined three times. *The Paika* counted the number of stretched-out sighs Ari Ara issued, waiting for the question or outburst that she sensed would soon erupt. She winced as she tried to reach behind her head to untangle the snarl at the nape of her neck.

"Can I help?" Ari Ara offered, turning to her.

The Paika nodded and lowered her arms with a sigh. She held out the comb to the girl. The elder tried to rise and stretch daily, but each day, it took longer to massage the stiffness out of her joints. She tried to totter out and join the family in their work. She would curl her gnarled hands around a knife and pretend to peel potatoes while the younger ones discretely did the bulk of the work. The time of chores and childrearing had passed for her. She participated to keep herself from collapsing in on her aching bones, but oh, how they ached, ever more so as the years weathered her away like the Grandmother and Grandfather Mountains.

These days, her duties lay more in remembering and reflecting, advising and directing. The Paika clans turned to her wisdom in troubled times. While the mothers and fathers, aunts and uncles had the task of caring for children and beasts, larders and tools, homes and hearths, they needed her to stare at the dancing flames until the answer to their problems came. In the Paika culture, each person played their part in the community's well-being and heroes came according to the needs of the times. They were given poets in eras when poetry was needed and warriors in periods when fighters were required. *The Paika* watched the current crop of children singing and dancing and took it as a good augury for their future. When a generation spent more time telling stories than stick fighting, it boded well.

The girl combed carefully, her hands surprisingly gentle, easing the tangles out so as not to yank out a single strand of the elder's thinning hair. *The Paika* was appreciative – she had seen Ari Ara wrenching at her own curls, her face screwed up in a grimace, a determined set to her jaw.

The girl should learn to care as tenderly for herself as for others, the old woman thought, drifting in the warmth and light touches of comb and nimble fingers. She fell into a half-lull until a sharp tug snapped her out of her musings.

"Ouch!" she cried out, more startled than hurt.

Ari Ara tumbled out of her thoughts, apologizing. She had been thinking of Finn, his pointy acorn chin, the shape of his muscles pressed against his shirt as he hefted an armload of wood, and his weirdness this evening. She began to comb again, but *The Paika* reached out a wrinkled hand and stopped her. She tugged the girl around to face her. The elder gestured to the carpet and bade the girl sit, trying not to envy the ease with which Ari Ara folded her legs beneath her and plopped down. If the old woman tried a motion like that, she'd break a bone.

"Tell me what's on your mind," *The Paika* invited.

Ari Ara's eyes turned the color of granite in a rainstorm. She wrestled with her words, the questions barraging her faster than she could express them. Her thoughts jammed up and spilled out of her eyes instead. She wanted to pick up a pillow and throw it across the room in one big, answerless question about *everything*.

The Paika waited with the patience of one who has spent long hours listening for answers to hard questions. The old woman gave the girl her complete attention, as if she didn't have dozens more pressing problems to think over. One never knew how important the smallest detail might be to the survival of the clans. Listening to a confused youth might seem less significant than determining the fate of the Paika, but time might prove her wrong. She had lived long enough to understand that, at least.

"Why is it so hard to grow up?" Ari Ara groaned out, at last. Her eyes swept up in an anguished appeal. "Is it always this confusing?"

"How many years have you seen?" the wrinkled, white-haired elder asked the girl.

"Fourteen - no, wait," Ari Ara corrected, remembering. "Fifteen."

Her birthday had come and gone. She wasn't used to celebrating it; the Fanten never did. Unless other people thought of it, she forgot that the frosts marked the completion of another year in her life. She certainly didn't feel a minute older. Everything still felt as confusing and frustrating as it had before. Ari Ara looked up at *The Paika* expectantly, hoping for some sympathy or wisdom or *something* to make her feel less miserable.

"Have you ever seen a caterpillar?" *The Paika* asked her.

Ari Ara blinked. Whatever answer she had expected, it hadn't involved bugs. She nodded. She'd seen those green, inching creatures chewing holes in leaves, forming cocoons, and emerging as glistening butterflies. Sensing where this conversation was headed, she rolled her eyes.

"Are you going to tell me I'll be a beautiful butterfly someday?" she grumbled. "Because I won't. I'll crawl out of the cocoon round, slimy, and still hungry."

The Paika chuckled at the thought. She doubted that very much. Ari Ara was more likely to break all the rules of nature and crawl out as a tiger.

"No. I was going to tell you about turning into goo."

Ari Ara let out a bark of laughter. She knew all about that! She'd felt gooey and weird all year long.

"Inside the cocoon, a caterpillar doesn't just grow wings. It

279

dissolves completely. It turns to mush and then, only then, does it reform into a butterfly."

Ari Ara scrunched up her nose; that sounded gross.

"I thought I was supposed to be done growing up," she complained. "I sang my Woman's Song. I completed my *druach*, my proving task. Why am I still goo?"

The Paika bit her lower lip, trying not to laugh. No youth enjoyed being laughed at . . . but no elder who had made the Crossing from child to adult to elder could help it.

"You're never done growing," she told the girl.

"You mean I'm going to feel *like this* forever?" Ari Ara screeched with horrified alarm. "I won't. I can't."

"Calm down," the old woman chided. "No, you won't always feel like you do right now. This is special to your age, I assure you. Nothing lasts forever. The Changes are the only thing that is constant. The Changes and the Crossings."

"What are those?" Ari Ara asked, mystified.

It was *The Paika's* turn to blink. But, of course, no one else talked of these any more. Not the Marianans nor the Harraken. And, evidently, not the Fanten . . . though perhaps the girl had been too young for this lesson when she lived with them.

The Paika clans believed that life was a long series of Changes and Crossings. It wasn't a journey with a destination. One did not arrive at adulthood like a town at the end of a road. Every person made endless Crossings through the Changes, from infant to toddler to walking child to adolescent to youth to adult to the first touches of silver in one's hair to the heat that rushed through a woman's body as she aged to a wrinkled elder like *The Paika*. The Wrinkling Crossing traded vigor for wisdom, and *The Paika* had not minded making the bargain.

"You've made the beginning of your Crossing from girl to woman, with your monthly blood arriving, your woman's song, and your *druach*," the old woman shared with a twinkle in her eye, "but think how many more lie before you on life's path. You may make the Mother Crossing one day and have a child. You may go through the Fire Crossing that will trade your monthly blood for the heat that burns away your foolishness and makes you smart like me. If you're lucky, you'll live long enough to go through the Elder Changes, and grow wrinkled and wise. But for certain, you will make the Last Crossing, the one that goes into the Unknown."

"Death?" Ari Ara asked, frowning. "I thought you joined the Ancestor River or Ancestor Wind when you die. I know you do. I've seen the spirits, spoken to them, dreamed with them."

The Paika shrugged. Every culture had their stories about what lay on the other side of the Last Crossing. But who really knew? Not her. Not yet. When she left this old body, she'd find out. *The Paika* grinned. It was something to look forward to, a new adventure that didn't require aching bones.

She fell quiet, though, sobered by how many people never lived through all their Changes and Crossings. Cut down by war. Felled by disease. Shot by arrows in bandit raids. Violence was always a tragedy, cutting short the journey through the Changes and Crossings. Far too few got to live like her, with a long life and the hope of a gentle Last Crossing. Even among the Paika, the wisdom of the Changes and the Crossings was being forgotten. One had to grow as old as she to truly understand this knowledge, to have experienced the profundity of its gifts. When she welcomed the clans' newborns, she always prayed for them: *May you make all your Changes and Crossings before the Last.*

She shook herself as an invisible draft traced an icy line down her back. The girl still stared at the hearth fire, lost in her thoughts. Sensing the elder's gaze, she turned her head with a determined look.

"So, how do I stop being goo?"

This time, the old woman laughed merrily. The answer was simple.

"Stop resisting your Changes and grow through them. Make your Crossings with courage."

CHAPTER TWENTY-FOUR

. . . . .

The Paika Guide

A few days later, the rain froze in the night. The forest shimmered. The clear gold of the dawn sparkled. Icicles bedecked the tips of twigs. When the wind lifted, every tree tinkled and chimed. Heavy, aching limbs groaned as the weight of the ice strained trunks. Lightning sharp cracks shot out as branches snapped. The echoes rolled across the mountains. Standing on the balcony, Ari Ara's breath caught in wonder then sighed out, white on the chill air.

Like a storm clearing, Finn had returned to teasing and jesting as usual. At breakfast, he bumped her hip over with his and squeezed into place on the bench. He tossed her a merry wink as he reached across her for the milk. He teased her about her dislike of curdled goat's cheese. His strange aloofness had rolled past like a mountain storm, dark and foreboding in one moment, clear and sunny in the next. Ari Ara decided to pretend it never happened.

She scanned the clouds, searching for the black speck of Nightfast. Shulen's latest letter was overdue. He usually replied promptly, but she hadn't heard from him in a week. The Paika also awaited Shulen's letters anxiously. Usually, they knew every leaf that turned color and every newborn elk that tottered across the alpine meadows, but the closure of the border and the ban on the Fire Peaks Region had cut them off. As anti-Paika sentiment intensified, they felt this loss keenly. One of their trackers narrowly escaped with his life when a band of men chased him. The Peace Force had talked several mobs out of attacking the Spires. Mahteni was still across the border, working hard to forestall any Harraken reprisals. Pressure was building on Mendren to arrest – or execute – Paika suspects.

A shout lifted from below. Ari Ara squinted down. Voices argued, some low and rumbling, another higher pitched, a third accented and . . . she gasped. She knew those voices!

Ari Ara darted for the second spire. Since a slip on the icy, stone-carved staircase could prove fatal, the ingenious rope-and-pulley lift was in use today, the squeaky gears shrieking as people descended. By the time she reached the ground, Paika sentries had surrounded a horse at the edge of the ice-coated forest. The tall, golden stallion stamped his feet in irritation. He wore leather guards to protect his ankles from the cutting edges of the ice. His rider - no, riders, Ari Ara realized as they raised their hands in the air and let the sentries search them for weapons - wore white tunics over their bundled layers.

"Ari Ara!" Minli's voice cracked with relief.

The sentries kept their notched arrows aimed at the intruders, but their eyes flicked to her. She slipped and skidded across the hard, slick crust of ice, trying to get closer.

"Stay where you are," one warned her.

She halted.

"Those are my friends," she called out.

"We walk in peace and mean no harm," Minli told the bristling, suspicious guards. "I am Minli of Monk's Hand, a member of the Peace Force."

"I am Tala, of the Harraken Tala-Rasa," the lanky figure seated behind Minli informed them.

One sentry flung up a hand and signaled to the others to lower their bows. Minli, bundled round as a little bear and barely recognizable under his thick woolen cap, explained that they had come in search of Ari Ara. They also carried a message from Korin de Marin. Tala held up a small scroll bearing the seal of the House of Marin. Ari Ara frowned at it, curious. They'd traveled on the cart road that splintered off the wide Garrison Road – a difficult journey, but still easier than the high-altitude trails Ari Ara had taken to the Spires.

"Ari Ara is our guest," Grindle Spireson said, walking toward them. His footsteps crunched steadily over the frost and ice. "As you are, if you walk in the way of Alaren's peace. Come, you look as though you rode through the night. Your horse needs rest and tending."

Zyrh did *look ragged*, Ari Ara noticed with some alarm. Beneath his bristly winter coat, he looked thin. His flank shivered. He was not too exhausted, however, to keep from snapping his teeth at the sentry.

"Er," Minli remarked with an apologetic expression, "perhaps we can help settle Zyrh into a paddock or stable? He's, uh . . . "

"A bad-tempered lout who ought to be more grateful for small kindnesses," Ari Ara remarked with affection and annoyance. Zyrh promptly waggled his tongue at her as he shook his head. She ducked under his muzzle and drew close.

"I missed you, too," she murmured, stroking his withers and scratching the spot that always itched.

In the stables, Zyrh came to swift friendship with the uncanny Mistress of Beasts. She was a tall and silent woman, more at ease with animals than people. Some claimed she spoke the hundred languages of the beasts. The elk followed her footsteps. The goats obeyed her requests. She could even entice the wild birds to eat seeds out of her palm. Once, Ari Ara had spied fox kits playing games with her at the edge of the woods at dusk. Zyrh flirted shamelessly with the Mistress of Beasts. He even held out his leg so she could slather salve on his ice cut. Minli, Tala, and Ari Ara watched in bemused silence as the bull elk and horse sniffed and snorted at each other until some unspoken negotiation settled them both.

"What news?" she hissed as she aided Minli with the saddlebags.

"Mostly bad," he breathed back. "Commander Mendren had the Peace Force arrested."

"What?!"

"Shhh," Minli urged, tipping his head toward the Paika. "They're fine. Technically, they've been detained and confined to the garrison for safety's sake. Mendren found out that the raiders were harassing us - they've come back and gotten worse. Nightly visits, though they never went so far as to actually hurt us. Unless you count sleep deprivation."

His voice dripped with annoyance.

"How'd you get away from the garrison?" she asked in a whisper.

"Well, no one could catch Zyrh," Minli explained, "and they didn't know whether to put Tala in with the men or the women, and while they were debating ze slipped loose. I talked my way out."

She had to smile at that.

"Before I left, Shulen told us to find you and stay put."

They had no more chances for quiet exchanges. Grindle guided them onto the lift - Minli studied it with fascination - and across the rope bridges to his family spire. Minli and Tala received all the courtesies due to guests. *The Paika* even came out of her quarters leaning on Finn's arm, eager to greet the young Tala-Rasa.

"I met the eldest when ze was young," she remarked with a twinkle in her eye.

While the young Tala caught their immediate interest, it was Minli who made the lasting impression, opening his saddlebag and offering gifts with a bow of respect. Wrapped in a length of fine desert silk lay three statues carved in obsidian-dark stone: an elk, a goat, and a shaggy horse.

"These are gifts from Tala and me," Minli explained, "in gratitude for your welcome, and on behalf of our friend Ari Ara, who has been your guest for these long weeks."

The delicately chiseled sculptures had been carved from High Mountain stone; Ari Ara felt a jolt at the touch of the black rock. The Peace Force had acquired them in the Stonelands, anticipating the need to speak with the Paika. The plan had been put on hold when Ari Ara disappeared, but came in handy now.

"I suppose you've come to take her, then?" Tessa demanded shortly.

"When we travel onward," Minli replied quietly, "we hope she wishes - and is free - to come with us, yes."

It was a dance of subtleties. The wrong inflection in a word could slam the door of welcome shut. None of them knew the steps to the dance, a misstep or blunder could trip them up at any moment. But, Minli and Tala had made an effort to learn the ways of the Paika, and to show respect accordingly. Tala brought a block of salt for the beasts. Minli offered news of the road as the meal cooked. Neither mentioned the purpose of their visit until bread had been broken and the plates cleared away. Tala offered a song as only one of the Harraken Tala-Rasa could, an old tune recalling a time of friendship between their peoples.

The Paika watched and listened with a lively gaze, taking the measure of the youths.

Itching with impatience, Ari Ara nearly burst out with questions numerous times, but she knew enough of the Paika to understand the insult of haste and the value of letting her friends break bread and build trust. She let her curiosity burn in her blood until the clan breathed easier about the unexpected arrivals. She shared stories of the antics she and Minli had gotten into at the monastery. She spoke of journeying across the desert with Tala. A bit of the trust she'd won over the past weeks transferred to her friends.

At last, the smallest children were hustled off to lessons and chores. A quiet fell. Into that space constructed of food and gifts, story and song, *The Paika* asked the question that had hammered in Ari Ara's heart since the moment Zyrh had emerged from the forest.

"What brings you here, young ones? Surely not just the love of your friend?" *The Paika's* voice suddenly turned hard as stone, uncompromising in the demand for truth.

"We bring news from the Great Lady's son, Korin de Marin," Minli explained. He pulled out the scroll and handed it to her. "He sent it to the Peace Force, but we felt you should hear what he has to say."

Silence hung like a held breath as she read the message, first to herself, then aloud so all could hear. Korin had taken his entourage north, through the Smithlands and into the Orelands. Rill sniffed around, listening at keyholes and poking into dark corners. She overheard many intriguing tidbits: Thornmar's relatives were annoyed at his prolonged absence, his wife wanted him home rather than in the Border Mountains, his sister grumbled that his schemes would come to naught, his inner circle hated the Paika and the Peace Force and cursed them with equal vehemence.

"Korin and Rill are searching for hard evidence that proves Thornmar's involvement in the raids," *The Paika* told the room, "but they have a suggestion for us."

In a sleazy tavern in the crookedest quarter of Thornmar's major city, Rill had heard a thief swear to a pickpocket that he'd seen Orelands soldiers at the Thieves Den last spring. The fellow hadn't stuck around to learn more; he feared a raid or an ambush. Rill thought someone should look into this.

The Paika tapped her fingers on the table thoughtfully. The room broke into noisy chatter. The elder let the questions and outbursts wash over her as she pondered the news. When a brief lull fell in the storm of voices, she spoke.

"Why are children delivering this news?" the old woman queried somberly. Her eyes turned sharp as a hawk. "Where are Shulen and the Peace Force?"

An uncomfortable silence fell. Minli gulped. Tala bit zir lower lip.

"They - the others couldn't come," Minli stammered. "Commander Mendren - at the suggestion of Commander Thornmar - has detained them at the garrison."

"He arrested them," Ari Ara blurted out.

Faces grew grim at this news. Mendren claimed it was for their safety in this time of unrest, but Ari Ara knew the real reason: Thornmar was trying to stop them. Without the Peace Force countering lies and seeking the real culprits, everyone would blame the Paika for the burnt villages. Worse still, Tala reported that the Mariana garrison was threatening to attack the Spires and arrest every last Paika to stop the raids. Angry cries and outraged mutters broke out. Protestations of innocence arose.

"*We* know," Tala assured them. "Shulen knows. Everyone in

the Peace Force knows it wasn't you. Korin ordered the garrison to stand down and not launch any attacks on the Spires. The Great Lady backs him in this matter."

Finn's family was not reassured. If a rogue force of Orelands fighters already ignored the orders of the Great Lady, what good was her word now? They muttered about tracking down the attackers and putting an end to them. They'd defy the ban on the Fire Peaks Region and the closed border. They'd leave those bastards' heads on pikes.

"You can't!" Ari Ara cried. "That's just the excuse they're looking for. If you kill Marianans, the army will attack you with all the force it has!"

Her words set off a roar of objection. *The Paika* let them flare up, then waved her hand for silence.

"We must get to the bottom of this and find out who these imposters are," the old woman declared, severe and stern.

"How?" Grindle burst out in frustration. "If everyone suspects us, they won't let us near the villages. If we violate the ban, Mendren will put our heads on pikes."

"With the Peace Force locked up," Tessa added, "who is left to help find the truth?"

"We're still here," Minli pointed out quietly, gesturing to himself, Tala, and Ari Ara.

The Paika's eyes grew distant. Wrinkles deepened around her face as she considered their options. Her mind stretched through memory and mountains, searching for some hope. She tilted her head slightly, listening to the voices of the ancestors. At last, she sighed and spoke.

"Someone must talk to Slygo. That means going to Thieves Den," *The Paika* stated with a touch of reluctance. "It's the only way."

"Who is Slygo?" Tala asked.

No one answered. Expressions grew guarded and closed. The mysterious woman lived at the crossroads of gossip and dark dealings. If there was anything to be learned at Thieves Den, Slygo would know about it. Slowly, Grindle shook his shaggy head of salt-peppered dark hair.

"One problem: Slygo won't break the Thieves Code for Paika business. She told me that the last time I tried."

The Paika held up her gnarled finger.

"It's not Paika business. It's Peace Force business. We'll send the young ones to ask. They aren't constrained by the ban."

"What if the garrison detains us?" Minli worried, shaking his head from side to side.

"They'd have to catch us first," retorted Tala. "Ari Ara can help us evade capture. She has Fanten training."

"Not much," Ari Ara sighed. "Not enough for three people, not in mountains I don't know."

"I'll guide you."

Finn spoke abruptly, an urgent fire burning in his stormy eyes. He could help them. He knew every hideaway and untrackable foxhole in this part of the Border Mountains. Grindle objected, arguing that someone more skilled should go, someone with more experience in fighting.

But the youths did not need fighters; they needed a guide, someone who wouldn't rouse suspicion, who could lead them over goat paths and deer trails unseen.

"Finn Paikason will go."

The crone's voice settled the debate with the brittle clarity of hard-earned wisdom. Like the Huntress guiding Alaren, Finn would help the followers of the Way Between find the path through the dangers of these mountains.

CHAPTER TWENTY-FIVE

. . . . .

The Crooked Wheel

The four young people journeyed light and swift. They saw no one, traversing paths through frost-etched hills. Bare branches rattled in the cold winds. Stray fallen leaves hissed and rustled. Early snows dusted the peaks. Before they left, Grindle advised them to keep to the lower altitudes.

"You'll have to follow the valleys and river passes," Grindle warned, pulling a roll of maps out. "Snow is piling up on the higher peaks."

He laid them across the Hearthroom table. Flattening the scrolls with his heavy palm, Grindle peeled back three layers, one after another.

Seasons! Ari Ara realized. *By month!*

The maps showed the build-up of glaciers and ice. They revealed the flood paths of spring snowmelt. They warned against perilous routes through avalanche zones. They pointed out potential mudslides. The maps marked the main roads, including the one that Minli and Tala had ridden as they came north from the garrison, but they also showed little-known trails that connected the roads together. When Ari Ara asked why they shouldn't just take the Garrison Road south then cut west to Thieves Den, Grindle traced a pair of sinuous lines marked in red.

"These routes will get you there faster and with less trouble," he told her in a deep, rumbling voice. "The main road takes a week to travel. Our route takes three to five days, depending on how fast you're moving."

The journey took them four days. A horse and rider galloping could make it in three days, but Finn's shaggy pony was built for endurance, not speed. Ari Ara and Finn rode together. Tala doubled up with Minli on Zyrh. The horses' breath turned white on the cold air. Minli's crutch clacked against the buckle on their travel sacks as they cantered. Overhead, the clouds gathered and clashed, dropping sweeps of snow flurries across the hulking grey heads of mountains. They slept lined up next to each other for warmth, sheltered only by the half-sheds the Paika hid in the underbrush for fellow trackers. The work of the Peace Force took on growing urgency with each day. They had to convince this Slygo to share her secrets. The lives of the Spires Paika hung by a thread.

Hurry, hurry, hurry, the wind hissed.

They arrived after dark. Thieves Den clung to a cliff's edge beyond the deep gorge carved by the Fool's Gap River. The town had a leer to its look. Thin slits of windows poured out smoky glares. The stone roofs canted at sloping angles like the brim of a hat pulled low across the brow. A long wooden bridge swayed in the wind, creaking mournfully over the deep, black chasm of the ravine.

"We can't take the horses over those bridges," Ari Ara pointed out.

"Nope," Finn agreed, unperturbed. "You'll stay here with them."

"Will not!" she protested.

He rolled his eyes at her objections.

"I can't take the *Lost Heir* into Thieves Den," he groaned. "You'd be kidnapped faster than *that!*"

He snapped his fingers.

"You two," he pointed at Minli and Tala, "can be disguised as Paika youth so the bridge guard doesn't hassle you. Paika come and go as they please in Thieves Den."

"Wait!" Ari Ara objected. "If they're going in disguise, I can go in disguise, too. No one will know I'm the Lost Heir. And besides, I'm the best at outer Azar. You may need me!"

Ari Ara folded her arms stubbornly over her chest, matching Finn glare for glare. Zyrh, she told him, could look after himself. Finn eyed the big horse and reluctantly agreed. He tethered the shaggy pony to the taller horse, trusting that they'd take care of each other.

With charcoal, he smeared grime across Minli's face and hands to hide his noticeably pale Marianan skin. He doled out his spare coat and shirts, swapped boots with Tala, and made Ari Ara give him her Fanten cloak.

"Don't lose that," she grumbled as she tucked her bright red curls up under Minli's thick woolen cap.

Finn studied them. By torchlight, no one would spot the giveaways like Minli's round face or Tala's ever blurring gender. Three Paika boys and a sister wouldn't be viewed strangely. Especially if they stuck to the story that they were entering Thieves Den in search of a wayward uncle.

"Keep your mouths shut and an eye on your valuables," he warned the others.

"We don't have any," Minli pointed out.

"No? How about your good leg? Or your eyes or ears or fingertips?" Finn retorted. He smirked at the wide-eyed horror on their faces. Strictly speaking, those were the penalties for breaking the Thieves Code, not dangers Paika youth would face, but an ounce of caution was worth a pound of regret.

Even Ari Ara looked suitably subdued as they approached the guards and stated their business. One guard demanded a crossing toll and Minli started to stammer that they had nothing. Finn cut him off contemptuously and glared coldly at the man.

"Since when do Paika pay fees to thieves?" he scolded. "Unless you consider this a small loan, collected tenfold on some lonely highway out there?"

The guard backed down from the demand, grumbling that the common thieves tried to dodge out of fees by pretending to be Paika. Tala, Minli, and Ari Ara shifted uncomfortably and turned their faces into the shadows.

As they stepped onto the swaying bridge, Finn rounded loudly on Minli, making a show of his scorn.

"Fool! Just 'cause you've never left the Spires Cradle is no reason to be stupid." In a lower voice, he hissed to Minli, "Don't apologize - just sulk. Paika never apologize when insulted."

Ari Ara filed that tidbit of cultural knowledge away to think about later - it would be useful for peace work - then focused on keeping her footing on the swaying rope bridge. It creaked and groaned ominously, bouncing perilously with their strides. Minli gritted his teeth as the end of his crutch slithered on a damp board. Ari Ara kept an anxious watch on him, one hand running along the rough rope, the other half-extended to catch him. The river sounded a long way down. In the darkness, they could see nothing. Ari Ara found this unnerving, but Finn assured them that it was worse by daylight when you could see the plummeting depths and the thinness of the boards. Tala chanted under zirs breath in a taut prayer to the Ancestor Wind to catch zir if the bridge broke. Minli muttered to Alaren's ancestor spirit that he would study twice as hard for the next month if only the bridge held. That promise swelled to a year as the slats sagged alarmingly at the midpoint.

Knees shaking, they climbed to solid ground on the far side, refusing to think about having to do it again upon departure. Thieves Den stretched along a single, twisting serpent of a road that switch-backed up the cliffs. A second row of buildings loomed over the taverns, and a third row above that. Finn told them it continued in that fashion all the way up to a lookout tower at the very pinnacle of the mountain. Ari Ara squinted up, but could see nothing of the upper levels. Finn followed her gaze and explained what night concealed.

"The second level holds trading posts where robbers can switch up gold for saddles and silks for supplies. Above that are the workshops of craftsmen and women who repair dirk hilts, worn boots, and such. Over that are the Burrows, the hideaways that every decent thief and robber needs. They go back into the mountain, too. The northside of the peak is riddled with passageways and tunnels, but you've got to know your way around or else you'll get lost forever."

Ari Ara could have asked a thousand questions, but Finn had warned them to keep their mouths shut. He led them toward the last tavern before the hairpin turn of the road. The Crooked Wheel hunkered against the mountainside like a squat toad. Dim lamplight filtered out through the two large, grimy windows that bookended a battered front door. The raucousness inside rattled the glass panes. A heavy thud shuddered against the door. A sudden crash of splintering wood followed it. The four leapt back as a body hurtled out, sprawling on the cobbled street.

"For the love of all that's wicked, Pete," a booming voice implored and warned, "go home or crawl in the bushes 'til you're sober. T'ain't my business to keep your head on your shoulders!"

Ari Ara started forward, but Finn held her back.

"Not your fight," he hissed, "not tonight. We've a task."

The woman in the doorway wiped her hands on a rag black with grease. She was easily as broad as the four of them lumped together. A tangle of curling brown hair piled up atop her head and tumbled down one side of her beaming cheeks. She wore a pair of knee-high boots that had seen some rough-and-tumble journeys. A brilliant red skirt was tucked up in a broad belt, revealing an emerald-green petticoat. Her biceps rivaled a blacksmith's. Beneath her skirts, she was clad in sensible trousers, ready as the next fellow to give better'n she got. Despite it all, a jolly air exuded from her.

"In or out, lads?" she thundered, shooting them an inquiring look. "Don't be afeared. The ole Crooked Wheel's not rough to all who visit. 'Melda will fix you up a drink that'll put a man's whiskers on those young chins of yours."

They scurried in as she waved her hand in a welcoming gesture. The Crooked Wheel seemed to shove the boisterous clatter of an entire town into a single room. Every battered, ale-stained table was occupied by disreputable-looking characters. The woman - whose name turned out to be Kitty - led them through the throng. She ignored the calls to arm-wrestle a big, muscled smuggler and knocked aside the hand of a light-fingered thief who tried to pick Minli's pocket.

"None of that, now," Kitty declared, glaring around the room fiercely. A lull in the clamoring din fell as eyes studied the four slight figures trailing in the barkeep's wake. "We're gonna treat the young'uns right, y'hear? If they misplace so much as a hair on their heads, all your tabs'll come due tonight!"

A collective groan shot around the room. The thieves and smugglers, bandits and swords-for-hire went back to their drinking and gambling, deal brokering and rumor swapping. Kitty elbowed her way to the bar and cleared room for the youths to hop up on the barstools' age-darkened, red leather.

"What'll it be for these lightweights?" asked a beautiful, petite woman behind the counter.

Finn and Minli gawked at her luminous dark eyes and cinnamon skin. Her black springlets of curls floated in a halo around her face. She set a delicate hand atop the full curve of her hip and watched the two trip over their tongues trying to answer.

"Emelda, m'love, best give 'em watered wine," Kitty laughed, "for they're half-drunk on you already."

"Sorry lads," she answered, "I'll break your heart, being happily married to Kitty these nine years past."

She tossed them a saucy wink.

"We're looking for Slygo," Finn said in a low tone.

Kitty and Emelda's eyes instinctively darted to a shadowed figure in the corner.

"What business do you children have with our partner Slygo?" Emelda asked with a sharp edge to her voice.

"That's ours to say, isn't it?" Finn replied, touching the brim of his hat and getting to his feet.

Ari Ara saw the two wives exchange a look of skepticism and raised eyebrows. The tavern owners ran a tight operation, obviously capable of fending for themselves. Tiny Emelda had to do no more than shoot a quelling look at a leering drunkard to get him to shuffle off. Kitty was a force of nature, alright, but Ari Ara suspected that it was this Slygo, brooding in the shadows, that no one wished to cross.

With trepidation, they followed Finn toward the darkened corner. Ari Ara's eyes adjusted swiftly to the gloom. She wondered how much the others could see of the mysterious figure. Her night vision had always been sharper than her friends; a side effect of Fanten herbs, so far as anyone could tell.

Slygo was a thin, whip-like woman with calloused knuckles and a long scar down one cheek that gleamed pale against her nut brown, wind-weathered skin. A leather hat pulled low over her forehead; a braid of dark hair hung over her shoulder. The turned-up collar of her coat hid most of her features. Ari Ara spotted three throwing knives - which Slygo no doubt wielded with accuracy - a short sword at her belt, and a fighting dagger in her boot. Then, she spoke, and Ari Ara knew in a flash that it was not for her weapons that Slygo was feared. It was her Sight, her uncanny knowledge of things beyond the glimpse of eyes.

"So, Finn Paikason," she remarked in a low, deep voice, still not lifting the brim of her hat, nor looking directly at them. "Why have you brought these three - and such a three, they are - to trade secrets with me?"

"How - how did she?" Ari Ara breathed in Minli's ear, astonished.

"I don't know," Minli answered.

"Because, Minli of Monk's Hand," Slygo answered, "I make it my business to know the names of all who wander these mountains, especially those who cross the threshold of the Crooked Wheel."

The hat tilted up. The travelers gasped. Slygo's eyes were white - no pupil, no iris, just a pair of round, stark white marbles in a scar-crossed face. She had always had the Sight, but when a gang of jealous rivals had tried to cut it out of her along with her once-hazel eyes, it sharpened her gift rather than vanquished it. Now, she navigated solely by it . . . and saw all the better for it. Slygo knew, for example, what no one else in the tavern had guessed. These were not four Paika youth standing before her, but as odd an assortment as ever she'd seen: a Paika lad, a Harraken Tala-Rasa, a one-legged Marianan, and *her*.

Slygo recognized the Lost Heir at once . . . and yet, her Sight faltered. Like a light shining in ordinary eyes, she winced and squinted. The girl was and wasn't who she thought she was. Slygo let it rest. Not all secrets were hers to know.

Many assumed that her blindness limited her awareness. In truth, it heightened it. She knew the one-legged boy by the step-clunk of his crutch. She scented the wild herbs of the desert in the Harraken youth's pouch, one a healing plant only the Tala-Rasa carried. The soft rustle of embroidered sleeves hinted that a Paika traveled with them. The boy's accent confirmed it, placing him as a Border Mountains lad, born and raised. She knew the girl, too, by her accent. That High Mountain lilt - same as the one-legged boy's - was rare in this region. Her Sight gave her the final details of their names.

"Sit."

It was a command more than an invitation. They obeyed, settling on benches around Slygo's small, round table. Ari Ara eyed the woman uneasily. She'd had odd experiences with seers and worse with prophecies.

"I am not an oracle, as the Paika well know," the blind woman told them. "I listen and hear . . . and trade in secrets and knowledge. What have you come for?"

Ari Ara bit back a gasp of sudden understanding. She peered over her shoulder at the tavern, realizing how the three women plied their trade - Kitty and Emelda running the tavern, and Slygo silently collecting the gossip of the entire Thieves Den, using her ordinary ears, extraordinary Sight, and her cunning wits, besides.

"There is a group of riders pretending to be Paika," Finn told her, "attacking villagers and undermining the Peace Force's efforts. We need to know who they are. I ask not just for my people, but for the sake of peace in these mountains."

Slygo nodded once, took a sip of her ale, and leaned back in the shadows, hat brim tipped down low once more. The Paika lad told the others to wait quietly. Like the seer Ari Ara had met in the desert, Slygo charged only for the telling of an answer. If she knew something of interest, she'd haggle for a payment. If not, she'd send them on their way.

Their question stirred up memories for Slygo, recollections of warmer times. She cast her memory back through months of buzzing conversations, searching for the hints and clues of what they sought. She remembered a day when the tavern door stood propped open and the fresh spring breeze mingled with the scent of Kitty's soap as she mopped the floor. Ah! That was it. Kitty'd been put out when a group of warriors, rough men, had clomped in. Their lowlands accents had been sharp and arrogant; Slygo hadn't forgotten that. She'd heard the clank of metal buckles and the jingle of coin. She could smell the reek of their horses and remembered their odd inquiries.

They needed Paika gear, they'd said, though they hadn't named a reason. It had prompted Slygo to tuck the incident away in her mental records. No good came of lowlanders meddling with the Paika. On the other hand, knowing who was impersonating the Paika was a gem of information. Someone would come asking for it, eventually. Slygo had no qualms about twisting those soldiers' secrets as barter for another deal. She could use it to blackmail commanders into leaving her favorite thieves alone, for example, or to get a friend off the gallows.

Her memory itched again. Kitty had sent the soldiers to Pete's Trade Post and . . . Slygo's smile curled, cat-like. Now *this* was something she could trade hard and well for. A pretty little tidbit, indeed.

"I don't know where they are now," Slygo told the youths, "but I have knowledge that's of use to you regarding the identity of those raiders. What can you offer?"

Finn dug something out of his pocket and laid it on the table. A nugget of gold. As Slygo hefted it, Ari Ara hissed in his ear.

"Where'd you get that?" she breathed.

"Lots of folks have a nugget in their pocket hereabouts," Finn whispered back with a shrug.

"You stole it," Ari Ara stated flatly.

His stony silence was his only reply.

"We're on Peace Force business, remember?" she hissed. "We can't use stolen goods."

"*You're* on Peace Force business. I'm on Paika business," Finn retorted.

"Don't tell *her* that."

Slygo shook her head. The gold wasn't enough.

"What I have will be precious as a hundred lives to you," she explained, her voice dropped so low that the four youths had to lean closer to hear her, "but it's a risk to my life and my loves to give it to you."

Whatever she had was valuable.

Two more gold nuggets, the second the size of a peach, slid across the table's mottled surface. Slygo's rough-knuckled hand flicked out and swept up the nuggets. She weighed their worth, bit them to test their purity, and sniffed the mineral scent. Then she gestured to Kitty.

"The young'uns are here for the letter Pete settled his tab with."

The buxom woman lifted her eyebrows high, but did not argue. She returned moments later with a rolled parchment. Ari Ara's breath caught in her throat as she recognized the insignia on the wax of the broken seal.

"Knew this would come in handy . . . if it wasn't the death of us," Kitty muttered. "Pete did, too. That's why he nicked it in the first place."

"And the letter'll pay back his tab twice over," Slygo assured her, putting the gold in her hands for safekeeping. "I'm not doing it for the pay, though."

"No?"

Even Kitty looked skeptical, but Slygo shook her head.

"Those imposters are trouble, not just for the locals and the Paika, but also for the one good thing that's happened hereabouts in a long time."

She nodded to the youth in a gesture that indicated the entire Peace Force. Ari Ara gaped; she'd never have suspected Slygo had a soft spot.

"Aren't you worried what they'll do if they find out you gave this to us?" Minli asked, tapping the letter.

"No, because you're going to say you stole it from Pete," Slygo remarked with a droll chuckle that held a serious edge.

Tala grinned, a gleam in zir eye, already composing the ballads about how the Lost Heir snuck into the Thieves Den and out-thieved the thieves to keep the peace.

"Now, away with you lot. Children have no business hanging out in Thieves Den."

Her sightless gaze landed on Ari Ara for an uncomfortably long spell. They took the hint, grabbed the letter, and hustled out the tavern door.

CHAPTER TWENTY-SIX

. . . . .

The Paika's Way

Ari Ara could hardly keep her explosion of anger and excitement contained. As soon as the tavern doors shut behind them, she hissed to the others:

"The insignia on the seal - that's the House of Thorn! I knew it."

Minli read the letter by the dim light from the windows. It issued orders to a company of Orelands warriors to pose as Paika and conduct raids in the Fire Peaks Region. It detailed the plan to steal Bergen's cattle in Gult, attack Hock, and burn Tillun. The Orelands warriors were warned to stay away from Commander Mendren, who wasn't sympathetic to their cause.

"Well, he's not sympathetic to us, either," Ari Ara grumbled.

"And to the Paika least of all," Finn sighed.

"Look, Moscam's on here," Minli said, pointing to the list in alarm, his stomach lurching over the thought of the town in danger. The weathered halls had withstood wars; they couldn't let them burn because they now stood for peace. "We have to warn them."

"Whose signature is that?" Tala asked, peering over his

shoulder at the bottom of the scroll. "We can expose who's doing it and let the garrison trap them at Moscam."

"Can't make it out," he answered, squinting at the scroll, "but it's paid in Oreland marks."

"I knew it," Ari Ara grumbled again.

The others shushed her as a dark-cloaked group banged past them into the tavern. Finn tilted his head. They'd read all they could by lamplight. They shouldn't talk in the open. He pulled them into the bushes at the corner of the street. They huddled in the dark, heads bent close together, conversing in whispers. Finn vowed through gritted teeth that he'd track them all down. He could find them; the Paika could find anything once they scented a trail. He wasn't afraid to defy the ban on entering the Fire Peaks Region. They fell silent as footsteps and voices approached. Two men's banter rumbled in the night.

"Garrison's looking for more swords. Gonna go?"

"Might, might not," the other replied in a lukewarm tone. "Paika are tough fighters. And the Spires? Huh, the garrison will never take them. Bloody waste of time."

"Still, the coin's good. The commander'll starve them out in the end, every last one of the filthy devils."

Ari Ara gripped Finn's arm to keep him from leaping out.

"Well, best make up your mind soon. The garrison'll arrive at the Spires in three or four days. We'll be late, but they'll be hiring on the spot when the siege starts."

"Bah, they'll still be polishing their boots by the time we get there."

The two laughed and turned the topic to the foolery of soldiers, climbing the road toward the hideouts on the upper levels.

"We have to warn the clans," Finn said at once.

"And Moscam," Minli added.

"We could send messenger hawks," Ari Ara suggested. Nightfast was far away in the south, but many towns kept hawks. Surely there were some in Thieves Den.

"There are, but they can't be trusted," Finn answered. "The birds are as crooked as their trainers. Unless you're bound by the Thieves Code, it's better to ride to the nearest town and send messages from there."

Then Finn sniffed the air. The sharp scent of snow clung to it. He cursed. By morning, the hawks would be huddled in aeries, waiting out the snow squall. It might last days. He shook his head. He couldn't afford to waste time hoping a hawk's wings would deliver the message. The mountain weather patterns were capricious. A snowstorm here would ground the hawks, while on the same day, the soldiers to the south were marching under a clear blue sky. The others continued their hushed discussion while his thoughts raced through Paika maps of weather patterns.

"Sending multiple hawks is our best option," Minli was saying. "One to the Spires, one to Moscam, one to Shulen, one to the Great Lady, and one to Commander Mendren on the road."

"We can't count on that," Finn cut in anxiously. "What if the storm delays them? What if the messages go awry? That happened to the headwoman of Serrat, remember? Someone's messing with the hawks. What if ours are intercepted?"

"We'll have to risk it," Minli argued. "What other options do we have?"

"I'm going north to the Spires."

"You might not get there before the soldiers," Tala told him. "They're already on their way."

"There's a faster route," Finn insisted, "but the horses can't come. Even a Spires goat wouldn't like it. I can leave my pony here."

"Then we'll split up," Minli said practically. "Ari Ara and I can ride Zyrh to find messenger hawks. Then we'll try to catch up to Commander Mendren with the letter. You and Tala can take this other route to the Spires and warn them."

Finn nodded . . . then hesitated.

"Maybe Ari Ara should come with me," he mentioned hesitantly, holding up a hand to forestall their protests, "for two reasons. First, too many people are looking for her. The Paika's Way is not . . . safer, per se . . . but no one will catch her on it."

"And the other reason?" Tala demanded.

Finn didn't want to mention it. His people needed the Lost Heir as a hostage. It was their last bargaining chip, their only protection. But he couldn't tell them that. Instead, he appraised the thin, lanky Tala. Then he swept a sharp gaze over the stockier, sturdier Ari Ara.

"Paika's Way is hard traveling. It takes two to traverse it. It's mountains all the way up and all the way down. Boulders and cliffs and sheer drops. I'd rather run it with a High Mountain shepherdess. No offense."

"None taken," Tala answered.

There was a fourth reason, too, another one Finn couldn't mention. The Paika's Way was his people's secret. He couldn't tell Tala. Ze was a servant of the Harraken and zirs knowledge was their knowledge. Just as Minli wouldn't be able to stop himself from recording the path on a Marianan map, Tala would wind up putting the trail into song. But Ari Ara? She'd wanted to know his Paika secrets. She'd earned *The Paika's* trust. And his.

Ari Ara hesitated. She remembered the look on Minli's face at High Summer when she had raced to the pool without him. She recalled the misery in his voice when he told Emir he wasn't going to the bonfire. She'd promised not to leave him behind.

"We should stick together," she stated, strongly and firmly.

"We'll all go back by the road, fast as we can, and send a messenger hawk to the Spires. Either we all go or we don't go."

Finn growled in frustration. This was the slowest route possible! He kicked the dirt and started to argue. Minli interrupted.

"No, Finn's right. We should split up in pairs. You go with him. You'll be faster than me or Tala. Besides," he smirked as he winked at the songholder, "we're faster on Zyrh and better at verbal Azar. If anyone's going to convince Mendren to stand down, it's us. You'd just lose your temper."

Tala snorted in agreement. Ari Ara hugged Minli. He squeezed her back, replying to her whispered thanks that this was different than before. She had given him a choice rather than just leaving him behind.

Finn escorted Tala and Minli across the bridge to Zyrh. He paid a passing thief to look after his pony and offered double to make sure the fellow didn't just run off with the horse. Then he sketched out Minli and Tala's route on the map, explaining the trail markers at each crossroad. Once they were safely on their way south, he jogged back to where Ari Ara waited. They climbed up and up the winding switchback road. They passed shuttered dwellings and shops with doors flung wide open. At the fourth level, Finn knocked on the silvered wood of an unmarked door wedged between the workshops of a leather worker and a fletcher. He rapped in a particular pattern, waited a beat, and tapped it out again with his fingertips. The door cracked open. A startlingly green eye peered out at them. A heavy chain prevented anyone from forcing their way in.

"What do you want?" the woman demanded, irate at the late hour.

Finn spoke in a swift whisper. Ari Ara caught only the words, *travel, way,* and *Paika*. The woman slammed the door shut and

Ari Ara thought Finn had spoken the passphrase wrong. Then she heard the muffled clunk and thud of chain and bolt unlocking. The door swung open. The woman's strong grip shot out and yanked them in by the front of their tunics. The wooden door shut behind them. Ari Ara stood blinking in the darkness. As her eyes adjusted to the dim light, she saw that the windowless corridor had been chiseled out of bare stone. It was scarcely wide enough for two abreast and Ari Ara knocked her shins against a stool. The woman slid it back into a wall niche and lifted a lit candle from the small alcove just above it.

"Does she just sit here, waiting for someone to knock?" Ari Ara hissed to Finn with an incredulous look.

He shot her a warning glance against asking questions. She was still dressed as a Paika youth. Her speech would give her away and the Gatekeeper would toss her out the door . . . or worse. Nary a soul in Thieves Den knew about the entrance to the Paika's Way, hidden behind a door so bland and unassuming, eyes simply slid past it without noticing.

The woman led them deeper into the mountain. The air smelled of stone and minerals. Ari Ara tried not to think of the crushing weight stacked above them. At the fork in the corridor, the woman paused. Handing the candle to Ari Ara, she opened a series of cupboards in the wall and passed out waterskins, candles, flint, a coil of rope, and a pouch of journey cakes.

"You know the Way?" she asked them, a scowl over their obvious youth furrowing her brow.

"I do," Finn answered. "I have traveled the route with Spireson himself. *The Paika* is my great-grandmother."

"And you?" the woman queried, jerking her head at Ari Ara.

"This is her first crossing," Finn replied.

"Then stick close to him. Do what he does. Do not wander off - not even for a step," the woman warned in a severe tone. "If you lose the way, no one will hear your cries for help. No one will even find your bones."

Ari Ara gulped and inched closer to Finn.

"Safe crossing, then," the Gatekeeper intoned. She touched her candle to Finn's, then cupped her hand around her flame and went back the way she came.

Finn shouldered the waterskin, looped the journeycake pouch over Ari Ara's arm, and shoved the flint stone in his pocket. He pointed to the northward fork of the corridor.

"Go north to go south, at the Undermountain's Mouth," he chanted, setting off.

Ari Ara's palms grew clammy. She hoped Finn knew what he was doing. They had no map, nothing but his memory to guide them. The darkness beyond the candle's small orb hung absolute. The bottom of the tunnel climbed gradually. The backs of her calves ached and she kept scuffing her feet on the rising floor. The tunnel curled over her shoulder, spiraling back the way they'd come.

"Uh, Finn?" she asked eventually. "You know where we're going, right?"

"Yes." Then, perhaps hearing the faint tremor of uncertainty in her tone, he added, "We'll be in this tunnel for a couple hours. This is the Undermountain-Overhill Road, the Paika's Way."

The name tickled something in her memory. She'd seen it on one of the maps at the Spires . . . but the name had been different.

"I thought it was the other way around," she said, confused. "Isn't it the Overmountain-Underhill Road?"

"That's the merchants' road on the maps," he answered. "We're on a different route."

Finn halted and turned around, holding out his hand with

the fingers spread wide apart. He handed her the candle and traced a trail over his knuckles, up and down the web of his fingers.

"Imagine that these are the Hand Mountains. The usual road crosses them below the Grandfather and Grandmother Peaks, but above the ridges of the Sons and Daughters. Then it dips down into the valleys where the villages sit. It takes forever to make that journey, especially with laden horses."

He pointed his finger in a straight line as if threading a needle through his knuckles.

"The path we're taking is not on any map. It's called the Paika's Way by my people and it goes under mountains and over hills."

Using secret tunnels, they would pass directly through the Hand Mountains. In between the peaks, they'd run narrow footpaths across the interlocked hilltop ridges that spread out in a maze. Not many people knew how to find their way through the forking and splintering crests of those hills. Finn did. The footpaths were kept open by mountain goats and Paika travelers.

"Here," he pointed to the hollow between his fourth and fifth knuckle, "we'll have to go across the Sword Blade. It's a thin, high mountain ridge, not wider than this tunnel, treacherous underfoot, with winds that can throw you off into the air and hurtle you down to death. I told you it wouldn't be easy."

"I can do it," she assured him stoutly.

They moved on. Time passed strangely underground. Without the moon or stars, Ari Ara had no idea how long they'd been walking. Her heart hammered in her chest, nervous at the intense weight and silence of the earth. Every now and then, the candle spluttered and her breath fluttered with it, afraid it would go out. After what felt like an eternity, she sensed a cold tendril of air wisping along the corridor.

"Are we nearly out?" she asked hopefully.

Finn shook his head.

"We're about halfway. There are air holes here; otherwise, we'd suffocate. On the surface, they just look like small animal burrows in a cliff."

As soon as he said the word *suffocate*, her breath shortened in panic. She gulped greedily at the cooler air and forced her mind to stop imagining cave-ins. She was shaking when they reached the end of the first tunnel. Finn insisted on halting near the entrance and sleeping until first light. They'd traveled hard the day before and they needed their strength and wits about them.

In the morning, they emerged from the tunnel, blinking and wincing as their pupils dilated. The door on this end arched so low they had to duck their heads as they exited. It stood unguarded, though a sign on the front warned of cave-ins and sudden drops in an old mineshaft. Through such disguises, the Paika's Way had been cloaked in secrecy for centuries. Each section had been painstakingly discovered or built by Paika route-finders. Over millennia of exploring old mines, unused tunnels, and natural cave systems, they carefully plotted their path through the mountains. They shifted rockslides to open passageways. They dug tunnels that connected miles of trails. They charted the geometry of the underground world to calculate the shortest routes. The Paika's Way was ingenious . . . even if treacherous.

When her eyes ceased watering, Ari Ara understood why this section of the Paika's Way was called an *Overhill*. Old mountain creeks had eroded the foothills into ribbons standing on edge. The gravely slopes fell steeply down each side, leaving a narrow strip at the curling top. While descending from the mountains to the eastern floodplain was a relatively easy downward stroll, traversing from south to north over the numerous crests seemed impossible. Finn led her onward, however, seeking out the hidden swales between the foothills, finding the passable trails down one ribbon and up the next. They crossed a precarious footbridge half-buried under a rockslide. They moved at a steady jog across the flat sections. They slowed as they scaled the heights. Ari Ara kept up, barely, and she knew she'd sleep like a stone that night. Her years running in the High Mountains sustained her pace. Tala would have faltered. Minli could not have made the journey at this speed.

By noon, they had crossed the gap between the two mountains. They ate in the shade and rested. Ari Ara pounded her muscles so they wouldn't stiffen. Finn eyed her as she stretched the exertion out of her limbs.

"Had enough or can you keep going?"

She could, she promised. She could hear the anxiousness in his voice, the burning need to reach his family. If they didn't keep going, he'd only spend the time pacing restlessly.

"The next section is an Undermountain," he cautioned her. "We can sleep below ground at a camp we leave stocked and prepared."

Ari Ara ignored her flighty nerves and nodded. She didn't like those tunnels, not one bit, but the safety of the Paika was worth her discomfort.

Finn led her up the trail as the afternoon swung lazily toward evening. The entrance to this passage was not a door. It was a low, narrow slit beneath a slab of overhanging stone. A twisted juniper hunched at the cavern's mouth like an old man leaning on a stick. Finn lay flat on his belly and wriggled in the gap. He was swiftly devoured by the mountain. Ari Ara balked.

"It's alright," he assured her, his head popping back into view and his arm reaching out. "It opens up just beyond here. It'll be like strolling down the East-West Road."

She gritted her teeth and lowered onto her belly, sliding under the rock into the dark.

"Finn?" she cried out as her body blocked the light and blackness seized her in its grip.

His flint sparked and caught the tuft of kindling he used to light the candlewick. The soft glow illuminated his face. She slithered toward him and scrambled to her feet. In the dim light, she could see shadowy outlines of stalactites and stalagmites. She shivered at the way they formed beastly teeth in the yawning cavern. A dull dripping sound punctuated the quiet. Toward the back, like a throat, the cave opening darkened as it curved deeper into the mountain.

"We call this the Jaw of the Beast," Finn explained, stepping over the loose rubble carefully. "It's not all monstrous, but it is a good deterrent for keeping out the faint of heart."

Down the Beast's Gullet they climbed, stepping over broken stones and squeezing between boulders. Ari Ara could not see a trail, but Finn led her unfalteringly. When she asked how the path was marked, he pointed out signs she hadn't noticed. Some had been carved into stones, others were made of rocks arranged in a certain sequence. Still more were marked with white slashes of paint made from the limestone seams that ran through the cave walls. But, Finn cautioned her, the Paika's Way was full of traps for the unwary. In the next cavern, every stalagmite bore a white slash. He pointed to the carved rune that marked the next section of trail. At the fork in the cavern system, the correct path was indicated by a marking hidden beneath the top stone of the two stacked trail guides.

"Even if someone managed to get this far," Finn explained, "these are meant to throw them off. You also have to know the teaching tale, the story of the path, which only *The Paika* tells."

"Why?" Ari Ara asked. "What's so important about keeping this a secret?"

"You'll see," Finn answered.

They stopped to sleep in a Paika camp in the belly of the mountain. It was well stocked, too far underground for even the mice to disturb. Ari Ara sank gratefully onto the thin cots that must have been carried down rolled up. Finn carefully replenished his supply of candles and borrowed a small lamp. He checked the stores of food and contributed some of their travel cakes. The Gatekeeper had given him an extra length of rope. He placed it on the upper shelf and carefully recoiled the length he would carry onward.

Ari Ara tried to settle the flutter of nerves in her stomach. The Fanten caves she'd grown up in were lighter. Tree roots ran through them, some thick as roof beams, others thin as hairs. The scent of the wind trickled down through the entrances. Even in stormy weather, when the roots groaned as the huge trunks swayed overhead, the presence of people filled the Fanten caves with laughter and chatter. In the winter, the Fanten slept and the caves grew drowsy, but never silent. The light dimmed grey, but gleamed with phosphorescent glowlights.

This was different. The Paika had made the camp comfortable, but she could not forget the crushing weight above them. Beyond the white limestone paintings of patterns on the walls and the carved spiral on one side, she could sense the mountain pressing down. The ground was swept clean, but it was still as death. She'd never realized how much the earth pulsed and reverberated on the surface, how soil sprang under one's touch, or how the warmth of sun enlivened stone. Ari Ara eyed the cistern of water and the stack of folded blankets. How long would they last if they were buried here? Not long enough. No one would dig this far down to rescue them. No one even knew they were here, save for the Gatekeeper. The heavy stillness choked the breath from her. She gasped a little.

"Ari Ara?" Finn asked, seeing her eyes darting around. "Are you . . . will you be alright if I blow out the candle?"

Fear shot through her, sharp and metallic. She swallowed and nodded anyway. They shouldn't waste the candles.

The blackness was shocking. Ari Ara's whole body clenched in sudden panic. She forced herself to breathe. Once, twice, thrice. On the fourth exhale, a sudden, terrifying thought shot through her.

"Finn!" she gulped, her voice squeaking. "What about air holes? There aren't air holes here like in the other tunnel. What if we suffocate?"

His fingers tapped her shoulder in the darkness. Her hand bolted up and latched on tight to his. When he spoke, it was with the voice he used to calm spooked elk and nervous goats.

"Hold out your hand and feel the air."

She reached up with her free hand. Her eyes strained sightlessly; she longed for Slygo's power. She couldn't even see her finger if she tapped her nose with it. But she could feel the air stirring, slipping past her skin, light as silk.

"Here, the mountain breathes. All the way along our path, the air moves through from one cavern to the next. It is our thread through the mountain. The Paika found it, long ago, using the Way Between. It guides us still today. Even if we lose the markings, we can follow the breath back to the surface."

He did not tell her that the caverns were so vast they could follow the air for weeks, running out of food and water. Only if a lost wanderer was lucky and careful could they follow the freshest breath to the surface. He told her the story of the Huntress' great-granddaughter following the Way Between through solid stone. With her fingers still entwined with Finn's, Ari Ara began to drift into sleep, thinking of ancient legends founded in surprising truths.

She slept deeply and dreamlessly. She had hoped to dreamwalk to find the Fanten Grandmother. She'd make any deal the silver-haired woman demanded, just to be able to warn Finn's family of the attack. But her eyes fell shut and she slumbered solidly. Perhaps it was the depth of the cave, but she did not dream at all.

She woke in the dark - the same absolute black they had entered when Finn blew out the candle. She felt his fingers slip away from hers and fumble to restore the light. Ari Ara curled the lingering warmth of where their skin had touched to her heart. The flint sparked. The kindling flared and settled. The wick caught. The light grew.

"Alright then?" he asked her, his face carved from shadows and glow.

She nodded, glancing away as the heat rose in her cheeks. They shared travel cakes and water for breakfast, then set off.

Rather than following tunnels, this underground trail threaded through a series of natural cavern chains that riddled the mountain. They crawled over boulder falls tall as houses and shimmied down rock chimneys. Finn lowered her down these with the rope looped through an iron ring set in the stone, the line tied around her waist for safety. Then they switched, Finn dropping down as she countered his weight from below. She held her breath until he landed next to her. Untying the rope, they coiled it again and traveled onward.

A fierce, gnawing urgency propelled them. Somewhere beyond the silent, heavy weight of the mountain, the world of wind and light, soldiers and schemes rushed forward. Tala and Minli hurtled down the road on Zyrh's heaving, golden back. Messenger hawks fought the blustery winds of blizzards. The

Paika waited anxiously for word of their search. The soldiers marched toward the Spires. Ari Ara and Finn traveled as fast as they dared over the treacherous terrain.

In some places, the path opened broad and level as a road. In others, they had to squeeze through narrow openings on their bellies. After several hours, Ari Ara heard a strange sound. She lifted her candle. The light hit solid rock, above, below, to the left and the right. Her heart lurched in her chest. They had reached a dead end. Panic thundered through her. The world spun. The ground seemed to ripple - no, wait! She squinted. It wasn't her nerves. The ground *was* moving, churning.

"Is that . . . " her voice squeaked in alarm. "Is that . . . a river?"

CHAPTER TWENTY-SEVEN

· · · · ·

Underground River

Finn lifted his candle, shining the light over the water. The river gleamed eerily, black and coppery in some places, greenish in others. It was not wide across, but the sound of the water hinted at depths. The current dragged its feet here, backed up by the rocks downstream. It slid under a narrow opening on one side and exited beneath a slice in the stone on the other. Ari Ara gulped at the sight of the black-edged hole swallowing the water like a throat.

"Um, where now?" Ari Ara squeaked, wrestling with her thundering heart.

The Paika lad took a deep breath. She wasn't going to like this next part, not at all. He uncoiled the rope and started to tie it around his waist and over his chest. Then he did the same to her, carefully checking the knots.

"There's a way through," he said calmly, "but we have to swim. See that glow?"

He pointed. Deep in the water toward the back wall, a luminescent green gleamed. She'd thought it was a reflection, but as she studied it, she realized it was an opening.

"We have to hold our breath, dive down, and go through the hole to the other side. The cave system opens up there and it's so beautiful! I promise it is worth it."

She swallowed the hard lump in her throat. Finn kept talking as he carefully stored the candle in a wall niche. There would be dry candles and supplies on the other side. Finn put their borrowed gear onto a shelf carved in the rock face. Paika traveling in the opposite direction would use it once they'd passed through the river. Then, seeing Ari Ara's uncertain expression, he told her of the luminescent algae that glowed in the incredible cavern beyond the river. It would be bright as a full moon, he said, she'd love it. The hole in the water was larger than a door. It wasn't that hard to swim through, but she had to be brave. Could she do it?

Ari Ara nodded. She had no choice, really. Finn would go first. She had to spool the rope out after him. He checked the knots again, nervous. He'd never been on the lead end of this crossing. His uncle Grindle had jumped in first and he had followed. The current tugged here, not strongly, but enough to confuse you in the darkness. The knots had to hold. If Ari Ara became disoriented, the rope would guide her through the passageway.

"Follow the rope," he explained. "When I get to the surface, I'll give the rope five hard tugs - hard enough to nearly yank you over. You won't mistake it for the pull of the current. You'll know it. Like this."

He demonstrated, heaving at the rope so hard, she toppled against him. She gripped his shoulders. A shiver ran through them both. Ari Ara let go hastily. She didn't know what to do with her hands. She tucked her curls behind her ears. She rubbed her nose. She clutched the rope.

"Spool it out as I go down, just like I did when lowering you down the rocks earlier. Not too tight, not too loose. We don't want it to snag on stone. When it's your turn, follow the rope and swim toward the light. Keep going toward that green glow."

She could read his nervousness in his face. They were trying - and largely failing - to conceal their fears and be brave for one another, knowing that if one cracked, they both would.

Make your Crossings with courage, The Paika had told her.

"Just go. Now," she croaked out in a hoarse voice.

The lanky youth turned toward the dark waters and the wall of rock. He took a deep breath and crouched for the dive. But, instead of plunging into the river, he whirled and - to Ari Ara's complete surprise - kissed her.

"Just in case," he murmured. "Wanted to do that for a long time . . . ask me how long on the other side!"

Then he dove, evidently more scared of her reaction than of the black waters and dangerous passage.

"Finn Paikason! You trickster!" Ari Ara muttered, astonished, letting the rope spool out through her hands. She watched him kick like a frog down to the green glow. Emir had said she'd always remember her first kiss . . . and the first one that really mattered. She cursed. She'd show that Paika boy, alright. *This* wasn't going to be the end of the story, not in this dark, dank cave, miles underground.

The rope tugged, cutting off her silent fuming. Had he made it already? She craned over the waters. The green glow was gone - no, wait, there it was. He'd blocked it with his body for an instant. Ari Ara held stock still as he slid through and disappeared. She counted the seconds, hoping he was alright, waiting with the eerie gurgle of the river churning in her ears, praying to all the ancestors.

Then the rope yanked, hard. She stumbled with the force of it and dropped the extra length in her hands. The loose coils spooled out fast, slipping into the water. Ari Ara could tell Finn was hauling up all the slack on his side because the knots at her waist grew taut. His forceful second yank toppled her to the edge of the water.

"Not so hard!" she shouted, but there was no way for him to hear her.

The third yank plunged her into the water. She floundered, taking a swift gasp of air. Then, before the fourth tug could submerge her, she dove and swam toward the green glow. The rope pooled around her as her strong kicks propelled her downward. Her heartbeat thudded in her ears as the current tugged at her limbs. She fumbled for the black edge of the portal, blurry with the water in her eyes. She slid through feet first, into a womb of glowing luminescence above, below, to every side. The rope coiled loosely around her like the umbilical cords that tied newborn babes to their mothers. She panicked, disoriented, confused by the loops of rope. Which way was up?

A half breath escaped her lips. The bubbles!

She watched them rise and followed, kicking in hard scissors for the surface. Just as she saw Finn's curly head peering down at her, the loose coils of rope behind her jerked. A loop had caught on a snag of rock in the portal. She thrashed, frantic, trying to yank it free. Her fingers fumbled with the knot at her waist, struggling to untie it, almost out of air.

The water exploded beside her. Finn dove in, searching for the tangle below her. Ari Ara forced herself to hold still. She didn't want to kick him. Her heart thudded. She felt the rope tug as he tried to free it. Finn shot up past her toward the surface, gasped a lungful of air, and returned.

He pushed the swirling tendrils of red hair away from her face and kissed her again. It was a messy thing of open mouths and bubbles. She jerked away then realized he was trying to give her air. She sucked it from his lungs. He surfaced, inhaled, dove again. This time, she felt the rope loosen. She kicked upward, bursting into the open air, gasping, coughing. His head bobbed up beside her, his chest heaving.

Floundering, half-tangled in the rope that pooled around them, they swam to the edge of the water. Finn hefted himself onto the ledge and grabbed her by the armpits with his wiry arms, hauling her out. She lay sprawled on the ragged stone, too tired to sit up until she'd gulped lungful after lungful of air. Then they sat, feet dangling in the water. Ari Ara wiped her sodden hair off her face, scrubbed the water out of her eyes, and managed to look around.

The luminescent glow shone like a moonlit night, just as he'd promised. It ran in streams of color down the cave walls. More than green, it shimmered with teal and gold, aquamarine and turquoise. Flecks of silver mica sparkled in the trickles of water. The cavern murmured musically, dripping and tapping. As Ari Ara's breath quieted, a deep calm settled in her body. Who could be afraid in such a beautiful place?

"The algae will shine from here almost to the surface," Finn said, smiling at the majestic space. "We're through the worst of the dark."

He dropped his head, suddenly studying his hands with fascination. Ari Ara bit her bottom lip, now remembering his words - and that kiss! - on the other side of the water. It felt like a lifetime ago, another world entirely. She almost dropped the subject, frightened to ask him what that kiss was all about. What if it was just a Paika trick to get her through the river? *The Paika's* words echoed in her heart, suddenly.

Make your Crossings with courage.

Ari Ara took a deep breath. This was it. She couldn't be scared of asking, not after nearly drowning in an underground pool far beneath the earth.

"So," she demanded, "how long, exactly?"

Finn sighed.

"From the first, long before you even knew I was hanging around Moscam," he confessed, looking up at the ceiling now, not meeting her eyes.

Ari Ara grinned. She'd sensed him earlier than he knew! The prickles between her shoulder blades had warned her.

"I almost stole a kiss at Market Day, but then I saw you dance circles around that lout of a boy," he admitted, "and I thought I'd best tread carefully around you."

She chuckled. He had that right!

"Then I was going to tell you at High Summer," he confessed.

"But I puked on you," Ari Ara groaned, burying her head in her hands. She thought she might just die of embarrassment instead of drowning.

"Yeah, well, for many reasons, it wasn't a good time to confess a - uh - um - feelings."

His voice cracked over the last words. He seemed as awkward and uncertain as she did.

"How come you never said a word about this when I was at the Spires?!" she burst out in exasperation.

"Oh, come on," Finn shot back, taking his turn at exasperation. "That's obvious. You're the *Lost Heir*. I'm nothing but a backstabbing Piker."

"That's nonsense. I'm not - you're not - " she stammered.

He didn't answer, but lifted his eyebrows, skeptical. He was a Paika. She was the Lost Heir. She had a thousand-mile journey ahead of her and royal heirs to bear one day. He didn't want any part of those worlds. He wanted his mountains and his clans . . . and peace . . . and her, if he was honest about his heart.

"And that kiss, back there?" she asked, a question that was a hundred questions crowded into one.

"I . . . well . . . I thought if anything went wrong, this was my last chance."

"You thought I'd drown?" she snorted.

"You nearly did," he pointed out, "but no, I was worried I'd drown, which would have been the death of both of us."

He shuddered. She sobered. Then a grin curled over his lips.

"And maybe I figured your curiosity and outrage would carry us through. I mean, you'd have plunged into the Ancestor River just to haul me back and demand answers about that kiss, wouldn't you?"

Ari Ara's grin suddenly shot out to match his.

"I would. For that and other reasons."

"Such as?"

"Well, Finn Paikason," she answered, "it may just be that I like you right back."

Then, in the hush of the cave with the green-blue glow shimmering and sparkling all around them, she grabbed the front of his sopping shirt and kissed him.

This was the kiss she'd remember . . . not that she'd ever forget the first two!

CHAPTER TWENTY-EIGHT

. . . . .

Paika Gold

As Finn had said, the last part of the tunnels glowed with light. Ari Ara was certain she was shining, too, gleaming with a giddy joy. She kept sneaking glances at Finn - and catching him looking back - and slipping into laughter. He stretched his fingers out and wove them through hers almost shyly.

"What about the clan secrets?" Ari Ara asked tentatively, not wanting to break their happiness, but remembering the fight. "*The Paika* told me there were many things you can't share - and that sharing's important for Paika lov - relationships."

She tripped a bit over the last word, wanting to say *love*, chickening out of the immensity of that concept, switching it out for something that wound up sounding as awkward as she felt.

"I've been thinking about that," he admitted. "How about this: I promise to tell you all the things that can be shared, and let you know if there's something I can't?"

He ducked around a low-hanging stalactite that shimmered silver-green.

"Fair enough," she agreed. "I can do the same."

"What secrets do you have hiding?" Finn exclaimed with a

329

laugh. She was an open book.

"None," she answered with a shrug, "but you never know."

As soon as she said it, she remembered her promise to the Fanten Grandmother not to tell anyone about dreamwalking.

"Everyone has one or two secrets," she amended.

"That's less than a newborn Paika," Finn sighed.

They scrambled up a set of hand-and-footholds in a huge slab of stone. A narrow passageway opened onto a long, deep cavern.

"And here's another closely-guarded Paika secret," he said, "one you've been itching to know about."

He stooped swiftly and picked up a stone, holding it out toward her in the palm of his hand. Ari Ara peered at it, then looked more closely at the scattered stones, the rock walls, the ceiling.

"Oh," she gasped, many perplexing mysteries becoming clear at once.

The caves were studded with gold nuggets.

"We're coin forgers, not thieves," Finn told her. "And you can't ever mention this to anyone."

This was how the Paika got their gold.

"We guard these caves carefully," Finn told her. "Otherwise, the Marianans and Harraken would mine the mountains down to rubble and wage endless wars to seize them. When we deal in nuggets, we tell the Marianans it came from the desert and tell the Harraken that we got it from the riverlands."

"But they accuse you of stealing it, of being bandits."

"It's the price we pay to protect the mountains," Finn declared as he gathered a few nuggets to give to the coin makers at the Spires. His jaw set in a determined-to-endure expression. "The mountains are our relatives. They offer the Paika what we need - and no more - and we keep their secrets safe. It's easy enough to pass gold off as bandit takings."

"Your secret is safe with me," Ari Ara assured Finn, and the mountains.

The gold caverns led to a narrow mineshaft with a rickety lift. Gingerly, they climbed onto the creaking platform and heaved at the fraying rope. The system of pulleys and weights groaned and screeched as they inched upward. At the top, the entryway was concealed behind a tumble of boulders. They crossed an Overhill section by dusk and spent another night in a Paika camp below ground. Ari Ara and Finn shyly twined fingers together. She didn't feel afraid of the pressing darkness, though. In this cave, phosphorescence gleamed on the walls and a trickle of fresh air carried the scents of the forests deep underground.

The next morning, they rose eager for the journey to end. Ari Ara had dreamed in the night - not Fanten-style, but ordinary dreams plagued with worry and desperate races to get to the Spires on time. She woke in a cold sweat, the stillness of stone weighty after such frantic dreams. Having traveled two and a half days in the eerie underground, Ari Ara longed for sunlight and wind. She and Finn hustled through the last sections of the tunnel, not stopping to eat, merely munching on travel cakes as they continued onward.

The final leg of the underground passage climbed steeply. Wooden ladders had been set into the walls with tiny wedges of landings to rest on. When they reached the top, Ari Ara whooped for joy at the sight of blue sky. She squeezed Finn hard. The brightness of midday watered her eyes. A blast of wind flung its arms around her and tossed her hair up and off her face. The exit from the caverns opened onto an escarpment riddled with holes. The wind howled and moaned and whistled through them like a set of shepherd's pipes. The Paika circulated rumors that the area was haunted, keeping outsiders away. Even without ghostly tales, the face of the mountainside would baffle the unwitting. A hundred holes opened in the cliff side; only one of them led to the Paika's Way. It bore no marking. Once they had picked their way down a complex series of handholds, Finn pointed back up to the pattern of the openings.

"Think of the night sky in reverse - instead of white stars twinkling in a black sky, look at the black holes gleaming in the paler stone. What do you see?"

She squinted, then shifted into the Way Between, looking for what wasn't obvious.

"Oh! That's the Huntress constellation," she exclaimed, recognizing the pattern.

"The entrance is the middle of her belt," he told her. "Just in case you ever need to take the Paika's Way."

"I hope I never do," Ari Ara answered with a shudder.

The last stretch of their journey was no less perilous than the others. It lay across a cutting ridgeline aptly deemed the Sword Blade. Barely a footpath wide, the cliffs plummeted abruptly on either side. The wind hurtled in gusts across the sharp stone ridge. More than one unwary traveler had been scooped up and tossed down to death below.

Finn led the way. Ari Ara stayed close on his heels. Their luck held. The storm clouds had skirted around the peaks of the Grandmother and Grandfather Mountains. The early snows had melted clear away. No lingering patches of ice threatened their strides. They had both grown up running the mountain ridges, leaping just like this from one boulder to the next, trotting a few even strides before springing up a rise and scrambling down a short slope. The hawks wheeled overhead. The landscape fell away in swells of mountains on all sides.

When the Spires crept into view, the dangers threatening the Paika returned to her thoughts. Worry gnawed at her belly. Had they come in time? How would they stop the raid? Could she convince the Paika to try to use the Way Between before they loosed their arrows?

She was so lost in those questions and the rhythm of her stride that she crashed into Finn when he skidded to an unexpected halt.

"Look!" he cried, catching her before they both toppled off the Sword Blade.

Down below, the Spires loomed above the valley floor. Curls of smoke rose from the chimneys. But Finn wasn't pointing in the direction of home. His arm extended south and east, toward the foot trails. A river thundered below them, curving in a crescent around the mountains abutting the Spires. A narrow bridge stretched over the plunging cascade. On it, a large golden horse stood crossways, white tail flicking in annoyance. Two slight figures, dwarfed by the horse, shifted restlessly on either side.

"Isn't that . . . ?" Finn trailed off, uncertain.

Ari Ara gasped, recognizing the pair: Minli and Tala!

"They must have galloped night and day to get here this fast," Finn exclaimed in an awestruck tone. *That* was a hard journey, even by Paika standards. "What are they doing on the bridge?"

Tala's hands were raised toward one side of the ravine, outstretched in a stopping gesture. Minli had cupped his hands to his mouth and was shouting toward the other embankment, the roar of the river swallowing his words. Ari Ara squinted at the shadows on the edge of the forest. A sinking feeling plummeted through the pit of her stomach as she spotted the soldiers.

"Finn," she said in a shocked tone, "we've got to get down there."

Minli and Tala were stopping the garrison's attack.

Rivera Sun

CHAPTER TWENTY-NINE

. . . . .

The Battle At The Bridge

They bolted like a pair of startled goats, skidding down the loose rocks and half-leaping from one ledge to the next. Lungs heaving, legs burning, calling up reserves of endurance they didn't know they had, Ari Ara and Finn sprinted through the tall forests. They leapt boulders and bounded across streams. They pounded through a meadow, sending up a cloud of birds. They whipped down a switchback deer path at a dizzying, breakneck speed.

Poised on the brink of battle, Paika fighters lined one side of the ravine, arrows notched and swords drawn. Across the river, the garrison soldiers stood among the trees, prepared to charge forward. Between them, holding back the two factions, stood two youths and a horse, blocking both groups from crossing the bridge. The ravine stretched just wider than an arrow's reach. The waters coursed too fiercely to forge. So long as Minli and Tala didn't budge, the battle couldn't erupt.

Ari Ara and Finn hurtled through the forest to aid them.

She knew that she and her friends could hold that bridge all day - all night if they had to. Neither side would attack them.

335

Killing four youths - a Harraken Tala-Rasa, a Marianan, a Paika, *and* the Lost Heir - was surely more of an international incident than anyone wanted. As she dodged branches and skidded down slopes, Ari Ara ran through their options. She could let the Paika hold her hostage and use her double royal blood to push for negotiations. She could relieve Minli and let him walk up the slope to try to persuade the garrison to back down. That was the best idea. But if the soldiers charged onto the bridge and tried to pull them off, then she'd have to use physical Azar to stop them. Ari Ara hoped it wouldn't come to that. She didn't have time for a better plan . . . they'd reached the bottom of the ravine. She and Finn burst out of the brush and raced toward the bridge.

They skirted through the narrow break between the trees and the edge of the ravine. Finn shouted out to the half-hidden Paika, warning them not to shoot. Panting, legs aching, they thundered onto the wooden boards of the bridge. Tala's face lit up in relief. Ze cried out to Minli over the horse's back. Craning around Zyrh's head, Minli broke into an exhausted smile at the sight of them. He had the letter from Slygo clutched in his hand.

"We never got to deliver it," he told them, not bothering with greetings. "We sent messenger hawks, but heard nothing. We raced Zyrh to the point of exhaustion, riding night and day, sleeping only when the horse had to rest."

They'd heard the garrison was a day's ride ahead of them on the main road, so they took a shortcut to the Spires, figuring it was better to arrive in time to warn the Paika than to chase the soldiers' heels. When they rode in last night, the Paika patrols had already spotted the soldiers. Every last Paika was preparing to fight. A select company was headed to the ravine, planning to pick off the soldiers one-by-one as they tried to cross the bridge. Hearing this, Minli and Tala had wheeled Zyrh around and rushed to avert the bloodbath by blockading the narrow bridge.

They'd been holding their position since last night, sleeping in rotation. The garrison arrived at dawn and halted in the trees, baffled by the two Peace Force members blocking the way.

"Commander Mendren's with them," Minli said. "I've been shouting at him about the letter, but he can't hear me over the water. When I tried to walk up and deliver it, one of the archers shot at me."

Ari Ara gasped, horrified.

"It was just a warning shot," he said, waving his hand dismissively. "They aren't sure whose side we're on."

"Peace," she muttered. "We're on the side of peace."

"We're running out of time, though," Tala put in, pointing at movement in the tree line. "They're getting restless."

Finn groaned. Ari Ara grabbed his shoulder.

"It's okay. We'll stop them," she promised, hugging him tightly and laying her cheek against his.

Tala's eyes widened, sensing the shift in their relationship.

"Wait! Are you two . . . ?"

Ari Ara and Finn nodded sheepishly. Tala crowed, thrilled.

"Focus!" Minli snapped, eyeing the stirring soldiers with alarm.

Ari Ara ducked under Zyrh's neck and strode toward the other end of the bridge. Finn followed at her heels. One of the garrison soldiers shouted and lifted an arm, pointing at her. An armored rider cantered along the tree line, kicking his heels into his warhorse's flank. From the stiff-spined posture and gold-trimmed uniform, Ari Ara guessed that was Mendren. He gestured with a gloved fist. A group of six men headed toward the bridge, swords sheathed. Finn crossed his arms over his chest, glaring stubbornly at them as they approached, legs spread in a wide stance.

"Looks like they're ready to talk," Ari Ara hollered, twisting over her shoulder to call to Minli.

He shook his tousle-haired head, mouthing something she couldn't hear. She jogged back toward him. Minli's face contorted. His hands gesticulated wildly, trying to get her to turn around. Ari Ara skidded to a halt and spun back to look behind her. Her hair flung across her eyes. She shoved it off her face impatiently.

"Get off that bridge or we'll drag you off!" the lead soldier shouted.

The soldiers burst into a run, approaching like a herd of charging bulls. The first soldier reached the wooden planks. Finn backed up hastily, colliding into Ari Ara. Her foot slipped on a slick, wet patch and they thudded painfully onto the boards in a tangle of arms and legs.

The soldiers were on them in a flash, strong hands gripping her arms and hauling Finn up by the back of his shirt. Ari Ara's blood ran cold as she heard the Paika raise a battle cry. Finn's mother, Tessa, burst from the pines, sprinting full tilt, roaring with the strength of a mother bear after her cub.

"Get your hands off my son!"

She thundered onto the bridge, an arrow notched and pointed at the soldier who gripped Finn. Suddenly, the woman froze, eyes locked on her son. Ari Ara's head whipped around. The soldier had shoved Finn backward over the bridge railing. The boy's toes scrambled futilely for the boards, eyes rolling down to the roiling waters below.

Time stalled. Every motion stretched, long and dreamlike. In slow motion, she saw Finn's stormy eyes snap toward her. The soldier's head spun, his mouth falling open. Ari Ara wrenched free, knocking aside the man's forearm and turning over her shoulder. Her breath sounded loud in her ears. Her hair fanned out slowly, suspended midair. The soldier gripping Finn bellowed in a low roar. She saw his hands clutching Finn's shirt, white-knuckled, the veins bulging. Then, to her horror, the man let go, his fingers splaying wide apart. Finn toppled, his hands scrambling for a grip.

Ari Ara's heartbeat thudded like a slow drum, pounding in the rhythms of her movements, one boom for every motion. She lunged . . .

Over a flailing hand that tried to grab her . . .

Under the arm of a soldier . . .

Around Finn's legs as he flipped over the rail . . .

Through the space emptied by his falling body . . .

. . . and snatched his wrist in the air.

Time lurched back into place. Her torso slammed hard against the railing. The breath was knocked out of her. She gripped Finn with both hands as he hit the wooden struts of the bridge. His lip split as his head smacked, but his instincts kicked in. He grabbed the rail with his free hand and scrambled for a foothold.

In the sharp clarity forged by danger and crisis, Ari Ara sensed motion behind her on the bridge. Minli's voice drew near. She could feel the click-thud of his crutch on the boards beneath her feet. Finn heaved his legs up and clambered over the rail, back to safety. Ari Ara spun around and spread her arms wide in front of him, ready to use the Way Between to turn aside anyone who tried to hurt him.

But she didn't need to. Minli wove his words quicker than she could move, waving the letter like a white flag of truce, backing the soldiers up to the end of the bridge, explaining what they'd found, telling the men to fetch Commander Mendren. Finn's mother came hurtling over. The soldiers tensed, but Tessa merely flung her arms around her son, hands shaking so badly she couldn't have notched an arrow if she tried.

As one of the soldiers ran up the slope to get Mendren, Ari Ara risked a glance behind her. Tala had both hands stretched out, trying to hold back a cluster of angry and anxious Paika at the far end of the bridge. A horn sounded from the forest. The Paika pivoted toward it, startled.

The Paika emerged from the trees. The dark skirts of the fir boughs closed behind her. The elder sat regally on the bull elk. Her head was high. Her spine was proud. Her white hair coiled on her head. Her cheekbones caught the sun. She swayed slightly, side to side, as the elk delicately picked his way down the slope, antlers dipping and rising. Her kinfolk parted without a word. Tala boldly stood firm until the old woman spoke to zir quietly. As the elk carried the elder to the middle of the bridge, the big golden horse surrendered his blockade, nickered softly, and slid up against the rail to let the woman pass.

Commander Mendren reached them a moment later. Minli exchanged a few words with him, handed him the letter, and let his horse step onto the bridge, keeping the soldiers where they were. The hoofbeats of the elk and warhorse clopped out counter-rhythms, slow and measured, closer and closer, until they stilled like statues. The mist of the river hissed and swirled around them. The rapid currents roared as the two leaders eyed each other in silence.

The tense moment stretched. One breath. Two. Another. Ari Ara thought of Shulen's lessons in stillness and slowness. Sometimes, doing nothing was the Way Between. Ari Ara counted her breaths and the galloping drumbeat of her heart. The blood still screamed in her veins, coursing at the speed of crisis. Her fingers twitched, impatient. The muscles in her legs spasmed, struggling to hold still. Waiting was one of the hardest things she'd ever done.

But in the breath of stillness, in the slow quiet of silence, the tension on the bridge eased. The pounding fear subsided. The elk sniffed the air. The warhorse flicked an ear. Commander Mendren sighed. *The Paika* spoke.

"Come, Mendren," she said gently, glancing at Finn, relieved beyond measure that Ari Ara had snatched him back from toppling to his death. "One tragedy has just been avoided by this girl's swift action. These young people say we can avert further tragedy by not attacking one another. Don't you think it's time we listened?"

He nodded, grudgingly and gruffly, but enough. He lifted his gloved fist and signaled to his men. The archers lowered their bows. The soldiers sheathed their swords.

Ari Ara breathed a sigh of relief. Now the real work could begin.

CHAPTER THIRTY

. . . . .

The Crown of Light

The sharp metallic scent of snow hung on the air. Clouds pressed low over the bare branches. The freezing night gnawed at the edge of the chill evening. Ari Ara and Finn crouched on a ridgetop overlooking a lonely, abandoned farm outside of Moscam. Minli sat beside her on a fallen tree, blowing warmth into his fingertips. Beyond, Tala hummed a tune under zirs breath, jiggling a knee in tempo and agitation. A small fire of twigs and dry branches crackled in front of them. They'd been tending it all day. The black earth hissed with steam as the heat melted the snow from the edges of the circle. Ari Ara's mitten-clad hand gripped Finn's leather glove as they watched the garrison soldiers and the Paika trackers encircling the old hay barn.

The raiders lurked inside.

Together, they had accomplished what none of them could achieve alone. Commander Mendren had lifted the ban on the Paika. Steady as wolves, the Paika trackers had stalked the raiders over the mountains, through towns and villages, across high pastures and deep ravines. As frosts stripped the branches bare, the Paika pursued the raiders south through bandit territory, following tips from Joss and his band. As the hush of snow blanketed the valleys, they nearly caught the raiders outside Knobble, chasing them at full gallop past the white-curtained Haystacks. Soon, it was clear where they were headed: Moscam.

Commander Mendren dispatched his soldiers and caught the raiders holed up in this abandoned barn. Following instructions from the Peace Force, the garrison didn't attack. They set up a watch so the raiders couldn't escape. By the time the Paika and the Peace Force arrived, the assailants had been surrounded for days. There was nowhere left to run, nowhere left to hide. Without food and water, they couldn't stay barricaded in the barn much longer. The garrison soldiers had wanted to torch the barn and smoke them out. But Grindle Spireson turned his steely gaze on them.

"If you do that, you're no better than they are," he growled.

So, they waited. The Peace Force took turns speaking to the men stuck inside. Shulen, Mahteni, and Solange stood in the open space of the clearing and used verbal Azar to try to convince them to surrender. The secret was out. Everyone knew they had been hired by the Orelands to cause chaos and disruption. They faced serious charges. They'd directly disobeyed the Great Lady's command to leave the Peace Force alone. They'd burned ten villages. They'd raided many more. They'd endangered innocent Paika. They'd brought two nations to the brink of war.

But the Peace Force and the Paika did not demand their deaths. Instead, they demanded their lives. The imposters would face neither the noose nor prison, but rather Harraken-style justice. It was far worse, Shulen warned them. He let their blood run cold in wild speculation before explaining the circle process of speaking stories, hearing truths, and repairing harms.

"You may have to help rebuild the villages," Mahteni cautioned them through the wooden slats of the barn door, "and the Paika, whom you so poorly imitated, have several bones to pick with you as well."

At first, the Paika had been in favor of old-style justice: heads on pikes. But Ari Ara, Minli, Tala, and Finn had talked the older generation out of it. Killing these men would make their nasty lies live on forever. Making them travel *with* the Peace Force to uproot each false rumor and weed out the misperceptions would be punishment enough.

Thornmar and the House of Thorn would face the wrath of the Great Lady Brinelle. She was furious over the whole affair. The incriminating letter from Slygo proved the House of Thorn's involvement. Korin and Rill had found Bergen after he had eluded the Paika during the Wild Hunt. Bergen had known it was Orelands fighters from the start. He'd been paid handsomely to let them "steal" his cattle. For the sack of gold, he had also started the rumors about the "Paika" raiders. The man had been holed up in the Smithlands, too scared to leave his safe house, trying to reach the Orelands and the dubious protection of the Thorns. Korin informed him bluntly that the Thorns would likely slit his throat to silence him. After that, the man accepted the protection of the House of Marin in trade for his written testimony identifying the raiders.

The Great Lady was beyond outraged that her own citizens – even if they were from the treacherous Orelands - had dared attack the Peace Force. Shulen strongly urged her to choose a kind of justice that didn't cause more problems down the road, but only time would tell how she would punish Rannor Thornmar. The House of Thorn already roiled with resentment toward the Lost Heir and the Way Between. Slapping the entire noble house into chains and locking them in a dungeon was unlikely to change anything for the better. As it was, the trade embargo the Great Lady was leaning toward imposing on the Orelands would pinch the ribs of every man, woman, and child in their territory ... most of whom had nothing to do with Thornmar's actions.

Ari Ara hoped her Lady Aunt would send a sizeable contingent of the Peace Force to the Orelands to speak truth and correct the false impressions Thornmar had planted in his people's minds. She'd like to go, although her exile still had not been lifted ... and she had other places to be.

Ari Ara leaned into Finn's warmth, a slow smile curling on her cold-brightened cheeks. Shulen had agreed to assign her to a winter posting at the Spires, along with a few other Peace Force members, including Minli. Tahkan Shirar had grumpily approved - though he informed *The Paika* that the Desert King would be making a visit soon.

Finn stiffened beside her.

"Come on," he urged in a breathless hush, whispering words to the Orelands fighters inside the barn. "Make your Crossing with courage."

The barn door creaked as the wooden boards barring it shut loosened. A voice called out. Mahteni, Solange, and Shulen nodded, waving at the others to lower their weapons. The soldiers and trackers ignored them. Until they could see the imposters' empty hands in the air, they would assume an attack was imminent. Ari Ara held her breath. Finn gripped her hand in a nervous clench.

The barn door cracked open. Another exchange of words shot back and forth. A silent moment stretched unbearably. Just when Ari Ara thought nothing would happen, the barn door swung wide. Shadowy figures inside held their empty hands high, unarmed.

"Come out," Mahteni called to them, "it's time for you to wage peace."

The four youths leapt to their feet as the men surrendered. Finn fanned the embers of the fire to life and picked up the torch stuck in the snow, waiting to be lit. On the crest of the ridge, a pile of kindling and logs waited like a somber giant. Across the valleys, north and south, lookouts scanned the snowy horizon as the evening faded from golden to pale lavender. Word had spread through the Border Mountain villages: the enemies of peace had been found. The followers of the Way Between were about to catch them. Messenger hawks had winged east and west, delivering the request of Ari Ara Marin en Shirar:

Prepare the fires on the heights, set a lookout, wait for the signal.

Hundreds of bonfires stood poised like sentinels atop the peaks and ridges of the mountains. For days, lonely lookouts, many of them Peace Force members in winter postings, had waited patiently, eyes fixed on the nearest ridgeline, a sense of hope kindling in their chests.

"I'll race you," Finn dared Ari Ara.

But she shook her head.

"We do this together," she told Finn, pausing as Minli tucked his crutch under his arm and Tala rose to zirs feet.

As one, they climbed the last steps to the ridge. With four hands on the torch, they lowered it to the stack of wood. The bonfire ignited, flaming bright against the gathering night. Light poured into the darkness, sending a signal as far as the eye could see. The four youths watched the sparks leap skyward toward the stars. The glow of the flames cast a golden circle onto the snow. They turned their gazes from the fire, blinking to clear the smoke and light from their eyes, scanning the distant and dark horizons. The mountains pressed the solid outlines of their crests against the night. They searched, breathless.

Finn spotted it first. Silently, he raised his arm and pointed south. A tiny pinprick of light flared up on the next ridgeline. A shiver of excitement ran through them. No one spoke, waiting, hope clutching at their hearts. A second light, smaller, more distant, grew on the peak beyond. As the kindling caught, the glow of the bonfires swelled and rose. All four youths exhaled in a whoosh as a third fire sparked on another peak.

A trill of joy broke loose from Ari Ara's throat. As if the mountains sang with her, it echoed off the slopes. She spun around. Like stars winking into sight at twilight, the northern ridges filled with flickering firelight. The horizon glimmered with tiny, fiery jewels. The Haystacks danced with a row of blazes. The ancient fire pits around Knobble gleamed.

Beyond, hidden by the shoulders of the mountains, from Hock to Shottam to Serrat, the fires flickered, crackled, and burned, one after another in a chain that stretched from the southern sea, north to the mystical frozen lands. After years of war and heartbreak, a spark of hope had returned to the Border Mountains. The promise of peace blazed on every horizon. Old legends roared back into life.

Ari Ara felt the sting of cold catch the tears brimming in her eyes. The shining fires stirred her deeply. Finn had teased her for being a double royal heir without throne or crown, but *this* was her crown - the hope of peace starting to gleam in these mountains. It wasn't made out of jewels. It was here, adorning the peaks as far as the eye could see. Her throne was wherever she sat down, in hayfields with humble villagers or in temples with quiet monks. Her palace was the rise and fall of mountains, the curl of rivers, and the expanse of desert lands. Her nation stretched across borders and resided in the heart.

If she needed a crown, it was forged by friendships near and far. It was built of hope and peace, shimmering in the dark night.

It was crafted from an old saying, one that rang in the memories of elders and the hopes of youths, alike.

Wherever mountains meet and the people stand united,
the Crown of Light shines.

The End

AUTHOR'S NOTE

It takes courage to work for peace. In a world plagued with war and violence, building peace can seem like an impossible dream. And yet, it is the sanest, most practical thing any of us can do. In *The Way Between*, Ari Ara learns to read with a collection of folktales about the peace-loving ancestor, Alaren. These stories capture her imagination and by the time she's twelve, she's dreaming of reviving the ancient legend of the Peace Force. In Ari Ara's fourth adventure, *The Crown of Light*, our heroine finally gets her chance. With friends, she embarks on a journey to diffuse the sparks of violence in a war-torn region.

The Ari Ara Series is fantasy, but the seeds of these stories are rooted in the real-life work that happens in neighborhoods, hot conflict zones, and embattled regions throughout our world. As Ari Ara drew inspiration from Alaren's stories, I draw many of my creative ideas from history and reality. (Believe me, even my wild imagination could not have dreamed up the remarkable escapades that peace teams get into.) From juggling to stop armed soldiers from opening fire on children to breaking up fights at festivals, the true stories I've heard from my colleagues who work with unarmed peacekeeping defy belief. They are the real heroes of our times.

From Badshah Khan's eighty-thousand person, nonviolent "Peace Army" to M.K. Gandhi's Shanti Sena, there are many historic examples of how organized groups have worked to halt violence, achieve justice, and wage peace. Today, unarmed peace teams like Nonviolent Peaceforce, Meta Peace Teams, DC Peace Team, Portland Peace Team, Cure Violence, and others continue the legacy, entering dangerous conflict zones to protect people, building skills to resolve conflict, and de-escalating violence. Each of these groups has a slightly different focus, approach, and methodology. Some work in war zones. Others protect vulnerable community members from assassination by governments, corporations, or armed groups. Still more operate in their local communities as people mobilize for protests, rallies, or public events, diffusing threats of violence from police or counter-protesters. Growing numbers of groups train local people to interrupt violence on the streets of their communities, particularly around gun violence in the United States.

In crafting this novel, I spoke with many colleagues who do this work, and researched how these efforts unfold. I've attempted to weave their hard-won lessons into my fictional Peace Force, incorporating humor and heart, individual and collective actions, respect for local knowledge and people, and much more. I encourage all my readers to read more about the real-life work, take trainings with peace teams, and watch documentaries about their endeavors. It is inspiring and empowering.

The other source of inspiration for *The Crown of Light* is the work of peacebuilding. This field of practice emphasizes building relationships, opening dialogues to foster understanding between groups, strengthening local resiliency, and addressing underlying grievances and injustices. It strives to weave a web of connections that keeps violence, injustice, and war from breaking out. I began to study peacebuilding in 2017 at the River Phoenix Center for Peacebuilding in Gainesville, Florida. To create peace at the local level of their community, they work with restorative justice, Police-Youth Dialogues, mediation, social-emotional learning, Nonviolent Communication, and community justice, among other practices. From them, I learned the importance of building relationships and fostering connections.

You will see this woven throughout Ari Ara's experiences in

the Border Mountains, including in her conversations with Nell Banderhook, at the gathering for the Summer Bonfires at Knobble, and in her determination to befriend Finn and get to know the Paika. When the bonds of social connection are severed, it is easier to fear one another. From there, it is a short step to reacting with violence. Many wars in human history have been precipitated by the alienation and dehumanization of our "enemies". To wage peace, we have to reverse that trend and reweave the threads that connect us all.

Peace is the work of a thousand hands. If we want to see it in the world, we have to build it, in every town, in every person, each and every day. Ari Ara's fictional story shows us what it looks like to intentionally build peace in places where war and violence have caused profound harm. *The Crown of Light* also activates our imaginations to envision the potential scope and scale of how we could wage peace. Millions of people participate in the military - imagine what our world would be like if all those people worked day in and day out for peace and justice. Each year, the US government spends a trillion dollars on war - imagine if we invested even a fraction of that in a Peace Force. Novels are the fertile ground in which our sense of possibility grows. I hope this book offers this to you.

As Ari Ara and her friends revive these skills in her world, we should all be inspired to revive them in our own. If peace is the work of a thousand hands, let's add ours to the effort.

In solidarity,
Rivera Sun

ACKNOWLEDGMENTS

Writing a novel is a far less solitary endeavor than you might think. In my journey with *The Crown of Light*, I've been blessed by remarkable companions every step of the way.

This year's beta-reader circle was the largest and most delightful yet. Thank you to my long-time readers, Cindy Reinhardt and Jenny Bird. And special thanks to David Gilman for bringing together a group of beta-readers who are Ari Ara's age, including Ronja Grundig, Lucien Ruiz, Petra Bitterman, and Estrello Mayo-Romero. Born of enthusiasm and curiosity, the feedback of these young readers was some of the most insightful I have ever received.

I owe a debt of gratitude to my friends and colleagues who do real-life peace team work. Mary Hanna, Stephen Niamke, Peter Dougherty, and Kim Redigan from Meta Peace Teams offered invaluable advice, tips, and best practices. All the best ideas in *The Crown of Light* emerged from their comments; all the foolish ones are my own. Tom Hastings, Adam Vogal, and the Portland Peace Team also gifted me with countless stories drawn from their in-the-streets work, de-escalating violence and keeping protests peaceful. I'd also like to thank peacebuilders extraordinaire, David and Jan Hartsough, for their lifelong inspiration, including initiating, with Mel Duncan, the incredible Nonviolent Peaceforce. My heartfelt appreciation goes back through history to Khan Abdul Gaffar Khan, Mohandas K. Gandhi, and those who followed in their footsteps to build peace "armies", the Shanti Sena Network, and more. Without these examples, Ari Ara's Peace Force would be far less interesting. Thank you.

My thanks goes out to the River Phoenix Center for

Peacebuilding and my fellow participants in the Peacebuilder Immersions. Heart Phoenix, you modeled what it looks like to "run to the rescue with love" and let everything else follow. Jeffrey Weisberg, the intelligence and commitment you bring to even the most challenging aspects of peacebuilding is a powerful example of the humble heroics that go into this work. You have both taught me so much about the work of peace. I am in awe of what you do in the world.

A special thanks for the fictional adaptation of the *I Am From ... Exercise* in Chapter Three goes out to a lineage of trainers, from Veronica Pelicaric (whom I learned it from) to Cathy Hoffman (whom Veronica learned it from) to Linda Christensen (who invented it). If you would like to connect with the original training, Christensen has published it in *Reading, Writing and Rising Up; Teaching about Social Justice and the Power of the Written Word* (2000) published by Rethinking Schools, Ltd.

More gratitude must be offered to: the Community Publishers of the Ari Ara Series, whose generosity over the years has kept these stories coming; the wonderful young students and readers, near and far, who tell me, with great frequency, how much they love these books; and the teachers, parents, and librarians who help the youth discover Ari Ara's tales.

And, last but decidedly not least, my heart swells with love for my partner, Dariel Garner, who read every word of this book seven times, weathered my frustrations with technology, cooked amazing meals, and did a hundred other tasks that helped this novel be born.

With love and thanks,
Rivera Sun

ABOUT THE AUTHOR

Rivera Sun is the author of the award-winning Ari Ara Series, *The Dandelion Insurrection,* and other novels, as well as theatrical plays, a study guide to nonviolent action, three volumes of poetry, and numerous articles. She has red hair, a twin sister, and a fondness for esoteric mystics. She went to Bennington College to study writing as a Harcourt Scholar and graduated with a degree in dance. She is a trainer in strategy for nonviolent movements and an activist. Rivera has been an aerial dancer, a bike messenger, and a gung-fu style tea server. Everything else about her - except her writing - is perfectly ordinary.

Rivera Sun also loves hearing from her readers:
Email: info@riverasun.com
Facebook: Rivera Sun
Twitter: @RiveraSunAuthor

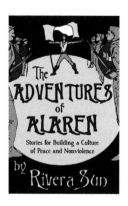

Read the folktales that inspired Ari Ara!

In a series of clever and creative escapades, the legendary folkhero Alaren rallies thousands of people to take bold and courageous action for peace. Weaving new epic tales from real-life inspirations, author Rivera Sun brings a new kind of hero to life. *The Adventures of Alaren* offers perfect stories to teach peace at home, conflict resolution in the classroom, and nonviolence in faith and peace centers. Each fictional folktale includes a footnote on the real-life inspiration and discussion questions for classrooms and small groups. For readers of all ages, *The Adventures of Alaren* warms hearts, opens minds, and gives us ideas for waging peace!

"What wonderful stories to share with my class of sixth and seventh graders. Right now, we are listening to Ari Ara's adventures and creating skits from *The Adventures of Alaren* as part of literature class. Important and hopeful new stories!"
– **Scott Springer, Class Teacher, The Bay School**

"To read the tales of Alaren is to be opened to a world of creative solutions to seemingly insurmountable challenges. Each tale is inspired by a successful nonviolent action in real life, reminding us of what's possible when we are committed to nonviolence and willing to be bold and brave in our actions." – **Leah Boyd**

Read all of the adventures in the Ari Ara Series!

The Way Between

Between flight and fight lies a mysterious third path called *The Way Between*, and young shepherdess and orphan Ari Ara must master it . . . before war destroys everything she loves! She begins training as the apprentice of the great warrior Shulen, and enters a world of warriors and secrets, swords and magic, friendship and mystery.

The Lost Heir

Going beyond dragon-slayers and sword-swingers, *The Lost Heir* blends fantasy and adventure with social justice issues in an unstoppable story that will make you cheer! Mariana Capital is in an uproar. The splendor of the city dazzles Ari Ara until she makes a shocking discovery . . . the luxury of the nobles is built by the forced labor of the desert people.

Desert Song

Exiled to the desert, Ari Ara is thrust between the warriors trying to grab power . . . and the women rising up to stop them! Every step she takes propels her deeper into trouble: her trickster horse bolts, her friend is left for dead, and Ari Ara has to run away to save him. But time is running out - can she find him before it's too late?

Discover more at:

www.riverasun.com

Find your next great book.
Read essays and excerpts.
Check-out behind the scenes stories.
Hear about new releases.
Join an upcoming book club.
Sign-up for Rivera Sun's fun and personal newsletter.

Love this book? Tell a friend!
Most readers discover the Ari Ara Series when a friend tells them about it. Spread the word among your family, friends, and fellow readers, in-person or on social media. Ask the librarians at your school and public libraries to put the series on the shelves.

Thank you!

Printed in Great Britain
by Amazon

42272030R00212